The Re

Cherith Baldry was born in Lancaster, England, and studied at Manchester University and St Anne's College, Oxford. She subsequently worked as a teacher, including a spell as a lecturer at the University of Sierra Leone.

Cherith is now a full-time writer of fiction for both children and adults. Her children's fantasy, the 'Eaglesmount' trilogy, was published by Macmillan in 2001. She has a special interest in Arthurian literature, and has published several Arthurian short stories in which she explores the character of Sir Kay. Other short stories have appeared in *Interzone, Marion Zimmer Bradley's Fantasy Magazine, 3SF* and various anthologies, and her Arthurian novel, *Exiled from Camelot*, was published by Green Knight in 2001.

Her next novel will be *The Roses of Roazon*.

CHERITH BALDRY

The Reliquary Ring

TOR

First published 2003 by Macmillan

This edition published 2004 by Tor
an imprint of Pan Macmillan Ltd
Pan Macmillan, 20 New Wharf Road, London N1 9RR
Basingstoke and Oxford
Associated companies throughout the world
www.panmacmillan.com
www.toruk.com

ISBN 0 330 49207 1

1 3 5 7 9 8 6 4 2

A CIP catalogue record for this book is available from
the British Library.

Typeset by SetSystems Ltd, Saffron Walden, Essex
Printed and bound in Great Britain by
Mackays of Chatham plc, Chatham, Kent

In memory of Peter Baldry

Scientist
Musician
Theologian

Acknowledgements

I should like to thank my agent, Bill Neill-Hall, my editor, Peter Lavery, and members of the Bromley and Brighton writers' groups for comment and criticism. Especially I would like to thank the members of the Milford Writers' Workshop who first thought there might be a novel here, and Liz Holliday who published some of the early material in *Odyssey*.

One

Gianni was hoeing the onion bed when the Reverend Mother herself came looking for him.

'Quickly, boy, put that away,' she said, clapping her hands at him as if she was scaring birds. 'Make yourself tidy and come in, come in right away. Messire Alessandro is asking for you.'

Gianni gaped, but he automatically cleaned the dirt from the hoe and leant it against the garden wall, while the Reverend Mother stood on the path, fuming at his slowness.

She clutched his elbow and hustled him along the path towards the house. 'There, scrape your boots, and you must wash your hands and comb your hair – such a thatch, Gianni! – and make yourself presentable for Messire Alessandro.'

Her crisp white robes rustled as she chivvied Gianni indoors; Gianni caught their fresh laundered smell.

He had grown up with that sound in his ears, that smell in his nose, here in the Hospital of the Innocenti, the only place in the city that fostered unwanted human children. Though Gianni was inexperienced, he understood what that meant, for what kind of children would be unwanted, when so few women were able to bear a child at all?

Children like Maria, with the face of an angel and a squat, bloated body, her delicate hands protruding from her shoulders. Domenico, who hunched up spidery limbs and crooned and drooled to himself in a corner. Gianni, huge and clumsy, with coarse, pitted skin and a deep purple stain that spread over his face and neck and most of his body.

'You are God's children,' the Reverend Mother told them briskly. 'You are precious in His sight.'

'It is a punishment,' said Father Battista when he brought them the Sacrament. 'A punishment on men who set themselves up like God and changed God-ordained humanity to create the genics, creatures outside God's law.'

Gianni could not help wondering why he and the others should be punished for something they had not done. He did not ask the question; he knew himself too stupid to understand the answer.

He did understand Father Battista's command, repeated almost every time he spoke to them. 'Children, never touch a genic. It is a grievous sin.'

Gianni knew that this was one sin he had no chance of committing. No genic would ever penetrate the sanctuary of the Hospital. He would have rather liked to see one, just once, to understand why a genic was so dreadful that even its touch was defilement.

Now in the scullery he sluiced hands and face in cold water and dried himself on the coarse towel the Reverend Mother thrust at him.

She examined his hands and drew in a shocked breath. 'Fingernails!' As he started looking round for something to scrub them she pushed him into the passage. 'No time, no time. Go and comb your hair, Gianni, and come straight down to my parlour.' As Gianni began to climb the stairs she called after him, 'And tuck your shirt in!'

In his haste he forgot to be nervous until he stood outside the Reverend Mother's parlour. He had heard of Messire Alessandro, but never seen him. He was a merchant, so wealthy that nobody could count his riches, or so they said. He gave generously, to the Innocenti among others. But there was a whiff of sin about him; Father Battista instructed the children regularly to pray for him, and not just out of gratitude, either. And this man was here, now, asking to see Gianni?

Gianni knocked, opened the door, and went in. And in that moment, without a word being spoken, he knew that his world had changed.

Messire Alessandro was seated in the faded brocade chair where the Reverend Mother always put her guests. He was a small man, so delicately made that Gianni was almost shocked, and felt his own clumsiness by contrast. Although from what Gianni knew of him he must be at least thirty, there was something childish about the pale face and wide blue eyes, the loose curls of pale gold hair. He was dressed in grey, with a dazzling white shirt under the velvet coat, and grey kid gloves on slender hands clasped around the silver knob of his cane. He sat erect, and contemplated Gianni.

Gianni was used to the cursory glances of those who saw him for the first time. The shock, and the revulsion. Messire Alessandro showed none of that. Gianni felt that the clear blue eyes were looking at him, not the lumpish body and disfigured face, seeing him as no one, not even Reverend Mother herself, had seen him before. He snatched his hands behind him, fearing that the penetrating gaze could not fail to notice his dirty fingernails.

'Say good day to Messire Alessandro,' the Reverend Mother told him sharply.

Gianni realized he had been staring like a clown. 'Good day, messire,' he mumbled, trying to bow in the way he had been taught.

'Your name is . . . Giovanni?' The first words Gianni had heard him speak. A cool voice, light and almost expressionless.

'We call him Gianni,' the Reverend Mother said. 'He's a good boy. Strong, and willing.'

'How old are you, Gianni?'

'Fifteen, messire.'

Messire Alessandro nodded. 'Good. Gianni, I need a servant. Are you willing to come to me?'

Gianni was startled. Surely a man as wealthy as Messire Alessandro would buy genic servants, or even constructs to do the heavy work that was all he himself was capable of. A hard knot of fear began to grow in his stomach as he saw that even the Reverend Mother was looking flustered.

'Gianni's a good boy, messire,' she said. 'He's led a sheltered life here.'

Messire Alessandro smiled, but a faint flush stained the pale cheeks as if he was not entirely at ease. 'Don't be afraid, Holy Mother,' he said. 'The tales they tell of me are quite inaccurate.'

It was the Reverend Mother's turn to blush.

'Well, Gianni?' Messire Alessandro prompted him gently.

Gianni thought it might be time for another bow.

Along with the fear he felt a rising excitement. 'I will come, messire,' he said. 'If I can do the work.'

Gianni did not know what he had expected when he left the Hospital of the Innocenti. Father Battista had always told the children that the city was a wicked place, and lived in daily expectation that the Good Lord would strike it with divine lightning as once He had struck the cities of the plain. But Gianni saw none of this wickedness in the house of Messire Alessandro. In its own way it was as ordered, and as dull, as the Innocenti itself.

Messire Alessandro had no wife or family. He lived in a suite of rooms over his warehouse, where Gianni, in the snug chamber he called his own, was awakened early each morning by the cries of the boatmen on the canal below his window.

Nobody else lived there except for Lucetta, the old crone who kept house. She was the ugliest woman Gianni had ever set eyes on, with a speech impediment that kept Gianni in a ferment of anxiety for the first few days until he learnt to understand her.

Lucetta did the cooking, and when Gianni came he helped her with the cleaning, hauled logs and water, and carried her basket when she went to market. He took messages for Messire Alessandro and rowed his boat when he wished to go out.

For a man of wealth, Messire Alessandro lived simply. He kept no body servant. Lucetta laundered and mended his clothes; Gianni cleaned his boots; he shaved and dressed himself.

He rarely dined from home, and the only regular

visitor was Dr Foscari, his man of business, a man so
spectacularly fat that Gianni could hardly keep from
gaping. He came to dine about once a month, and played
chess with Messire Alessandro after supper. Gianni waited
at table; all the conversation was of business.

Gianni had been surprised that Messire Alessandro
wanted a human servant; as he settled in he realized that
Messire Alessandro owned no genics at all. Gianni and
Lucetta, the clerks and warehousemen, even the crews of
Messire Alessandro's own ships – all were human.

Nor did Messire Alessandro frequent the Imperial
Hostel, where the merchants from the Empire in the
north brought their cargoes of genics and constructs, and
the machines made by cunning Imperial craftsmen whose
skills were unknown in the city. As he listened to the
gossip of the clerks, Gianni heard that there was great
wealth to be made there for men like Count Dracone,
who was said to be a broker for the Imperial merchants.
Messire Alessandro would have none of it.

Gianni might have thought that Messire Alessandro
was one of those exceptionally pious men who distanced
themselves from even the possibility of sin, except for one
thing that troubled him more as time went on. Every
Sunday he was free to attend Mass at the Innocenti, but
Messire Alessandro did not attend Mass at all.

Gianni had heard of men so lost that they denied
God, atheists like Count Dracone, whose wickedness,
Father Battista always said, was outstanding even in this
wicked city. Gianni had never seen the Count, but he
could not imagine Messire Alessandro as wicked.

His master was gentle, remote but kind, and every
charity in the city, not only the Innocenti, was grateful

for his wealth. But he did not go to Mass. Gianni suspected that he did not even pray.

He was troubled, and more so when, fearing that he had forgotten to slide the bolts on the door to the counting house stairs, he padded past Messire Alessandro's bedchamber late at night. In the silence he could make out the slight but unmistakable sounds of weeping.

Gianni had no chance to speak until the evening, when he served Messire Alessandro's solitary supper. Pouring water – Messire Alessandro drank wine only on the rare evenings with Dr Foscari – he said, 'Sir . . .'

Messire Alessandro looked up inquiringly. Gianni felt the heat of blood rushing to his face and neck. 'Sir, I have seen – forgive me – I have seen that you never go to Mass.'

A slight flicker of the blue eyes was all that showed Messire Alessandro was startled. He did not reply.

'It might give you great comfort, sir,' Gianni said, fearful of having offended.

Slowly, Messire Alessandro shook his head. 'It is not for me.'

'Sir . . .' He was committed now, and Messire Alessandro showed no signs of taking offence. 'Sir, do you believe in God?'

'I . . . do not know.' He sighed; the blue eyes, unfocused, looked at something far away. 'Gianni, do not speak of this.'

There was no anger in the command, but no room for disobedience, either. Gianni set down the water jug and went back to the kitchen.

*

Even while he feared for Messire Alessandro's immortal soul, Gianni had no wish to return to the Innocenti. He could still visit on Sunday after Mass; all he really missed was the garden. He liked the feel of earth and the bite of spade into ground; he liked watching things grow.

One day he went to the market and bought with part of the wages Messire Alessandro paid him an earthenware pot. He carried it to the Innocenti and filled it with earth from the garden, and planted in it a slip of the sweetscented jasmine that scrambled over the garden wall.

Then he hauled the whole thing home and placed it on Messire Alessandro's balcony. Messire Alessandro often sat there of an evening, turning over the pages of a book or watching the shimmer of light on the canal. Gianni watered the green shoot hopefully. Soon it would twine around the balcony rail, and shed the scent of its flowers.

'Gianni?' Messire Alessandro had come quietly up behind him as he watched the water soak into the dark earth. 'What's that?'

Gianni straightened up, feeling embarrassed. 'It's a plant, sir. Jasmine. It's pretty when it grows.' Daringly he added, 'It's a present, sir. For you.'

Messire Alessandro stiffened, his lips slightly parted. For a horrible minute, Gianni thought he had done something wrong, made his master angry, though he was never angry, hurt him in some inexplicable way.

Then he sighed out a breath. 'For me – truly?' He sounded bewildered. 'Thank you, Gianni. It's beautiful.'

He stared down at the pot for a few seconds longer and then turned abruptly and went back into the room.

Gianni also stared at the pot, frowning. The cutting

was not beautiful, though it would be. Then he shrugged.
There was no understanding Messire Alessandro.

2

Stumbling over fallen masonry in the heavy darkness,
Serafina groped her way along the wall, and pounded on
the door. She leant against it, panting, feeling the peeling
paint beneath her palms, and was raising a fist to knock
on it again when she heard the faint sounds of approaching footsteps from the passage beyond.

The door edged open. A burly figure appeared against
the light, and a guttural voice spoke, mangling the accents
of the city. 'What do you want?'

'Dr Heinrich? Countess Dandolo is . . . very ill. Will
you come, please?'

A guttural sound came from the doctor's throat.
'Dandolo? The old woman's rat-poor. Where's my fee
coming from, hey?'

'Please!'

The door swung suddenly wider, and Serafina got a
good look at Dr Heinrich for the first time. He was tall,
and broad to the point of clumsiness, with an untidy
shock of hair framing a reddish face.

He spoke abruptly. 'You're the Countess's genic?'

'Yes, sir.'

'Come in.'

He slammed the door shut behind Serafina and led
the way along a narrow passage and up a flight of stairs.
Serafina said, 'Sir, the Countess . . .'

'All in good time, girl.'

The room at the head of the stairs was long and

narrow, with bare, whitewashed walls that shone in the light of a dozen lamps. On a table under the shuttered window an array of metal instruments glittered alongside jars packed with shapeless things.

Serafina looked away, repressing a shiver. Everyone said that Dr Heinrich practised forbidden arts, or perhaps only the forbidden science of the Empire he came from. Holy Church had excommunicated him when he refused to abjure his practices. Serafina's mouth twisted a little in bitterness. Perhaps she and Dr Heinrich had something in common after all, though she doubted that the doctor would admit it.

She waited while Dr Heinrich pulled on a pair of thin, transparent gloves, and searched, muttering, among the instruments on the table. The room reeked of antiseptic and preservative, and underneath it all a sweetish odour Serafina could not identify. Her eyes were drawn to the far end of the room, where on a trestle table, under a sheet, lay a shape that . . .

'They fished a genic out of the canal this morning,' Dr Heinrich said, startling Serafina. 'Near the Palazzo Dracone. Died of drowning, but there were other injuries . . .' He grunted, half disgusted, half amused. 'Makes you wonder what Count Dracone has been up to.'

A picture flickered into Serafina's mind as he spoke. Darkness, and someone blundering along the canal side, terrified, perhaps looking back, missing a step, falling . . . And perhaps a slender, scarlet coated figure standing at the edge, watching as the genic's life bubbled away in the filthy water.

Serafina shuddered. Who would care what was done to a genic?

'Roll your sleeve up, girl.' Serafina flinched at the

order. 'I won't hurt you,' the doctor said impatiently. 'I only want a blood sample. Then I'll come with you to the Countess, and call my fee paid.'

Serafina pushed up the sleeve of her gown and tried not to shrink, even when the doctor plunged a needle into her arm and drew her silver-pale blood, the mark of her genic heritage, into a tiny chamber of glass. 'What will you do with it?' she asked.

'Nameless rites at the full moon.' Dr Heinrich laughed. 'Don't be a fool, girl. I shall study it. I want to know . . .' He pulled out the needle and slapped a pad of linen onto Serafina's arm. 'Hold that. The bleeding will stop in a minute.' Turning away to his worktable, his back to Serafina, he went on, 'Never mind why I want it.' A snort of contempt. 'A genic, and a woman . . . you wouldn't understand.'

'Sir . . .' Serafina began nervously. 'When you have looked at that, will you be able to tell me why I was made?'

Heinrich swivelled to stare at her, eyes bright under bushy brows. 'Don't you know, girl? Most genics are made for a purpose. What does the Countess use you for?'

'Her servant, sir. But she found me, when I was a child. I was a beggar in the streets. I don't remember how I came there.'

'Hmm . . . I wondered how a woman as poor as the Countess could own a genic.' The doctor came and stood over Serafina, staring at her with the look another man might have given a jewel he suspected held a flaw. 'You look healthy enough, but not bred for strength. You're very beautiful.'

Serafina felt the blood rising in her face, but the words

were not spoken with admiration, or even with disgust. The doctor shrugged. 'Who can say?'

He spoke as if it did not matter. To him it did not, Serafina thought, even though he studied her and her kind as another man might study the dogs he bred, or she herself might trace the ruined embroidery it was her task to repair for the Countess. She could not expect him to feel the hunger that she felt herself, to know what she was, why she was in the world, and what her life might mean. If she had tried to tell him, he would have laughed at her. A genic had no right even to ask questions, much less to expect the answers.

Dr Heinrich had already turned away. 'Well, girl,' he said, 'why are we standing here?' He picked up a coat thrown over the back of a chair. 'Let's go and see your mistress.'

There were no boatmen for hire on this narrow side canal, so Serafina steered a route between heaps of tumbled stone and refuse, with no light except for the moon, half veiled by scudding clouds. There was a reek of rotting fruit, and cats. Dr Heinrich, stumbling in her wake, cursed graphically.

At last they came out beside a wider canal where market boats lay moored, their awnings tightly battened down. At the corner a late opening tavern spilled out torchlight and raucous music. A drunkard, lurching through the door, opened his arms for Serafina. 'Here, my pretty—'

Catching sight of the genic badge on her cloak, he veered off with a curse, and as she hurried on with head lowered Serafina heard him vomiting into the canal behind her. Dr Heinrich caught her up, grunting something, and she realized that he was briefly embarrassed. Serafina could not see why. She had not expected his protection, or needed it.

She crossed the canal at the next bridge, and took out a key to open the door of a tall, narrow house on the far side. As she entered with the doctor, an inner door opened and a woman bounced out into the passage. 'Who's that you're bringing in? This is a respectable house, I'd have you know. And what about my rent?'

Serafina sighed. 'Donna Violetta, Dr Heinrich. Come to see the Countess.'

The landlady sniffed. She was a fat woman, with untidy, fading hair pushed under a cap, and a black gown of rusty silk, straining at the seams. 'Countess!' she snapped. 'And her without two sequins to rub together. You'll get no fee, doctor, you can be sure of that.'

'My fee is paid, madam,' said Dr Heinrich heavily. 'And now if you'd be so good . . .'

Donna Violetta had been standing at the foot of the stairs. Still muttering, she drew back; if she had tried to block the way she would have had to lay hands on Serafina. There were advantages, Serafina supposed, in lodging with such a respectable woman. Donna Violetta would never have tolerated a genic under her roof, if she had not been able to boast of having a Countess.

Serafina and the Countess lived at the top of the house, under the eaves. Dr Heinrich was blowing uncomfortably by the time they climbed the last flight of stairs. Serafina pushed open a door, said, 'Countess—' and broke off.

A smoky oil lamp lit the room, which was mostly filled by a vast bed, covered in mulberry coloured brocade

with ravelled gold embroidery. Brocade hangings were
looped back at the bed's head. In the bed, tiny against a
mound of pillows, lay the Countess Dandolo.

Her wrapper of peacock silk was stained and
crumpled. Tiny parchment hands like claws poked out
from the embroidered sleeves. Her lined face was sunken;
the beak of a nose and crest of wispy white hair made her
look like a parrot. Her eyes were closed; Serafina could
scarcely believe that the fierce life in her had ebbed away.

Serafina sat beside the bed while Dr Heinrich made
his examination. After a few minutes she poured water
from the carafe on the bedside table and swallowed a few
mouthfuls. She felt quite cold.

No one could have said that her life with Countess
Dandolo had been easy. There had never been enough
money, and often Serafina had been at her wits' end to
meet her demands. The old woman had screamed at her
and slapped her, but there had been a warmth even in
the slaps, and the Countess had laughed raucously when
her confessor had tried to lesson her. It was more than a
genic had any right to expect, and more than Serafina
could expect now.

Finally the doctor straightened up, and pulled the
brocaded cover over the old lady's face. 'Who will see to
her burying?' he asked.

'The Count, her son.' Serafina found it hard to keep
venom out of her voice. Sanctimonious skinflint, who
had allowed his mother barely enough to live on, when
she had refused to join the holy sisters at Corpus Domini
on her widowhood. 'I will send word to him in the
morning.'

Thinking of Count Dandolo brought on a sudden

shaking in the depths of her stomach, though she tried to
keep it out of her voice. 'Sir, he is his mother's heir.'

Heinrich snorted, and glanced round the poky little
room. 'Little enough.'

'Sir, there is me.' Heinrich gave her a piercing look,
and in sudden panic she reached out to him. 'Sir, Count
Dandolo is a pious man. He will never keep a genic. He
will sell my rights. Sir . . . I'm afraid.'

For a moment, Heinrich stared at her, frowning. *See
me*, she begged him silently. *Me, not just a genic.* Then he
said, 'I'm sorry, girl. Maybe a decent woman—'

'Decent women do not keep genics. The Countess
was not decent.' Not decent, but warm and alive and
passionate. And now she was dead. 'Sir, will you buy me?'
Gathering her courage, before he could refuse, she went
on rapidly, 'I could cook and clean for you. And you
could study me. I would be useful to you.'

Dr Heinrich laughed uneasily. 'They would say you
were my mistress.'

'Do you think I care? Do you care, with all the rest
they say of you?'

His eyes slid away from her. She almost screamed with
frustration, anger driving out her fear. He was like all the
others. Stupid and petty-minded and afraid of talk.
'Please, sir—'

He was shaking his head. 'I can't afford you, girl.
Even supposing the State would assign your rights to me.
But if you like, I'll speak for you to the Count.'

Serafina rose and made him a respectful curtsey. 'I
thank you, sir, but no.'

'I'm sorry . . .' He sounded uneasy, but Serafina did
not expect the uneasiness to last. He would have shrugged

her off by the time he had reached the bridge over the
canal. 'Will you be . . . all right, here alone?' he asked.

'Of course, sir. Did you not see, I have Donna Violetta
to guard me?'

Now she did not trouble to keep the sarcasm out of
her voice. Heinrich grunted, muttered something inaud-
ible, and backed out of the room, closing the door behind
him.

Serafina listened to the clatter of his boots on the
stairs. It died away, and was followed by the dull thud of
the outer door closing, far below.

Once she was sure he had gone, Serafina trimmed the
lamp, coaxing a steady glow out of the dying wick. By its
light she took pen, ink and paper out of the drawer in
the bedside table, thought briefly, and began to write.

3

Manfred crossed himself and knelt stiffly on the sanctuary
steps before the altar. A damp wind whistled through the
cracked windows in the chapel, and through the crack
close to the main doorway, where part of the wall had
collapsed the day before. The ancient frescos were peeling
in the damp. Withered leaves were scattered over the
broken tiles of the floor and drifted against the steps and
the base of the marble altar, stripped now of the hangings
and silver that had graced it in the days of old Count
Loredan.

Kneeling in the watery light, Manfred addressed a
God made in the image of the old Count. Not young
Leonardo's father, the degenerate who had diced away his
patrimony, but his father, Ercole Loredan. The old Count

had known how to value the name and the wealth of House Loredan, even to this humble hunting lodge in the hills above the city.

Those days were gone. Count Ercole's son had gambled away these lands to the upstart Dracone, who had not even bothered to visit them, though he had gutted the house of most of its furnishings and the chapel of its silver, and paid off the servants, leaving only a couple of constructs, with Manfred as steward.

Manfred had expected him to sell, before the neglected property fell into ruin, but he had not sold yet.

'Dear God,' he murmured, 'of your grace, restore us, or grant us an ending.'

As he rose from his knees he heard the distant sound of an engine, gradually drawing nearer. He watched from the chapel porch as Count Dracone's flyer circled and set down neatly on the lake below the lodge. A construct lumbered down to the lake side, caught the mooring rope and drew the flyer to rest, bobbing against the landing stage. The pilot got out and strode up the hill.

Manfred let him come. He would not go to meet a man such as this, one of Dracone's bravos, or give him any honour. He could not help a tiny stirring of uneasiness, deep inside him, as he wondered why the man had come, and what new demand of Dracone's he might have to meet.

The pilot was blowing a bit as he reached the chapel, Manfred noted with satisfaction. He was a short, thick man, with a bullet head and black hair cropped close to his skull. He thrust his chin out pugnaciously. 'No more honour than this for Count Dracone?'

Manfred gazed blandly around. 'The Count? I do not see him.'

'His representative.' The pilot poked himself in the chest and then seemed to realize that he was making a fool of himself. He grunted. 'The Count needs gold.'

'Then you're in the wrong place,' Manfred said drily. 'The Count took all we had years ago. What does he expect to find here now?'

'Are you telling me you haven't a pot of savings under the hearthstone? You must have been bleeding the estate for half a lifetime.'

Manfred drew himself up stiffly. 'I would not demean myself to cheat House Loredan.'

'And House Dracone?'

'There is no House Dracone.'

The pilot drove a fist into his stomach. Manfred doubled over, choking for air, and reeled against the wall where the stonework had started to collapse. Groping for support, he felt a stone give way beneath his hand, and another bounce on his shoulders. Mortar showered down. When Manfred raised his head, bruised and winded, his eyes stinging, he saw that the crack of the day before had become a gaping hole.

Where the stonework of the outer wall had crumbled away, an ancient doorway was revealed. The door itself was made of thick oak planks, studded with iron, but they were rotting; the framework had shrunk away from the stone surround. Manfred realized, intrigued, that what he had taken to be the outer wall had been a later addition, to cover up the door.

The pilot thrust forward, pushing the old man away, and set his shoulder to the door. It burst open, and he staggered forward, letting out a curse as he grabbed at the doorpost to stop himself plunging forward into blackness.

Manfred peered over his shoulder. The pilot stood at

the head of a flight of steps, leading down into darkness. The pale daylight lit only the first few of them.

'A crypt . . .' he said.

The pilot stepped back, brushing wood splinters from his leather coat. 'Go and get a light, old fool.'

When Manfred returned from the lodge, a lamp in his hands, the pilot was waiting beside the collapsed wall, stamping his feet against the raw cold. He jerked his head, ordering Manfred to go first down the steps.

Raising the lamp, Manfred started downwards. The steps were crumbling, worn in the middle from countless feet, and though there were metal rings in the wall to hold a rope, there was no rope there. Manfred steadied himself with his free hand, while the pilot muttered impatiently behind him.

The steps led into a small stone chamber with a vaulted roof. Once it must have been the chapel crypt. In alcoves around the walls, beneath the crumbling shields of House Loredan, cobwebs festooned the marble sarcophagi of the ancient Counts.

Manfred brushed aside a clinging curtain of spider-silk, and stepped forward. The yellow lamplight revealed a bier standing in the centre of the room, the shape upon it half hidden in the sweeping folds of the pall. Tarnished silver thread glinted on half seen armorial bearings.

As he drew closer Manfred could see that on the bier lay a skeleton, the empty eye-sockets fixed on the hidden sky, the wasted hands still folded in an attitude of prayer around a sheet of parchment. On one bony finger still remained a ring, of gold set with lapis, winking in the lamplight.

Manfred stood still in wonder, but the pilot pushed roughly past him and grabbed the ring; the skeletal hands shivered into tiny bones and powder. The parchment drifted into the dust that lay in the folds of the pall; Manfred set down the lamp and unfolded the sheet so that he could read what it said.

His heart swelled as he traced the faded script. He read to the end, and then read it again, aloud, for the pilot to hear. 'The ring herewith contains the most holy of holy relics, a hair of the Lord Christos when he lived on earth. Yet now the world changes, and all that is holy is derided and disregarded. I have decreed that when I die the ring shall be buried with me, and hidden from the profane, until God shall be pleased to reveal it, or the world shall end. Written in my own hand: Leonardo, Count Loredan.'

Manfred's mind whirled. His prayer this morning; he had barely considered his words, or expected a response. Yet the ring had come, now, in the time of another Count Leonardo; what might that mean? And what was God's purpose for it in a time when so many still derided and disregarded the teachings of Holy Church?

As Manfred read, the pilot had let out a snort of disbelief, and now he was muttering over the ring, turning it in thick fingers as he tried to discover how it might hold a relic.

'With your leave, messire . . .' Manfred murmured. He took the ring and flipped back the stone, which hinged up to reveal a compartment set with crystal. Both men peered down into the depths; even in the poor light Manfred thought he could discern a single tendril of hair trapped beneath the crystal.

'" . . . the most holy of holy relics",' he whispered.

He pressed the lapis covering back over the crystal, and closed his hand around the ring. 'It must go to the Holy Father,' he said.

The pilot encircled the old man's wrist with blunt fingers and tightened his grip until pain stabbed up Manfred's arm and his hand grew slack. He cried out as the ring fell and the pilot thrust him aside.

He snapped up the ring and wiped the dust away on his sleeve. 'No,' he said. 'It must go to Count Dracone.'

Two

I

Father Augustine stepped into the boat, unfastened the painter from the ring let into the presbytery wall, and leant on the single oar, driving the craft out into the main waterway. The black prow reared up against a reddened sky; the canal reflecting it became a sea of blood. The ripples of his passing disturbed water creatures that writhed in his wake; averting his eyes, Father Augustine made the sign of the cross.

Ahead was a bridge, the black arch springing from its reflection, but the arch was broken, the circle eternally incomplete. Fallen masonry blocked part of the channel, but Father Augustine negotiated it with the skill of long practice. At the end of the bridge was a stone lion, its mane softly curling round a face filled with wisdom, an open book in its paws. Father Augustine whispered the carved words it was too dark to see. *Pax tibi, Marce, evangelista meus.* His boat skimmed beneath the bridge.

He remembered his dream of the night before, when the lion had led him by twisting paths up a mountainside, pacing gravely before him, its wings half raised, while he panted to keep up. The sky was dark; Father Augustine did not know by what light he walked, unless it came from the lion. It led him to the wall of a city, that covered the mountain top. The wall was built of translucent stone, and beyond it Father Augustine could see towers and pinnacles, their shapes wavering as if he saw them through water. A river flowed through the city, and on either side of it grew groves of trees, but all was dark and silent. The lion took wing, soaring higher until it became no more than a tiny, scintillating pulse in the darkness. Left alone, Father Augustine had stumbled along beside the wall, groping with one hand on the smooth surface until he encountered something else, the intricate filigree of a gate . . .

Beyond the bridge the waterway twisted sharply, and as he rounded the bend Father Augustine was confronted by the blazing lights of the Palazzo Dracone.

He stopped rowing, letting the boat glide slowly forward. With the light, music came jangling over the water, a popular tune that delivery boys whistled and drunkards bawled in taverns. By the palazzo's doors, a flyer was moored, bobbing on its floats. Father Augustine could not restrain a faint intake of breath. Count Dracone made no secret of how he trafficked in the science of the Empire. But then, he told himself, the vast wealth it brought Count Dracone made it all the more likely that he would give what Father Augustine had come to ask.

At last the boat nudged gently against the palazzo steps. Father Augustine made fast to a pole striped in scarlet and gold, the colours of House Dracone, and stepped out. Bronze doors were closed against him; he seized the knocker and struck down with it.

The doors swung slowly open. A creature stood there, wearing a scarlet livery laced with gold, incongruous beneath the thrusting jaw and lowering forehead, the hair sweeping over small, sunken eyes: no human door-keeper, but a genic, or more likely a construct, adequate for an undemanding task.

Father Augustine repressed a shudder of revulsion, and said, 'I wish to speak to Count Dracone. Please tell him that Father Augustine of I Frari asks for a few minutes of his time.'

The creature turned without speaking, and shuffled through the doors, closing them again behind him, and leaving Father Augustine to wait on the steps.

He glanced around him, and shifted from foot to foot. He was a young man, tall, with a countryman's rawboned body that seemed incongruous in his priest's black. As he waited, he had time to admit the nervousness that had been growing ever since he had known that he must come. He was uneasy in the face of Count Dracone's wealth; he did not know the proper courtesies, and he proposed asking for much more than a few minutes of the Count's time. He murmured a prayer, and the door opened once more.

The liveried construct shambled ahead of him down a corridor towards a flight of stairs. Lights dazzled from the ceiling; after one glance at the frescos which rioted across the walls, Father Augustine walked with his eyes cast down.

The chamber to which the construct took him was huge, pillared and echoing. The marble floor shone, so that the furniture, couches gilded and cushioned with velvet and brocade, seemed to float in light. As Father Augustine entered, his host the Count rose to greet him.

He was a small man, dark, serpentine. His hands glittered with rings. Thin red lips smiled as he said, 'Father Augustine. You're welcome. How may I serve you?'

Father Augustine took off his broad-brimmed, black

hat, revealing untidy, strawcoloured hair, laid it against
his breast, and bowed awkwardly. 'My lord Count—'

'But this won't do!' the Count interrupted. 'Take off
your cloak, Father, sit and be comfortable. And then you
can tell me all about it.'

Father Augustine felt the construct's hands fumbling
at his shoulders, easing away the cloak; he gave it the hat,
too, and perched on the edge of a chair that the Count
indicated. The construct was at his elbow again, offering
a silver goblet. The liquid it contained looked like water,
but when Father Augustine sipped it, he was sure it was
not water; he put it aside on a small table.

Count Dracone was seated opposite him, leaning
forward and smiling. 'Now, Father . . . Augustine?'

He broke off as an inner door opened. Father Augustine caught his breath. The most beautiful creature he
had ever seen had entered the room and was coming
towards him; while he knew it to be wholly evil, he could
not tear his eyes away. His hand moved involuntarily in
the sign of the cross.

It was a genic, an altered human, and Father Augustine would not have cared to guess whether it was male
or female. Below medium height, slender, delicate. The
hair was a fleece of silvery curls, and the skin had a silver
sheen, as if the pale genic blood, the mark of its separation, coursed just beneath the surface. It wore a robe of
silver mesh, a chlamys falling straight from its shoulders
like rain. The long, tilted eyes were aquamarine.

The Count was watching Father Augustine with an
amused expression. 'You like Rafael?'

Father Augustine stared at him. 'How can you call
this – this abomination,' he burst out, 'by the name of
one of God's archangels?'

Count Dracone still kept his amused look, but his eyes were cold. He stretched out a hand; the genic came to his side and curled up on a stool at his feet. It gave Father Augustine one wondering look from wide, sea-green eyes, and then lowered its lashes, as if it dissembled submissive modesty. The Count stroked and played with the silver curls. 'You're a young man, Father,' he said. His voice was silk. 'Inexperienced. May I suggest you come to the purpose of your visit?'

Father Augustine felt his throat dry. Inadvisedly, he took a gulp from the goblet beside him. The Count smiled.

'My lord, word came to the presbytery today . . .'

'Yes?'

'Word of a ring. A ring that your servants found and brought to you. A ring of – oh, my lord, of incalculable value!'

His eagerness drove away some of his misgivings. The Count was nodding.

'It is true?' Father Augustine breathed out.

'My dear Augustine, it is true that a wall on my property collapsed and revealed a burial vault. My pilot, Cesare, brought me a ring that he had taken from a dead finger – a finger wasted to bone. What more you may have heard, I cannot say.'

'I heard,' Father Augustine said softly, 'that the ring is a reliquary. That it contains a hair – a hair, my lord, of Christos when He walked this world as a man.'

Now the words were out the room was silent, as if the very air assimilated them. The genic Rafael had raised its head, and was gazing at Father Augustine again with those wonderful eyes.

The Count still smiled. 'Indeed.'

'Indeed? Is it – is it so, my lord?'

Slowly, the Count drew off a ring. It was gold, set with lapis; the Count flicked at the stone, which hinged back to reveal an inset crystal, and within the crystal . . . Father Augustine leant forward, eagerly reaching out, but the Count made no move to give him the ring.

'So precious . . .' Father Augustine whispered.

'So,' the Count said. 'You have ascertained that your rumour is true. If that is all—'

'No.'

The Count's brows lifted. His smile had vanished. 'No? What, then?'

Father Augustine swallowed. He knew what he wanted, but it was not easy to put words to the thought. 'My lord Count, it is . . . it is clear that such a treasure should be in the keeping of the Church.'

'It may be clear to you, Father,' the Count said, 'but it is far from being clear to me. Are you proposing to buy it from me?'

Father Augustine could not help smiling. 'You are a rich man, my lord, and we are poor. Besides, who could buy it? Who could presume to put a price on it?'

'I see.' The Count was smiling again. His teeth were white, sharp, his look predatory. 'You are asking me to give it to you.'

'We would pray for you day and night, my lord.'

The Count closed the ring and turned it in his fingertips. 'The ring is mine,' he murmured. 'But I have many rings. You would be better advised, Father, to convince me this one is worthless. Then I might give it to you.'

Father Augustine frowned; he was not sure he understood, or that he believed the Count meant what he seemed to mean. 'My lord . . .?'

'Deny your God, Father. Tell me the relic is trash, no more than the superstition of an age long gone. At best, a curiosity. Tell me that.'

'My lord, I cannot!'

The Count shrugged, a fluid, dismissive movement. 'But I regret, Father, that is the price of this ring.'

Father Augustine found it hard to answer. He had no experience of great men, nothing to tell him whether Count Dracone was playing a game with him, or whether he was serious, or whether, perhaps, he meant to trap him into blasphemy. Steadily, he said, 'Forgive me, my lord, it is a price I cannot pay.'

For a moment the Count made no reply. He went on turning the ring to and fro, watching the play of light on the gold and the rough surface of the lapis. 'The ring is mine,' he repeated. 'Certainly I might give it if I choose. And I do choose.'

A sudden joy expanded in Father Augustine's heart. It had been a game, then, or a test of his faith. Yes, a test, to see if he was worthy to possess – no, not possess, but even touch – the reliquary ring. Then joy turned to ice as Count Dracone let the ring fall, and the genic Rafael turned a palm up to receive it.

Father Augustine sprang to his feet. 'No!'

'No?' The Count's murmur had a cutting edge. 'Do you tell me I cannot do what I wish with my own?'

'No. Not that. You have no right. You defile what is holy beyond your understanding. No man has the right.'

Father Augustine stared down at Rafael. He had a wild impulse to snatch the ring and flee. The genic had not moved, had not even closed its hand, as if it had not understood what the ring was, or what the Count had done. Father Augustine wondered if it was an idiot, wondered if there was any mind at all behind that beautiful exterior.

While he stood, indecisive, the Count had risen. If he had given any signal, Father Augustine had missed it, but he heard movement and looked up to see two more constructs entering the room, to join the one that had been in attendance all along. They drew close to him, hemming him in, and Father Augustine looked from one to another, beginning to feel a fear deeper than his anxiety at mishandling the situation.

'Your Lord Christos was crucified, was he not?' the Count said. 'You should feel privileged to share the manner of his martyrdom. Unfortunately, perhaps, I have no cross, but I might perhaps provide a suitable substitute.'

He made a signal to the constructs. Two of them laid hands on Father Augustine and bore him backwards until he fetched up against the nearest pillar. He began to struggle, but their strength was greater, though their touch was curiously gentle, with hands that felt soft. He shuddered. 'You dare not do this,' he said. 'In harming me you do harm to Holy Church herself. You do harm to God.'

The Count's eyelids drooped. 'You overwhelm me.'

Father Augustine had lost sight of the third construct, which now approached its master again, carrying what looked like a hank of thin cords, though they writhed and lashed back and forth in its grasp. Father Augustine let out an involuntary exclamation.

'Bioropes,' Count Dracone said. 'You have seen them

before, perhaps. You know how they work? They respond to movement, Father. Any movement, however slight, makes them contract a little. Fight against them, and they contract very quickly indeed.'

He nodded to the construct. As the creature drew close to him, Father Augustine gave way to another spasm of violent struggling, but it was useless. With inexorable strength, the constructs bound him to the pillar, with bioropes around his wrists, lashed above his head, around his throat, his waist, and his ankles. He stood still, trying to control his gasping breath. He could feel the bioropes as a cool, silky touch, not even tight as yet.

'Go on struggling,' the Count said, 'and you will finish it quickly. And that might be merciful. But if you keep still, and very, very quiet, then it will take you hours to die. And help may come, although I doubt it. Or I might release you myself, Father. For you don't know that I mean to kill you. Perhaps I only test you. Perhaps I'm playing a game. Perhaps after all I mean to let you live. There's no way you'll ever be sure, Father, until it happens.'

He made a dismissive gesture towards the constructs, which withdrew through the outer door. He himself moved towards the opposite door, flicking his fingers for the genic Rafael to follow him. It rose obediently, passing so close to Father Augustine that he felt himself shrinking in revulsion at the thought that the thing might reach out and touch him. Then it was gone, following the Count.

Alone in the vast, bright room, Father Augustine forced himself to think coolly. The impulse to struggle, to shout for help, was very strong, but he resisted it. That would end in a swift, helpless choking, and then death.

He was not ready to give in yet. The rope around his wrists felt loose. If he could get one hand free ... Delicately he slid one wrist against the other, but the biorope's response was instant: a slithering against his skin, a tightening. Father Augustine grew still, the rope firm around his wrists now. Silently, he prayed.

He tried not to move, tried to make each breath as shallow as possible, but he knew very well that each tiny movement of throat and chest, even the thrumming of blood through his veins, would cause the infinitesimal tightening of the cords. How long before he was aware of it? How long before it became discomfort, and then pain?

He could feel sweat trickling down his face. His skin pricked under his cassock. His vision dimmed and there was a thundering in his ears. He needed more air. But if he took a deep breath his bonds would tighten. If he fainted and sagged in the cords, they would tighten and hold him there. The temptation to finish it quickly returned with overwhelming force.

As his senses swirled away, he thought himself back on the mountainside of his dream. The gate was locked against him. The streets of the city beyond it were dark and empty. Augustine did not know why, or why the gate would not open to him. He dared not stay. He dared not go back down the mountain. Leaning against the gate, he wept, and felt the bioropes cut harder into his chest and throat.

He did not know how long he had been held there when he heard the inner door open again. He blinked to clear his vision. Hope leapt within him. The Count had returned, then. It had been a game after all. A cruel game, played by an evil man, but no more than a game. Even

so, Father Augustine dared not try to turn his head, and
when at last the newcomer moved into his field of vision,
it was not Count Dracone, but the genic Rafael.

It came close to Father Augustine, looking up at him
with lips parted, its breath coming unevenly. It raised one
hand, and Father Augustine saw that it held a thin-
bladed, glittering knife. On the same hand it bore the
reliquary ring.

'Father,' it whispered. 'I'll release you, if you promise
to take me with you.'

'What!'

The single word came almost as a shout. Father
Augustine had not even been sure that the genic could
speak, and those were the last words he would have
expected it to utter. He felt a warning tug on the bioropes
around his throat, and schooled his voice to a low, flat
muttering. 'Is this another game of the Count's?'

'No!' The creature glanced fearfully over its shoulder.
'He doesn't know – if he found me . . .'

The whisper died away in a gasp of terror. Father
Augustine had not thought the thing sentient enough to
feel fear. 'Then why are you here?'

'I told you!' The whisper had grown more urgent.
'Take me with you. Give me a place to stay where he
won't ever find me. Oh, please . . .' Its voice was breaking.
Pleadingly it reached out, not quite daring to touch
Father Augustine's face. 'Take me with you, and I'll give
you the ring.'

Father Augustine thought rapidly. He wanted to live.
This was a genic; to promise and then break faith with it
would be no sin. Yet if he kept the promise, he would
gain the ring, rescue it from defilement and bring it into
the protection of the Church. Sanity returned. There was

nowhere, no safe place, in the city or out of it, where he could take a genic with Rafael's looks, not when Count Dracone owned its rights and could petition the State for its return. Promise, then, and break faith, and live . . . The sea-green eyes, so close to his, were brimming with tears.

'Please . . .' Rafael whispered.

Father Augustine had lost control, the bioropes were tightening, and he fancied the constriction around his throat was already cutting off his breath. In seconds the knife could slice through it . . .

'No,' he said. 'How can I? Where could I take you? And how can I make a bargain with a genic, a creature outside God's law?'

The eyes suddenly blazed at him. 'A genic? Is that . . .?' The voice was still low, but suddenly vibrating with disgust. 'Is that what you think? Look!'

The creature took the knife and dug the point into its own forearm, slashing upwards. Behind the point a gash opened up in the silvery skin, like a scarlet mouth gaping. Blood welled out and splattered to the floor. Rafael – no genic, but human, a boy scarcely out of childhood – stared at what he had done, trembling and whimpering.

Now, when he really looked at him, Father Augustine could see the signs that might have told him the truth before this. The boy's teeth were uneven, his hands broad, with stubby fingers – flaws that would make a genic unsaleable, at least to a connoisseur like Dracone.

'Why?' Father Augustine asked. 'Why stay here if you're not—'

'What would you do?' Rafael sobbed out. 'Where would you go if you looked like me, and you had no one . . .'

Father Augustine had jerked against the ropes, and they were cutting into him, tighter and tighter now. He fought for breath enough to speak. 'Yes,' he choked out. 'I'll help you. Be quick . . .'

For a few seconds Rafael did nothing. He seemed to quiver on the edge of hysteria. Father Augustine was suffocating. His vision drowned in a roaring, red haze. Blood drummed in his ears. Then the bonds were gone, and he pitched forward on to his knees, shaking his head to clear it, retching and massaging his throat, while the scraps of biorope writhed harmlessly around him.

Rafael was crouched beside him. He dragged the ring off his finger, and pressed it into Father Augustine's hand. Father Augustine thrust it almost disregarded into his cassock pocket, pulled Rafael to his feet and across the hall to the outer door, snatching up his cloak from a chairback as he passed it. He flung open the door; in the corridor stood Count Dracone.

Rafael shrank back. The Count smiled. 'Did you really think, Father, that I would not be watching?'

Father Augustine stood quietly. He knew it would be futile to plead, or protest, and he would not even try to attack. He waited, and had the satisfaction of knowing that his waiting disconcerted the Count.

'You have done well, Father,' he said. 'Better than I would expect for a priest and a peasant. Suppose I reward you? Suppose I let you take one of my treasures – the ring, or Rafael? Which is it to be?'

He was looking past Father Augustine at Rafael, the promise in his eyes more venomous for being silent. Father Augustine could hear Rafael's shuddering breath. His hand went to his cassock pocket, pressed around the hard shape of the ring.

He took it out, looked at it, weighing it in his palm, and held it out to Dracone. The Count's nails scraped his palm as he took it. His upper lip lifted in a snarl. Father Augustine turned from him, folded his cloak around the weeping Rafael, and began to walk down the corridor.

2

Serafina sat in her own tiny room under the eaves. Her hands were folded in her lap; she gazed out of her window to where she could just catch a glimpse of the distant domes of the basilica, dark against an evening sky barred with cloud.

Today Countess Dandolo had gone to her entombment. Serafina could not go with her; she had said her own farewells already. Now she wondered whether the Countess's God, who was not the god of the genics, would hear her if she offered Him a prayer. She did not even know how true humans prayed, or what form of words would be acceptable.

'If You are listening . . .' she murmured aloud, half nervous that divine lightning would strike her down for presumption, half ashamed that she was speaking into a void, 'if You are listening, welcome the Countess into Your house. Forgive her for what the Count calls her impiety. She loved life, and You gave it to her. And I loved her,' she added, hurriedly, more ashamed still.

The reddening sky beyond her window remained unresponsive. Serafina wondered what response she had expected.

Some time later she heard voices and doors banging below, and then a single set of footsteps on the stairs. Her door was flung open; Count Dandolo, the Countess's son, stood on the threshold, a black pillar of rectitude. He was alone; he would not expose his equally pious wife to Serafina's company, or their carefully nurtured daughters.

Serafina got to her feet and dropped him a respectful curtsey. He stared at her from cold eyes under jutting brows. As if his mouth was soiled by even speaking to her, he said, 'Follow me.'

'Where are you taking me, sir?' Serafina asked.

Count Dandolo's mouth set like a trap. He did not find her worthy of an answer; he simply gestured irritably for her to obey.

Serafina stood her ground. 'Am I to serve you, sir? Now that I belong to you?' She fixed her eyes on her demurely folded hands, hiding amusement. 'I'll try to please you well, sir . . . in everything.'

She heard his hiss of outrage, though she did not look up at him.

'Girl,' he said, 'a man in my position cannot keep a genic. I have made other arrangements for you.'

Terror clawed deep in Serafina, though she fought to maintain her outward calm. 'What arrangements, sir?'

'You are to be maidservant to Countess Contarini's daughter. The Contarinis are somewhat . . . less strict in their views, but a great House, nonetheless. You should think yourself fortunate.'

Some of Serafina's terror dissolved. She did indeed think herself fortunate, though not in the exact way the Count had intended. But to serve the Countess Contarini's daughter — or anyone's daughter — was no part of her plans. She said, 'Did my lady the Countess leave no orders about me? Have you looked at her papers?'

'Papers?' Count Dandolo's voice was suddenly sharp.
'What papers?'

Serafina caught the glitter of greed in the hard eyes.
He had assumed that his mother had no wealth – other
than one slightly embarrassing genic – and in that he was
quite right. But Serafina had guessed that he would never
resist the possibility that there was more.

'I'll show you, sir. Come.'

She liked the way he started back from her as she
passed him in the doorway, the hem of her gown trailing
over his freshly polished boots. Would he order them
polished again when he got home, she wondered, or
simply give them to a servant?

She led the way into the old Countess's bedchamber.
The great bed was stripped of its hangings now, gone to
adorn some lesser bed in House Dandolo. But the bedside
table still stood in its place. Serafina opened the drawer
and stood back to let Count Dandolo look.

He pulled the drawer out and laid it on the mattress,
impatiently turning over the contents. Writing materials;
wax and seal; a few unpaid bills which he crumpled and
tossed aside. And one other sheet. Serafina's stomach
lurched as he picked it up, and it took all her self-control
to remain with her eyes modestly lowered.

After a pause, Count Dandolo read aloud, ' "The last
will and testament of Caterina Dandolo. Being of sound
mind, and having no property to dispose of but the genic
Serafina, I bequeath her to Dr Heinrich, in gratitude for
his medical services." Have you seen this, girl?'

Serafina raised wondering eyes to his face. 'How
should I, sir?'

Of course, how should she? Count Dandolo would
never imagine that a genic would be able to read and

write, or that the Countess might have confided in her genic. He snorted, displeased. Serafina watched him. The handwriting, even the signature, should not rouse his suspicion, for Serafina had written all the Countess's meagre correspondence in the last few years.

At length, very deliberately, the Count laid the document down. 'This is not legal,' he said abruptly. 'There are no witnesses, and no notary's seal.'

'The Countess had no one to witness it,' said Serafina, 'and no money for a notary. But it is her last wish, sir.'

'My mother, sadly, was too ill to know her own mind.' His movements still deliberate, the Count took a lucifer from the tray by the lamp, struck it, and held the corner of the document in the flame.

'Sir!' Serafina exclaimed as it flared up.

The Count watched silently until the sheet was consumed and the flames died. He blew away the ash and dropped the spent lucifer to the floor.

'The document never existed,' he said, his voice betraying a tight satisfaction. 'If you speak of it you will be whipped for lying. Do you understand me, girl?'

Inwardly raging, Serafina bobbed another curtsey. 'Yes, sir. I understand.'

'Good. Now follow me to the Countess Contarini.'

3

Manfred stumbled as he turned into the alley alongside the Palazzo Loredan. His head swam with exhaustion; he had not eaten since the day before. He supported himself against the wall as he struggled towards the doorway of the palazzo.

The alley was pitch black, except for a faint light showing at the far end, where the waters of the canal glittered under the moon. There was a rank smell. Manfred trod in something soft and disgusting; an eerie yowl sounded from somewhere close to his feet and he caught a glimpse of green eyes as the cats fled. He did not want to know what they had been feeding on.

Count Dracone's pilot had left with the ring and the parchment. Manfred had left the same day, but it had taken him much longer to reach the city on foot, with only the occasional lift from a donkey cart. In the last day or two, he had wondered whether his strength would serve him.

He had done with Count Dracone. He was returning where he belonged, to House Loredan, and he wondered why he had not done it years ago.

The heavy doors of the palazzo were closed, and no lights were burning. Manfred stumbled up the steps and banged his fist on the door. Silence was the only response. What were the servants thinking of, Manfred asked himself angrily, or the steward for not lessoning them in their duties?

He knocked again. This time he heard brisk footsteps approaching from beyond the door, and it opened a crack, though all was dark inside. A slender young man, fair hair blanched by the moonlight, stood in the opening.

'Let me in,' Manfred said, striving for the crisp tones that had sent servants scurrying to do his bidding in years gone by. 'Tell your master Count Loredan that Manfred wishes to speak to him.'

'Manfred?' The young man looked puzzled, and made no attempt to obey the order.

As he drew breath for a scathing rebuke Manfred remembered where he had seen that pale, arrogant countenance before. The young man was the image of old Count Ercole, as he had been a lifetime ago. Wild thoughts of the old man's by-blows fled through Manfred's mind, but he let them go. He knew who was standing before him. 'Count Leonardo!'

His knees began to give way, from shock or respect he was not sure, and he felt the young man's arm about him, drawing him in through the door.

'Hold up, man!' the Count said. 'Here – sit.' He let Manfred fall, like an inconvenient sack, on a bench just inside the door, and turned to shut it. 'Manfred – from the hunting lodge?' he asked. 'I remember now. What can I do for you?'

Manfred's head was spinning; he shook it to clear it of the dark fog that threatened to overwhelm him. 'I have left Count Dracone's service,' he said.

Count Leonardo gave a short laugh, and stood with his back to the door, looking down at Manfred. He sounded almost embarrassed. 'And come to me,' he said. 'Manfred, I'm sorry. My father left me with nothing. I can't afford to employ you.'

He spread his arms and showed Manfred the hall. Apart from the bench where Manfred sat, it was empty. The plaster was peeling from the walls. There were no lights, except for the moon shining through the transom window. Count Leonardo himself was dressed in the threadbare black that at first had made Manfred take him for a servant. Manfred began to realize why it was that the Count should answer his own door.

'Your father—' he echoed stupidly.

'Left nothing but his debts. I sold everything to clear

them, and preserve the good name of House Loredan. I'm sorry, Manfred, you will have to go elsewhere for employment.'

The old man rose to his feet. He was afraid that he might faint at the young Count's feet, and he was determined not to do that. Mustering dignity, he said, 'I have nowhere else to go. I will work for food and lodging, until your House rises again.'

'Rises?' The firm mouth suddenly shook, and Leonardo bit his lip to hide it. He stepped forward and rested his hands on Manfred's shoulders. 'I accept your service,' he said gravely. 'And you shall share in the fortunes of House Loredan, good or bad.'

Manfred bowed his head.

'And now,' said the young Count, 'tell me what led you to forsake Count Dracone.'

4

'He will never let us go!' Rafael was still sobbing, terrified, as the door of the Palazzo Dracone closed behind him.

'He made a bargain,' Father Augustine said, but even as he spoke the words he was afraid that Rafael was right. He could not believe that Count Dracone would give him a real choice, or that he had ever meant to let him keep Rafael or the ring.

His boat was moored where he had left it, next to Count Dracone's flyer. He helped Rafael into it, slipped the painter, and began rowing out into the main channel. Rafael huddled at the opposite end of the boat, shivering and cradling his wounded arm.

Father Augustine was not sure where they could go.

He could not return to the presbytery. There would be no protection there from Count Dracone. Besides, Father Augustine knew that when he dropped the ring into Count Dracone's hand, he had stepped outside the protection of Holy Church.

He wondered if that was what his dream had meant, when he stood alone, outside the gate of the darkened city, and found it locked against him.

Here and there along the sides of the canal lights flickered from behind shuttered windows, or from shrines where statues gazed blindly down, casting a momentary, uncertain gleam on the surface of the water. Once, as they slid beneath a bridge, they caught a gust of raucous singing, and once a wisp of music, a faint violin, floated on the air and was gone. They met no other boats.

If they could survive until morning, Father Augustine thought, they might petition the Duke. There was still law, of a sort, in the city, though Father Augustine wondered if the Council would believe him, in preference to a wealthy man like Count Dracone. They certainly would not believe Rafael.

The moon was rising behind cloud as Father Augustine rowed his boat into the square. The sea was high, water covering the paving stones; a cold breeze ridged the surface as the moonlight turned it to wrinkled steel. Beyond the sheet of water rose the basilica, the golden domes floating insubstantial as clouds.

The distant sound of a flyer engine sent Father Augustine towards the basilica, rowing swiftly, at the risk of grounding on the pavement below. As he approached it, the pale light changed, grew brighter, and a wing of shadow swooped across the boat as Count Dracone's flyer screamed overhead.

Rafael, who had sunk into a stupor, roused up; the boat rocked dangerously as he clutched at the side.

'Keep still,' Father Augustine said.

He sent the craft skimming into shadow, and crouched low as the flyer doubled back and slashed its trail of light once more across the square. Before it was out of sight, he dug the oar into the water again and began to propel the boat towards the steps, and the refuge of the basilica, only to change course sharply as the flyer came swooping down again, almost touching the surface.

A jet of fire spat out of it, setting flames dancing in the black mirror of the water.

The flyer drove them away from the basilica, along the dark frontage of the Ducal Palace. It seemed to swerve from side to side like a hunting bat, herding them always towards the quayside and the deeper water of the lagoon.

Father Augustine felt the moment when the deeper surge took them, tossing the frail boat. Fire raked the waves and seared over their heads. Rafael screamed and flung himself to one side, away from the licking flame. The boat tilted and filled, pitching him and Father Augustine into the sea. The flyer screamed overhead and the jet of flame hissed as it met the surface.

Father Augustine gasped, trod water, and looked for Rafael. Terrified, he thought the boy had gone down for good until he reappeared a yard or two away, struggling and choking as he tried to scream for help. His cries were lost in the snarl of the flyer engine.

Striking out towards him, Father Augustine knew despair. Between fire and water, what could he do, to save himself and Rafael? He reached the boy as he was sinking again, and fought to hold him up as Rafael clawed blindly at him.

He was swallowing water. The sodden folds of his cassock clung round his legs. Rafael's weight was dragging him down, and the boy's frantic grip on him hindered his efforts to swim. He did not know where the flyer had gone. All he could hear was Rafael gulping and retching as he drowned.

Then beyond the sound, Father Augustine thought he could make out something else, a highpitched call that was repeated close by. He turned his head; something else was in the water beside him. The red glare reflected off a face not human. The voice cried, 'Dive!'

Father Augustine obeyed, less out of trust than because the jet of fire was upon him again, sweeping over his head as he plunged for the depths. Rafael thrashed spasmodically and then was still. A hand fastened round Father Augustine's wrist and drew him down; his hand brushed the ooze of the bottom and he had a momentary terror of being held under, of twining limbs enmeshing him like weeds. Then his fingers were guided to a rope; he fumbled and found it looped through a metal ring in the wall. Lungs bursting now, he pulled himself along. Just as he thought he could bear it no longer, he surged upwards into air.

Steps led up out of the water; the rope he was clinging to continued up the wall to a landing above. The flames were gone. Yellow light slanted down from a lamp hanging from the roof. Beside him, the other head broke surface and for the first time he saw the genic clearly as it followed him up the steps and turned to face him.

It was a genic, he was sure of that this time, in the form of a woman. Her skin was pallid white, roped with blue-green veins. Her face was flat, with a wide gash of a mouth and protruding eyes with thick lids half covering them. Her fingers were webbed, and her toes were long and prehensile and webbed also. She was ugly beyond imagining, except for a long fall of silky, blue-green hair, plastered now by the water to her body as far as her waist. She was completely naked.

Kneeling on the lowest step clear of the water, she reached out and slid her hands round Rafael's shoulders. He was limp, his head sagging, his eyes closed. Sheathed in the silver chlamys, he looked like some exotic fish taken from the lagoon.

The genic dragged him out of the water, and Father Augustine, following, helped her to lift him as far as the top of the steps. Here she pounced on him, covered his mouth with her own and breathed for him. Father Augustine knelt beside him, gasping air into tortured lungs.

No more than a moment passed before Rafael stirred, moaned, and opened his eyes to see the genic bending over him, her face close to his own. He tried to scream, convulsed, and coughed out a gush of water before subsiding into terrified sobbing. Father Augustine caught hold of his hand. 'Don't, Rafael. It's all right. You're safe.'

The genic was watching him with an expression which, on a human, he might have thought conveyed curiosity and amusement. Belatedly, he thought to thank her.

'You have a powerful enemy,' she said calmly. 'I'd like to know what you did to deserve that.'

'Dracone,' Father Augustine said. 'I took the boy from Dracone.'

For a moment the genic's amusement deepened, and then was gone. 'He will believe you dead – drowned,' she said. 'But you cannot go back.'

Father Augustine looked at her, and then at the still weeping Rafael. Relief at their escape gave way to uncertainty, mixed with fear. Where could they go, how could they live, and be safe from Dracone? Even his hope of petitioning the Duke seemed pitifully frail now. Safety lay in this small circle of yellow light; outside was only darkness, slashed by gouts of flame. Yet they could not stay there for ever.

Painfully, he said, 'Mistress, there is nowhere we can go.'

She went on regarding him for a little longer, her slitted features unreadable now. At last she unhooked the lamp, and holding it high began to walk along the passage that led away from the top of the steps. Over her shoulder, she said, 'Follow me.'

'Where?' Father Augustine asked, though he was already hauling Rafael to his feet, beginning to panic that the genic would leave them behind.

She did not answer him.

Supporting Rafael, who was barely conscious through fear and exhaustion, Father Augustine hurried after her.

The floor of the passage was rough stone, the walls whitewashed, with narrow windows closed by shutters. Father Augustine guessed they were in one of the abandoned buildings along the waterfront, but he had no idea where the genic was taking them.

Soon they reached a door. The genic hung the lamp on another hook beside it, and blew it out. In the darkness Father Augustine heard her thrusting back bolts, and then moonlight flooded into the passage as the door swung open.

Beyond was the dark glitter of water: a narrow canal, with the blind wall of another building beyond it. A small fishing boat was moored there, its sail neatly furled.

The genic woman stepped down into it. 'Come,' she said.

As Father Augustine stepped out of the shelter of the building, he half expected to hear the snarl of Dracone's flyer, see its flame spitting down on him, but now the night was dark and quiet. He lowered Rafael into the boat, and clambered down after him, with more speed than dignity.

Whispering urgently now, he asked, 'Where are you taking us?'

The genic pushed off and began to paddle softly towards the canal mouth. With a half smile of her lipless mouth she answered, 'You will see.'

Father Augustine opened his mouth to protest, and closed it again. They were in her hands. Whatever was to come, he could do nothing about it, except offer up a silent prayer.

Once away from the quayside, the genic hoisted the sail, and the boat went skimming out into the lagoon. Father Augustine sat in the stern, looking back as the city dropped away behind them.

With one webbed hand on the tiller, and the other on the rope that controlled the sail, the genic woman guided her craft expertly along the channels that separated the inner islands, keeping her prow pointed towards the open sea. The cool wind struck chill on Father Augustine's wet cassock, and he shivered, but not all from cold. A great fear fell on him, of night, and sea, and the secrets in the genie's eyes.

At last he realized that the boat was drawing closer to an island, so distant from the city that when Father Augustine turned to look back he could see nothing but a dim line on the horizon.

Ahead was a tumble of ruined buildings, falling away sharply on the western side. As the boat drew nearer, Father Augustine saw that the land had collapsed, or the sea had risen and engulfed half the abandoned village. Waves lapped in the streets and as he looked down he saw the shadows of rooftops.

When he first noticed the pale light he thought it was the reflection of moonlight on water, until he realized that it was striking upwards from below, illuminating groves of seaweed and the undulating fronds of sea anemones, rocks or the ruined walls of buildings encrusted with shellfish. In a flash of pearl he saw limbs cleaving the water beneath the boat, the swimmer's hair a floating cloud. Shivering, he remembered the old tales of mermaids who drew sailors to their death, and then in a moment all was gone, dropping behind as the boat sailed on.

A low moan drew his attention back to Rafael. The boy lay uneasily in the bottom of the boat; his eyes were closed, and when Father Augustine spoke his name there was no response. Father Augustine reached down and touched his forehead; a feverish heat was rising in him. The gash in his arm had stopped bleeding, but his flesh was beginning to puff up, and his skin was stretched and shiny. Father Augustine knew he needed a physician, but not all his prayers would be enough to provide one out here.

With his eyes still doubtfully on Rafael, Father Augustine was suddenly aware of something dark looming out of the water ahead of them. A cry was stifled in his throat, as the genic woman sent the boat skimming under an archway.

The wind was cut off, the sail flapped, and the boat glided to a halt, rocking gently on the sea swell. Father Augustine stared around him in wonder rising to dismay.

They lay becalmed in a vast, walled space. Veined marble columns rose out of the sea, stretching up to a domed roof. Fixed to them, or set in niches around the walls, coiled shells served as lamps, shedding a pale, nacreous light. From balconies overhead, twisted vines of sea-wrack looped or hung trailing into the water. Everything was silent except for the soft lapping of the waves.

Father Augustine gazed up into a dome covered in dim gold. Darker blotches spread across its surface, and as his eyes became accustomed to the light he gradually discerned other eyes, gazing gravely down at him, and realized that he was looking at an enormous mosaic, Christos and His Mother, marred by decay but still recognizable. And he knew where he was.

'The ancient cathedral . . .' he breathed out. 'You live here?'

'Some of us.' The genic woman's face bore that same look of detached amusement. 'This troubles you . . . Father?'

No mistaking the irony as she addressed him by the name of his calling. Father Augustine's hand moved almost automatically in the sign of the cross. He knew that he should be denouncing her for blasphemy, and yet more than his need of her kept him silent. He was filled with wonder.

The genic took up a paddle and began propelling the boat along the length of what had been the nave, their wake a momentary dark slash in that lake of shimmering pearl.

As they moved slowly on, Father Augustine began to see movement on the balconies above, a shape printed briefly against the night sky visible through a clerestory window, a head bobbing in a distant apse, a rustle from the dangling vine ropes. He gradually realized that the cathedral was not as empty as he had thought at first. 'Some of us,' she had said.

'How many of you are there?' he asked.

The genic paused in her paddling to consider the question, and shrugged. 'We do not count our numbers.'

'Then you are—' Father Augustine broke off with an inarticulate sound in his throat as a dark head broke surface beside the boat in a shower of glittering droplets. A hand reached upwards, the arm naked and roped in pearl, and grasped the side of the boat. Another genic woman clung there, her hair floating around her, her skin lustrous from the sheen of light on water. In a flash of altered vision, he almost saw that what he had taken for grotesque could be pure beauty, but the insight was gone again before he could capture it.

Then they were all around the boat, men and women, swimming closer in curiosity, while the air was filled with echoing sounds of wonder and soft laughter.

'What have you there, Tethys?' someone called.

'Fugitives from the city,' their rescuer replied.

More laughter, more comments – some of them hostile, Father Augustine realized. *What will they do with us?* he wondered. *What will we do if they cast us out?*

The boat slid onwards, between the shattered panels

of the rood screen, surrounded now by an escort of the sea genics. As they approached the apse at the end of the sanctuary, one of them swam ahead, and pulled himself up on to the bishop's throne, which still stood, half in and half out of the water, so that the man himself sat poised between the two elements.

Father Augustine saw that he wore a short tunic, of dark silk shot through with silver, moulded to his body by the water, and a circlet made of pearl and coral on his blue-green hair.

'You have a king?' Father Augustine asked.

'We have a Duke,' Tethys said, 'as you do. Here we are the true republic of the sea.'

She pulled the paddle out of the water and let the boat glide to a stop in front of the throne.

'Well?' the sea-Duke said. 'What have we to do with fugitives? Why are they here?'

Murmurs from the crowd of genics around the boat echoed the question. The Duke looked down with hooded eyes; Father Augustine, beginning to read expressions on the alien faces, saw displeasure there.

'Help us,' he said. 'We have nowhere else to go. I think the boy is dying.'

The sea-Duke's voice was as cold as the waves that surrounded him. 'Why should that matter to us?'

A sudden anger sparked in Father Augustine. He rose unsteadily to his feet, and turned his face upwards, to where those shadowed faces looked gravely down from the golden dome. 'How can you ask that, living as you do, in sight of the Lord Christos?'

The sea-Duke did not bother to look up. 'You humans teach that there is no god for genics.'

Before Father Augustine could think of a response,

Tethys cut in, with the same self-possession she had shown all along. 'Dracone hunts them. Dracone who traffics in genics for profit and his own lusts. You should thank me for the chance of serving him an ill turn.'

A gleam lit in the sea-Duke's dark eyes. Father Augustine expected him to berate Tethys for her lack of respect; instead, he looked amused. He waved a hand. 'Take them, then. Find them a place. Later you will tell me more of this.'

Overwhelmed by relief, Father Augustine stammered out, 'Thank you, my lord.'

He sank down in the boat as Tethys expertly turned it and began to paddle out of the Duke's presence. The hushed vastness of the ruined cathedral oppressed his spirit. Rafael still moaned and whimpered at his feet.

Smiling, Tethys said, 'Now you have seen more than any human living.'

Three

Gabriel gazed up at the domes of the basilica, floating like soap bubbles, dim gold against grey cloud. By some trick of the light, the skin of water that covered the square shone brighter than the sky, as if the whole expanse were paved with silver.

Perched on a chunk of shattered masonry, Gabriel waited for the single cracked bell that announced the end of the service, and pulled his thin jacket around him against the raw wind that swept in from the sea.

The congregation began to trickle out of the narthex through the central archway. Gabriel half rose as he saw his master, only to settle back on the stone as he saw that the Count was not alone. The Procurator of the basilica had him by the elbow, and the two men were in earnest conversation as they drew closer to Gabriel.

'. . . a ring which holds a priceless relic, a hair of the Lord Christos when He walked this earth as a man,' the Procurator was saying as he came into earshot. 'One of Count Dracone's men found it in an ancient tomb.'

Gabriel heard his master let out a snort of contempt. 'On land which my father diced away to Dracone.'

Count Leonardo Loredan flaunted his aristocratic lineage in his pale, high-nosed face, his ice-blue eyes and silk-blond hair, carelessly drawn back into a queue. His shabby black garments spoke of his poverty. His inheritance was no more than a crumbling palazzo, a few pitiful rents that dwindled year by year as his properties fell into disrepair, and Gabriel.

The Procurator inclined his head respectfully as he listened to him. 'The ring may once have been a treasure of House Loredan,' he said. 'But Count Dracone has offered to gift it to the Church if his name is inscribed in the Book of Gold.'

Leonardo straightened and came to an abrupt halt a few yards away from Gabriel. 'You refused, of course.'

'The decision is not mine.' The Procurator spread his hands; he was a thin, greying man, his black gown of office billowing in the sea wind. 'The matter must come before the Council.'

Leonardo gave him an icy stare. 'What have we come to? Dracone is an upstart, who bows and scrapes to the men of the Empire. For the sake of this ring – that House Loredan would have gifted to the Church without strings attached – we would write his name in the Book of Gold and give him the right to a perpetual place on the Council? Him and his descendants?'

The Procurator's mouth quirked. 'Count Dracone's mode of life is not such as will provide him with descendants. Come, Leonardo, for the sake of such a treasure . . .'

'No.' Planted on the silvery paving stones, Count Leonardo looked like a spiky rock surrounded by the sea – as amicable, Gabriel thought, and about as easy to shift. 'I'll remind you, messire, that I have a veto in Council. Dracone will never sit there while I live.'

The Procurator glanced nervously from side to side. Leonardo had not lowered his voice, and the congregation were still leaving the basilica. 'As well not let the Count know that,' he said.

Leonardo, who had begun to stride away, stopped and swivelled. 'A threat, messire?'

'A warning.' The Procurator caught him up, and they walked on side by side. 'They say Count Dracone has spies everywhere, and I for one believe it.'

Leonardo laughed, and signed to Gabriel, who rose and bowed as the two men came closer.

'So this is your genic?' the Procurator said, peering at Gabriel with interest overlaid by a faint revulsion. Gabriel kept his head bent, his eyes fixed on the water pooling at his feet. He had endured many such stares. 'I have seen few genics,' the Procurator went on. 'Holy Church, of course, may not make use of them. Forgive me, Count Leonardo, but is it entirely wise? Your reputation . . .?'

Leonardo's head went up arrogantly. 'A Loredan does not need to worry about his reputation.'

'Of course . . .' The Procurator sighed. 'Where, may I ask, did you obtain your genic?'

'I thought the whole city knew that, messire.' Bitterness warred with amusement in Leonardo's voice. 'My father won Gabriel on a throw of the dice. Gabriel is quite a trophy – the only time the old Count won anything at the gaming tables.'

The Procurator looked faintly shocked. 'Indeed . . .' He waved a hand, dismissing Gabriel from his mind, if not from his whole universe. 'On that other matter, my young friend, think well. Count Dracone is a determined man, and he greatly desires this place on the Council.' He paused, and added, 'The holy fathers at I Frari saw fit to send a young priest to ask Dracone for the ring. An inexperienced young man, totally unfitted for the task, in my view. He went to the Count's palazzo, and he has not been seen since. Count Dracone professes to know nothing of the matter.'

Leonardo snorted. 'And you think I am likely to disappear too? Messire, there have been Loredans in this city since it was founded. Whoever heard of this Dracone until a few years ago? He doesn't frighten me.'

He snapped his fingers at Gabriel, who fell in behind him as he stalked away across the square. 'All the same,' the Procurator called after him, 'he is a dangerous man to cross.'

Gabriel bent over the canvas, tentatively dabbed at it with his brush, and raised his head to gaze out of the window at the arch of sky over the canal. He let out a small, despairing sigh. How had the ancients, faced with such pure, quivering light, managed to translate it into paint? How had they dared to try?

The marble floor of Gabriel's studio was stained, and the flaking frescos that had once adorned the walls and the high ceiling were now barely visible. Along one wall was a trestle table that held Gabriel's experiments with pigments and brushes, and beside it the mattress where he slept at night. His single blanket was wrapped around him, clumsily pinned to leave his hands free for painting. The huge window had long since lost its glass, and the shutters were pulled back to let in the light.

Gabriel worked on until his concentration was broken by the sound of the door opening. For the space of a breath he was motionless, his brush poised; then he turned.

Count Leonardo kicked the door shut behind him. He was carrying a thick, pottery mug that steamed in the icy air. 'Here.' He waved the mug at Gabriel and then set it down on the edge of the table so there was no possibility that their hands would touch. 'Dear God, Gabriel, it's cold enough in here to freeze hell.'

Gabriel shrugged, set his brush down, and rubbed paint-stained hands through his hair. He was stiff with cold and concentration. He grasped the mug thankfully, sipping the hot cordial it contained, and watched his master as he examined the painting.

At length Leonardo stepped back and let out a long breath. 'It's wonderful.'

'No, it stinks.'

Count Leonardo gave a faint sound of amusement. 'When will it be finished?'

'I don't know. I need more oil.'

'More? What are you doing, bathing in it?' As Gabriel went to pull closed the shutters against the failing light, he added, 'It may be a choice between oil or dinner.'

'Oil, then. No paint without oil.'

Count Leonardo laughed. 'Then we may have to boil the bindings in the library for soup.'

Seeing him like that, in good humour, Gabriel could not help a smile tugging at his own mouth. 'Don't despise your library, my lord. It was there I learnt to do this.'

'Yes.' The laughter faded quickly, as it always did, and left a look of calculation. 'We shall eat well, Gabriel, as soon as we sell the painting.'

Gabriel groped his way through the dim room and struck flint to set light to a single taper. Shadows leapt in the corners and hung from the ceiling like tattered banners, while by the wavering yellow light Gabriel threw a linen cloth over the unfinished painting and set his brushes to soak.

'You're tired tonight,' Leonardo said.

Gabriel shrugged. He was about to reply when there was a knock at the door; the old steward Manfred opened it. 'My lord, Dr Foscari is here.'

'Foscari? At this hour? Damn – will he expect to dine with me? There's nothing—'

'My lord, he said he must speak with you urgently.'

Leonardo cocked a brow. 'Urgently? That doesn't sound like Foscari. Very well, Manfred – bring wine and candles to my study. Gabriel, come with me.'

Gabriel blew out the taper, unpinned the blanket and let it drop, and followed his master downstairs. Dr Foscari, the genial old lawyer who handled Leonardo's affairs, such as they were, was waiting in the great hall below. He heaved himself up from a spindly, brocaded chair as if he was relieved it had not collapsed under his huge bulk. 'My boy,' he said, 'we need to talk.'

He flourished a leather document case. Leonardo greeted him courteously and ushered him into the study, where Manfred was already setting a branch of candles. Gabriel followed them in, and took up a silent stance by the empty fireplace.

Foscari settled himself in a more solid chair behind the desk, and extracted a single sheet of paper from his case. 'A clerk from the Judiciary delivered this to me,' he said, handing it to Leonardo.

Leonardo read it, glanced up at Dr Foscari, and read it again. The very stillness in his face warned Gabriel, and he felt the icy clutch of fear inside him.

He watched Leonardo, who waited until the steward had brought wine, poured it, and withdrawn. At last he said, 'I thought we settled the last of my father's debts when he died.'

'So did I, boy,' Foscari said, sniffing the wine and taking a judicious sip. 'But it seems he borrowed from the State. That document has been quietly working its way through the files for the best part of three years.'

'And it comes to light today,' Leonardo murmured. 'Why today, I wonder?'

Gabriel could not repress a slight intake of breath. Leonardo's eyes flashed towards him, and away again. 'Dr Foscari,' he said, 'have you heard the latest news about Count Dracone?'

Swiftly he repeated the tale of how Dracone had offered to barter the relic of Christos for a place on the Council. Foscari sighed, and gave him an exasperated look.

'So, my boy, you threaten to use your veto – in the middle of the square and with half the city listening, I don't doubt. Did it never occur to you that Dracone might object?'

Leonardo peered suspiciously at the document. 'It's my father's seal. It looks like his signature. If it's a forgery, it's a good one.' He slapped the paper down. 'Fifteen thousand – I can't raise that.'

'Then the State will seize your property and sell it.'

Leonardo shrugged. 'It still won't—' He broke off.

'You see it now,' said Dr Foscari. 'If you're bankrupt, the State can sell you into bondage. No bondman can sit in Council.'

Leonardo had gone white, but he managed a thin

smile. 'I thought Dracone might stick a knife between my ribs. I would have had more sense than walk the streets at night.'

'But Dracone is a good citizen,' Foscari said. 'He destroys you in the daylight. And think of this, boy,' he added. 'If you become a bondman, who will buy the rights in you, do you think?'

'*What?*' Count Leonardo's mouth tightened into a furious line. 'I'll see him damned first. Dr Foscari, arrange the sale of the rented properties. And this house. I'll sleep under a bridge before I'll serve Dracone. What's left of the wine cellar. The library might fetch something . . .'

'We thought of that, my lord,' Gabriel reminded him, managing through surging fear to keep his voice level. 'It's how we discovered—' He shot a glance upwards; he knew Leonardo would not wish to tell Dr Foscari about the painting, not yet. 'Damp has got into the books.'

'I'll send a clerk to make an estimate,' Foscari promised. 'But it won't be enough.' He paused, and added, 'You have another asset, my boy. Your genic here. What about him?'

Gabriel wanted to make his eyes meet Leonardo's, but could not. He was too afraid of what he might see there. After a moment, sounding unsure of himself for the first time, the Count said, 'Not – not yet. I'll think about it.'

'Think about this, boy,' the old lawyer said heavily. 'If you break, the State will sell the rights to both of you. You could both find yourselves serving Count Dracone.'

While Leonardo showed Dr Foscari out, Gabriel withdrew to the studio and lit the taper again. In its uncertain light he could not paint, but he set himself to cleaning up, and mixing colours for the following day's work. Before long, as he had known it would, the door opened to admit the Count.

'What Foscari said . . .' he began without preamble. 'What do you think, Gabriel? If I find some decent man to buy the rights in you . . .?'

'What decent man would buy the rights to a genic?' Gabriel asked. He had intended to be calm, and sensible, and respectful as was his lot in life, but he could not keep back the bitterness. 'You heard what the Procurator said. What about his reputation?'

'The Procurator is a pious old fool.'

'He says no more than all the city thinks. A genic is man made, outside God's law. Not even human. Its very touch defiles.'

'Rubbish!'

Gabriel flung up his head. 'When have you ever touched me, my lord?'

Leonardo strode towards him. For one unimaginable moment, Gabriel thought that he would grasp him by the shoulders, but at the last instant he checked and turned away. Without looking at Gabriel, he said, 'Let me sell you somewhere you will be safe.'

'Let you sell me? My lord, I was Countess Contarini's page. She staked me on a throw of the dice and lost me to your father. Then I was his page, and now yours. Do with me what you please.'

'I want you out of Dracone's hands.'

In the silence that followed, Gabriel walked over to the painting and took off the linen cloth. Quietly, he said, 'Whoever bought me would not allow this.'

'No, probably not.' Leonardo came to his side, and they looked at the unfinished painting together. Leonardo said, 'What will it fetch, do you think? Enough?'

'Fifteen thousand? No.'

'I can raise half that.' Laughing suddenly, the ice-blue eyes alight, he said, 'I'll invite all the nobility, all the ones who look down on me now for my poverty. I'll hire a construct to serve the wine, and—'

'No need,' Gabriel interrupted. 'I'll do it.'

'You will not! No, Gabriel, you're going to dress in a good suit and make polite conversation with rich ladies.' His eyes gleamed in the taper's light. 'It's your painting, Gabriel. You're going to sell it for me.'

Gabriel took a step back. 'No,' he said. 'Please.'

'But it's your work,' Leonardo insisted. 'The art was lost until you found it. There has been nothing like this for hundreds of years.' He paced rapidly away into the shadows, and swung round. 'Those fools can't resist a new thing. They'll fall over themselves to pay me for it. Enough to settle the debt – more than enough, perhaps.'

Gabriel felt mingled fear and disgust beginning to close his throat. 'You know how it will be!' he cried, while he could still form the words. 'They will treat me like a pet monkey or a lapdog. They will wonder at me, not at the painting. Because I'm a genic, a made thing, something no decent man would touch.'

He drew himself up, and set his teeth on the desperate weeping that would break out if he weakened for a moment. Count Leonardo stared at him, and then spat a curse as he strode towards the door. With his hand on the handle, he paused. 'Today week. Will you be ready?'

'Yes, my lord.' The words came out tightly, barely controlled. 'I live only to serve you.'

2

Serafina bent over the silk and set in another stitch. One hundred and fifty tiny roses on the border of Giulietta Contarini's petticoat. Serafina had counted them as she traced the design onto the delicate fabric. Before she had embroidered half of them, she thought, she would be screaming mad.

She had settled into the routine of House Contarini as if she had always lived there. After that first evening, when Count Dandolo had led her there, and handed her over as if she were a basket of fish, she had seen little of Countess Contarini. The Countess rarely appeared before mid-day, when her chamberwomen had assembled her beauty to face the outside world. The rest of the day she would spend in making calls and receiving callers, at the gaming tables, and in the entertainment of her cavaliers. Such a great lady could not be expected to take much interest in the humblest addition to her household.

Instead, Serafina found herself in the service of Giulietta Contarini, the Countess's daughter. Not as a maidservant, where she would have to brush Giulietta's hair or stroke perfume onto her body. But Giulietta and her parents could reconcile themselves to a genic embroidress, and Giulietta was happy to wear the clothes she stitched, if they were pretty enough.

Serafina bit off the end of the silken thread. One more rose. She almost wished that she could hate and despise Giulietta. Her vapid little face, among its sheaves of golden hair. Her mind so full of silks and jewels that there was no space left for ideas. Her tinkling laugh and fluttering gestures, eyes peeping slyly from beneath curled lashes.

Human blood runs in her veins, Serafina thought. But she is not human. She is a doll they have made, and she is content to be a doll.

But Giulietta was, in her own way, kind. She had ordered a pleasant chamber for Serafina, and given her cast-off dresses. She talked to her, when there was no one else to talk to, though she always remembered what was proper.

She was here now, in the boudoir where Serafina worked in a corner by the window to make the most of the light. Giulietta lay on a chaise longue, wrapped in a foam of lace and yawning prettily over a handful of letters.

'Count Leonardo writes a vile hand,' she said, holding one of the letters at arm's length as if it would yield up its secrets more easily like that. She sighed. 'But he is *so* handsome! Don't you think so, Serafina?'

'I've never seen the Count, that I know of,' Serafina said. 'Is he one of your suitors?'

Giulietta's laugh chimed out. 'He would like to be, I think,' she said complacently. 'But Papa would never allow it. House Loredan is ruined. Count Leonardo has no money *at all*.' Her eyes grew round. 'Isn't that dreadful, Serafina?'

'Dreadful,' said Serafina. 'But he writes you letters?'

'Only to say that he will come to our *soirée* tonight. He is a Loredan, after all. One must notice him. Oh, and Serafina—' Giulietta half sat up, scattering her letters, 'he has the most *delicious* genic! You must see him!'

Annoyed, Serafina could not shut out Giulietta's tinkling laughter. Sharply, she said, 'What's that to me?' She bent over her embroidery again.

'Gabriel used to belong to Mama,' Giulietta told her. 'But Mama lost him at dice to the old Count Loredan – Leonardo's father. Serafina, I was *devastated*! Gabriel is so *beautiful*! But I think Mama was getting tired of him, and soon after that papa bought Hyacinth for her, so she doesn't miss Gabriel at all.'

'Hyacinth?' Serafina asked. She had not been aware of another genic in the Contarini household.

'Our musician. He is beautiful too, of course, but *so* arrogant! Papa says that he must teach me to play the lute.' She gave a mock shiver, and cast a glance at the beribboned instrument propped on a chair in the corner of the boudoir. To the best of Serafina's knowledge, since she joined the household, Giulietta had not touched it. 'Papa says that my husband will expect me to have accomplishments,' Giulietta went on. 'But I don't think so. My husband will just want me.'

And she could be right, Serafina thought. Giulietta's beauty, and her family's wealth, and her seal of fertility, brought every marriageable man in the city buzzing around her. 'So have you given up your studies?' she asked.

Giulietta shook her head. 'Hyacinth has been away with Papa, and I haven't practised.' She giggled, and stretched out one hand to admire her rings. 'Hyacinth will be *so* angry. And that makes him even more beautiful. Serafina, I could just *die*!'

Serafina threaded her needle with gold silk for the centre of the next rose. Count Contarini had returned home the night before, very late, from a mission to the

Holy Father. He had gone with others from the Council and the Church, to report on the ring, the reliquary of Christos, that was now in Count Dracone's possession. Serafina knew that the ring had nothing to do with her, though she had felt vaguely disturbed at the tale of the young priest who had disappeared. She wondered if his body was floating somewhere in a canal, like the body of the genic she had seen in Dr Heinrich's rooms.

Remembering Dr Heinrich reminded Serafina of how she had tried to have her rights assigned to him when the old Countess died. In the comfort of the Palazzo Contarini, she was sometimes in danger of forgetting. Ever since Countess Dandolo had taken her off the streets, once she had time to think of something except where she could beg her next piece of bread, she had hungered to know what she was. Why she had been made. What purpose a genic could find for her life. Not this, surely, not here, embroidering Giulietta Contarini's roses?

'Silly thing!' Giulietta said, jerking Serafina back to the present. 'Don't look so sad. Hyacinth always scolds me. And he'll scold me even more today, because Papa took him to sing before the Holy Father. That's *so* unusual, for a genic. It's because Hyacinth's voice is so wonderful. He'll be quite *insufferable*. But I don't care. He's only a genic, voice or no voice.'

Unaware of the insult, she gazed helplessly at the notes scattered on the floor, with little fluttering movements of her hands, until Serafina put aside her work, gathered them up, and laid them on the arm of the chaise longue.

Giulietta sorted through the papers with rosy tipped fingers. 'Count Leonardo will come tonight,' she said. 'And Count Dandolo – *such* a bore, Serafina! And Count Dracone.' She gave another delicious shiver.

'That man!' Serafina said sharply.

Giulietta gazed at her with wide, china-blue eyes. 'Don't you scold me, Serafina! Mama invited him. She owes him money, I think.'

'Does your father approve?'

A pout from the pretty lips. 'Papa might be cross. But it's too late, anyway, the Count accepted, and he's coming. Besides, I don't believe half the gossip, Serafina. Count Dracone is different, that's all. Not a pious bore like most of Papa's friends. And he's handsome, too, Serafina, and very, *very* rich.'

Is the silly little floozie thinking of Dracone as a husband? Serafina asked herself. She would get more than she bargained for. But Count Contarini would surely never allow it, however rich Dracone might be, even in the unlikely event of Dracone asking for his daughter. The Count's tastes, so Serafina had heard, ran another way.

She was half inclined to soil Giulietta's delicate ears with a few choice items of gossip, but just then Giulietta sat up, dropping the notes again, and clapping her hands in delight. 'I know, Serafina! You shall come to the *soirée* tonight, too.'

'Don't be ridiculous,' Serafina said. 'A genic, your sewing woman? Your father would fall down in a fit.'

'Not as a *guest*, silly! Hyacinth will sing; you can turn over his music or something. I'll find you a dress – you could be really lovely, Serafina, if you bothered with yourself. And you'll see all the guests, and Gabriel, and hear the music. Serafina, you don't want to shut yourself up in your room for ever and just *sew*, do you?'

'No.' Serafina was not sure what she did want, except that it was not a *soirée* at the Palazzo Contarini. But

Giulietta had made up her mind, so she did not have much choice. 'As you please, lady,' she said. 'I am here only to serve you.'

3

Father Augustine sat on the wharfside and let the sea wind lift his hair. He had lost count of time since he had come to this distant island; here the cathedral bell-tower was fallen into ruin, the cathedral itself the haunt of godless genics, and there was no angelus to divide the days, no calendar to mark one from the next. Looking down into the water, he saw a scrap of wood, drifting close in to the wharf, nudging against the stones and being drawn away again. He was much like it, drifting.

After the sea-Duke had dismissed them on the night of their arrival, Tethys the genic woman had found them a place to stay above the waterline, in one of the disused warehouses that backed the wharf. In the days of the city's greatness this island had been the first stop for merchants from the east; now it was deserted, save for the sea genics.

For the first days of his stay here, Father Augustine had thought that Rafael would die. The boy's terror of the genics, the effects of near drowning, and the loss of blood from the wound in his arm, had all combined to weaken him and sap his will to fight back. Father Augustine and Tethys had fought for him, and in the night that was just past he had slept deeply, without fever, for the first time. That battle was won. Father Augustine did not look forward yet to the battles that still lay ahead.

A footstep along the quay alerted him and he looked up to see Tethys striding along the wharfside towards him. Without thinking of her as woman, as desirable, he admired the fluid movement, the ripple of blue-green hair, a strength and freedom that was in its own way grace.

She joined him and sat down, folding her arms over her knees and letting the webbed hands hang loosely. She smiled with her lipless mouth and eyes like the deep places of the sea. 'The boy does well.'

Father Augustine sighed, not bothering to hide his weariness. 'I think so.'

'And now? What will you do now?'

He shrugged. 'I don't know. I can't go back.'

He had told her of Count Dracone and the ring. He had told her that Holy Church would never accept him again, when he had given the ring in exchange for Rafael. He had wondered as he told the story, and wondered again now, whether the Count would have pursued him if he had chosen differently, whether he could ever have returned safely and handed the ring over to his superiors.

He wondered what stories were being told about him, back in the city.

Tethys seemed unconcerned. She said, 'Stay here, then.'

Father Augustine started to get to his feet, winced at the aches of weariness that still stabbed through his body, and sat down again. 'With you and your people? Mistress, I am a priest. What is there for me here?'

'I don't know. Why don't you tell me – priest?'

Father Augustine wished he could. He had asked himself the same question over and over, in the darkness, struggling to fan the frail flame of Rafael's life. He had demanded an answer from God. Neither God nor his own mind had provided him with one.

Wryly, only half serious, he said, 'I can sweep floors, make a pot of bean soup, stitch a torn garment. Are these skills you would value, mistress?'

Tethys raised one shoulder in a shrug that set the indigo shadows shifting in the folds of her robe. 'Perhaps. And Rafael?'

'Truly, mistress, I do not know. But if he returns to the city he will fall prey to Dracone, or some other like him.' He sank his head into his hands and felt his hair still sticky from sweat and dried sea water. The bright sunlight hurt his eyes. 'We are driftwood, mistress, thrown up on your shore. Do with us as you will.'

For a long time Tethys was silent, gazing across the water to where, on the horizon, a faint line showed where the city stood. Father Augustine cast stealthy glances at her.

At last he said, 'In the city they tell tales of you, mistress, of the sea people who live in the lagoon, and rescue drowning sailors. Or who lure sailors to their death, depending on who is telling the tale. I confess, I'd thought you no more than that.'

A chuckle of genuine amusement came from Tethys. She turned the sea deep eyes full on him. 'That would suit your rulers, I daresay. They would not have it known that they traffic with genics.'

Father Augustine became aware that he was gaping, and clamped his mouth shut. When he had his astonishment under control, he said, 'Mistress, you tell me that the Council *know* you are here?'

'Your Council put us here.'

As he tried to protest and only managed to splutter, she said, 'Oh, not your present Council. We have been here for many years, many lifetimes. No doubt your Councillors are as ignorant as the rest of you, with one or two exceptions.' She smiled again, not amused this time, her mouth a closed triangle. 'We come under the jurisdiction of the Master of the Waters.'

Father Augustine stared at her and spread his hands helplessly. 'Tell me.'

Tethys shifted her position to get more comfortable, one leg with its webbed foot extended. 'We were made – as you can tell – for life in the sea. We were placed here to guard your coasts, from the enemies of wind and tide. If we did not regulate the water levels, you might find your city sliding under the sea.'

Her explanation explained nothing, and left him just as astonished as before. 'How can you do that?'

'Generations ago,' Tethys said, 'great sluice gates were placed beneath the sea, at the entrance to the lagoon. We keep them in repair, and open and close them so that the water does not rise too high, or drain away. More than that, we guard the bays and inlets and sandbanks, we shape the coast so that the currents run where we would have them.'

To Father Augustine, she spoke of wonders still, and yet her matter-of-fact air told him that to her all this was ordinary.

Tentatively he asked, 'Are you . . . slaves?'

'Are not all genics slaves? However you cover it with a skin of law. The city owns our rights, and yet they pay us for our work – not in money, but in goods, like food-stuffs, fabrics, and the tools we need.' She shrugged. 'We live better than your city genics, I think. And yet there are still some of us who crave for the open sea, and perhaps will go there one day.'

Thinking of what she had said, Father Augustine found himself shivering. 'And leave us to sink, mistress?'

'Who knows? Not today, or tomorrow, but – who knows?' She gazed over the water as if she herself might have heard the call to the distant deeps, but after a moment she spoke again in a much more practical voice. 'You're fortunate I was there to help you the other night. We come inshore so little – only to collect our payment, and sometimes to inspect the seawalls, as I did then. We have little interest in what happens on land.'

'And are you happy?' Father Augustine could not repress the question. 'Is it enough – the far islands, and the sea? Do you not feel you are in exile?'

'Exile?' Tethys looked amused. She raised an arm and gestured towards the low smudge on the skyline that was his city and his world. She said, 'That is the exile.'

4

Serafina's misgivings about the *soirée* did not disappear as evening approached. Giulietta, as she had promised, gave her a white silk dress, worn once and then discarded. Serafina snipped off most of the knots of ribbon and loops of pearl, but even so, she felt self-conscious as she put it on. It was too fine for a genic, and too revealing for a woman whose charms, by her very nature, were forbidden.

She knew she had been right when she came nervously down the stairs to the huge salon, and met young Paolo

Contarini on the landing. Giulietta's brother, the Count's only heir, had missed his sister's beauty without acquiring the saving grace of intelligence. Serafina felt herself colouring as he gawped down her bodice. His slack mouth moved into a grin.

'Pretty Serafina . . .' He sounded half drunk already.

He moved towards her; Serafina thought he was going to reach out and maul her. She recoiled and felt the banister rail hard against her back. She could smell the scented pomade he used on his hair. His skin was unhealthily pale; he breathed wine into her face.

'Messire, I am not—' she began.

'Paolo!' His mother the Countess had appeared on the landing in a rustle of silver tissue. 'Paolo, go and make sure Alvise understands which wines are to be served.' She spun him round and thrust him in the direction of the salon. 'Serafina, what are you doing here – and dressed like that?' Her delicately rouged features were set in lines of disapproval.

Serafina said, 'My lady Giulietta requires my presence, Countess. She gave me the dress.'

The Countess's disapproval deepened. 'Giulietta is far too frivolous. But since you are here . . .' She waved Serafina in front of her into the salon. 'Come and make yourself useful.'

The salon shimmered in the light of slender beeswax candles. Messire Alvise, the steward, almost suffocating in his own dignity, was lecturing the pages and serving women, and trying to listen to Paolo at the same time. He had no leisure to notice Serafina. Nor had Count Contarini, warming his rump in front of the fire and sipping a glass of wine while he listened to whatever his chaplain, Father Teo, had to tell him.

Serafina, naturally, had seen little of the chaplain. Holy Church would not deign to notice a genic. Though Father Teo was no ascetic; he was a small, elegant man, with silvering dark hair, who liked his glass of wine as well as anyone, and gave, so Giulietta said, easy penances. He wore a cassock of figured black silk, and fingered a silver pectoral cross as he spoke to the Count.

Serafina looked away, suddenly afraid they would see her staring. She stood behind one of the cushioned couches, hands lightly on the gilded frame, and wished herself somewhere else.

The couches were loosely grouped around the Countess's harpsichord, where she would sit from time to time and amuse herself with little tinkling tunes. Now single notes or chords were coming from it, and the occasional wisp of melody, but the raised lid concealed the player from Serafina. Could this be Hyacinth, the musician, she wondered, and was edging forward curiously when the experimental phrases ended in a crashing discord, a hand slammed down on the keys, and one word, loud and blasphemous, exploded into the salon.

The Count's head came swivelling round. Father Teo looked faintly shocked. Then the Count laughed, and called down the length of the salon, 'Hyacinth, spare my poor instrument! My guests will be here at any moment.'

A reply from the unseen musician, in a furious alto. 'If you want your instrument in tune, Count, you must heat this room every day.'

The Count's only reply was a dismissive gesture as he returned to his conversation with Father Teo. After a moment's silence, during which Serafina could almost see outrage rising like a wave of heat from behind the harpsichord, the offending phrase was repeated. This time

she could hear what was wrong, the note slightly off
pitch, and for some reason the sudden understanding
excited her, and she took the step that brought her around
the end of the instrument so that she could see the
musician. 'Sir—' she began.

The musician stopped in the middle of the phrase.
His head turned. Clustering golden curls framed the most
devastatingly beautiful face Serafina had ever seen on
anyone, man or woman, human or genic. Huge violet
eyes looked her up and down with an expression of frozen
disdain.

He finished the interrupted phrase, and let his hands
drop into his lap. His fingers were long and slender, bare
of rings, though a great jewel, a sapphire, flashed at his
throat. He wore a strange garment, a robe with tight-
fitting sleeves and a high standing collar like the calyx of
a flower; a single sweep of midnight blue silk fell from his
shoulders to the floor.

'Well?'

Serafina could not help dropping a curtsey, even
though there was no need, for another genic. She said,
'Sir, I am Serafina, Lady Giulietta's genic. She thought
you might wish me to help you tonight.'

'Thought?' Hyacinth was icy. 'Lady Giulietta thought?
Perhaps Holy Church should proclaim a miracle.'

The unexpectedness of that made Serafina slap a hand
over her mouth to keep back a giggle. Was Hyacinth so
outrageously rude to everyone? When he was no more
than a genic, however beautiful?

He looked her up and down, and said, still in the
same freezing alto, 'Help me to do what?'

'Turn your pages over, sir.'

'You can read music?'

'No, sir.'

Hyacinth sighed. 'Stop calling me "sir". Wait a minute.'

He played the flawed phrase again, took a tuning key, and adjusted one of the tuning pegs in the body of the instrument. Every movement was graceful, precise. When he took his seat again and played, the note sounded true. Serafina found herself smiling. 'That's beautiful.'

Hyacinth slanted a look at her from under thick lashes. 'You can hear that?'

'Yes, of course.'

He fell silent, looking at her more attentively, the disdain replaced by careful appraisal. If a man had looked at her like that, Serafina thought, she would have felt embarrassed, but from Hyacinth ... She paused in her reflections, realizing that without trying she had defined for herself something of Hyacinth's true nature. They had made him for the music. Every cell of his body served that, and nothing else. She met his eyes, and did not know whether she ought to feel awe, or pity.

Hyacinth seemed indifferent to what she felt. His scrutiny over, he flipped open a book of music on the rack in front of him. 'Very well. You will be no worse than the Count's pages, I don't doubt. At least you know you're ignorant. Look, these are the pieces ...'

Serafina stood beside him so that she could see the music too. Hyacinth began to show her how the markings in the book corresponded to what he played on the keyboard.

'Six months' lessons in five minutes,' he muttered fretfully. 'It won't work, of course. I'll nod when I'm ready. And remember that—'

Serafina, fascinated, had not noticed that the Countess was bearing down on her again. 'Serafina, don't stand there dreaming! The guests are beginning to arrive. Go down into the hall and help to collect their cloaks.'

Serafina dropped a curtsey, hiding her frustration. As the Countess glided away on another errand, she cast a glance at Hyacinth, who lifted his shoulders in a tiny shrug and said, 'Come back when they ask me to play.'

In the hall of the palazzo, a doorman announced the names of the guests as they arrived, while Count Contarini's footmen and maidservants took their cloaks. Serafina joined them, a little embarrassed to be dressed as she was and yet doing the tasks of a servant, though none of the others paid her any attention.

As she arrived, Count Dandolo, dressed in the rich mulberry velvet of his House, was ushering his wife and his bevy of daughters through the doors of the palazzo. Serafina advanced and bobbed a curtsey; the Count gave her a frosty look with no sign of recognition, but his youngest daughter, Caterina who was named for her grandmother, smiled and said, 'Serafina – are you well?'

When the old Countess lived, Caterina had been the only one of her family to visit her in the attic rooms. Even though she was escorted by a servant, Serafina had gathered that her father did not approve of these visits, but dared not neglect his mother totally, for fear of his reputation. Caterina had always brought some tiny gift – flowers, or sweet cakes – and the old Countess had given to her the last of her jewels, an emerald ring which she was wearing now.

Serafina curtsied again. 'Thank you, Lady Caterina. I am very well.'

'Caterina!' Her mother, the present Countess, reproved her daughter. 'Remember where you are. Girl, take my cloak.'

Obediently Serafina detached the cloak, careful to touch only the fabric and not the lady's white shoulders, aware all the while of Caterina's mischievous and friendly gaze.

As she turned away with her arms full of mulberry coloured velvet, the doors of the palazzo opened again, and the doorman announced, 'Count Leonardo Loredan!'

A young man stepped into the hall and paused, his head arrogantly raised. He was tall, slender, with ash-blond hair pulled back from a pale face. He nodded stiffly to Count Dandolo, who returned the nod and herded his women folk rapidly towards the stairs. Caterina cast a glance back over her shoulder, and was snapped at for her forwardness.

Serafina looked on interestedly. Why was Count Leonardo so undesirable? Was it just his poverty – evident in the threadbare evening coat and lack of jewels? Or was there some other reason for a careful father to guard his daughters from him?

Her gaze fell on the young man at Count Leonardo's shoulder. Not so tall as the Count, a pale, intense face framed by heavy black curls. It was a second or two before she saw the badge on his jacket and realized that this must be the genic Giulietta had told her of, the page who had belonged to Countess Contarini. What was his name – Gabriel? He had a wary look, as if he was uneasy to return now to the house where once he had served.

Count Leonardo had unfastened the clasp of his cloak and tossed it to Serafina with scarcely a glance. Serafina dropped him a curtsey and said, daringly, 'You're welcome, sir.'

Ice-blue eyes flicked onto her face. A faintly puzzled frown gathered between his brows, and she guessed he might have asked her – if Count Loredan ever condescended to ask – why she was dressed as a guest and collecting cloaks at the door.

She curtsied again. 'I am Lady Giulietta's genic, sir.'

Count Leonardo smiled, and Serafina caught a whiff of the devastating charm that had Giulietta sighing over him, money or no money. As if he meant it, she thought wonderingly, as if he might think of a genic as someone who deserved a smile, deserved attention, who might share the rights of true humans to human warmth and contact.

Or perhaps, if you were Count Loredan, you saw little distinction between genics and the rest of the human race who belonged to inferior Houses.

'Show Gabriel where he can wait for me,' Count Leonardo said. 'Somewhere they won't stare. Gabriel, I won't stay long.'

The genic bowed as Count Leonardo turned away and ran lightly up the stairs towards the entrance to the salon where the Count and Countess were receiving.

'Gabriel . . .?' Serafina said, when he had gone. 'Would you like to sit in the kitchens?'

The genic turned the same wary look on her. He shook his head. 'I can wait outside on the loggia.'

'But it's a cold night.' His jacket was thin, and he looked as if he hadn't had a good meal in a month.

Gabriel shrugged. 'It doesn't matter. And I want to look at the sky.'

'It won't go away,' Serafina said tartly, 'if you sit where it's warm for an hour and have something to eat.'

Gabriel shook his head, and smiled, but stiffly, as if courtesy was something that did not come easily to him. Without saying any more, he withdrew through the open doors and out into the night.

Serafina watched him go. Looking at the sky? Was he, perhaps, not quite right in the head? Strange things could go wrong with genics, she had heard. Or perhaps it was the effect of serving Count Leonardo, who could not be an easy master.

Turning away into the hall, Serafina realized that the flood of guests had died into a trickle, and the footmen and maidservants could cope with those who were still arriving. Not even Countess Contarini could object if she went back to the salon and Hyacinth.

The great room was crowded now, noisy with chatter and laughter. It took Serafina some time to navigate as far as the harpsichord without brushing against the guests.

While she was still some way away, Count Contarini came to stand beside it, and clapped his hands for silence. The noise sank a little, but he had to raise his voice to make himself heard.

'Dear friends, welcome! You grace our house tonight. Of your courtesy, be seated, and allow me to offer you the trivial entertainment I have prepared for you.'

Trivial! thought Serafina. That should please Hyacinth.

As the guests began to dispose themselves on the chairs and couches grouped around the harpsichord, she managed to slip through and reach the musician's side. 'What must I do?' she asked.

Hyacinth gave her a startled look, as if she had dragged

him out of deep concentration. 'Nothing yet,' he said, after a pause where she guessed he was reminding himself who she was. 'I shall sing without music. After that, the keyboard.'

Serafina stepped back to listen, while Hyacinth advanced in front of the harpsichord and let his gaze rake across the chattering guests until he had achieved something like silence. Then he lifted his head and sang.

Serafina drew breath painfully. She had heard music before, raucous bellowing in taverns, or the sweet untrained voices of beggar children singing for coppers. This took her by the throat and would not let go.

She had never heard a voice with the power and range of Hyacinth's. Never one so flexible and expressive, as if the tragic love he sang of had broken his own heart. The music soared with a passion she had never imagined could exist in this world. The voice itself was scarcely something that could exist, or come from any human blood and bone.

When the sudden shock began to ebb, Serafina had the chance to look around her and pick out the guests she knew. Count Dandolo, sitting bolt upright with an expression of black disapproval. She hid a smile. If she herself was too scandalous for him, whatever must he think of Hyacinth! His Countess looked frankly bored, and the clutch of daughters were whispering and rustling among themselves, all except Caterina, who caught Serafina's eye and acknowledged her with a tiny smile and lifted hand.

Serafina felt warmed, but knew she could not safely respond. She and Caterina would both be scolded if anyone noticed friendly gestures between a genic and a daughter of House Dandolo – and in the middle of the Countess Contarini's salon, of all places!

Not far from the Dandolos was Paolo Contarini, slumped against the head of his couch and apparently asleep. Beyond him was Giulietta, excessively pretty, Serafina had to admit, in an azure gown with silver embroidery she herself had worked. She did not even pretend to be listening to Hyacinth, but giggled and flirted behind her fan with the young man sharing the couch with her. From the green velvet he wore, the colour of House Venier, Serafina guessed that he must be Lucio Venier. Another suitor of Giulietta's, and just as hopeless as Count Leonardo, for though House Venier was wealthy, Lucio was a younger son.

On Giulietta's other side was Count Leonardo, sitting immobile with a frosty look on his face. Was he jealous, Serafina wondered, at the favour Giulietta was showing; did he think of Lucio Venier as his rival?

Close to the balcony windows Serafina could see Father Teo, gravely attentive, but then her eyes were drawn to a slash of scarlet by the main doors of the salon. She recognized Count Dracone.

He must be a late arrival, she thought; she had not seen him in the hall. Now he moved forward, quiet but as if he was oblivious of the music, and wove his way through the gilt chairs until he reached a place just behind Giulietta. Serafina saw him lay a hand on her shoulder; somehow she wanted to shudder as if it was her own body he touched.

Giulietta turned and let out a squeal. 'Dear Count!'

Hyacinth never faltered, but Serafina caught a flash of fury in his eyes. Count Contarini was looking annoyed, and there was a rustle of disturbance among the other guests. Dracone, smiling, said something to Giulietta; she shrugged and pouted, but was silent.

Lucio Venier, who had previously been the target of her coquetry, was staring ahead, looking sullen. Countess Dandolo had half started up, scandalized, to be pulled down by the Count, who was speaking into her ear. Serafina guessed they would both have preferred to walk out, but for offending House Contarini.

Hyacinth brought his song to an end in a triumphant flurry of notes, and stood with bowed head. There was a polite spatter of applause.

Count Contarini said fussily, 'Play something, Hyacinth.'

Hyacinth bowed to him and took his seat at the harpsichord. Serafina moved towards him, ready for her task. His face was white, fierce, and he had to pause for a moment to make sure his hands were steady. Serafina thought no one else saw it; if they had, they would have found it presumptuous, amusing, even, that a genic might care whether or not he was appreciated. She wanted to offer comfort, but the outrage in every line of him was an impregnable shield.

As she took her place beside him he said, 'Turn when I nod. Keep your hands out of the way.'

He reached for the keyboard, and suddenly he was all concentration again, and no more than a conduit for the music that poured out of him. Watching for his signal, dreading that she would make a mistake, Serafina still could not help her heart lifting.

When at last the recital was over, Serafina felt that she could not stand the heat and glare of the salon any longer, or the inane chatter in the wake of the music. She wanted to think about it in quiet.

Glancing around to make sure that no one was observing her, she fought her way between the thick velvet folds of the curtains, and through the open windows to the head of the outer staircase that led, a pale spiral, down to the courtyard garden.

The night was cool. Serafina leant on the stair rail and gazed down into the garden, to where the moon blanched twining jasmine that scattered silver petals on the grass. She let out a long sigh.

A faint rustling sound to her right alerted her; she turned. At first she could see nothing in the shadows, but gradually her eyes made out a dark figure, a dark head bent: Father Teo in his black silk cassock, sitting on the stair and murmuring prayers from the tiny breviary open in his hands.

Partly she was embarrassed, half inclined to leave, partly fascinated to think that this worldly, sophisticated little man would withdraw himself from the Countess Contarini's *soirée*, and find a quiet place where he could pray.

While she hesitated, Father Teo crossed himself, closed the breviary, and looked up. He smiled at her. 'Serafina.'

Awkwardly, she said, 'I'm sorry, Father. I didn't . . .'

He waved a hand, dismissing her apology, and tucked the breviary away in the pocket of his cassock. 'You liked the music,' he said.

Liked? Stupid word, Serafina thought, for what she had experienced. Meekly she said, 'Yes, Father.'

His eyes widened, and he gave her a penetrating look. Somehow he reminded her of Count Leonardo, and at first she was not sure why, for two men could scarcely be more different in looks and demeanour. Then she realized that he was truly looking at her, as Count Leonardo had, as though she were a woman and not a genic. From a priest, who ought to believe her an abomination, it was even more startling. She felt as embarrassed as if he had caught her naked.

Quietly, Father Teo said, 'No, not "liked" I think. Such music entraps the soul.'

'Do you mean it's wrong to listen, Father?' Slightly bolder, when he seemed to be considering her question, she added, 'I know little of what Holy Church would teach.'

Still thoughtful, Father Teo shook his head. 'Not wrong to listen. But to become completely obsessed by such beauty ... That would be wrong. Yet that is not what I meant, or not all of it.'

Serafina waited, hoping he would say more.

'It cannot be right,' Father Teo went on at last, 'to create such a being as Hyacinth.'

'A genic? You would say—' Serafina rushed into speech, not even sure of what she intended to say, and breaking off at the priest's impatient gesture.

'Not that he is a genic, but ... Hyacinth was created to have that voice, that ... blazing genius for music. But what of the rest of him? He is not whole. I ask myself, what would it be like, to be Hyacinth, and only truly live in the music? What of the times when he may not sing?' There was pain and compassion in his voice. 'In the dark hours, when he wakes, and there is nothing but God and the silence—'

'There is no God for genics, Father.' Serafina could not keep back the words.

'So Holy Church teaches us.' He sighed out the words, half raising one hand. He had beautiful hands, narrow and well-kept, with a heavy silver ring. 'What do you think, Serafina?'

She was almost tempted to answer rudely, to ask what a genic could be expected to know of God, but the compelling dark eyes would not permit that.

'I do not know, Father,' she said.

'Nor I.' Surprise kept Serafina silent as he went on, 'But I believe that this is a world where every question has its answer, even if we do not know what it is. We know what Holy Church believes about such as you and Hyacinth, my daughter. But what God Himself believes? No, we do not know that yet.'

Serafina's initial surprise was deepening into incredulity. Her breath came short. She found it hard to imagine that she was standing here on the stairway of the Palazzo Contarini, discussing theology with the Count's chaplain, and, unless she was mistaken, listening to heresy. However did Father Teo dare? And yet, she thought, she was only a genic, and it did not matter what he said to her, for no one would believe her if she denounced him.

And having had that thought, she was ashamed of it. If he, a human and a priest, had shown her a little of his heart, was she to reject it, out of cynicism? She felt almost as disgusted with herself as if she had spoken the thought aloud.

'Father—' she began, but at that moment she heard the harpsichord strike up again, a dance tune this time, and following it the movement of feet and rustling of silken gowns beyond the curtains. 'I'm sorry, Father,' she said. 'I must go. I may be needed again.'

He nodded to her, his eyes bird-bright. 'Perhaps we will speak of this again,' he said.

Four

The great hall below the studio shone in the soft light of candles. It was almost possible to ignore the peeling gilt on the panelling, the frayed brocade covers to the chairs. In the centre, Count Loredan had placed a stand, and on it the finished painting in a gilded frame. Gabriel stood looking down at it, and wished he could banish his sick apprehension as he thought of the evening ahead.

Dr Foscari had lent a couple of his construct servants: almost faceless, silent presences, moving about their tasks with swift efficiency. No one would recoil from them as they would from a genic, for they were clearly made things, with no pretence of being human.

Nervously Gabriel adjusted the cuffs of his silk shirt. In the end, Leonardo had opted for simplicity: the open-necked white shirt, black velvet trousers, no ornament of any kind.

'You look fragile,' he had said, grinning, as he inspected Gabriel's appearance. He flicked his fingers so close to Gabriel's neatly combed black curls that Gabriel could not help jerking his head away. 'All the ladies will fall in love with you.'

Gabriel had moved away uncomfortably, and come downstairs to wait beside the painting. Leonardo might be right, at that. There was a delicious whiff of sin at the thought of embracing a genic. Even a virtuous lady might enjoy it, so long as it went no further than a thought.

He shifted the stand slightly, imagining the light fell better on the painting. What would the guests see, he wondered. The canal, the crumbling buildings they saw every day, the sky silvered by pale sun behind cloud? No more than that? Or a pleasing pattern of shape and colour, all the more intriguing because it had been created by a genic?

Would any of them see what he had felt as he painted it – that yearning for the light, and the desperation because what he could depict with paint and brushes was so much less than he saw painted on the sky itself? Had even Leonardo seen that? Gabriel shrugged. He doubted it. Genics were not human. They were made to satisfy desires. They were not supposed to have their own.

Gabriel's first memories were of the hot, scented bedchamber where the Countess Contarini received her cavaliers, the silken rustle of her gowns and the sickly taste of the sweetmeats she gave to him, holding out the silver comfit box with white hands that never touched him to slap or to caress. She had lost him in the dice game with less chagrin than she would have handed over a jewel or a fan.

Gabriel had often wondered whether that was all he had been meant for: to fetch and carry, to speak softly and to look decorative. He had never found an answer. But he was sure that this hunger to express himself with paint on canvas had not been part of his making. Who would ever have thought of it, or thought that such a useless talent would enhance a genic?

He only knew that as he rediscovered the lost techniques among the mould and mice of Leonardo's library, he had found himself. The prospect of losing it again was more than he could bear.

He started as Dr Foscari's constructs glided past him to welcome the first of the guests. Beside the doors of the hall, Leonardo had appeared, bending over the hand of a lady who blushed and simpered, captivated by his courtesy and his good looks. Gabriel straightened, ran his hands through his hair, and prepared to face them.

As the evening crawled by, Gabriel's head began to ache. He was sick of smiling, of bowing, of explaining for the fiftieth time how he had found the secrets of painting as he examined Count Loredan's books. He was sick of the admiring glances the fine ladies tossed at him, particularly when he knew that if he had merely brushed the hand of one of them she would have shrieked and ordered him a whipping.

Thankfully he turned to Leonardo as his master threaded his way through the guests towards him. 'How much longer?' He kept his voice low. 'Have you an offer yet?'

'Several. Enough to clear the debt. And more commissions.' The look Leonardo gave him was exultant. 'Keep smiling, Gabriel; let them wonder if—'

He broke off. There was a stir at the doors as a late arriving guest walked in and paused in the doorway, his thin red lips curved into a smile.

Gabriel glanced at Leonardo. 'You invited Count Dracone?'

Leonardo frowned. 'No, I didn't.'

Dracone was drifting gracefully forward, bowing here and there, exchanging a word with this guest or that, slowly moving towards the centre of the hall, and the painting. Behind him were two huge constructs, dressed in gold and scarlet livery, hunched shapes with low foreheads and the muzzles of animals.

'My dear Leonardo.' Count Dracone inclined his head as he stood before Leonardo. 'How delightful. And this is the wonder we have all come to see?'

He stood before the painting. Gabriel drove his nails into the palms of his hands. It took more self control than he knew he possessed to compose himself into a proper picture of submission.

To his relief, Count Dracone gave him no more than a moment of his attention. To Leonardo he said, 'I congratulate you. I see little that is truly new.'

'Gabriel rediscovered the ancient techniques in the library.' Leonardo's voice was neutral. 'It is interesting, don't you think?'

'Fascinating. Is it sold yet?'

'Not yet,' Leonardo said. 'But I have several offers. Regrettably, I have to clear an old debt of my father's. Tedious, but necessary.'

He sounded exquisitely bored, as if the words would mean nothing to Dracone, as if he had not just slipped out of the trap that the Count had set for him. But his eyes were dancing, as he looked at the frustration in Dracone's face.

Dracone's serpent gaze rested on him for a moment, and then flicked back to the painting. 'I will buy it. What is your price?'

Gabriel wanted to cry out in protest, but he knew he could not. Leonardo drew himself up and coolly named a sum that was twice what he had speculated the painting might fetch. Gabriel drew a breath of hope; Leonardo would never deny Dracone, but he might set the price so high that he would refuse to pay it.

If that had been his intention, it failed. Count Dracone nodded. 'Done.' He held out a hand, and after a moment's hesitation Leonardo shook it to seal the bargain.

As if at a signal, the guests began to take their leave. A few of them spoke courteously to Gabriel, and hoped there would be more paintings. After a few minutes, Leonardo and Gabriel were alone, except for Count Dracone and his servants. Count Dracone snapped his fingers at the nearest construct. 'Pay him.'

The creature pawed open the capacious pouch at its waist and extracted a purse, which it held out in soft fingers. Leonardo was forced to take the three paces which brought him to its side, and take the purse from it. Gabriel heard the chink of coin.

'So . . .' Count Dracone murmured. 'The painting is mine. What is your price for the genic?'

In the silence that followed his question he came close to Gabriel, and with one thumb traced the line of his jaw. Gabriel could not stop himself from flinching. The black, glittering eyes mocked him; the curved red mouth was ready to fasten on his own.

Ever since Gabriel could remember, ever since he had been a child who could not understand, he had hungered for this, for a hand to reach out to him. He would have prayed, if he had dared to offer prayers to a God who could not be his own. Or was this how an angry God would answer the prayers of a genic – that the hand should be Dracone's, and what it held, pain and humiliation?

Terror seized his throat and almost stopped his breath

as he turned his head to look at his master. Frostily, Leonardo said, 'The genic is not for sale.'

Once again Gabriel felt Dracone's touch against his face, the lightest impress of the claws that tipped the caressing hand. It bore a heavy ring, gold and lapis; was that the reliquary, Gabriel wondered, that held the hair of the Lord Christos? Were the faint lines graven on the lapis the ancient crest of House Loredan? He shivered.

'Such beauty . . .' Count Dracone whispered. 'What else was it made for? Such a waste, Leonardo, to let it daub and dabble with paint on canvas. A monkey could do as much.'

Leonardo's hand was clenched white around the Count's purse. 'Dracone, you are offensive.'

'Surely not? The thing is but a genic, after all.' Still with his eyes on Gabriel's face, he drew off the great ring and held it out to Leonardo on the palm of his hand. 'I will give you the reliquary ring.'

For a minute Gabriel thought he could see into the twists of Count Dracone's mind. He had offered the ring to the Church, to buy himself a place on the Council. But that plan had failed now, when Leonardo was free to use his veto. The ring was useless, except as the instrument of a most exquisite revenge.

Gabriel dared not look at Leonardo. He could recover the ancient treasure of his House. He could give it to the Church. He would be honoured throughout the city, and be rid of the scandalous genic that defiled his household. He would ensure that the name of Loredan would be remembered for ever.

After an eternal moment Gabriel heard a stir of movement as Leonardo took the step that brought him to his side. 'I thought you had another purpose for that,' he said. 'Or have you begun to learn that the ring will buy you nothing? Not power, not respect, and most certainly not Gabriel. Take what belongs to you and go.'

An ugly fury in his eyes, Count Dracone swung round to face the painting. For a moment he looked down at it, the ivory profile set in a sneer. Gabriel could not help thinking that if he could paint that look he would have captured the soul of evil.

The Count snapped his fingers at the construct once again. 'Destroy it.'

A cry broke from Gabriel before he could snatch it back, and he burned in the look of triumph the Count turned on him. Leonardo, white with fury, was silent as the construct shambled across the hall. A tensile strength invaded its limp hands as they flexed around the frame; the gilded wood splintered; the canvas buckled and twisted, its light quenched. The creature let the scraps fall.

Count Dracone watched with a thin smile until the work was done. Then he bowed to Leonardo. 'Your servant, Count Loredan. My thanks for a most ... instructive quarter hour.'

He gestured to the constructs to precede him out of the hall. Leonardo followed. When he was alone, Gabriel stumbled to the wreckage on the floor and dropped to his knees. He reached out a hand, but could not touch.

At a distance he thought he heard the echo of footsteps, and realized that someone was standing beside him. Leonardo said, 'Don't weep.'

Gabriel looked up. Brushing at tears with the palm of his hand, he said, 'I'm not.'

'He is vile. Unutterably vile.' Leonardo was forcing out the words through his teeth; then he stopped and took a breath. 'Gabriel, you can paint others. You—'

'No. Please. I can't. I have no right.'

'What do you mean?'

Wearily Gabriel rubbed his hands over his face. 'You heard what he said. "What else was it made for?" Not this. I have no right to this.'

Leonardo made an impatient gesture. 'You actually listened to that . . . filth?'

'Why not?' Gabriel reached out again, and touched, not the painting, but a splinter of gilded wood from the frame. For a moment he wanted to drive it into the palm of his hand and see the gush of genic blood. 'If your guests had seen, would they have blamed him? Or thought he was right to punish a genic for presuming to—'

'Stop it!' Leonardo snapped. 'You belong to House Loredan. What do you care what the rest of them think? Or . . .' He broke off and then began again. 'Gabriel, you didn't think I would sell you to him?'

Gabriel stifled bitter laughter. 'For the ring? When it should have been yours? When it would set House Loredan among the city's great ones again?'

'House Loredan stands where it has always stood.' Leonardo's chin went up arrogantly. 'Unlike Dracone, I do not need to bribe my way to honour.' He paused, and the arrogance seemed to dissolve. 'You do not trust me.'

'Why should I? When have you ever forgotten what I am?'

Though Gabriel asked the question, he did not care what the answer would be, or even if there was an answer. He was silent, fighting the pain of his genic heritage, of the unimaginable gulf between what he was and what he wanted to be, of sheer loneliness.

Leonardo stood gravely looking down at him. After a moment he stretched out one booted foot and stirred the wreckage of the painting. 'You will do others,' he said. 'When the debt is cleared there'll be enough left to buy canvas, oil, anything.' He held out a hand to Gabriel. 'Let's go to the studio and see what you need.'

Gabriel stared, frozen. He could not reach out to take the offered hand. 'You can't. It's forbidden.'

'To hell with that,' said Leonardo. His voice was shaken but suddenly joyful. He gripped Gabriel's wrist, pulling him to his feet, and forced his head back so that Gabriel had to look at him. 'A Loredan does what he damn' well likes.'

Gabriel choked back laughter that could easily have turned to tears. Leonardo's grip was fierce, bracing him, a world away from Count Dracone's poisonous caresses. He suddenly felt as if light were springing up inside him, ready to flow out through his fingers. He knew what he was and what his life would mean; he was centred, whole.

He said, 'For a minute I thought you were going to throw Count Dracone's purse back in his teeth.'

Leonardo laughed. 'Don't think I wasn't tempted. But I've more sense, Gabriel, I promise you. Let Dracone pay for destruction, if that's what he wants.' He leant forward and drew one hand down the side of Gabriel's face, erasing the last memory of Count Dracone's touch. 'You and I, we pay for life. We pay whatever it costs.'

2

Serafina stepped out onto the loggia of the Palazzo Contarini, and let out a long sigh as the doors closed behind her. After the cushioned warmth of the palazzo, the cold air of the city braced her and spoke to her of freedom. She could even bear the faint stench that rose from the canal, so long as she could walk under the open sky.

She pulled her cloak around her, and made sure that she had her purse in her inner pocket, fat with the coins the steward Alvise had given her to buy fresh thread and ribbons for Giulietta, along with the scraps of silk she needed to match.

Quickly she threaded through the alleys behind the palazzo, and came out near where the market boats spread their awnings, their decks piled with melons and oranges and bundles of herbs. A few of them sold cloth; sometimes she had bargained fiercely to buy for the old Countess, but nothing there would be fine enough for Giulietta. Serafina would need to visit the silk warehouses of the merchants' quarter.

She was walking in that direction when she heard a voice behind her. 'Serafina! Serafina!'

Turning, she saw Caterina Dandolo, waving to her and hurrying to catch her up, dodging around the heaped baskets of produce on the canal side. A footman in the mulberry livery of House Dandolo followed her more slowly; Serafina recognized the boy who used to accompany Caterina when she visited her grandmother's rooms.

'Serafina, where are you going?' Caterina asked as she came up. 'Shopping? Shall we go together?'

Serafina dropped a curtsey. 'No, lady. Your father would be angry.'

Caterina cast a laughing look over her shoulder at the footman. 'Giacomo won't tell. And if any of Papa's friends see us, I shall tell them I'm helping you find what Giulietta needs. You are shopping for Giulietta, aren't you?'

With no other choice – except to flee, and make herself and Caterina ridiculous – Serafina fell in beside her and they made their way towards the merchants' quarter together.

'I saw you at the *soirée*,' Caterina said. 'I'm sorry Papa wouldn't let me speak – so stupid, when I used to see you so often at Grandmama's. But it would not be seemly.' She let out a little chuckle, and glanced mischievously at Serafina. 'Papa is anxious that we should all be very seemly. Or we will never find husbands, and then what would become of us?'

'You are young for a husband, lady,' Serafina said. Yet such things were done, she knew, if the girl was well-born and had her seal of fertility, and the prospective bridegroom was desperate for an heir.

Caterina shrugged. 'I am to be tested soon. Maria was to be betrothed to Francesco Foscari, but she failed her test, and so Papa thinks that I might do instead.'

'And you *want* that?'

'My sister's betrothed? No.' Some of the brightness faded from Caterina's face. 'Maria truly loved Francesco, and he loved her. But he cannot marry her, because he will be Count Foscari when his father dies, and he must have a wife who will give him sons. Papa says Maria must go to the sisters at Corpus Domini, and she weeps in the night when she thinks no one can hear.' Her hands clenched. 'It sickens me, Serafina. Are we cattle, to come together only so that we can breed?'

Serafina glanced back at Giacomo, who walked two or three paces behind them with an expressionless look on his broad face. A convenient young man, she thought, who must be very conveniently hard of hearing, for Caterina to talk so.

'Holy Church would say it is your duty, lady,' she murmured.

Caterina's eyes flashed. '*That*, from you, Serafina?' She made a faint, disgusted sound, which Count Dandolo would no doubt have felt was very unseemly indeed. 'Papa takes us to hear Father Battista preach at the Church of the Innocenti. He says that we are cursed in our seed because we sought for knowledge that belonged to God alone, and spewed out abominations on the earth.'

'Genics,' said Serafina, tight-lipped.

'Oh, Serafina, don't be angry. It is Father Battista who says so, not I! And he is very strict in his ideas, even for a churchman; that's why he pleases Papa. I just wish that Maria and Francesco could marry and be happy, and – and I wish that you and I could be friends, Serafina.'

Serafina stopped in surprise and faced her. She was even more surprised to feel Caterina timidly laying a hand on her arm. 'Lady, you should not—'

'That's just silly superstition, Serafina, and I won't have any more to do with it.' She looked up into Serafina's face, her own bright and questioning. She was no beauty, not like Giulietta, but she had an openness and truth in her face that Serafina thought was more beguiling. Would any man think so, though, and would it matter? Caterina's husband would choose her for the name of House Dandolo – provided she could produce her seal of fertility.

She began to walk on as Caterina gave her arm a little tug and then released her. 'Let's do our shopping and be comfortable,' Caterina said. Her warm laughter bubbled up again. 'And not be seen doing anything Papa would find unseemly.'

She took Serafina to one of the great silk warehouses, not far from the Imperial Hostelry where Dr Heinrich's countrymen trafficked in genics and the strange machines, like Count Dracone's flyer, from the Empire in the north.

Were they giants and magicians in the north, Serafina wondered, as the common people said? Or the grubby labourers Count Contarini called them, or impious usurpers of the power of God, as Holy Church would have everyone believe? Serafina could not help suspecting that they were people not much different from those she saw around her every day.

Caterina herself was choosing stuff for a new gown. As the construct assistant was spreading out the shimmering lengths of silk for her to see, she whispered to Serafina, 'I should have liked to go to Messire Alessandro's. He has much the prettiest. But Papa has forbidden it, because, you know, Messire Alessandro is not quite respectable.'

'No, I didn't know.' House Contarini was not quite so fussy, and Serafina had seen nothing, on the one or two visits she had made to Messire Alessandro's, that anyone could reasonably object to.

'Well, he lives alone, but for his servants,' Caterina said. 'He does not entertain guests, or go if he is invited anywhere.'

'He sounds extremely respectable,' said Serafina.

Caterina giggled. 'To be respectable you must do as everyone else does.'

Serafina matched the silks she had brought with her, and paid for the embroidery threads she needed and the ribbons that would prettify Giulietta's nightgowns. While she waited for Caterina to finish choosing, she wandered over to the warehouse door and stood looking out over the canal.

She had not been there long when she saw a boat draw away from the landing stage in front of the Hostelry, rowed by a construct in a livery of scarlet and gold, and seated in the bows another scarlet figure, Count Dracone. He was staring ahead of him, oblivious of the other traffic on the canal.

Even the sight of him made Serafina feel uneasy, although she would not have cared to admit it. She was drawing back into the shadow of the door when she saw someone else she recognized – the broad, burly shoulders and blundering walk of Dr Heinrich.

In a few seconds he would pass her; Serafina froze, not wanting to be noticed by him or to have him remember the attempt she had made to gain his interest. She had begun to realize she had been wrong, or perhaps thrown off balance when the old Countess died. She had been foolish, to think that a man like Heinrich might hold the answers to her questions about herself.

But before Dr Heinrich drew level with the warehouse door, he stopped. He had seen Count Dracone's boat, and hailed it. The Count glanced his way, seemed as if he would ignore the shout, and then gave an order to his construct, who changed course and brought the boat gliding neatly up to the wharfside.

Dr Heinrich bent and spoke to the Count. Knowing

she was being very stupid, but overwhelmed by curiosity, Serafina edged closer, into the shelter of a stack of silk bales, until she could hear what they were saying.

'. . . my ring?' she heard the Count say as she approached. 'What is it to do with you, Doctor?'

'Is it true,' Heinrich asked, 'that it contains Christos's hair?'

There was a hunger in his voice that Serafina could not understand. He was excommunicated; he had deliberately flouted the teachings of Holy Church. What should he care for the relics of Christos?

'Indeed.' Count Dracone sounded indifferent, but he raised one hand and displayed a heavy gold ring, set with lapis. He flipped open the stone; Serafina saw a glitter of crystal; Heinrich crouched over it, staring.

'Count,' he said, 'I could show you how to use this ring to give you power. Great power.'

A sneer settled on Dracone's face. 'In this city?'

Heinrich's voice dropped almost below the level of Serafina's hearing. He glanced from side to side, but did not notice Serafina, shielded from him by the bales of silk. 'Especially in this city. I will show you how.'

Perhaps it was his certainty, or perhaps the sudden fire that leapt in Dracone's eyes, that chilled Serafina. Dracone, Heinrich and the ring. She felt she was standing at a point of unimaginable consequences, like a tiny spring in the mountains which holds within itself the seeds of a great river.

'And what do you want in return?' Count Dracone asked. 'Everyone wants something, my dear Doctor.'

Heinrich passed his tongue over his lips. 'To do my work. And to share in what will come to you.'

There must have been an assent from Dracone,

though Serafina missed it, only seeing Heinrich begin, clumsily, to lower himself into the boat. At the same moment she heard Caterina's voice.

'Serafina! Now that really *is* unseemly! Staring at men in the open street! Come and tell me if you like the silk I've chosen.'

Murmuring something, Serafina followed her back into the warehouse, only glancing back once, to see Dracone's boat manoeuvring out into the canal once again, while Dr Heinrich leant close to the Count, talking rapidly.

3

Jasmine flowers were starring Messire Alessandro's balcony rail when Count Dracone came. The first Gianni knew of him was when he saw his flyer, bobbing at the wharfside, and a man who must be his pilot leaning lazily against a bollard. No one but Count Dracone flaunted so openly the machines of the Empire.

The pilot noticed him staring; uncomfortably Gianni turned away and went into the counting house. Near the door Count Dracone and Messire Alessandro were talking together. Gianni had never seen the Count before, but he had heard enough about him to know who the visitor must be. He stood waiting, just too far away to hear the low-voiced conversation.

Count Dracone was a small man, though taller than Messire Alessandro. He wore a scarlet coat faced with black brocade, and his hair was shiny black, shaped to his head as if it had been varnished. As he spoke he gestured with claw-tipped hands. Gianni could not see his face.

Messire Alessandro was looking up at him, adding no more than a word or two to their talk, his expression polite but detached. After a moment he shook his head and half turned away.

Count Dracone drew closer to him and put a hand on his shoulder. Gianni bit back an exclamation. It took him a few seconds to realize why the gesture should seem so shocking.

Messire Alessandro did not like to be touched. Gianni thought that his fear of touching a genic was so great that he kept himself safe by refusing to touch anyone.

He was looking uneasy now. A thought came to Gianni so daring that he could hardly entertain it. Could Count Dracone be a genic? This powerful, impious man – could he have added to his crimes the ultimate sin of pretending to be human when he was not?

Gianni cleared his throat. He stepped forward, deliberately clumping his boots on the wooden floor, and held out the message that had been his errand. 'The note from Dr Foscari, sir.'

Messire Alessandro moved away from the Count and took the paper. Gianni fancied that his hands shook slightly. 'Excuse me, Count,' he said. 'This needs my attention.'

Count Dracone turned. Gianni had a brief glimpse of an ivory face like a curved sword blade, slashed by a scarlet mouth. The Count was furious; he pushed past Gianni and was gone.

'Sir, was that Count Dracone?' Gianni asked.

Messire Alessandro nodded. He was abstracted, tapping the note slowly against his hand. 'He wanted to borrow money,' he said, surprising Gianni that he should speak so freely. 'I told him to go to a money-lender.'

He broke the seal and began to read. Though Gianni waited, his master said no more about Count Dracone.

That was not the last of him, however. The next day an invitation came for Messire Alessandro to dine at the Count's palazzo.

'You'll never go, sir?' Gianni, who happened to be there when the messenger came, could not hold back the question.

'Why not?'

'Sir, he's an evil man!'

Messire Alessandro smiled faintly, sadly. 'There are those who would say that of me. Yes, I think I will go.'

'Then take me with you!'

Messire Alessandro looked startled. Gianni was startled himself. He was not sure why he thought that Messire Alessandro was going into danger, or why he should feel the overwhelming need to protect him.

'It's – it's my duty, sir,' he stammered, confused. 'To escort you . . .'

Messire Alessandro looked up at him with that clear, blue gaze. He was still smiling. 'To escort me . . . no, Gianni. The Palazzo Dracone is no place for you.'

Or for you either, Gianni wanted to say, but could not. Before he could frame a protest, Messire Alessandro had withdrawn down the stairs to the counting house.

That night, Gianni sat up to wait for his master's return. He felt sullenly angry – with Count Dracone, for pushing himself in where he had no business to be; with Messire Alessandro, for letting him; with himself, for doing nothing.

Messire Alessandro did not return until after midnight. Gianni heard his feet dragging on the stairs. He paused in the doorway, leaning on the frame. He was

flushed; Gianni caught the reek of wine. Yet Messire
Alessandro did not look drunk; exhausted, rather.

Gianni stepped forward, ready to guide him to his
bedchamber. Seeing him, Messire Alessandro straightened, startled and defensive.

'No!' He moved away from Gianni's outstretched
hand. 'Go to bed, Gianni.' His voice was sharp. Then he
smiled, and repeated more softly, 'Go to bed.'

'Are you all right, sir?'

His master frowned as if he did not understand the
question. Gianni would not have been surprised if he had
crumpled to the floor at his feet. Then without another
word he stumbled down the passage to his bedchamber.
Gianni was left staring at the door, anxious and frustrated.

A few days later, Messire Alessandro sent for Gianni to
come to the counting house. Somehow, when the sum-
mons came, Gianni already knew that Count Dracone
would be there.

Messire Alessandro was seated at a table beneath an
open window. A faint breeze filtering through it lifted the
papers on the table, and brought the scent of spices along
with the shouts of men unloading on the wharf, and the
more distant cries of boatmen on the canal.

Count Dracone was smiling. He stood beside the
table; one hand played with Messire Alessandro's hair.
Messire Alessandro's look was guarded, and his voice crisp
as he said, 'Come, Gianni. I have a document I want you
to witness.'

'Yes, sir.'

Gianni knew better now than to stand gaping. He was
even learning to read and write with Malatesta, the chief

clerk in the counting house, and so he could sign his name. But he did not know why Messire Alessandro should ask him to do this.

'The freak can write?' Count Dracone said thinly. 'You amaze me, Alessandro.'

'Gianni has many talents.'

The Count shrugged, sinewy muscles shifting under the scarlet silk of his coat. 'I wonder you can bear to set eyes on him. In my house you will see none such.'

Messire Alessandro made no reply, but held out the pen for Gianni to sign. He was very faintly flushed; Gianni did not think he was at ease.

Gianni looked at the document. From what he had heard Dr Foscari say, he knew how important it was to read before you signed. He heard the Count make an impatient noise, but he still read it.

It was the record of a loan, from Messire Alessandro to the Count. Gianni had to stop himself exclaiming when he read the sum. He had not thought so much money existed in the entire city. And yet the Count was supposed to be a wealthy man!

He looked up and met Messire Alessandro's eyes. If they had been alone, he would have asked his master if he really wanted to do this. But they were pinned down by the Count's mocking gaze, and when Messire Alessandro said, 'Sign, Gianni,' he scrawled his name in the space for the witness without making any protest. But as he put the pen down he felt as if he had done a shameful thing.

'Thank you, Alessandro,' the Count said. 'And the security . . .' From one white claw he drew a heavy ring, made of gold and lapis. 'I will redeem it,' he said, 'for not all your wealth and mine together could purchase this ring.' He flicked it and the stone hinged upwards to reveal a crystal compartment beneath. 'In this crystal,' he went on, 'is a hair of the Lord Christos when he lived on earth as a man.'

He let the ring fall to the table, where it rolled and stopped near Messire Alessandro's hand. Then he crossed himself; Gianni gasped as if he had witnessed the deepest blasphemy.

'You wonder at it, freak?' the Count said. 'Wonder on, for you will see nothing so rare in all your life. Take it, Alessandro.'

Messire Alessandro was staring at the ring as if a scorpion crouched near his hand. 'Gianni,' he said, 'you will wear this for me. Put it on.'

Gianni stood with his mouth open. 'Messire, I cannot,' he stammered at last. 'It is not for me . . . it is too holy.'

Messire Alessandro reached out; for a wild instant Gianni thought that he would take his hand and himself put the ring on his finger, but he drew back. Softly, he said, 'Put it on, Gianni. Keep it safe, I beg you.'

Gianni heard a snicker of laughter from the Count. Slowly, he reached out and closed his hand around the ring, and wondered at the relief that he saw in Messire Alessandro's eyes.

That night, as Gianni was thrusting home the bolts on the outer door, he heard heavy footsteps approaching, followed by a thunderous knocking.

He hesitated. He had no orders from Messire Alessandro about what he was to do if visitors arrived after the door was locked. No one had ever come before.

While he hesitated, Messire Alessandro came down

the stairs behind him and paused half way, a hand on the balustrade.

'Shall I let them in, sir?' Gianni asked.

The knocking was repeated, and a voice shouted, 'Open in the name of the Duke!'

Messire Alessandro whispered, 'No!' Gianni stared; Alessandro was pale, eyes wide with terror. As a splintering crash came from the door, he turned and fled up the stairs.

Another crash and the door gave way. There was a rush of feet. Three constructs in the Duke's livery drove their way in, almost overwhelming Gianni as he tried to stop them. They pursued Alessandro up the stairs. A human sergeant, following, paused for a second to tell Gianni, 'Keep out of this, lad.'

Ignoring the order, Gianni pounded up the stairs after him. The constructs had trapped Messire Alessandro on the balcony. Gianni could not get near him. He heard a thin shriek, saw Alessandro struggling vainly in the grip of two of them, and heard another crash as the balcony rail gave way and the jasmine pot plummeted into the canal.

The constructs brought out Messire Alessandro slumped between them as if he was unconscious. He did not reply when Gianni cried out to him. The sergeant took Gianni's shoulder in a hard grip. 'Don't get involved, lad,' he said.

'But what are you doing?' Gianni wished he had better words to protest. 'You can't just – where are you taking him? Why?'

'Your master's a genic,' the sergeant said. 'Someone denounced it. There's nothing you can do.'

He turned away, following the constructs and their prisoner. Gianni stumbled after them, down the stairs

and onto the wharfside. They were loading Messire
Alessandro into a boat.

'Take me with you!' Gianni begged.

'No.' The sergeant nodded to the construct oarsman
to push off. His voice raised as the boat drew away, he
added, 'For your own good, lad.'

Gianni stood watching the boat as it pulled out into
the canal and slowly diminished. Then, in a cold calm,
he went to Dr Foscari's house, where he kicked and
thumped the door until a servant came to protest.

Gianni pushed his way inside. 'Dr Foscari!' he called.

The servant grabbed him, trying to throw him out
again, but Gianni stood his ground, calling out until a
light grew from the top of the stairs and Dr Foscari
appeared, a vast figure in a black brocaded bedgown,
holding a taper and blinking sleep out of his eyes.
'Gianni? All right – ' he flapped a hand at the servant –
'you can go. Close the door.'

'Dr Foscari!' Gianni gasped out, his calm deserting
him again. 'They've taken Messire Alessandro – they say
he's a genic!'

Dr Foscari did not seem surprised. He scratched a
wart on his chin. 'So it's come, then,' he said.

'You knew?'

The lawyer lumbered to the foot of the stairs and
looked Gianni up and down. 'No, I didn't know. I
guessed. Sit down, boy, and tell me what happened.'

Gianni perched on the edge of a spindly gilt-framed
couch at the side of the hall. Dr Foscari did not trust his
weight to it, but stood listening while Gianni told his
story.

'Someone denounced him,' he repeated when Gianni
had finished. 'Through the lion's mouth.'

'What do you mean?'

'At the top of the steps in the Ducal Palace,' Dr Foscari explained, 'there's a stone box shaped like a lion's head. If you've an enemy, post your denunciation through the lion's mouth. No need to sign it. He'll be arrested. It's not law as I was taught it, but it's law here.'

'Then what have they done with Messire Alessandro?' Gianni asked.

'He'll be held in the Palace. He'll be tried tomorrow.'

'Then—'

Dr Foscari shook his head sombrely. 'He's a genic. Law or no law, what defence against that? There's no hope for him now, boy, no hope at all.'

Five

The rickety gilded table in Giulietta's boudoir was spread with scraps of silk. Giulietta sorted through them, discarding this, pouncing on another, prattling away happily about colour and weight and pattern. She was choosing a new gown for her father's birthday celebrations, and Serafina was to stitch it.

She held out a scrap of cyclamen pink and let it flutter in front of Serafina's face, where she sat on the rug by the table. 'This one, Serafina?'

'Not with your hair,' Serafina replied mechanically.

She scooped up the scrap as Giulietta let it fall, and replaced it on the table, trying to disguise her screaming boredom. Whatever fabric the stupid girl chose, she would be the centre of a crowd of admirers. 'Your father likes to see you in white,' she said.

Giulietta wriggled, pouting. 'I *hate* white.' She held up one sample of sea green threaded with silver, and one of violet. 'These are pretty. Which one, Serafina?'

'The sea green,' Serafina said, on the grounds that she liked it better and she would have to look at it for longer.

Giulietta bit her lower lip. 'Yes, but it's one of Messire Alessandro's. We might not be able to get it now.'

'Why not?'

Giulietta sat upright. The table rocked and half the

silks slid to the floor. 'Serafina, haven't you *heard*? Messire Alessandro is a genic! He was denounced yesterday.'

Serafina stared at her. She had accompanied Giulietta once or twice to Messire Alessandro's warehouse. The little merchant had always treated her courteously – so courteously that she wondered whether he realized she was a genic. The idea that he might be one himself had never crossed her mind.

'What will happen to him?' she asked.

'He's being tried today. That's how I know, because Papa was called to the Council this morning. And then . . .'

Her voice died away. She obviously had no idea what would happen to a genic who pretended to be human, and for once Serafina could not blame her for ignorance. She had no idea either. She had visions of the gentle little man being tortured or put to death; no one would protest at what was done to a genic, and there would be no one in the whole city to speak for him or help him.

She retrieved the dropped silks and arranged them carefully along the edge of the table. Carmine, rose, indigo . . . Had the trial taken place, she wondered. Where was Alessandro now?

'I shall send Roberto,' Giulietta decided, turning the sea green scrap in her fingers. 'With so much trouble, he might be able to get the silk cheaper, and that will please Papa. Put all these others away, Serafina.'

Serafina took the box and began to lay away the samples, bending her head to hide the rage that shook her stomach and her hands. If she lost control now she would scream at the empty-headed little bitch, and she could guess what would happen then. Is this all? she asked herself despairingly. Silence and self-control and grovelling for the favour of Giulietta Contarini? For ever?

The door of the boudoir opened and closed. Serafina did not look up to see who it was until she heard the fluting alto. 'Lady, it is time for your lute lesson.'

Hyacinth. Serafina looked up at Giulietta, not at him, to catch her in another pettish wriggle. 'I don't *want* a stupid lute lesson.'

'It is your father's order, lady.' Serafina glanced at him at last to see his face set in a fierce disdain. She was almost surprised not to see Giulietta curl at the edges and start to shrivel. But she was oblivious, sliding into a sulk, making no move to fetch the lute.

Serafina finished packing away the silk samples as Hyacinth waited out the silence; she was surprised when he reached a hand down to help her to her feet. She had not thought he realized she was there, or if he did, he might just as well have walked over her.

She thanked him, and took the box to her sewing corner by the window, where she sat down. If Giulietta dismissed her she would have to go, but she had a fancy to listen in on the lute lesson. It might, she thought, be amusing. She did not wish to admit to herself the fascination she felt for Hyacinth.

He had opened up a leather portfolio of music and set a sheet on the stand. 'I have a new piece for you, lady,' he said. 'But first play me the exercise you learnt last time.'

With a petulant flounce, Giulietta picked up the beribboned lute from the chair where it always lay, seated herself, and plucked out a sequence of notes.

Hyacinth winced. 'Tuning.'

Giulietta held out the instrument without a word, and Hyacinth took it from her, careful, Serafina noted, not to touch her hand as he did so. While he tuned it, Serafina took up her needle and began to repair a ripped lace edging on one of Giulietta's morning gowns. Neither teacher nor pupil was paying her any attention.

When Hyacinth had finished, he handed back the lute and Giulietta repeated the exercise. A frown was wrinkling Hyacinth's perfect forehead as he listened. 'No, lady,' he said patiently. 'The stress is wrong. Like this.'

He hummed a phrase. Even at that faint suggestion of his singing voice the room came alive. The dust motes danced to a livelier tune.

Giulietta tried again; to Serafina's ear there was no difference from the first time she had played. Can't she hear it, she wondered.

'Lady,' Hyacinth said, 'you might find it easier if you altered the position of your left hand. Bring it further round the neck of the instrument. Arch the wrist.'

Giulietta frowned. 'It makes my hand look ugly. Oh, there then . . . like that?'

'No.' Serafina could tell that Hyacinth's patience was fast running out. 'Lady, if you would permit me to place your hand correctly . . .'

'Touch me?' Giulietta's voice was a squeak of outrage. 'No! Don't you *dare* – filthy genic!'

The rings on Hyacinth's slender fingers flashed as he clenched his hands and then slowly relaxed. 'Then give me the instrument and let me show you.'

Giulietta handed the lute over, but when Hyacinth had demonstrated she made no attempt to copy his placing. Please don't slap her, Serafina begged him silently. Remember what they will do to you. She reminded herself that Hyacinth was used to this; all he did was let out a long sigh. 'Play the exercise again, lady.'

The same unravelling sequence of notes. 'Have you practised at all since last time?' Hyacinth said sharply.

'No. Why should I? It's so *boring*.'

'If you don't practise, you won't learn.'

'Do you think I care?'

Hyacinth's lips tightened. The wonderful violet eyes were dilated; his voice had tightened with fury as he said, 'No, I don't. But your father wishes you to learn, and you will do so. If you will not do as I tell you, then he must be brought to lesson you.'

To Serafina's surprise, Giulietta broke out into tinkling laughter. She let the lute fall in a jangle of strings. 'Hyacinth, you are *funny*!' she said. 'I *love* it when you get angry with me! Do you think Papa would listen to you? When you're just a genic?' She fluttered a hand at him. 'I've had enough now. You can go.'

Hyacinth had flushed and then gone white. He said, 'The lesson is not over.'

Giulietta jumped to her feet. 'It's over when *I* say it is.' She stamped her foot. 'Go *away*!'

The musician stood his ground. Serafina watched; she had given over all pretence of mending Giulietta's gown.

Giulietta waited for a moment, facing Hyacinth. When he did not move, she said quietly. 'Get out.' She took a step towards him. 'Or I'll tell Papa you wanted to touch me.'

Hyacinth hesitated a few seconds longer. He was paler than chalk, but his eyes smouldered. Stiffly he turned and stalked out; Serafina found that she was shivering.

When the musician had gone, Giulietta turned to her and giggled. 'Stupid thing, don't look so shocked! He wouldn't dare lay a finger on me. And he won't say anything to Papa. *I* know!' She picked up her skirts. 'I'm going to find Roberto and send him to Messire Alessandro's.'

She danced out in a rustle of silk.

Serafina let out the breath she had not been aware of holding. After a moment she retrieved the lute, meaning to put it back in its place. Giulietta's rough treatment didn't seem to have damaged it. Serafina plucked the strings; they sounded still in tune. She couldn't help wondering what Giulietta found so difficult, and sat down to try holding the lute in the way Hyacinth had demonstrated. Yes, it felt awkward, but nothing to make such a fuss about. Unless, like Giulietta, you enjoyed fusses.

Serafina hummed to herself the phrase of the exercise. How would you get those notes from the lute? She plucked experimentally, working out where to place her fingers on the frets. After a few minutes she felt confident enough to try the exercise. No – again. And again. She wasn't sure that she was remembering it properly.

One more try, before someone came along and found her wasting her mistress's time. As the last notes died away, she heard Hyacinth humming the phrase again.

He was standing in the doorway. Awkwardly, Serafina got to her feet. She felt as if she ought to apologize, though she wasn't quite sure why.

He still looked furious, and very much on his dignity. Stiffly he advanced into the room and picked up the sheet of music he had left on the stand. He said, 'I forgot this.'

Serafina found her ready tongue had deserted her. She held out the lute and began, 'I was trying—'

'It was dreadful,' Hyacinth said. 'Who taught you?'

'No one. I—'

Hyacinth's eyes narrowed. Serafina suddenly felt like a fish, gutted and laid out on a slab. 'No one taught you? Then—'

'I listened to you and – and my lady Giulietta. It didn't seem difficult, so . . . Are you angry?'

He advanced on her. 'Sit there. Hold the lute.'

Nothing to do but obey. Hyacinth bent over her and adjusted her hands with cool fingers. 'Like that. Now play it – no, listen first.'

He hummed the phrase again and Serafina did her best to copy him. He was looking thoughtful, the faintest crease between his brows. She felt herself growing red under the intensity of that violet regard.

'You'll need to learn the proper fingerings,' he murmured. 'Don't think it's easy. And you . . . Give me the lute again.'

Not daring to say a word, Serafina obeyed him. He struck a note. 'Sing that.'

'But I—'

'Sing it.'

Feeling completely stupid, she sang the note.

'Again. Now this.'

He made her copy single notes, and then short phrases. At last he put the lute aside and sat on the couch Giulietta had vacated. He looked puzzled.

Nervously, Serafina said, 'I'm sorry if—'

He waved her absently into silence, and then said, 'Don't you know you have perfect pitch?'

'I don't even know what perfect pitch means.'

Hyacinth stared at her, shocked, and covered his eyes theatrically with one hand. Then he said, 'It means that a human or a genic with your talents would have learnt music from a child, as I did. We must hope not too much time has been lost.' Curiously, he added, 'You must have been made for this. Why were you never trained?'

Serafina's lips were parted, her breath coming unevenly. Was this the answer she had looked for? Not in Dr Heinrich's analyses, but here, so simply, in a phrase of music? Crossly she told herself, He must think I'm a complete fool! She said, 'I was a street beggar. I don't remember anything before that.'

Hyacinth was looking outraged. He whispered, 'The waste . . .' He stood up, straightening himself. 'I will speak to Count Contarini. You must lose no more time.' His eyes flashed scorn over the sewing corner and the torn gown. 'Any idiot can sew.'

Serafina felt laughter bubbling up. 'My lady Giulietta won't like it,' she said.

'Serafina,' said Hyacinth, 'I do not care in the slightest whether my lady Giulietta likes it or not. I shall speak to the Count.'

He took his music and went out. His footsteps had died away before it occurred to Serafina that he had never asked her if that was what she wanted.

2

Gianni waited until morning outside the Ducal Palace, hugging himself in an effort to keep warm. Dawn came cold and bright, with a wind fluttering the surface of the flood waters in the square.

By the time the doors were opened, a crowd had gathered. Gianni let them carry him through the archway, up the stairway and past the stone lion whose mouth gaped to swallow treachery, and into the hall where the trial would take place. He thrust and wormed his way to the front, but had to stand there for hours, with head and shoulders aching, while other cases were heard.

The hall was large; light washed over the faint remains of frescos and the floor where cracks seamed the marble. A throne stood on a dais at the far end, and from there the Duke sat in judgement, looking to Gianni like a remote, golden figure from a holy icon.

At length the door which led to the cells opened to admit Messire Alessandro. He was conscious now, able to walk, but still held between two construct guards. Of course, Gianni thought. No one human touches a genic.

He felt his heart wrenched as he looked at his master. Alessandro was ghost pale, a drifting wraith of white and silver gold, with a tensile grace beside the bulky constructs. Had they tortured him, Gianni wondered. What could you let yourself do to a genic if you did not believe it was human?

Alessandro flinched at the avid sound that rose from the crowd as he appeared. Someone read the accusation: the genic calling itself Messire Alessandro had passed itself off as human, had consorted with them, traded with them. And prospered among them, Gianni thought silently. That was what they could not forgive.

The Duke gave an order. A single swordsman detached himself from the Duke's retinue and moved down the steps to where Alessandro stood in the middle of the hall. He tore open the front of Messire Alessandro's shirt, and drew his sword. For a moment Gianni thought that he was an executioner.

The swordsman raised his weapon. Gianni cried, 'No!' in a voice so hoarse he did not recognize it. The blade flashed. It opened up a shallow cut across Messire

Alessandro's chest, and from it trickled the pale genic blood, the mark of his separation from humanity.

The crowd swayed and hissed their triumph. Messire Alessandro cried out, writhed convulsively in the constructs' grasp, and slumped between them in a faint. They stood there holding him up until at a word from the Duke they dropped him to the floor.

Gianni stood and stared at the tiny, crumpled figure. Somewhere in the echoing spaces of the hall a highpitched legal voice was speaking of the disposal of Messire Alessandro's property. Gianni did not listen.

Until the guards came, he had not known. That for months he had given his service and loyalty to a genic had never crossed his mind. And yet in all that time he had never touched Messire Alessandro, had never been allowed to touch him. Alessandro had kept him safe.

Gianni started forward, uncertain what to do now, and was prevented by a scarlet blur in front of his eyes which resolved itself into Count Dracone. The Count said, 'Freak, give me the ring.'

Gianni's first reaction was to close his fist, to protect the holy thing.

'Don't be a fool,' the Count said. 'A genic owns nothing. I owe it nothing. Give me the ring.'

Gianni stood staring at him in a vast enlightenment. 'It was you who denounced him,' he said. 'For the sake of his gold.'

The Count did not confirm or deny; it was not necessary. He merely held out a hand. Gianni drew off the ring and dropped it into the cupped fingers.

The Lord Christos did not need his protection. Not even the Count's evil could stain that transcendent holiness. And Gianni had something else to do. He knew, as surely as if he had heard the divine voice, that he was not leaving the Lord Christos behind him, but going to meet Him in Alessandro.

He crossed the hall, knelt beside Alessandro and raised his master's head, letting it rest on his own knees. He knew he should feel revulsion at the touch. Alessandro's skin was cool, slightly damp, his hair fine as floss silk. Nothing to fear; nothing to disgust.

Gianni examined the chest wound; it was barely more than a deep scratch, and the blood had already ceased to flow. Gianni's skin crawled, until he found a slow, faint heartbeat.

Footsteps stumped across the hall and stopped beside him. Dr Foscari was looking down at him, leaning on a stout stick. 'You can't do this, lad,' he said. 'They'll take him away now.'

'Where?'

'To the Ghetto. He'll have to stay there, unless someone claims him as a bondman.' Suddenly furious, he added, 'He's a genic, lad. There's nothing anyone can do.'

'I can go with him,' said Gianni.

If Dr Foscari replied, Gianni missed it, because just then Alessandro's eyes flickered open. He murmured, 'Gianni,' and closed them again as if he was exhausted. Gianni bent over him, intent for signs of life returning.

The court was breaking up, the crowds pushing out through the main doors. The Duke's golden throne was vacant again. A couple of construct guards marched across to Alessandro, thrusting Dr Foscari aside. Alessandro, reviving, let out a whimper of terror.

'Get back!' Gianni spat.

The constructs paused, their small eyes puzzled by the

conflict of orders. A human guard – Gianni recognized
the sergeant who had come to the house – strode over to
them. 'Leave it, lad,' he said to Gianni. He did not sound
unsympathetic. 'If you try to stop us, you're risking arrest
yourself.'

'Arrest me then. I'm going with him.'

The sergeant hesitated, shrugged, and said to the
constructs, 'Bring it.'

They stretched out their hands for Alessandro. His
breath came in sobbing gasps. Gianni placed himself as a
shield between them, and said, 'Don't touch him. I'll
bring him.'

Gently he raised Alessandro to his feet. Alessandro
clung to him instinctively; he could not stand alone. He
seemed dazed, as if he did not understand what was
happening. As they came to the glimmering expanse of
the square, he murmured, 'Gianni, no . . . oh, no,' but
Gianni still did not know what he meant.

The daylight was dying. The square stretched out like
a vast crucible of molten silver. Against it, a curved black
shadow, the boat with the guards waited at the quayside.

Gianni helped Alessandro on board and held him,
shivering, as one of the constructs leant on the oar and
the boat glided away from the steps. A pale sky arched
over them. Gianni felt as if he was leaving behind
everything he had ever known.

The boat drew up to a landing stage near the gateway to
the Ghetto. The construct guard reached for Alessandro,
who shrank whimpering into Gianni's arms.

'Leave him!' Gianni snapped. 'I'll do it.'

He half lifted Alessandro out of the boat; his master

was barely conscious. Ignoring the constructs, salvaging what little dignity was left, Gianni guided him towards the gate.

Two human guards, in the gold livery of the Duke, flanked the gateway. They raised their spears to allow Gianni and Alessandro to enter.

Alessandro roused a little. 'You can't come with me.'

'You can't go alone.' Gianni spoke to the guards, roughly because he was afraid they would keep him out. 'I'm human; let me pass.'

One of the guards relaxed his stone face into a look of disgust. 'Come and go as you please.' He spat. 'You'll go, soon enough.'

Gianni led Alessandro through the gateway. Ahead of them were streets of ruined houses. The shapes of splintered wood were printed on the fading sky. Shadows settled beneath humped stone.

Stagnant water stood in the streets, green with weed and water plants. Rough plank bridges crisscrossed it. There was a rich smell of decay.

Uncertainly, Gianni turned back to the guards. 'Where should we go?' he asked.

There was no response.

Still uncertain, Gianni led Alessandro on. Most doors were closed and barred, as if the houses were deserted, or the occupants hiding away. There was silence except for bubbling from the water, as fish or something like fish rose to flies, and sometimes a pattering footstep as if something crept up to observe them, and fled. Once a shadow grew up behind them, a monstrous thing with head far too large for the spindly body, but when Gianni whirled to face it there was nothing there.

Alessandro was sinking under terror and exhaustion

when they came to a courtyard. A wooden verandah, half
its planks torn away, was built round all four sides. The
courtyard itself was under water and from the centre rose
the statue of a bronze lion, its wings raised in a benedic-
tion. Roses and jasmine and clematis scrambled over the
rooftops and the verandah posts in a wild profusion.

'This isn't so bad,' Gianni said. 'We could stay here,
if there's a place.'

Near one corner, a doorway gaped open. There was
no door. The floor sagged and bloomed with rot. The
room was empty except for a wooden bed with a rope
mattress.

'Lie down,' Gianni said, letting Alessandro sink onto
the bed. 'You can rest here, sir, till morning. Then I'll see
if we can find somewhere better.'

Alessandro turned his face to the wall, drawing himself
into a tight knot. For a second Gianni felt desperate hurt,
until he realized that Alessandro was not rejecting him,
only the world that had racked him into unimaginable
pain.

Gianni laid a hand on his shoulder and went to keep
watch by the door. He knelt on the rotting floorboards
and said his prayers as he had been taught to say them as
a child at the Innocenti. Then he lay down across the
doorway to keep out anything that might try to enter in
the night.

Before he was able to sleep he heard a soft footfall
along the verandah. He sat up. A figure was approaching,
lit by the rising moon. It was unnaturally tall and thin, as
if a man had been thrown together out of straw, and it
moved jerkily. The face was bony, with a single large eye,
and a slit where the nose should have been.

Gianni sprang to his feet, but before he could strike

out the creature knelt in front of him and laid on the floorboards a blanket and a piece of bread. Gianni stared after it, trying to stammer out thanks, as it retreated the way it had come.

The creature had disappeared before Gianni could drag himself out of his stupefaction. He took the blanket and tucked it around Alessandro, who seemed unaware of him. 'There's bread, sir; do you want some?'

No response. Gianni divided the bread scrupulously and ate half of it, before settling down to sleep.

He woke in the night to hear crying, a thin wailing sound, like a sick child. He got up and went over to the bed. Alessandro lay with his face hidden in the blanket, hands clutching it around him. Very gently, Gianni rested a hand on his shoulder. 'Don't,' he said awkwardly.

Alessandro rolled over, away from him, and stared up at him. Tears glimmered on his face. 'You can't touch me,' he said. 'No one touches a genic.'

'I can,' Gianni said.

He sat down on the side of the bed and took the genic into his arms. Alessandro fought against him briefly, and then clutched at him, with wrenching sobs that shook all the frail body.

Gianni held him. 'Don't. Sandro, don't,' he said. 'You're with me. I won't leave you.'

The terrible sobbing went on, until it seemed that Alessandro was too exhausted to cry any more. His breath was a convulsive gasping; the thin hands still clung desperately.

Gianni stroked his hair. 'Lie down,' he said. 'Go to sleep. See, I'll stay with you.'

He pulled the thin blanket around him and lay down beside him on the narrow bed, letting him rest against his shoulder and in the crook of his arm. There could be no sin, he thought. Genic or human, this was a tortured creature.

In the end, Alessandro slept, but Gianni lay awake beside him until watery light washed through the doorway and around the gaps in the shutters. It was a blue, quiet day. Gianni held the sleeping genic and tried not to think what they would do when he awoke.

At length Alessandro stirred. Gianni watched him, seeing memory flow back into his face, and the realization of where he was. He sat up and drew away from Gianni. 'Forgive me.'

'It's nothing, sir.'

Alessandro's pale gold hair was tangled around a white face. The skin around his eyes looked as if it had been smudged with ash, but the eyes were very bright. His loose white shirt was torn, and stiff where the pale blood had dried. When he spoke his voice was a frail thread, ready to snap.

'I was a genic child,' he said. 'Do you understand? Created to be a child, no more. We – creatures like me – we are not meant to grow up.' His mouth twisted bitterly. 'We have a beautiful deathbed, surrounded by elegant mourning dresses, but never a memorial, for who would wish to remember us?'

He turned his head away. Gianni moved to take his hand, but Alessandro pulled away from him. The laws of his genic heritage, swept away in the night's agony, were in place again.

'My foster father was a very rich man,' he went on. 'I won't tell you his name, or his city. He paid for a dispensation from the Church, and bought me for my

foster mother, for she was barren, and she wept for a
child. She was very beautiful, and not much more than a
child herself. When I was a baby, a small child, I was like
a doll that she could play with. But as I grew older, she
remembered – and the training goes very deep. I could
see her shrinking from me . . .

'I had never questioned that I was human. No one
touches a genic.' His voice quavered out of control, but
he mastered it. 'And then I saw my mother look at me
. . . as she looked at the genic bondservants. And then I
knew . . .

'When my father saw I would not die, he told me I
must go away.' Again the bitter twisting of the lips. 'That
was kindness. He could have sold me into bondage, or
killed me. Who would have blamed him? I was a genic,
and I was his. Instead he gave me money, and told me to
go to another city.' He shrugged. 'I came here. I prospered. But I have tried . . .' His voice quivered again, and
this time it was beyond him to control it. 'I did not touch
the ring. I did not defile the Lord Christos. I have tried
not to give offence . . . but it's so cold.'

Gianni thought he would break down then, and
reached out to grasp his shoulders, but Alessandro drew
back. 'No. I have no right. Last night . . . you saved my
reason. But you will need to confess your sin to Holy
Church and be absolved.'

Gianni sat and looked at his hands. He wanted to say
that he would not worship a God who called what he
had done a sin, or a God that would call Alessandro's
touch defilement, but his tongue felt thick in his mouth.
He had not the words. He wished that he was not so
clumsy. He looked down at the broad, coarse hands that

could fetch and carry, dig, row a boat swiftly down the canal, build a fire, even, of late, hold a pen, but were useless to give comfort now.

'Gianni, listen.'

He looked up in astonishment. That was almost the old Alessandro, the cool, crisp voice he knew.

'Gianni, you must go to see Dr Foscari. All my property has been forfeit to the State, but he has my papers. He's an honest man. There's money, and a house . . . I bought it in your name.'

'I don't want them.'

'No, you must. For Lucetta, too. I think I always knew what would happen in the end. I made provision. But you must deal with it now.'

3

Giulietta Contarini's bedchamber was like the heart of a pink rose. A lamp with a rose tinted shade threw out a soft light. The hangings of the bed were of rose coloured lace. The bedcovers were pink silk, edged with ruffles and covered with gold embroidery. Pink silk hung at the windows and festooned the toilet table, the ottoman and the prie-dieu. The scent of roses hit Serafina in the throat as she stepped inside.

Giulietta was lying back on a mound of silken pillows, one languid hand extended to her maidservant, who was manicuring her nails. Her hair was loose, spread in shining golden snakes over her shoulders and the rosy lace of her nightgown. Her eyes were pink, too, swollen with crying.

'Serafina,' she said fretfully. 'Come and talk to me. Everything's horrid today.'

Serafina had not seen her mistress since that morning, when they chose the silk for her gown. She stayed in her own chamber, diligently stitching, not letting herself think about what Hyacinth might be saying to the Count. No one sent for her.

Towards evening she heard movement from the family's private rooms: running feet, doors slamming, and Giulietta screaming. At first she wondered if Giulietta was ill. Then as the raised voices and banging doors and shrieks continued, she came to the conclusion that the girl was in the middle of a spectacular tantrum. She had not thought it worth trying to find out why.

Now she closed the bedchamber door behind her and asked, 'What's the matter?'

Giulietta screwed up her face and spoke with an artificial sob in her voice. 'Everything!' Her face changed as she snatched her hand away from her maid. 'You poked me, clumsy thing! Get out!'

The maidservant rolled her eyes at Serafina in what might almost have been a look of friendly commiseration. Without speaking she packed away the manicuring tools into their leather case and placed it in one of the drawers of the toilet table. Curtseying to Giulietta, she went out.

'Well?' Serafina asked. 'What is all the fuss about?'

Giulietta covered her eyes with one hand and sighed theatrically. 'I'm ill, Serafina. Bathe my forehead.' She flapped her free hand at a silver bowl and crumpled silk handkerchief on the table beside the bed. 'Don't touch me, mind.'

Serafina wadded up the handkerchief, wetted it in the

rosewater the bowl contained, and dabbed Giulietta's temples. She deliberately did not ask again what had upset Giulietta, and after a moment her mistress said, 'Count Dracone asked Papa for my hand in marriage.'

Serafina paused with the handkerchief poised; rose-water dripped on Giulietta's nose, but Giulietta was too deep into her grievance to scold her for it. 'Is that anything to get so worked up about?' Serafina asked.

'But you don't understand!' Giulietta's voice rose to a wail. 'Papa *refused*!'

'Are you telling me you want to marry Count Dracone?'

Giulietta wriggled. 'He's handsome. And rich. And I want to be married. Living here at home is *so* boring.'

'Well,' said Serafina, 'you wouldn't be bored if you were married to Count Dracone, that's for sure.'

Giulietta peered up at her suspiciously. 'Don't you like Count Dracone, Serafina? Why don't you?'

Serafina touched the scented cloth to her mistress's brow. Why not? Because a genic was pulled out of the canal near the Palazzo Dracone. Because a priest disappeared when he went to visit the Count. Because the Count's tastes did not run to marriage . . . Because he and Dr Heinrich were partners in something she could not put a name to.

She let out a little sigh. How much of that could you tell to this hothouse orchid, and expect to be believed? Especially when Dracone was handsome, in that serpentine way, and certainly he was rich.

Carefully, she said, 'He is a newcomer to the city. His name is not written in the Book of Gold.'

Giulietta wriggled further down among her pillows.

'Papa is on the Council. He could make them admit Count Dracone – if he wanted to.'

Perhaps that, Serafina thought, was why Count Dracone had asked for Giulietta's hand. She could not imagine that he wanted Giulietta for herself. But Serafina was fairly sure that even Count Contarini would not have the power to inscribe Dracone's name in the Book of Gold, unless the rest of the Council agreed. Still, there was no point in arguing with Giulietta, especially when Count Contarini – with more common sense than she had given him credit for – had refused Dracone's offer of marriage.

Giulietta was still sniffling away, squeezing out a tear or two, making the most of being ill-used. Bracingly, Serafina said, 'You can do much better than Count Dracone. You're not in love with him, are you?'

Giulietta looked shocked. 'A lady is not in love with her husband before she is married, Serafina. It isn't proper. But you wouldn't know that.'

No, Serafina thought. Genic, ex-street beggar – marriage would not come her way, and she was thankful for it. She had no wish to be bargained over like a fish on a slab.

'Then think of all the other young men who will come to ask for you,' she said. 'Younger than Count Dracone. Richer. Handsomer.'

She could see she had given Giulietta something to think about. Her mistress gave one final sniff. 'You can stop doing that now, Serafina. Put the handkerchief away – and tell me about Hyacinth.'

Serafina felt an unpleasant jolt in her stomach. To hide her uneasiness, she took the bowl and the handkerchief and laid them on the toilet table for the maid to clear away in the morning. 'What about Hyacinth?' she asked.

'Papa told me, he says you must study music.' Giulietta giggled. 'As if you ever could!'

Irked, Serafina said, 'Hyacinth says I have perfect pitch.'

Giulietta shrugged; probably she didn't know what it meant either. Curiously, she said, 'Do you want to learn music, Serafina? Really?'

Something told Serafina not to seem too eager. There was a cruel streak in Giulietta, or perhaps it was no more than thoughtlessness. At any rate, Serafina was used to keeping her own counsel. She would not seem to desire something, in case it was denied. 'It might be interesting,' she said evenly.

Giulietta giggled again. 'I see! You're in love with Hyacinth!'

Serafina felt blood rush to her face. Stupid little floozie, she thought furiously. Does she think there's nothing else in life but throwing yourself after some man?

'You're embarrassed!' said Giulietta. 'Serafina, you *are*! But it's no good, you know, not with Hyacinth. Anybody can see that.'

Though she could not control her face, Serafina managed to keep her voice level. 'It's not that at all. But your sewing doesn't keep me busy all day. Learning music would help to fill my time. And your guests might be pleased if Hyacinth and I could sing together.'

Giulietta waved a hand dismissively. 'You'll never be good enough to sing with Hyacinth. And if you haven't enough to do, you can sew me some new hangings for this room. I'm sick of these old things.'

'Whatever you want, lady.'

Giulietta lowered her eyes and peeped up at Serafina through the lashes. 'Don't be cross, silly thing! You shall learn if you want to. Papa doesn't mind – but you're to do *my* work first, remember.' Suddenly she laughed, and clapped her hands. 'I know! I'll give you my lute. Then *I* shan't have to play the horrid thing any more. Isn't that a good plan, Serafina?'

'Excellent,' Serafina said, hiding a pulse of excitement under a dry tone. 'Your generosity overwhelms me.'

Six

I

It was still early as Gianni went to see Dr Foscari at the Judiciary. The market boats were only just beginning to unroll their awnings. A couple of late revellers were lurching home. A skinny cat basked in a pool of sunlight.

Gianni's footsteps echoed as he paced across the stained marble floor of the ante-room. He wished he had been able to shave, or put on clean linen. But the petitioners who waited by the walls, or squatted on the floor, paid no heed to him.

A bored clerk, his desk a frowsy oasis of disorder in the ruined splendour of the room, cocked his head towards the archway that led to Dr Foscari's office and said, 'You can't go in there. You'll have to wait.'

Gianni groped in his pocket for a bribe. The clerk watched him, flat-eyed, and slid a hand over the coin Gianni placed on the desk. 'I didn't see you,' he said.

As Gianni strode through the archway he saw a man standing with his back to him, leaning over Dr Foscari's desk, his hands flat on it. He recognized the varnished hair and scarlet brocade of Count Dracone.

In a soft voice the Count was saying, 'I wish to claim rights in the genic Alessandro. I wish to claim him as my bondman.'

Gianni opened his mouth to yell a protest, and caught

it back. He needed time to think. Protest would be useless. He needed to be clever as Count Dracone was clever, but with a sick fear he knew he was not.

He understood. He had believed that the Count's denunciation had been for the sake of money, so that he need not repay the debt. Maybe that was true. But another reason, the reason that flaunted itself now in front of Gianni's eyes, was that the Count had wanted Alessandro in his power.

Gianni's breath came short. Between the Hospital of the Innocenti and the Palazzo Dracone there was a world of knowledge and experience. Lacking it, he could barely speculate on what the Count would do to Alessandro when he had him. But he knew that it must be evil.

In the seconds he had delayed, Dr Foscari was muttering and shifting papers around on his desk. Gianni stepped forward and bowed. 'Good day, Dr Foscari.'

Count Dracone whipped round to face him. 'Get out, freak,' he said. 'Don't interrupt your betters.'

'A moment, Count,' Dr Foscari said. 'Gianni, what can I do for you?'

'I've an errand from Messire Alessandro, sir.'

'Messire Alessandro!' Count Dracone gave way to sneering laughter. 'The genic Alessandro. Bondman Alessandro. Street sweepings . . . filth of the sewers . . .'

Gianni wanted nothing more than to take the Count by the throat and choke the sneering into silence. He knew he must not; he did not even move, but the Count read the longing in his face and took a step back. Nothing had ever given Gianni greater satisfaction.

'Get out!' the Count repeated. 'Do you want me to call an officer?'

Gianni ignored him, and spoke urgently to Dr Foscari.

'Sir, can the Count here truly claim Messire Alessandro as a bondman?'

'He can.' Dr Foscari's voice was a bass rumble; his pudgy hands shifted papers again. With a breath of hope Gianni realized that he was not happy; perhaps he would help Messire Alessandro, if there was a way he could do it. 'Any citizen in good standing can claim a genic as bondman.'

'No!'

Foscari shrugged, and Count Dracone moved forward, purposeful again. Gianni thought furiously. A citizen in good standing . . . was Count Dracone truly that, when all the city knew how evil he was? But the laws saw only his title, his wealth . . .

'Draw up the documents,' the Count ordered, slapping a hand down on the desk.

Gianni saw that on the claw-tipped hand Count Dracone once more wore the reliquary ring. 'That ring . . . that was your pledge to Messire Alessandro,' he said. Every word was like a step forward down a dark passage. Gianni was feeling his way; he was not sure where the passage was leading. 'The debt you owed him was never repaid. Since his property fell to the State, the debt is owed to the State now. Is that right, Dr Foscari?'

The lawyer was watching him, bright-eyed. 'Oh, yes, that's right,' he said. 'We'll make a lawyer of you yet.'

Count Dracone's crimson mouth curved into a sneer. 'I've a parrot that can babble as much law as that,' he said. 'Foscari, send this peasant to the devil and sign me the rights to the genic.'

Dr Foscari flashed a sideways glance at Gianni, but it was to the Count he spoke. 'But the law also states,' he said, 'that no one in debt to the State may claim rights to a bondman. Does your parrot know that, Count Dracone?'

The Count took a single step forward. Gianni almost recoiled at the look in his eyes, but he held fast. The look meant that he had won.

'Of course,' Dr Foscari said comfortably, 'you could always repay the debt . . . if that's convenient.'

Everything drained out of Count Dracone's face except the fury in the burning eyes. Without a word, he spun round and stalked out.

Dr Foscari grinned until his eyes disappeared into rolls of fat. He let out a wheezy chuckle. 'You've made an enemy there, boy.'

Gianni shrugged. 'So have you, sir.'

'Don't worry about me, boy. He'll have to get up very early in the morning if he wants to stick a knife into old Foscari. And now . . . I take it you want to do business with me?'

He called the clerk and sent for Alessandro's deedbox. The day was wearing on to noon before Gianni had finished reading and signing all the documents in it, and listening to Dr Foscari as he carefully explained Alessandro's disposition of his wealth.

At the end of it, Gianni realized that while he was not rich as Count Dracone pretended to be rich, or as Alessandro had been, he was the owner of wealth far beyond the dreams of a simple lad from the Hospital of the Innocenti.

No, he told himself, not the owner, but the guardian. And he was not the simple lad from the Innocenti any longer. He knew that Alessandro was still in danger, for who in the city would care about what was done to an unbonded genic? And while he saw the danger he saw the remedy. He knew what he had to do now.

'Well, Messire Giovanni?' the old lawyer said, with another fat grin. 'What next? You'll need to buy a decent suit and find some old granny to sweep your floors and cook your suppers.'

Gianni was startled at the courtesy, but not embarrassed as he would have been only days ago. The title fitted him as the new suit would fit him. He picked up the keys to the house Alessandro had deeded to him.

'Not yet, Dr Foscari,' he said. 'Before that, there's just one more piece of business . . .'

2

'Leo, stop fidgeting.' Gabriel looked up, exasperated, as Count Leonardo shifted his position for the hundredth time, and the light changed on his face. He threw down the brush. 'Oh, take a break then, if you must.'

Count Leonardo Loredan grinned at him as he unfolded himself stiffly from the chair by the studio window and chafed his hands together. Even though summer crept upon the city, a cold breeze was flowing in from the sea. There was a charcoal brazier in the studio now, but it did little more than take the worst of the chill off the room, when the shutters were wide to let in the light.

'The first thing I do,' Leonardo said, 'when we sell another painting, is to pay for glass in that window.'

'You can't sell this one.'

Leonardo crossed the floor and stood beside him to

look at the portrait. It must be a curious thing, Gabriel reflected, to confront yourself like that. To see not just the face that met you each morning in the mirror, but your own features filtered through another consciousness, another set of rules.

The face in the portrait was unsmiling, but not sombre. In painting his master Gabriel had striven for an absolute security that went beyond arrogance. The ice blue eyes looked out beyond the studio, as if they were fixed on something approaching from afar off. The features were expectant, the lips folded, but as though laughter danced beneath the calm surface. At least, Gabriel thought, sighing, that was what he had wanted.

By his side, Leonardo was still. In a moment, he said, 'Do I look like that?'

'God knows.'

Leonardo passed a hand over his face, almost as if he was wiping it. Daring to look at him, Gabriel saw he had a puzzled expression, as if he did not know what to make of the likeness in front of him. He said, 'You're right, Gabriel, we can't sell it.' He let out a short spurt of embarrassed laughter. 'What shall we do with it?'

Gabriel went over to the table by the wall and started to mix more of the ochre he was using for the background. He could fill in that until the light died; no need to trouble Leonardo any further today.

'We exhibit it,' he said. 'Think of it, Leo – everyone will want one. Wives and daughters. Stuffy old Councillors in their robes. Rich merchants and—'

'Gabriel!' Leonardo had turned to watch him, laughter in his eyes. 'Do you want to paint stuffy old Councillors and their overdressed ladies?'

Gabriel shrugged. 'I want to paint.' In any case, it was

line, light, colour; the subject was less important. Except
for this one portrait. 'Besides, Leo, we need the money.'

'That's true enough.' He tore himself away from
Gabriel's easel and began to pace restlessly up and down
the studio. 'Giulietta Contarini. Now there's a face you
could immortalize in paint. Her father can pay, too.'

With his back to him, Gabriel said, 'I thought you
wanted to marry Giulietta Contarini.'

His stomach tightened as he heard Leonardo's pacing
suddenly stop; the silence was broken by an explosion
of laughter. 'Giulietta? Well, I wouldn't mind marrying
her father's coffers, at that. But you know very well
that Count Contarini would never let me near her.
Whoever marries Giulietta will have to be very rich
indeed.' He paused and added, 'Gabriel, why does it
upset you?'

Gabriel went on mixing paint. 'I'm not upset.'

The Count must have moved very softly, for Gabriel
was surprised to feel his hands resting on his shoulders
from behind. The touch still felt strange to him. 'Liar,'
said Leonardo.

'You must marry, my lord, to get an heir for House
Loredan.'

Leonardo's grip tightened a little. 'Ah, well, there you
have it,' he said. 'What noble maiden would look at me
when I have no money? More important, what noble
maiden's father would give her to me?' He let out a sigh;
Gabriel felt the breath warm on the nape of his neck.
'Gabriel, nobly born girls with their seal of fertility are
rare as snowflakes in hell. I will have no heir.'

Carefully, Gabriel said, 'That pains you, to be the last
of House Loredan.'

The grip tighter still, fingers digging into his

shoulders. 'Yes. But I can bear it. Gabriel, stop fiddling with that damn' paint!'

He spun Gabriel round and looked into his eyes. I shall weep, Gabriel thought, if I'm not very careful. It was the portrait that had done it. Engaging with Leonardo on the canvas had meant that he had to strip himself, bring all his defences down. What hope for him, then, when the living man was so much more compelling?

Leonardo said, 'Gabriel, what is it?'

He knew his voice was shaking. 'If you marry, my lord, your wife would not . . .' No, that was not what he wanted to say; he began again. 'These last weeks, I've been happy. Everything is different. You have made me into . . . into something real. I cannot go back.' Now I'm whining, he thought furiously. He will despise me. He said, 'If Giulietta Contarini saw you touch me, the scandal would be all round the city.'

Leonardo was giving him a lopsided smile, his eyes very bright. 'Gabriel, I don't give a damn what Giulietta Contarini might see. How many times do I have to tell you, a Loredan does not care for scandal. Let them gossip.'

Gabriel gave a helpless gesture. 'They would ostracize you.'

For some unimaginable reason, Leonardo seemed to think that was funny. 'Oh, yes! Poverty-stricken and over-familiar with my genic! Could I be a worse marriage prospect?' Suddenly he was serious. 'Gabriel, no one is going to hurt you. I promise.'

Gabriel believed him. He thought that Leonardo must have seen his face change, for he clapped him on the shoulder and said, 'Do you want me in that damn' chair again?'

'No, not today.'

'Good. In that case, I shall take a walk to warm up. I'll see you at dinner.'

He went out. Gabriel went on mixing paint. He believed what Leonardo had told him, but belief was not enough. Easy for Leonardo now to claim that he could accept the lack of an heir. He was young, and he had an incurable way of assuming that life would rearrange itself to suit a Loredan. But as years went by, as he grew older, and there was still no heir . . . Would he accept then that he was the last of House Loredan?

I can paint for him, Gabriel thought. I can make money enough for us both to live on – to live in comfort, even. But not the kind of money that would make Count Contarini consider Leonardo as a husband for Giulietta – or any other noble father to entrust his daughter to him.

He rubbed a hand over his forehead, trying to banish a lurking headache, and went back to face the picture.

'I love you,' he said aloud. 'You are my heart's lord. And I can give you nothing that you really want.'

He could not have spoken so to Leonardo himself. It was no comfort to say the words to unresponsive paint.

3

The moon was rising by the time Gianni came through the gate. The verandah was deeply shadowed, but the dark pools rippled silver. The roses were carved from light.

As Gianni approached the room he could hear nothing, but as he stood in the archway, blocking out the light, a gasp of terror came from the darkness. 'It's only me, sir,' he said.

He stepped forward so that light flowed in again, painting the shadows of overhanging leaves on the bed-cover and on Alessandro's face.

'Why did you come back?' Alessandro asked.

Until then Gianni had not understood that his master had not expected him to return. He felt a tightness in his throat. He sat down at the foot of the bed, carefully distant so that Alessandro need not fear his touch. 'It all went well,' he said, 'but it took a long time.'

He had not decided what to tell Alessandro about Count Dracone. His master might never have realized what the Count had meant for him, and Gianni did not want to be the one who had to enlighten him.

To his relief Alessandro did not ask questions. 'Dr Foscari, earning his fee,' he said.

'Yes. So much to sign! Then when he gave me the keys I went to look at the house.'

'I've never seen it.'

'It's above water level, that's the main thing. It needs repair, but I can do that. There's enough furniture to be going on with. There's even a little courtyard, with a fig tree. You can lie there in the sun and get well.'

Alessandro's eyes widened. 'But I can't come with you, Gianni,' he said. 'You know I can't. I can't ever leave here. No genic can leave here, unless—'

'Unless he's bound,' Gianni finished for him. 'Listen, sir – listen, and please don't be angry with me. It was the only way. That's why I'm so late, because it took a long time to arrange. You're my bondman now.'

He saw shock like lightning in Alessandro's face, and

went on hurriedly, stumbling over the words. 'It won't make any difference, sir. I did it so that you can come with me. Oh, sir – Sandro, don't!'

Alessandro buried his face in his hands. He was shuddering spasmodically. Gianni wanted to comfort him, but he did not know how. 'Don't, please don't,' he repeated. 'I promise, everything will be just the same.'

Alessandro raised his head. His face was starred with excitement; wonderingly, Gianni saw that the spasms had been laughter, not tears.

'Oh, Gianni, you fool,' he said. 'Of course it won't be the same. Do you think I'm going to lie there and let you work for both of us?' His excitement faded to concentration. 'I still have my wits, and my experience. We can start again.'

Deliberately, Gianni held out a hand. 'Sandro,' he said, 'it is no sin.'

Half fearfully, his hand shaking, Alessandro reached out to him. Gianni leant forward. Their hands clasped.

'Can you walk, if I help you?' Gianni asked. 'I've a boat waiting, just outside the gates. We're going home.'

Seven

'Good,' said Hyacinth. 'Try it again, a little faster this time.'

Serafina watched him as he gave her the beat, and bent over the lute again. Though she had been learning for so little time, she knew she was making progress. Hyacinth did not give praise for nothing.

They sat in Serafina's own bedchamber, the only place in the house she had to work in private. It would have been scandalous, of course, to allow a man over the threshold, but no one would gossip when it was only Hyacinth. Serafina wondered if he knew that, and whether he cared.

When she came to the end of the tune again, Hyacinth nodded. 'Practise for next time. Now I want you to look at this.'

He took a sheet of music from his portfolio, and laid it on the stand in front of her. Serafina examined it. It was a song – a duet for soprano and alto. The words were the usual rubbish about beauty and cruelty and unrequited love; the music was complex and demanding, and Serafina's interest quickened.

'Who is to sing this?' she asked.

'You and I. At Count Contarini's birthday festival.'

'But I can't sing that! Especially not in public.'

Hyacinth brushed away her objections with a graceful, irritated gesture. 'Certainly you can. I wrote it for our voices. Look carefully, and you see that most of the difficulty is in the alto part. The soprano is cool, remote, measured – much as you are, Serafina.'

Serafina stared at him. He had never before said anything personal to her, or given any indication that she was a person and not just another, perhaps more complicated, musical instrument that he must fashion to his liking. And she did not feel cool, remote or measured. Was that how she appeared to him?

As if unaware that he had thrown her off balance, Hyacinth picked up the lute, adjusted the tuning, and played the first few bars of the accompaniment, humming the alto part along with it. 'Now you,' he said. He plucked a string. 'There's your note.'

Hesitantly, Serafina launched into the first phrase, and repeated it more confidently. Hyacinth added the alto part, and for a few seconds Serafina got a faint insight into how the piece should sound when it was sung properly, the interlacing of the two parts, the division of the melody between the two voices, the tossing back and forth of pleading and denial, warmth and coldness.

'Again,' said Hyacinth. He was smiling.

He began to play the introduction, but before he came to Serafina's entry the music was interrupted by a furious voice. 'Serafina!'

Giulietta, standing by the door. She stamped her foot. 'Serafina, why do I have to come looking for you?'

Hyacinth stopped playing, hissed out a single expletive, and stalked across the room to stare out of the window. Serafina cast a glance after him and dropped a curtsey to Giulietta. 'Your pardon, lady. We are rehearsing the music for your father's festival.'

'But you're *my* servant,' Giulietta said, still furious. 'I told you when you started this silly game, you're to do *my* work first. The stupid music doesn't matter when I haven't even got the silk for a festival gown!'

Serafina wanted to say, You have a hundred gowns, and only one Hyacinth, but she knew very well what Giulietta's reaction to that would be. She dropped another curtsey, and said to Hyacinth, 'If you leave the music, I'll practise it later.'

Still with his back to her, he tossed his golden curls but gave no other answer. There was nothing Serafina could do but follow Giulietta downstairs into her boudoir.

All the silk samples were scattered once again on the *chaise longue* and the floor around the table. Giulietta walked over them and plumped down among the cushions, with a sulky look on her face.

'*All* Messire Alessandro's silks are locked away until his sale,' she complained. 'Roberto couldn't buy the one I want, stupid creature.'

'Then choose one from another warehouse,' Serafina said.

'But I want *that* one.' She picked up the sea-green sample she had chosen at first, and tossed it down again.

Serafina suppressed a sigh. 'When is the sale?'

'Tomorrow, Roberto says.' Giulietta pouted. 'Papa refuses to go. He says the Contarinis are not merchants.'

'Then once the sale is over,' Serafina said, 'I'll go and see if I can find who bought it.' She could not have cared less which silk Giulietta wore, but she seized eagerly on

the chance of getting away from the girl's hothouse world
and her peevishness on an errand outside the palazzo.

Giulietta's expression cleared. 'Oh, Serafina, you are
good! Now, go and fetch the pattern books, so I can
choose the style and the embroidery.'

Later, when Giulietta had decided on the style and the
decoration and all the interminable trivia of her new
gown, Serafina hurried back to her bedchamber. She had
no expectation of finding Hyacinth waiting for her, but
he would have left the music, and she could practise.

In her haste she did not see the door of the Contarinis'
chapel opening, and cannoned into Father Teo as he
came out. Trying in the last second to avoid him, she
stumbled, slipped on the highly polished floor, and would
have fallen but for his hand under her elbow, steadying
her.

She drew away, blood rushing to her face. 'Father, I'm
sorry.'

'It's nothing.'

'No, I have been . . .' She sought for, and found, a
phrase that old Countess Dandolo's confessor had been
fond of using. 'I have been the occasion of your sin.'

Father Teo smiled faintly, almost regretfully, she
thought. 'Serafina, do you think that the Most High God
looks down on a moment's accident, and calls it sin?'

'It's said, Father, that He cares even for the fall of a
sparrow.'

Father Teo drew himself up. He was a small man, no
taller than Serafina, but she saw in him suddenly an
immense dignity, and a presence that could not be
disregarded.

'Who has told you that, Serafina, that God seeks to trap us with errors we never meant and could not have avoided? The words do not mean that at all. They tell us that God is aware of our pain and has compassion for us. Even the pain of the least of us.'

'Even the pain of a genic, Father?' The words were out before Serafina had given herself time to think of whether speaking them was a good idea.

Father Teo did not seem angry. He drew his brows together, the faint crease between them speaking of bewilderment. 'Truly, Serafina, I do not know.'

He motioned to a bench by the side of the passage, beneath a window, and after a second's astonishment it seemed quite natural to Serafina to sit beside him and continue with their talk.

'Holy Church tells us,' said Father Teo, 'that the genics were created outside God's law, and so can have no part in Him. And yet – if you ask me to contemplate a God who can see the suffering of a sentient being, whether human or genic, and disregard it, I can only tell you that is not the God I worship.'

'Is that heresy, Father?' Serafina asked, troubled. It was not the first time he had spoken so to her; on the night of the *soirée* he had questioned the Church's teaching.

'Certainly.' His smile returned, warmer and almost mischievous. 'Don't look so anxious. We do not burn heretics in these enlightened times.' Growing serious again, he added, 'Though I would not speak so in the hearing of my lord the Patriarch, or the Holy Father.'

'Or in the hearing of Count Contarini?' Serafina said.

That should have made him angry, but it did not. He sat silent, contemplating his clasped hands, slender and well-kept, and the silken folds of his cassock. Serafina thought she could read him well. He was a compassionate man, an intelligent man, and one who thought about the meaning of his faith, instead of parroting its precepts.

But he was not the stuff of martyrs. If he spoke his heresies aloud, in the hearing of anyone but a genic, what would happen to him then? The Church might not burn heretics, but the princes of the Church would never tolerate a heretic in their midst. And if they stripped Father Teo of his priesthood, what would be left for him?

He raised his head again, and now it was he who looked troubled. 'You shame me, Serafina.'

'Father, I'm sorry—'

'No, you are right. For I believe, truly, that God cares for you, for all genics, and yet I do nothing.'

'What could you do, Father?' Serafina expected the answer 'nothing', because she could not see anything that he could do. He was one man, and not a very powerful one at that, Count Contarini's chaplain. If he spoke openly, he could destroy himself, and no more.

The answer was not the one she had expected. 'I can pray.'

That was something Serafina knew nothing about. In all her life she had formed one tentative prayer, in her attic room above the city's rooftops, for the soul of the dead Countess, and she had no way of knowing whether that prayer had been heard or answered.

She asked, 'What prayer, Father?'

'For God to make His will known. Or to show me a way.'

He fell again into a contemplative silence, as if he was already forming the words with which he would approach his God. Serafina did not know what to say to him, or whether she should speak at all. To go away without saying any more seemed rude, and yet she was becoming anxious about what would happen if any of the servants – or, worse, one of the Count's family – should come along and see her sitting with Father Teo. She was sure the Count would not be pleased with either of them if he knew it.

As she hesitated, for some reason she could not fathom she thought about her errand for Giulietta, and the last time she had ventured into the city in search of fripperies for her. She recalled the busy traffic on the canal while she waited for Caterina, and the scarlet clad Count Dracone in his boat, and the meeting with Dr Heinrich. She recalled her disquiet.

As a genic, the reliquary ring had nothing to do with her, and yet she knew how powerful it might be in any man's hands. When the hands were those of Dracone, she could not believe that the power would be used for good. And there was something that made her profoundly uneasy in the thought of Dracone and Heinrich together.

At the time she had not seen anything that she might do. None of it was her affair, and she had no way of making it so. But now she realized that there was one thing; she could share the experience with someone who would listen to her, who could advise her, and might be able to find out how the Count and the Doctor meant to use the relic of Christos.

When a tiny sigh from Father Teo suggested that she might safely speak, she said, 'Father, there is something I would tell you.'

2

The tiny courtyard garden behind the house caught the
sun for most of the day. Paving stones surrounded a dry
fountain with a bronze seahorse, green with age and
neglect, and a basin with a few dead leaves in the bottom.
Around the walls was little except weeds and one stubborn
fig tree; although this was his first day there, Gianni was
already planning how he would dig and nourish the soil,
and plant jasmine and roses to scramble over the walls
and scent the air.

He had brought out a chair and a footstool for
Alessandro, and sat himself on the edge of the fountain,
looking up at the man who had been his master. Alessandro lay back against the cushions, weary and yet with a
bright look that Gianni had not seen in his face before.
He was still wearing the stained, torn clothing in which
he had been taken from his house, with Gianni's jacket
around his shoulders.

'You need something decent to wear,' Gianni said.
'And we must buy more furnishings. I asked Lucetta to
make a list of what's most urgent.'

Alessandro smiled. 'As you wish, Gianni. All this is
yours, remember.' He leant forward. 'But there is one
thing you must do. All my property fell to the state, and
they will sell all the goods that are stored in the warehouse. You must go to the auction and bid, Gianni, if
we're to set up in business again.'

Gianni felt a brief panic. 'I shan't know what to buy.'

'There'll be a catalogue. Dr Foscari will know where
you can get one – you should go and see him right away.
Then I can tell you what to bid for, and how much to

pay.' His faint smile returned. 'No one will take bids from a genic.'

'You'll be all right if I leave you?'

'Yes, of course. And Lucetta will be a dragon to keep the door, if anyone should come. All the same – ' the brightness looked out of Alessandro's eyes again, and Gianni realized wonderingly that he was happy – 'all the same, Gianni, I think you're going to need a boy to run errands for you. Perhaps you could go to the Innocenti. You can find very good servants there.'

Laughing, Gianni clasped his hand and went out, saying goodbye to Lucetta as he left. He had found her the day before, wandering desolate around Messire Alessandro's old lodgings, and brought her here to be house-keeper. She was already fiercely scrubbing her new kitchen, muttering at the last owner who had let it get so filthy.

As he walked briskly along the alley towards the canal, Gianni murmured a prayer of thanksgiving. He could not imagine anything he lacked now.

Dr Foscari was not at the Judiciary, but his clerk had copies of the sale catalogue.

'The master expected you,' the clerk said. 'He left a message.' He gave Gianni a sly, sideways look; under-standing, Gianni slid a coin across the desk. 'The lease on the warehouse is for sale. You're to let him know if you want it.'

Panic assailed Gianni once again. If he bought goods at the sale, he would need somewhere to store them, and yet he had no idea of how much the lease would cost, or whether he could afford it. But then, Dr Foscari knew these things; he would not have suggested buying the lease if there was not enough money to cover it.

'Yes,' he said, trying to sound confident. 'Tell him that we – that I would like it.'

He made arrangements about coming in to sign the documents, and stepped out into the street again. He found that his confidence was not entirely assumed, with one successful piece of business behind him.

Instead of going straight home, he walked down to inspect the property that was almost his. The warehouse itself was shut up, but the counting house was open, deserted except for Malatesta, Messire Alessandro's chief clerk, who was bent over an account book, his pen racing, unaware of Gianni until he went and stood beside his desk.

'The catalogues are over there, messire,' he said, and only looked up when Gianni spoke to him.

'Good day, Malatesta.'

The chief clerk got to his feet, almost knocking his chair over in his haste. 'Gianni! God be praised! Where have you been?'

'With Messire Alessandro,' Gianni said. He had not known Malatesta well enough, in what he was already thinking of as the old days, to guess what he would think about Alessandro now.

The old clerk frowned, sat down again, and scratched his cheek with the end of his pen. 'Where is he?' Hurriedly, as if he was half ashamed, he added, 'Have they harmed him?'

'A little.' An idea had entered Gianni's mind, and for it to work he would need Malatesta's co-operation. He explained the facts of what had happened, at the trial and afterwards. 'He is my bondman now,' he finished. 'We mean to start up the business again.' Catching Malatesta's eye, he added, 'We shall need a chief clerk.'

To his astonishment, Malatesta threw down the pen and gave way to soft, breathy laughter. 'So, lad,' he said when he had control of himself again, 'you're to be a great merchant?'

Gianni felt himself flushing. 'If I can earn our living, that's enough,' he said. 'Messire Alessandro will tell me what to do. Do you wish to join us?' He tried to sound firm, testing out that new confidence. 'At the same salary as before. And if you wish, you can live in the rooms that were Messire Alessandro's.'

'Well, that's a fair offer.' Malatesta was grinning, and after a second's pause he stuck out a hand. 'A bargain, Messire Giovanni.'

After supper that evening, Gianni and Alessandro put their heads together over the catalogue, and Alessandro marked the best lots to bid for, and how much Gianni ought to pay. Gianni attended the sale the next day, though he had arranged that Malatesta would bid for him. He was still nervous of making a fool of himself, in front of the shrewdest financiers in the city.

Towards the end of the sale, however, he ventured on a few bids of his own, and returned home jubilant. 'Sandro! Sandro, come and see!'

There was no reply, but standing in the narrow passage Gianni saw the door to the garden standing open. He set his bundles down and went out.

The sun was going down, and twilight covered Alessandro's chair. His eyes were closed, one hand dangling to the paving stones; as Gianni hesitated he tossed his head from side to side, and a murmur of distress came from his parted lips.

Gianni took a step forward and stopped, suddenly realizing that they were not alone in the garden. What he had thought was thickening shadow had taken on a form, a figure unnaturally tall and attenuated, wearing darkness like a cloak, with a hint of flame beneath.

As Gianni watched, frozen in primitive terror, the thing stooped over Alessandro, and tendrils of shadow seemed to coil outwards from it and enfold him.

Gianni let out a hoarse cry. As he started forward the thing whipped round with the speed of a striking snake, and melted back into the shadow of the courtyard wall. Gianni could just make it out as it flowed up and over the wall, snakelike still, but too lithe and silent for any embodied creature.

Stumbling across the courtyard he sprang up and gripped the coping of the wall so that he could peer over. In the alley beyond he could see nothing but the ordinary shadows of approaching night.

Behind him a voice said, 'Gianni?'

Gianni dropped to the ground and turned to see Alessandro sitting up, a hand to his head. He looked confused, drowsy still, as if waking from a nightmare. But what nightmare, Gianni asked himself, could take form and show itself in the waking world?

'Is something the matter?' Alessandro asked.

Gianni started towards him. As he held out a hand to help Alessandro up, he felt a burning sensation. Looking down, he saw his hands covered with something sticky, like a snail's trail; it was over his clothes as well, where he had caught the wall and pressed himself against it.

Drawing back, he pulled off his jacket, wiped his

hands on it and discarded it on the edge of the fountain. Forcing a laugh, he said, 'Nothing's the matter, Sandro, except I'm filthy from standing in the sale room all day. Come and see what I bought.'

Alessandro followed him back into the house. The boatman who had brought Gianni to the end of the alley was waiting, his arms still laden with Gianni's purchases. Gianni realized that only moments had passed since he stepped unsuspecting out into the garden.

'Your clothes, Sandro, and books,' he said, trying to sound cheerful. 'All your own things, from—'

Alessandro's eyes widened. 'Gianni, you shouldn't . . . I don't need all of that. Can we afford them?'

In truth, Gianni had paid little; no one wanted possessions that had been used by a genic. But he felt that it would be too hurtful to say so. Instead he drew himself up, and mimicked the pompous tones he had heard among the wealthy citizens and noblemen who used to patronize the warehouse. 'My bondman will not show himself like a street beggar.'

Alessandro stifled laughter, and Gianni, aware of the boatman staring, relieved him of his bundles and paid him off. Lucetta pounced on the clothes, exclaiming over creases in the velvet and fine linen, and bore them away to the kitchen, where Gianni could hear her clattering irons into the fire. He rescued a bedgown of faded, rose-coloured velvet, and placed it round Alessandro's shoulders.

Alessandro had picked up one of the books, caressed the leather cover, and turned over the pages wonderingly. 'I thought all would be lost . . .'

'Nothing is lost,' Gianni said firmly. 'Nothing that matters.'

Alessandro let out a sigh. In sudden alarm Gianni saw
the brightness in the blue eyes fade to a vague bewilderment, and flung an arm round Alessandro's shoulders as
he swayed and began to sink. Alessandro leant against
him, his breath coming fast and shallow.

'Sandro, what is it?' Gianni asked. 'Are you ill?'

Alessandro stirred, looked up at him again. 'No – no,
it's nothing.' He rubbed his forehead, as if he tried to
wipe away pain. 'Don't look like that, Gianni. It's tired-
ness, no more. I'm well, Gianni, I promise you.'

But he needed Gianni's arm, supporting him to a
chair. Even later, as they sat over supper and he told
Alessandro everything that had happened that day, Gianni
could not entirely crush down his fears, or forget the dark
thing he had seen in the courtyard.

3

Serafina reached the merchants' quarter to find Messire
Alessandro's warehouse open, and a bustle of activity
around the shop and the counting house. There was no
sign of the upheaval of the last few days. It was almost as
if the little genic had been wiped away completely, and
life was going on as if he had never been.

She was struggling with sharp anger and compassion
as she went into the shop and produced her silk sample
for the hulking youth who was in charge. She remembered seeing him now and then when she had come to
the warehouse in the past; you could hardly mistake the
clumsy body and the disfiguring purple birthmark.

Now he was wearing a good black suit and held

himself with some authority; he had come up in the
world, she reflected, and wondered what he had needed
to do to achieve that.

He greeted her courteously, however, and examined
her scrap of silk. 'I'm not sure, mistress. We bought a lot
of silk in the sale.' He turned, and bellowed into the back
part of the warehouse, 'Sandro! Sandro!'

A moment later, Messire Alessandro appeared through
the doorway. Serafina's anger gathered, became an arrow
she wanted to let fly. He was a bondman now, that was
clear enough, serving where he had once commanded.
Everything, his wealth and authority, even his freedom,
had been taken away because he was a genic.

He bowed, one hand on his breast, to his master and
then to Serafina. 'Messire Giovanni. Mistress. How may
I serve you?'

'Did we buy this green silk, Sandro? I can't
remember.'

Alessandro took the scrap from Serafina. Her percep-
tions were suddenly shifting wildly. His words, his gestures, were totally correct, and yet there was something
here she did not understand. Though he was grave-faced,
his eyes were laughing, and the young man – Giovanni –
had a broad grin on his face. They were like a couple of
children, Serafina thought, playing some delightful game
with rules that the adult world would never understand.

'Yes, I think so,' Alessandro said. 'That silver thread
in it is quite distinctive. I'll fetch it for you, mistress.'

'No, I'll go,' said Giovanni. 'The bale will be far too
heavy for you to carry. Where is it?'

'In the last bay on the right.'

Giovanni nodded and went, leaving Serafina with

Alessandro. She was not quite sure what to say to him, but for the sake of their shared genic heritage she could not stand there and say nothing, as if she was a fine lady.

She asked, 'Are you well? Have they hurt you?'

Alessandro smiled, and cast a glance at the doorway where Giovanni had disappeared. He looked tired, and desperately frail, but his face was suddenly luminous with happiness. 'Yes, mistress, thank you. I'm very well.'

Serafina gave up trying to understand what was going on. It was nothing to do with her, after all. She said, 'I'm glad.'

Then Giovanni reappeared, hefting a bale of Giulietta's coveted silk, and spread it out on the counter for Alessandro to measure and cut. Admiring the foam of sea-green and silver, Serafina said, 'This is for Giulietta Contarini, to be a gown for her father's birthday festival.'

'I'm sure I wish the Count a happy day, mistress,' Giovanni said.

'The Count means to refurbish his ceremonial barge and have his guests rowed out to the garden isle for feasting and music.' Playing at shepherds and shepherdesses with silk ribbons on their crooks, she added to herself.

'Then I hope for good weather, mistress,' said Giovanni.

Serafina hoped so too. She could hardly imagine singing her duet with Hyacinth in the pouring rain. 'I thought,' she said, 'that if you sent some samples up to the palazzo, Messire Alvise the steward might buy from you. He will need to make a splendid display, to grace House Contarini before their guests.'

Alessandro bowed. 'Thank you, mistress. We shall do so.'

He packed the silk for her, with ribbons and thread, and Serafina paid. She left the warehouse still feeling bewildered, still wondering at the alchemy that had turned apparent disaster into such joy. It cost her a pang to leave the warmth behind her, and return to her service in the Palazzo Contarini.

As the day of the Count's birthday festival approached, Serafina almost despaired of being ready in time. There was Giulietta's gown; there was her mother's gown; though the Countess had her own sewing woman make it up, only Serafina's embroidery was good enough. It was an accolade Serafina could have done without.

There were also costumes for herself and Hyacinth. They were to sing on board the barge, and perform Hyacinth's new duet as part of the birthday feasting on the island. It would be charming, thought the Countess, if they could appear in the dress of an ancient shepherd and shepherdess.

Hyacinth refused to be seen dead in the dress of an ancient shepherd.

The Countess insisted.

Hyacinth pointed out that he could not sing in such a garment, much less play the lute, and that was that.

There were to be new, matching robes for Hyacinth and Serafina, the design to be approved by Hyacinth. Serafina was to stitch them in her spare time. She thought she would go screaming mad.

Apart from all that, Hyacinth was demanding more practice, more rehearsals, and throwing exquisitely modulated tantrums at regular intervals. Serafina, losing her initial awe of him, stopped herself from throwing the

music at him, and channelled her exasperation into her
singing. He praised her expressiveness.

Giulietta changed her mind about the sleeves on her
new gown.

On the night before the birthday celebrations, Serafina
sat up late in Giulietta's boudoir, putting the finishing
touches to the new gown. It was beautiful, she knew,
taking pride in her skill. When she put it on, Giulietta
would look like Venus rising from the waves.

Alessandro had sent a gift, a packet of tiny, exquisite
roses in silver tissue, which Serafina was now stitching to
the flounces on the skirt, with a knot of them at the
bodice. There were more of them than she needed, and
so she had filched three or four of them to ornament her
own new robe. Though she castigated herself for being
stupid, she could not help feeling that the gift was more
hers than Giulietta's, or stop herself from wanting to
share the generosity that had sent it.

She was almost finished, racing her stitchery against
the tapers that were burning low, when Giulietta's maid,
Rosalba, came into the room. She was wearing a bedgown, with her hair loose.

'Serafina, you're to come to our lady at once.'

Serafina set in the last stitch that secured the last rose
to Giulietta's gown. She couldn't help saying, 'What,
now? It's after midnight. What does she want?'

Rosalba shrugged. She had never made a friend of
Serafina – Serafina would not have expected it – but they
shared Giulietta's demands, and that created a bond.
'She's ill. She's asking for you.'

'Ill? She was all right when we fitted the dress this afternoon.'

She shook out the folds of silk and laid the gown carefully on Giulietta's *chaise longue* to wait for morning. Then she blew out the last of the tapers and followed Rosalba out into the passage and up the stairs which led to Giulietta's bedchamber.

'One of her admirers sent her sugar plums. She stuffed herself all evening, and now she's throwing up.' Rosalba did not sound sympathetic.

'Have you sent for her physician?' Serafina asked.

Rosalba paused with her hand on the handle of Giulietta's door. 'Do you think I should? At this hour?'

Serafina nodded. 'If it's serious, then the sooner the better. If it's nothing, he can send the Count a bigger bill.'

Rosalba looked as if she wanted to laugh, and sped off to rouse a footman, leaving Serafina to go in alone.

The reek of vomit seized her by the throat as soon as she stepped inside the rose-coloured chamber. Giulietta was propped up on her pillows. Her face was an unhealthy shade of green, and her golden hair was plastered to her forehead and neck.

'Serafina!' she wailed.

Serafina went over to her. She wasn't sure why she had been sent for, or what she was supposed to do. She could not even touch Giulietta to comfort her, even supposing Giulietta wanted her comfort.

On the bedside table was a basin, and a filigree comfit box, empty now except for the silvery wrappings and a few sticky smears from the disgustingly sugary sweetmeats that Giulietta adored.

'Stupid stuff,' Giulietta said vindictively. 'There's something wrong with it, and now I'm ill, and I'm going to miss Papa's party!'

She clapped a hand over her mouth and flapped the other wildly at Serafina, who grabbed the basin and thrust it at her. She waited while Giulietta puked miserably; her eyes tactfully averted, she noticed the comfit box again and wondered which unfortunate admirer had sent it. There was no card there, no note with protestations of undying love, though Giulietta might have already thrown that away. Whoever the man was, Serafina thought, he had better give up his hopes and stay well away in future.

Choking, Giulietta handed back the basin and accepted in return a silken cloth soaked in rose water to wipe her face and hands. She flopped back against the pillows, sniffling miserably. 'I can't go tomorrow, Serafina. You will have to stay with me and amuse me.'

'But I can't!' Serafina was jerked out of her usual deference. 'I have to sing.'

'They have Hyacinth to sing,' Giulietta said. 'What do they want with you?'

Serafina already felt tired from her late work on the gown. Now it was as though a leaden hopelessness settled over her; she could have sunk down on the rug at Giulietta's side. What was the point in arguing? If Giulietta said stay, she would have to stay. There would be no duet; Hyacinth would have hysterics. Serafina hardly liked to admit to herself how much she had looked forward to singing, and even to the festival itself. Instead, she would be prisoned in these walls again, with Giulietta sick and querulous.

'But we've rehearsed . . .' she began, knowing perfectly

well that whatever she said she would not change Giulietta's mind.

The girl heaved herself up from the pillows. 'How often do I have to tell you, Serafina, you're *my* servant? I'd think you'd be ashamed, running after Hyacinth as you do. Well, tomorrow you will be *here*, with *me*, and I—'

The tirade was interrupted as she started retching again; Serafina held the basin for her.

A cool voice said, 'What is this?'

Serafina turned to see the Countess, standing in the doorway in a cloud of silk and lace, her hair artfully dishevelled. She curtseyed deeply. 'Lady Giulietta is ill, Countess.'

The Countess came further into her room and looked down at her daughter, disapproval rather than concern on her sculptured features. 'Giulietta? Ah – too many sweetmeats, I dare say. Where is Rosalba?'

'Gone to find a footman, Countess, to fetch your physician.'

The Countess nodded. 'And the day before the festival, too. How vexing! Your father will be most displeased.'

Giulietta looked up; Serafina took the basin and carefully dabbed at her face with the scented cloth. Giulietta jerked her head away. 'Mama, tell Serafina she must stay with me tomorrow.'

'Stay with you?' The Countess's thin eyebrows arched. 'Nonsense. Serafina must sing. Do you want to ruin your father's birthday celebrations completely?'

For a moment, Giulietta stared open-mouthed at her mother. There was time for the thought to flit through Serafina's mind: had she intended all along to spoil the celebration, if she could not be there herself? Or was that too calculating, for someone like Giulietta, who barely thought beyond the moment's gratification?

Giulietta let out a wail. 'You all hate me!' She buried her face in the pillows and began to sob.

'Giulietta—' Countess Contarini broke off in exasperation. 'Serafina, is all ready for tomorrow?'

'Yes, Countess.'

'Then go to bed. You will need to be up early. If Giulietta is not well enough to go, Rosalba will sit with her.'

As she spoke, Serafina heard Rosalba's step in the passage, and the maid came into the room. She bobbed respectfully to the Countess and said, 'Roberto has gone for the physician, ma'am.'

Serafina curtseyed in her turn and made her escape. Her last thought, as she prepared for bed, was that all the trouble of the sea-green gown had gone for nothing.

Eight

Sunlight dazzled through the leaves and made shifting patterns over Serafina's robe and her clasped hands. All white and gold, Hyacinth looked like something the ancient gods might have let fall from Olympus. He plucked a white, starry flower – Serafina did not know the name of it – and twirled it in his fingers.

Count Contarini's birthday celebrations were following the course the Countess had planned. The ceremonial barge of House Contarini had sailed majestically out to this garden island, decked out in silken drapery and the glitter of gold leaf, packed with the city's nobility who were the Count's guests.

Hyacinth and Serafina had performed their duet, to an audience who were more interested in the lavish food and wine the Countess had provided, or in flirting or gossiping with each other. When the performance was over, the Count had dismissed them in a breath, in the midst of discussing with Alvise the steward whether the wine was sufficiently chilled.

Hyacinth had stalked off into this clearing where he sat in the grass and sulked.

Serafina did not know what to say to him. He had written the music, coached her, rehearsed and driven himself half demented in his quest for perfection. And it was all for this. The polite spatter of applause, the relief, no doubt, that they did not have to pretend any longer that they were listening.

And that was nothing new. He had never had the audience he deserved; he never would have. Perhaps it did not even exist, that intensity of devotion to music that would recognize it in him. Serafina could not even claim to give him what he wanted from herself. He knew it, but there was nothing he could do.

Serafina had still found no real answer to her questions about herself. Her music was important, but it did not fill her. Hyacinth knew what he was, and knew that no one wanted the uniqueness that was in him.

Laughter and chatter still reached them from the company in the clearing. Serafina supposed that no one would want them now, until the time came to sail home. But shortly she saw two figures approaching through the trees. The first was the steward, Alvise, with a tray, and the second, following him, dark and elusive, Count Loredan's genic, Gabriel.

The steward deposited his tray on the grass beside Serafina. It was piled with delicacies from the picnic – pasties and little spiced cakes and sweetmeats. She had always suspected that beneath his impregnable dignity Alvise concealed a kind heart.

'Thank you, messire,' she said; Hyacinth was still brooding.

Alvise smiled. 'Perhaps you might entertain the Count's page,' he said, and withdrew.

Gabriel had brought a bottle of wine and three glasses; he set them down beside the tray, but awkwardly, and he did not sit; he looked as if he might slip away into the woodland.

'Sit down,' Serafina said, indicating the grass beside her. 'We won't bite you – not even Hyacinth.'

There was a flash of violet eyes, but no reply to that.

Gabriel said nervously, 'The Count my master gave me a message for you. He thanks you for your music. It was beautiful,' he added, with such sudden intensity that Serafina was startled. He sat on the grass, but warily, as if he was something wild that might start away at any moment.

Hyacinth emerged from behind his barrier, enough to look him over curiously and say, 'You are the painter.'

Gabriel's eyes lit. 'Yes.' Stumbling a little in his speech, in what Serafina suddenly recognized as appalling shyness, he added, 'I would like to paint you.'

Hyacinth's mouth twisted. 'I cannot imagine Count Contarini wishing for a painting of me. Of the Countess, perhaps, or Lady Giulietta.'

Gabriel stiffened, and cast a glance over his shoulder to where the bright silks of the Count's guests showed through the trees. Serafina did not know what he thought he saw. Hesitantly, he said, 'I will do so, if he speaks to Count Loredan.'

An excellent idea, thought Serafina. To have her picture painted, when the art was so new that no one else in the city could boast of it, would feed Giulietta's vanity, and keep her nicely occupied. It must take many days, she imagined, to transfer the living face to canvas.

'I should like to see that,' she said. The gossip about his first painting – bought and then destroyed by Count Dracone – had gone all over the city. There were those who commended Dracone for teaching a genic what his proper place should be; Serafina wondered how much it

had hurt. 'The Count has a few paintings, but they are
old, all dark and faded.'

She poured wine into the glasses, and offered one to
Gabriel, and to Hyacinth. They shared something, she
thought, apart from their genic heritage, and wondered
whether they would be able to reach out to each other, at
least to exchange their understanding of the fierce fires
that consumed them.

As for herself – nothing in her life consumed her like
that. It was more comfortable. But looking from one to
the other, the musician and the painter, she wondered if
they would see it like that, or whether they would change
places with her.

The sun was going down as the Contarini barge set out
for the mainland once again. The city lay low on the
horizon like a bar of cloud. The oarsmen steered a course
between flat, brownish mats of reed, where white birds
flew up, disturbed by the boat's wake, crying in lonely
voices.

The Countess had hired other musicians for the day,
and they played as the barge returned. After a while,
Hyacinth spoke to their leader, and motioned to Serafina
to join him in singing.

He had relaxed during the meal they had shared with
Gabriel, and now his professionalism had taken over
again. He was a singer; he would sing. That would not
change, even if there was no one to listen to him.

They sang the barge back into home waters, with the
last of the islands dropping away behind, and the quayside
beginning to take on definition. A few of the guests had
taken up Hyacinth's song.

Then there was a splintering crash from one side of the boat. Someone screamed. Someone else shouted, 'We're holed! We're sinking!'

As the cry went up, Serafina felt the boat shudder and lose momentum. The music faltered and died. Some of the musicians threw their instruments aside and stumbled across the lurching deck to the rail. She heard a cry and a splash as someone, in a panic, threw himself into the water. Around her, people began to scream and run.

Hyacinth had stopped singing and sunk down on a bench. He was shaking. His face was chalk white and the violet eyes wide with fright. 'I can't swim, Serafina,' he whispered. 'I'm going to drown.'

'No.' Serafina sat beside him and spoke low and soft. 'I'll help you if you do as I tell you.'

'You can swim?' he asked. 'But you're a genic.'

'I was a street beggar, remember? They used to throw coins into the canal for us to fetch. If you play that game, you swim well, or die. Take off your robe, and your shoes.'

As she was speaking, she was tearing at the fastenings of her own gown, letting the ruined folds slip down to her feet. Hyacinth only stared at her, too paralysed by fear to do as she said. Exasperated, she ripped the jewelled clasps away from his robe.

All that worried her, as panic swirled about her, was her guess that few of this noble company could swim well enough to save themselves. She and Hyacinth might be swamped by the drowning unless they could make a clean escape.

Gripping Hyacinth's wrist, she pulled him towards the rail of the boat, feeling it settle under them. Hyacinth gave way to frightened sobbing as a surge of water washed around their feet and receded again. Slipping and stumbling on a deck that was suddenly canted and slick with water, Serafina ignored his tears and went on dragging him to the side.

She saw Gabriel flung against the railing as the boat lurched again, caught there by the sudden press of bodies thrown off balance. The rail splintered; she caught a glimpse of Gabriel's face, white and shocked, as he was thrust outwards and fell.

Behind her she heard a shout. 'Gabriel! Gabriel!' Count Loredan was there, pulling off his coat, diving neatly from the deck where the rail was broken into the knot of struggling swimmers below. Even among her own rising fear, and the need to stay calm for Hyacinth, she had the time to think how interesting that was.

By now the stern of the barge was dipping below the water, and most of the passengers were frantically scrambling upwards, away from the encroaching waves. Serafina grabbed Hyacinth and thrust him downwards; he let out a shrill cry as the surge took him, and began threshing helplessly as he tried to reach the broken end of the rail.

Serafina launched herself after him, dived to evade his clutching hands and came up behind him in time to grab him as he went under and support him with a hand under his chin.

Hyacinth's breath was coming in uneven gasps of terror. The slender hands that were so adept on lute or keyboard thrust helplessly at the surging waters of the lagoon as if he could push it away.

'Keep still,' Serafina snapped.

'You won't leave me? Serafina, you won't let me drown?'

'No, but do as I tell you.'

To her relief, he was quiet, except when water splashed into his face and he started to weep and jerk his head up, snatching for air. Serafina concentrated on reaching the safety of the quayside, the clamour and turmoil of the sinking boat dying away behind her as she swam steadily.

Her strength was ebbing as she reached the quayside. She managed to grasp an iron ring let into the stone above her head, but the edge of the quay was too far above that for her to reach it and pull herself out, especially encumbered as she was by Hyacinth. There were steps further along the quay, but in the gathering darkness she could not see them, or remember just how far away they were.

'Hyacinth,' she said, 'can you hold on here by yourself if I—'

'No!' He was panic-stricken, clutching at her, not the iron ring. 'Serafina, you said you wouldn't leave me.'

'Yes, but—'

A gurgling cry interrupted her, and she saw Paolo Contarini floundering awkwardly towards the quayside. She doubted he would reach it. He was weakening visibly, flailing but making little headway as he gasped and gulped and looked around for rescue.

Still supporting the terrified Hyacinth, Serafina could do nothing. She looked on helplessly as Paolo went under and fought his way back to the surface, splashing and coughing water.

Then she saw another swimmer cutting through the water towards him with crisp, assured strokes. Paolo saw, too, and reached for him, babbling out his pleas for help.

As the swimmer closed with him, Paolo's face changed to stark terror. He threw up an arm, clutching impotently at the empty air. His mouth distended as he tried to scream, and choked on the water that gushed in as the swimmer pulled him under.

The water swirled. Paolo rose once, thrashing. An arm clamped round his neck and dragged him down. The surface grew still, and neither man reappeared.

Hyacinth had started to whimper in renewed terror.

'Hush,' Serafina said. 'He didn't see us.' She was not sure that was true. She had seen enough to identify the man again: the bullet head with short hair lying dark and sleek from the water, the blunt nose and broad mouth. *We saw*, she thought silently. *Does he know we saw?*

The added fear made her realize how cold and stiff she was. She knew she had to get out. 'Hyacinth—' she began.

Another voice interrupted her, from just above her head. 'Here, take my hand.'

She looked up. A man was lying flat on the quayside above; Serafina could see nothing of him but his head, outlined against the dying light, and the arm he reached down to her.

Serafina pushed aside the thought that she ought not to let him touch them. She managed to rouse the half fainting Hyacinth, who clutched at their rescuer's hand, and was dragged up and over the edge. Relieved of his weight, Serafina thought she could have managed for herself, but the man leant down again, gripped her wrist and got his other arm around her shoulders until he brought her scrabbling onto the flat stones of the quay.

She looked up, seeing him properly for the first time. He was a tall, raw-boned young man, with longish fair hair plastered to his head. He looked embarrassed – by her body outlined by her wet slip, Serafina realized – and sketched an awkward bow. 'Your leave, lady? The others . . .'

Serafina murmured thanks. The man turned and took a smooth dive off the quayside. Serafina saw him swimming strongly out to where some swimmer's head was bobbing in the waves.

Too exhausted to move, she sat shivering and looking down at Hyacinth, who lay on his face beside her, his body shaken by sobs. Automatically she put out a hand to comfort him, but she could do nothing more.

The whole of the waterfront was scattered with survivors, some lying still, others crouched weeping or staring out at the lagoon in silent horror. A few were blundering around as if they needed to do something but did not know what.

Further along the quayside, Serafina saw a small group of men dragging a limp body out of the lagoon and up the steps. Paolo Contarini. They laid him on the ground and one of them bent over him, trying to breathe for him. Another stood over them, watching. Serafina recognized the man with the bullet head, and lowered her eyes in case she should catch his attention and he might remember.

She was not surprised when all the efforts to revive Paolo failed.

In the hours that followed, the survivors dragged themselves back to the Palazzo Contarini. They all had stories to tell.

Father Teo had been with the Count and Countess as the boat began to sink. As the Countess clung to him, shrieking, the Count clutched at his chest. Colour drained from his face. His knees buckled and he fell to the deck, dragging the Countess with him.

Teo bent over him but could not rouse him. He was breathing stertorously, oblivious even to the Countess as she screamed at him to wake and save her.

As the boat settled Teo had pulled her away and towed her through the water to safety, in a dead faint by then and mercifully unable to struggle. He had tried to go back for the Count, but by then the lagoon was dotted with failing swimmers, and he could not leave them to drown. He chivvied them or hauled them to the quayside until his own strength started to give way; he was fortunate to be dragged on board one of the rescue boats that by then had begun to arrive.

Alvise, the elderly steward, had thrust his panicking staff into the water with benches or scraps of broken rail to bear them up. No one had seen him after that, and he had not returned to the palazzo by the time darkness fell.

Count Contarini's body had not been recovered.

In less than a day, House Contarini was destroyed.

Nine

Giulietta Contarini, pale and heavy-eyed, tugged at the tight sleeve of her mourning gown and said, 'I am heiress to House Contarini.'

To do her justice, Serafina thought, she did not look as if she took any satisfaction in the thought of her sudden wealth and independence. She sounded bewildered, as if she did not know what to do with it.

When word came to the palazzo, she had screamed herself into hysterics, only calmed by a sleeping draught from her physician. Now, on the morning after the disastrous festival, she had to come to terms with what was left. Serafina could find it in her heart to pity her.

She lay on the *chaise longue* in her boudoir, with the blinds drawn and the only light a taper for Serafina in the sewing corner, where she was rapidly stitching a black mourning gown for herself.

Father Teo sat beside Giulietta, trying to offer what comfort he could. He himself looked exhausted; he had not been to bed the night before.

He said, 'My daughter, your mother and I will advise you what to do.'

'I don't wish to do anything.' Tears welled out of Giulietta's eyes. 'I want Papa and Paolo. I want everything how it used to be.'

As Father Teo leant forward to clasp her hand, the door opened; one of the footmen stood there. He said, 'Count Dracone wishes to offer his condolences, lady.'

'Thank the Count in Lady Giulietta's name,' Father Teo said sharply. 'She can't be troubled now.'

Messages like this had been coming in all morning; there was no need for Serafina to feel a chill that Count Dracone should express his sorrow, except that she doubted he felt any. But she felt chilled, more so when the footman added, 'He begs the favour of a word with you, lady.'

'Tell him he may not,' said Father Teo.

The footman looked trapped. Serafina could guess how he felt at the thought of refusing anything to Count Dracone.

'No. No, I'll see him,' said Giulietta. She dabbed at her eyes and patted ineffectually at her trailing hair. 'Serafina, I look *hideous*!'

'How should you look, at such a time?' said Father Teo. 'Count Dracone presumes too much. You should not see him.'

But the footman had already gone, and a moment later reappeared to usher in Count Dracone.

The Count's scarlet coat was like a splash of blood in the dim room. He bent over the hand that Giulietta extended to him, murmuring the conventional phrases of condolence, but Serafina did not miss the serpent glint of his eyes when he saw Father Teo. He totally ignored her.

'Dear Count,' said Giulietta. 'You're *so* kind. And everything's *so* wretched!' Her tears overflowed again and she hid her face in the folds of her lace handkerchief.

Serafina could not help suspecting that now, with the entry of the Count, Giulietta had begun to use her genuine grief in her automatic response to him; there was a hint of theatricality now, as if she was conscious of the effect she was making. Serafina exchanged a glance with Father Teo. He had been right; Giulietta should not have seen the Count.

Dracone, however, remained respectful. He said, 'My dear Giulietta, I would offer you more than my sympathy. You may know that not long ago I asked your father for leave to address you as my future wife. I regret that Count Contarini did not find me worthy. But things are different now. I beg that you will allow me to renew my addresses and offer you the protection of my name and House.'

Nothing could have been more correct. Serafina sat frozen, her needle poised above the fabric. Giulietta's lips were parted, a faint colour creeping back into her face. Her breath was coming more rapidly. 'Dear Count . . .'

Father Teo interrupted by rising to his feet. 'All that is different, Count Dracone, is that Lady Giulietta is now the heir to her House, and has no father to protect her.'

Count Dracone turned to him. His manner remained correct, but Serafina could see an ugly anger peeping out of his eyes.

'Father, I don't recall asking your advice, or your leave. This is not your affair.'

'As the lady's chaplain and spiritual adviser, it is very much my affair. She is not as unprotected, Count, as you might think.'

'But, Father Teo—' Giulietta began to protest, and broke off as Father Teo strode across the room and tugged at the bell-rope. The footman reappeared so rapidly that Serafina guessed he had been listening at the door.

'Roberto,' said Father Teo, 'go and fetch the Countess at once.'

The footman gaped. 'She's in her bed, Father.'

'Then get her out. This is urgent.' When the footman had gone, he turned back to Count Dracone and said, 'Count, if you truly care for my lady, and have her good at heart, then go now, and renew your offer at another time.'

Count Dracone inclined his head. 'With respect, Father, it is now that Lady Giulietta needs support.'

'Yes, yes, that's true, Count.' Giulietta held out her hand to him again, and he clasped it between both of his. 'Dear Count, you understand *so* well.' She averted her eyes with exactly the right degree of maidenly modesty. 'If Mama agrees, it . . . it would not be hateful to me, to be your wife.'

The Count raised her hand to his lips. 'You do me great honour.'

Stupid girl! Serafina thought, driving her needle viciously into the neck of the mourning gown. Can't she see the sort of man he is? Can't she imagine the sort of life his wife will have?

And then her annoyance turned to fear, as she realized that if Giulietta married the Count, she herself would have to go with her to the Palazzo Dracone.

There was silence in the boudoir until rapid footsteps and the rustle of skirts heralded the arrival of the Countess. When she came in, Serafina could hardly avoid staring at her. She had never seen Countess Contarini unless she was delicately rouged, exquisitely dressed, like a jewel of gilt and enamel. Now her hair was drawn back into a snood, and she wore no paint on her face. She looked old.

Wearily she sank into the chair Father Teo placed for her. She had barely noticed the Count's existence. 'What is it?' she asked.

It was Giulietta who replied. 'Mama, the Count has asked for me in marriage.'

Countess Contarini drew herself up. Her brows arched; briefly Serafina caught a glimpse of the beautiful aristocrat whose slightest whim had governed the household until now. 'Count Dracone, this is not a fitting time.'

'It seems most fitting to me,' said the Count smoothly, 'when House Contarini stands so deeply in need of friends.'

'I wish to be married, Mama,' said Giulietta.

'Countess,' said Father Teo, 'may I speak with you alone?'

'No need, Father,' said the Countess. 'Count Dracone, I thank you for your offer, and your goodwill. But it is not so long ago that you made this offer to Giulietta's father, my lord Count who now lies dead in the lagoon.' She pressed her lips together and went on, 'He refused, and I will not go against his wishes now that he is dead. Giulietta is not for you, Count.'

Count Dracone released Giulietta's hand, ignoring her attempts to cling to him. Her face puckered, and she buried it in the cushions of the *chaise longue*, sobbing wildly.

Quietly, with no expression in the black eyes or on the thin scarlet mouth, Count Dracone crossed the room to stand beside the Countess's chair. He took a sheaf of papers from inside his coat. 'Gambling debts . . .' he murmured. 'To the gaming house on the Campo San Luca . . . not a very respectable place. You must have worn a mask that night, I fancy, Countess. Bills from the silk merchants, the perfumers . . .'

He riffled through the pages. The Countess was staring at his hands and what he held with an expression of fascinated dismay. Father Teo moved to her side. Serafina's hands lay still in her lap, her sewing forgotten.

'And letters . . .' Count Dracone went on. 'To Count Mocenigo's younger son. House Priuli's private chaplain . . . think of the scandal . . . the Captain of the City Guard . . . scarcely the taste of such a highborn lady as yourself.'

'Where did you get those?' the Countess whispered.

'Money, my lady, will obtain most things, I've always found,' Count Dracone said. He threw up a hand in warning as Father Teo took a step towards him. 'These are copies, Father. The originals are lodged with my lawyer. I'm not quite a fool.'

Now he was letting his triumph show. 'Countess, I could create such a scandal that you would be ruined, and Giulietta with you. What son of a noble House would wed the daughter of such a mother?'

'And what about the scandal I could create?' Father Teo asked. 'If I were to make public what you have just said and done?'

Count Dracone laughed. 'Who would believe you, Father? Even the Countess would say you lied. Would you not, Countess?'

The Countess had still not taken her eyes from the papers in Dracone's scarlet tipped fingers. 'You want Giulietta,' she said.

'On the day we are wed, Countess, you shall have these – all of them, the originals as well – to burn if you choose. I think we should have the wedding quite soon, don't you, and quietly? Too much rejoicing would be inappropriate.'

Giulietta had emerged from her cushions, and was gazing from her mother to Dracone with a puzzled look. While she wept she could not have heard what Dracone had said to the Countess, and Serafina could see she did not understand what was going on.

'Giulietta,' her mother said, 'do you truly wish to marry Count Dracone?'

Father Teo made an inarticulate sound of protest. Giulietta ignored him. 'Oh, *yes*, Mama!'

Serafina wanted to scream at her, to make her see what the Count was, and what she was doing. Yet she could not; she was a genic, and who would listen to her? Besides, Count Dracone was right; it might well be that no one else would take Giulietta, seal of fertility or not, if her mother was shamed. Giulietta would prefer the Count as her husband, even if she knew the worst of what he had done, to no husband at all.

'Then . . .' As Dracone waited, the Countess sighed, and her hand fluttered to her breast. 'Then I give my consent.'

The Count smiled, and drew a ring from one white hand – a heavy ring made of gold and lapis. Serafina stared. Could *that* be . . .?

'To show my goodwill,' said Count Dracone, 'I give this to my promised bride as her betrothal ring. No lady in the whole world ever had one more precious.'

Smiling still, he took Giulietta's hand, and placed on it the reliquary of Christos.

2

Gabriel fought impotently to breathe. He was sinking
below the waters of the lagoon, into the cold and dark. A
hand clutched at his shoulder, dragging him deeper. He
was drowning among a cluster of panicking swimmers
who had no idea he was a genic, who would not care if
he was a genic, if only he could bear them up into the
light and air.

But he had never learnt to swim, and he could not.

'Gabriel! Gabriel!'

Leo's voice. Gabriel struggled to raise his head, to
breathe and cry out. He thrashed and clutched an arm,
and suddenly his eyes snapped open and he saw light –
the soft shimmer of tapers, not the cruel sunset of Count
Contarini's birthday.

Leonardo Loredan was bending over him, shaking his
shoulder. 'Gabriel – for God's sake! Gabriel . . .' The last
word was sighed out on a breath of relief. 'Gabriel, are
you awake?'

Panting and trembling, an icy sweat breaking out over
his body as the nightmare loosed its grasp, Gabriel began
to realize where he was. He lay not on the hard mattress
of the studio, but half sunk in a vast feather bed,
mounded with pillows. The light of the tapers glinted on
tarnished gold thread in the hangings. The posts that
supported the canopy were carved into luxuriant leaves
and flowers. The Count's own bedchamber, far too good,
too intimate, for a genic.

'Leo?' He struggled to sit up, but he felt weak and his
head swam, and his tongue felt too big for his mouth,

choking back the words as the waters of the lagoon had choked his cries for help.

Leonardo pushed him back into the pillows. 'Lie still. Rest. I'll go and get you something to drink.'

'No.' Gabriel tried feebly to cling to him. If he went, the nightmare would return. 'Leo, you came for me . . . but I don't remember.'

'I thought I'd lost you.' Count Leonardo's voice was suddenly shaken, all its arrogance dissolved away. 'I thought . . . oh, God, Gabriel . . . When I got you out you were unconscious. I couldn't wake you. I brought you home. I sent Manfred for a physician, but no one would come for a genic.' He broke off, the blue eyes lambent with pain. 'I thought you were dying.'

Gabriel was bewildered. 'How long . . .?'

'The wreck? Yesterday.' He tried to laugh. 'Gabriel, you terrified me.'

Gabriel thought how worn he looked, his face gaunt, his eyes shadowed. He wore nothing but a silken bedgown, and his pale hair unbound. Wonderingly Gabriel realized it was true; Leo had feared for him. He reached out to him again, trying to embrace him in an outpouring of gratitude and a hunger that he could not repress any longer. He felt Leo's hair against his face and his breath warm against the curve of his neck. Turning his head aside, he sought Leo's mouth, fumbling, desperate for his kiss.

Leonardo stiffened, and moved to hold him off a little way, hands gripping his shoulders, blue eyes searching his face until Gabriel felt they would draw out the very essence of him. He said, 'Gabriel . . .?' He half smiled, and Gabriel saw with overwhelming pain the pity in his eyes. 'Gabriel, I'm sorry.'

Gabriel felt his tears spill over. He tried to draw away from Leonardo's touch, and the Count let him sink back into the pillows. He said, 'I meant never to tell you. I know it's mortal sin for you, Leo, twice over.'

Leonardo repeated, 'I'm sorry.'

Gabriel could not go on looking at him. He hid his face in the pillow, clutching at it as he tried to choke back desperate weeping. Black exhaustion and despair washed over him. He had thrown away so much. Leo would not want him now. He would send him away.

He felt Leonardo's hand, gently resting on his hair. He said, 'Gabriel, don't.'

'I am . . . no more than Dracone called me.' Words spewed out of him like vomit. 'You should have let me die.'

'No!' Furious anger suddenly in Leo's voice. His grip was painful as he pulled Gabriel round to face him again. 'Never say that. Never listen to Dracone's filth. You are more than that. Gabriel . . .' Quiet now, and earnest. 'You are more than that to me.'

Gabriel lay looking up at him, limp and helpless, his breath still shaken with the aftermath of tears. Darkness was swirling around him like the smothering waters of the lagoon. He fought for consciousness as Leonardo pulled the bedcovers round him. In a voice more like his own he said, 'You're ill, Gabriel. Not strong enough for this. Later . . . we'll talk later.'

Gabriel was already sinking back into the dark again. For an instant the old terror gripped him, the nightmare threatening to surge back. Blindly he reached out, and felt Leo's hand firm around his own. Leo said, 'You're safe with me, Gabriel. Do you understand?'

He was not sure what he wanted to reply, but in any

case the weight of exhaustion took all words from him, and with something like relief he let the darkness engulf him.

3

The whole city mourned. Even the sky wept as the black-shrouded barges carried the bodies of the dead to their last resting-place. More tears yet for those like Count Contarini, whose bodies had still not been found. A muffled drumbeat gave the rhythm to the oarsmen. Silent crowds gathered along the quayside in the rain. The single remaining bell of the basilica tolled out its cracked note.

As the barges returned, the waiting crowds parted respectfully to allow the noble mourners room to pass. The Duke himself was the first to disembark, carried in a chair by four construct bearers of the Ducal guard, huge creatures with the heads of heraldic lions. Caterina watched from the barge of House Dandolo, and shivered involuntarily. The city's disaster had drained what life was left to the old man. His face and hands were like crumpled parchment, his eyes empty as those of the bodies left behind among the tombs and cypress trees of the Island of the Dead.

When the ducal party had cleared the quayside, Caterina stepped ashore, behind her father and Maria, and moved slowly towards the basilica. She drew her black cloak more closely against the chill of the rain, but nothing could drive away the chill inside her.

Her throat ached from crying. Her mother and her other two sisters, Agate and Pia, lay cold among the cypress trees. Maria lived only because her father had

refused the Contarinis' invitation on her behalf; such
frivolities were unsuitable for one so soon to be a holy
sister. Caterina had told no one about how she herself
had survived, for she knew that no one would believe her.

The bell tolled on. Caterina caught a glimpse of
Leonardo Loredan, his pale hair conspicuous among the
dark-robed crowd. He had lost no one, there had been
no funeral barge from House Loredan, and yet he had a
haunted look that spoke of grief, or some great anxiety.
As she wondered what it might be, his glance crossed
hers, and he inclined his head gravely to her. Feeling
herself colour, she returned the bow. What would Papa
say if he saw her? Gazing at a man, and on such a solemn
occasion, too!

Since the wreck, Caterina had lost what little esteem
she had had for her father, but she would not give him
an excuse to reprimand her in public. Casting about for
something respectable that she might look at, she saw
some way ahead the back view of Count Dracone, his
scarlet covered for once by a black cloak, but his varnished
black head unmistakable, and leaning on his arm a
woman whose hood had fallen back to reveal the golden
hair of Giulietta Contarini. Soon to be plain Giulietta
Contarini no longer, but the Countess Contarini-
Dracone.

Worse and worse, Caterina thought. Papa had been
scandalized at the plans for the rapid marriage, so soon
after Count Contarini's death. And to a man of such
reputation! Why would the Countess permit it, unless to
cover some sin of Giulietta's, no more than to be expected
from a House of such lax principles? Caterina was no
longer to visit Giulietta, or to call her friend.

Since there was nowhere Caterina could look without risking Papa's displeasure, she lowered her eyes modestly and looked at her own feet. So she almost collided with her father's back as he halted to speak to the man who had stepped in front of him.

'Sir?' Count Dandolo sounded disapproving, and Caterina could well understand why. The man who was bowing to him was Francesco Foscari, who had been her sister Maria's promised husband.

Caterina moved closer to Maria, and took her sister's hand. Maria turned her head aside, hiding her face in the folds of her hood.

'Count Foscari, at your service,' Francesco said. Caterina remembered that his father had drowned in the Contarini wreck. 'Sir, forgive me for a time and place that may be inappropriate. But I wish to reopen the question of my marriage to your daughter Maria.'

Caterina felt Maria's grip on her hand become suddenly painful, and heard her indrawn breath.

'The time is inappropriate,' Count Dandolo retorted frostily, 'and so is the question. You know that my daughter can bear no heir to House Foscari. She is to vow herself as a holy sister at Corpus Domini.'

'That is why I speak to you now, sir.' Francesco Foscari sounded respectful still, but quite determined. 'Before she makes vows which will part her from me for ever. As to an heir for House Foscari, my younger brother is already wed, and has two sons. If Maria gives me no heir, I will adopt one of them; my brother has agreed.'

'And your father?' said Count Dandolo. 'Your father who is scarce cold in his grave? Would he allow this, if he lived?'

'No, sir, he would not, as we both know well. But he is dead, and though I grieve for him, I live. I would wed your daughter in love and honour.'

'It is impossible,' said Count Dandolo. 'It is grotesque and impious.'

Caterina saw a spark of anger in Francesco's stolid features. 'Sir, I—'

Count Dandolo waved him aside impatiently and turned to his daughters. 'Come, Maria, Caterina.'

'Maria!' Caterina whispered, agonized. Was her sister really so dutiful that she would let Papa do this?

Maria released her hand, and put back the hood of her cloak to look at Francesco. Though Caterina had no illusions – she and her sister were not beautiful – Maria looked beautiful then. Her mouth was trembling, and her eyes shone. 'Sir,' she said, 'if you truly wish this, I will be your wife.'

'Nonsense!' her father snapped. 'You will do your duty.'

'I will not take vows at Corpus Domini, Papa,' Maria said. 'The Reverend Mother would not accept them, if she knows I am not willing.'

Count Dandolo looked from her to Count Foscari, and back again, in black frustration. Foscari bent over Maria's hand, and touched his lips to it. 'Go home with your father, *cara*. I will arrange everything.'

Caterina had always thought him, too, to be a plain young man, but his face shone now with happiness and relief. She smiled at him. 'I will help Maria be ready as soon as may be, sir.'

Her father caught her arm, and swept the two girls in front of him towards the basilica, leaving Francesco Foscari looking after them, and, Caterina thought, very well satisfied. She caught her sister's hand and clasped it hard.

Maybe Maria will take me with her when she weds, she thought. For truly, I do not think I can bear the Palazzo Dandolo, alone with Papa.

As they reached the square, and the open space before the basilica, she heard a cry from the crowds ahead of her. People surged forward, but more were pressing backwards, and for a moment Caterina was swept up with them.

The first cry was answered by others, and became a swell of sound, with words growing clearer. 'The Duke! The Duke is dead!'

As the crowd pressed Caterina forward, she caught sight of the ducal chair, held high above the heads of the people as the bearers tried to fight their way to the basilica. The old Duke, who had sat so erect through the ceremonies, had slid sideways, and now he lay flopping over the arm of the chair like a rag doll. His head lolled, and one eyelid was twitching madly, the only sign that he still lived. As Caterina watched, horrified, his jewelled cap of office slipped sideways, fell, and was swept away into the crowd.

Ten

I

Serafina waited on the bench where once she had spoken with Father Teo, while in the Contarinis' private chapel, Giulietta was wedded to Count Dracone.

Father Teo had refused to perform the ceremony, and the priest in there now was one brought by the Count. Serafina did not know where Father Teo had gone, only that he had left the palazzo on the same night that Giulietta and her mother had accepted Count Dracone's offer.

Giulietta had begun to recover from the shock of her father's death in the excitement of her approaching marriage. She had driven Serafina to distraction with her complaints that she would have no proper wedding gown, and a private ceremony like this instead of a grand display in one of the city churches, or maybe even the basilica itself. The Count himself had barely mollified her, with a promise that she should have all the gowns she wished for when the mourning period was over.

Serafina folded her hands in her lap, and tried to still her nervousness, wishing for her lute or some sewing to keep herself occupied. She did not wish to go to the Palazzo Dracone, but she had no choice. She belonged to Giulietta now, and must go where her mistress went.

Further down the passage, Hyacinth was pacing restlessly, the heavy folds of his silken robe swirling around him as he turned back towards her.

'What are they doing in there?' he asked. 'How long does it take to get married?'

The questions obviously required no answer, and Serafina did not offer one.

Pace, turn, pace. 'If Lady Giulietta had been married in the basilica,' said Hyacinth, 'I should have written music for her.'

'They would never let you in there to perform it.'

A shrug from exquisite, silk-clad shoulders. Hyacinth was flushed as if in a fever, his violet eyes looking huger than ever. He had never recovered from the terror of the wreck; now he was strung tight as his own lute.

'I must consult with Count Dracone,' he said. 'What music will he need? What pleases him best?'

Not music, Serafina thought wryly. If all she heard was true, Count Dracone would be delighted to welcome Hyacinth into his household, but not for music. Looking at him now, his fretting ready to tip over at any second into hysteria, she realized that Hyacinth knew it too.

He paused beside her. 'Serafina, I'm afraid.'

Serafina reached out for his hand, and held it. At the same moment the doors of the chapel began to open. Hyacinth pulled away from her, and started back.

From the chapel Count Dracone, scarlet clad as always, led his bride Giulietta, Countess Contarini-Dracone. She was leaning on his arm, looking up into his face with a smile of sickly adoration. Behind them came her mother, still in the plain black she wore to mourn her husband; she had not deigned to adorn herself for her daughter's wedding.

At the end of the procession, a small straggle of

servants, those who remained to the shattered House Contarini. Giulietta's maid Rosalba, the footman Roberto, and others Serafina did not know. As they began to disperse, the Count raised a hand. 'Wait.'

He laid a hand possessively over Giulietta's, smiled, and let his glance travel over the Contarini household. He said, 'You are all dismissed. The Palazzo Contarini will be closed up now that my bride comes with me to her new home.'

An uneasy murmur came from the servants. Countess Contarini said, 'But I do not come with you, Count. I wish to remain in my own home.'

'You, Madam?' The Count's voice was scathing, though the scarlet lips still smiled. 'You will go to Corpus Domini, and contemplate your sins.'

The Countess gasped. Her hand fluttered to her throat, but she drew herself up, and said, 'You mistake, sir. You have no right to command me.'

Smoothly Count Dracone said, 'Do I not, Madam?'

The Countess's lips parted, her face white. 'You promised me—'

'I have reconsidered.'

Serafina was not at all surprised, except perhaps that Countess Contarini had ever believed that Dracone would return her letters to her once he was married to Giulietta. Who could ever believe that he would give up a scrap of power when he had it in his hands and could use it?

'But you—' Serafina saw pride warring with fear in the Countess, and losing the battle. Countess Contarini held out her hands to her daughter. 'Giulietta, don't let him—'

Giulietta had not really been paying attention, admiring the new ring on her hand while her new husband talked with her mother. Before she could work out what her mother's appeal meant, the Count said, 'My bride will obey me. She knows her duty.' He looked down at Giulietta, still smiling, and said, 'Surely you are not a child to wish for your Mama to live with us?'

Giulietta's eyes widened. 'Oh, *no*, dear Count.'

'Then, Madam,' said Count Dracone, 'you will observe a decent modesty and withdraw to Corpus Domini. There will be no one here to care for you. I cannot afford the expense of keeping two establishments.'

Wildly Countess Contarini glanced from side to side, looking for support, but there was none. Certainly not from the rat-faced little priest of Count Dracone's, who smiled and bowed as the Count said, 'Father Tommaso, you will escort the Countess. A boat is ready, Madam, and you will find the Reverend Mother expecting you.'

Countess Contarini measured glances with him. Play for time, Serafina urged her silently. Take your jewels and sell them. Find a room as the old Countess Dandolo did. Hire yourself as a seamstress, or anything, to save yourself. For she knew little about piety, but she could imagine the convent as no better than a prison, for those who did not choose it freely.

But the Countess Contarini's cushioned existence had not fitted her for defiance. It trickled away from her like water. She lowered her eyes and took a pace backwards, and the little priest came to stand at her shoulder like a gaoler.

'Let us go,' Count Dracone said to Giulietta.

He led her down the passage towards the stairway. The other servants had melted away by now, but

Giulietta's maid Rosalba was still hovering nervously at the head of the stairs. She bobbed a curtsey as Giulietta and the Count drew level with her.

'My lord Count, am I to accompany my lady?' she said.

The Count gave her a look of distaste. 'Did you not hear what I said, girl? You are dismissed with the rest of the servants.'

Giulietta let out a squeal. 'But Count, I must have my *maid*!'

Count Dracone paused, looking down at her, his lips a scarlet line. 'It does not please me.'

'But who will see to my *clothes*? And my *hair*?'

'You have your genic woman, have you not? Let her take care of you. Come.'

Giulietta balked on the top step, resisting the Count who would have led her down to the hallway. 'But she would have to *touch* me!'

By now Serafina could see the cruelty that underlay the Count's surface correctness, a deep satisfaction that in any disagreement with his bride, he was bound to win. She wondered if Giulietta could see it, too. *Stupid!* she thought. Stupid that you never saw until now, when it's too late.

'Surely,' the Count said coldly, 'you are not so superstitious as all that? I will have my wife conduct herself with more discernment.'

For a few seconds Serafina wondered what Giulietta would make of that. Her normal reaction, if denied anything, was to scream or weep; that was usually enough to ensure she had her own way. Serafina was fascinated to see what an appeal to her maturity would do, even if she doubted that discernment was what the Count really cared about, or anything except blind obedience.

A smile touched Giulietta's lips. 'If *you* think so, dear Count. Come, Serafina, Hyacinth.'

She allowed the Count to lead her down the stairs to the hallway where his constructs were pulling open the main doors of the palazzo. Serafina followed, urging Hyacinth into motion; the musician had listened to all this exchange in rigid silence, his look inward and fearful.

So far Count Dracone had shown no interest in either of them; Serafina wondered whether that was a good sign or not, or whether it meant anything at all.

Count Dracone and Giulietta passed through the doors. Serafina stepped out after them into the cool air of morning. A faint breeze, with a tang of salt and the sea, touched her face, but now there was nothing of freedom in it for her. She passed from one servitude into another.

Beside the steps that led from the loggia, two boats were moored; a larger one in the scarlet and gold trim of House Dracone, and a smaller one that was presumably intended to convey Countess Contarini to Corpus Domini.

As the Count led Giulietta out, Serafina heard a gasp from Hyacinth; glancing at him she saw the violet eyes fixed in terror. His mouth trembled. He whispered, 'Serafina.'

'What is it? What's the matter?'

The only reply was a sobbing intake of breath. Serafina followed the frightened gaze to Count Dracone's boat. His boatman was standing ready to cast off. Count Dracone handed Giulietta down onto scarlet velvet cushions, braided with gold.

He said, 'Cesare, welcome your new mistress.'

The boatman bowed. Serafina felt as if ice was crystal-
lizing in her veins. She recognized the bullet head and
cropped black hair: the man she had last seen in the
lagoon, when he had drowned Paolo Contarini.

2

Gabriel stepped back from the easel and contemplated his
work. He had begun to paint again the view from his
studio window, the same subject as the painting Count
Dracone had destroyed. He could still remember the
lucid light he had tried to capture there. This new picture
was grey, brooding, as if it reflected the darkness of his
own spirit.

The showing of Count Leonardo's portrait had been
cancelled, out of respect for the city's grief. No one would
commission work until the first shock was over, and life
could go on again.

The portrait itself was stacked against the far wall; no
one had seen it yet but Dr Foscari, when he came to dine
one evening, and he had said little. He was not a man for
extravagant praise, but Gabriel did not need it. The
portrait itself was all that he had wanted, the pride of
House Loredan, coupled with the bright spirit that was
Leonardo. If he painted nothing else, Gabriel thought, he
had justified himself in that.

He had stopped work as the light failed, and was
cleaning his brushes when the door opened and Manfred
came in. 'My lord Count wants you in the study.'

'Do you know why?' Gabriel left the brushes to soak
and reached for an oily rag to wipe his hands.

Manfred gave him a sour smile. 'Young Count Foscari is with him,' he said. 'And his uncle, and the Procurator. No, I don't know why they want you.'

Gabriel glanced at him nervously. He had never been sure what Manfred thought of him; the old steward had no interest in his painting. But as one of the belongings of House Loredan, he was at least tolerated.

He went downstairs, tapped on the study door and let himself in. For a moment, none of the four men in the study paid him any attention. They were seated around the table; Dr Foscari had his back to the door, and the Procurator of the basilica was seated opposite him, contemplating his clasped hands with an expression of disapproval on his narrow face.

Count Leonardo had half risen, and was speaking vehemently to the fourth man, who vainly tried to get a word in to interrupt him.

'... madness to let Dracone sit on the Council,' Leonardo was saying. 'Who is he? Who knows who his father was? Where is the name of House Dracone in the Book of Gold?'

The Procurator raised his head. 'Count Dracone sits as proxy for House Contarini, by virtue of his marriage to Lady Giulietta.'

Leonardo made a disgusted noise.

'I wish it were not so,' said the fourth man, Francesco Foscari.

Gabriel studied him curiously. He had seen the new Count from time to time, but he had never spoken to him. He was a tall, gangling man, with a youthful air, though he was older than Count Leonardo. He had thick, sandy hair and a plain, unremarkable face: nothing to show the resolution he must need to carry through his marriage to Maria Dandolo, who had no seal of fertility. What is she, Gabriel wondered, to be loved like that?

'Gentlemen,' said the Procurator, 'we are straying from the point. Sit down, Leonardo. The law of the city gives Count Dracone the right to sit on the Council until Lady Giulietta has an heir of an age to take his place, and that will be many years from now. The issue is what we propose to do about it.'

'Be damned to him.' Leonardo took his seat again, and tossed off the wine in the glass in front of him.

'The Duke is dying,' the Procurator said, 'and there must be an election to decide which of the Council will replace him. We all know this. So I ask you again, Leonardo, are you prepared to offer yourself?'

Gabriel caught his breath. Leo to be Duke? His heart swelled with rejoicing at the thought of the honour, but at the same moment he caught the Count's blue gaze flashing on him for a second, a look of doubt and pain, and realized that it would not be as easy as that.

'I'm poor as a Ghetto rat,' Count Leonardo said. 'I've never thought of holding office.'

'Then think of it now,' Dr Foscari said. His voice was a bass growl dredged up from the depths of his belly. 'That damned Contarini barge has cut a swathe through the Council. Good men died. Others lost their wives or their heirs. Men with their Houses shattered, or men like Francesco here, newly come to office and inexperienced – how can we ask one of them to be Duke?'

'The city needs a strong hand,' said Francesco Foscari. 'Leonardo, you could give us that.'

Leonardo was twirling his empty glass in his fingers, seeming fascinated by the petalling of the dregs of wine along its sides. 'If not me, then who?'

'Count Dandolo would stand,' said Dr Foscari. 'Idiot though he is, God defend us.'

The Procurator coughed. 'But a pious man,' he said. His voice sharpened. 'Many of the Council would vote for him in preference to a man who lives openly with his genic.'

Leonardo sprang to his feet. His chair crashed over behind him. 'Procurator, would you like to expand on that remark?'

'If you wish.' The Procurator was unmoved. 'The appearance of sin will lose you the Dukedom. No need for the sin itself.'

Gabriel crossed the room and set the fallen chair on its legs again, just as an excuse to move closer to Leonardo. Suddenly he felt afraid.

Leonardo nodded thanks to him as he sat down. 'That's why I sent for you, Gabriel. I knew this would come up sooner or later, and you deserve to hear it. Procurator, Count Foscari—' He spread his hands. 'I have no interest in gutter gossip. Gabriel is mine, he belongs in House Loredan, and here he will stay.'

The Procurator hissed in annoyance.

Dr Foscari said, 'Well, so you'd let Dandolo be Duke.' He shrugged. 'So be it. But what would you think of Dracone?'

Leonardo's gaze swivelled. '*What?*'

'It's not impossible. He has expressed a willingness to stand.'

Leonardo suddenly let out a shout of laughter. 'Dracone! And you talk to *me* about sin!'

'Count Dracone is very respectably married,' the Procurator said. 'Whatever the rumours about him, they will be laid to rest now.'

'He has the ear of the Imperial merchants,' Dr Foscari said. 'I dealt through him when I bought my constructs. Plenty of Councillors want what he has to offer, and be damned to whether the Church approves or not.'

'Bribery?' Leonardo said swiftly.

'Bribery?' A sardonic laugh rumbled from the old lawyer. 'Nothing so crude. But men who support Dracone might find their contracts come easier – and cheaper.'

'And think of this,' Count Francesco added anxiously. 'How many men are there who sit in Council as Dracone does, as proxies for a young child, or a woman who has yet to transmit the blood of her House. They will vote for Dracone to be Duke if he promises them a way to keep their power.'

'The Contarini wreck did Dracone no harm at all,' Dr Foscari said. 'I happen to know that he owed money to the State. We could have stopped him there. But now he has the wealth of House Contarini.' He shrugged. 'He has become a citizen in very good standing.'

'And the two genics in his household?' Leonardo challenged him.

'Exactly,' said the Procurator. 'His household. He has servants, and a wife. He does not live alone with a genic who . . .' The Procurator's eyes travelled over Gabriel; he was not condemnatory, but he spoke with a hard realism, and Gabriel felt as if the look stripped him to the bone. 'Who is extremely attractive, although no doubt he knows his place.'

'Gabriel is a painter,' Leonardo said brusquely.

'Indeed.' The Procurator's brows lifted. 'But there are many people in the city, Count Leonardo, who see that as no more than an interesting fiction. A cover for sin. Count Dandolo is one of them.'

'Count Dandolo sees sin everywhere,' said Leonardo. 'I would hate to disappoint him.'

There was a snort of laughter from old Foscari, but the Procurator did not share his amusement. 'I am reasonably certain,' he said, 'that Count Dandolo would not stand for election, but support you against Dracone, provided he felt satisfied with your mode of life.'

'A Loredan?' Count Leonardo sounded outraged. 'A Loredan submit to the approval of House Dandolo? Never while I live.' He rose to his feet again. 'Gentlemen, enough of this nonsense. Take me as I am, or not at all.'

Gabriel stepped forward. He had known this must come, but he had hoped to find an escape. Now he knew there was none.

'I will go,' he said. He could stop himself from shouting in the face of Leonardo's obduracy; he could not prevent his voice from trembling.

'Go – where?' Leonardo snapped at him.

'I don't know.' It was all Gabriel could do to remain standing erect among them. 'Somewhere I will not shame you.'

'You'll do as you're damn' well told,' said Leonardo.

'Assign his rights to someone who has no political ambitions,' said the Procurator thinly.

'I'd take him myself,' Francesco Foscari said, 'but my marriage is causing problems enough, and my prospective father-in-law—'

His uncle interrupted him with a contemptuous snort; he shrugged helplessly and fell silent.

'Now, listen, boy,' the old lawyer said to Gabriel, leaning across the table, 'you—'

'No, listen to me.' Count Leonardo was white-faced, furious. 'If you think I would stoop to take up the

Dukedom, if it meant losing my honour, if it meant I must betray—'

'Betray a genic?' said the Procurator. 'My dear Leonardo!'

Count Leonardo swung round on him; before he could damn them all to the lowest deeps of hell and lose his chances for ever, Gabriel interrupted. 'My lord . . .' His tongue felt thick in his mouth. He wanted to go to Leo, to take his hands, to compel his understanding, but he could do so little, here, in the presence of these others, when he must not overstep the bounds of a decent formality.

Leonardo stared at him. 'Well?'

'It is best I go. It is what I wish. My lord Count . . . you must be the new Duke. You must. Without you, the city will be torn into shreds. It will go down into the dark. You must take it up, or leave it to Count Dracone.'

Softly, old Foscari said, 'Well done, boy.'

Gabriel remembered the first time Leonardo had touched him. His lord had said to him, 'We pay whatever it costs.' He knew now that it was true. Leonardo must have the rule of the city, he must have honour once again for House Loredan, he must marry for wealth, for an heir, for the love that he could not accept from Gabriel. If the cost to Gabriel was his own life or his sanity, Gabriel knew he must pay it.

He said, 'My lord, let me go.'

The ice-blue eyes held him compellingly, and then looked away. Gabriel felt as though a cry was torn out of him, though he remained silent.

Leonardo said, 'Go and wait in the studio.'

Gabriel knew then what his decision would be. It was what he had wanted, what he had begged for, and yet he

did not know if his heart could bear the anguish. He
bowed and went out.

As he closed the study door behind him, he heard the
Procurator's voice. 'The boy knows his duty, Leonardo.'
Old Foscari's bass rumble began to reply, but Gabriel did
not wait to hear.

He fled up the stairs to the studio, and stood staring
at the paints and brushes and the other equipment
scattered on the table by the wall, the canvases made
ready, the new painting on the easel. If he was to leave,
he would need to take it all with him, but he did not
know how he would transport it, or where he was to go,
or whether he would be allowed to paint at all.

From its place against the wall, the eyes of the portrait
smiled at him. Had he really painted what he had seen,
Gabriel wondered, or only what he wished to see? Had
Leonardo only defended him because of what he thought
was due to House Loredan? Was he, perhaps, thankful
for an excuse to let him go?

Behind him, the door opened and closed. He braced
himself, thinking it was Leonardo, but when the newcomer spoke it was in the gruff tones of Dr Foscari.
'You're to come to me.'

Gabriel froze. He dared not turn, or ask if Leonardo
had agreed.

After a pause, the old lawyer went on. 'Leonardo will
lend you to me. There's a room you can use. I'll send my
constructs to pack all this up; you can supervise them
yourself and make sure it's done properly.' When Gabriel
still did not reply, he added bracingly, 'Come on, boy,
it's not the end of the world.'

The kindness broke Gabriel down as indifference
could not. He felt sobs rising in his chest and breaking

out against all his efforts to hold them back. 'I can't—'
he gasped out. 'Not when you don't understand . . . I
love Leo, I want him. But it's mortal sin for him, and
besides, he will never want me, not like that . . .' He was
not sure if he was making himself clear and he did not
know any other words to say that would not be obscenity.
Besides, his sobs were wrenching him so fiercely now that
he could not speak in any case, and he let himself fall to
his knees, utterly shamed and beaten.

After a while, he gradually became aware of the floorboards creaking as Dr Foscari moved around the studio.
When he looked up, the lawyer was standing in front of
his painting of Leonardo, studying it with head thrust
forward and hands clasped behind his back.

Gabriel dared not interrupt the scrutiny, and shortly
Foscari turned to look at him. He could have borne
contempt, but he shrank from what he saw in the old
man's face – not even compassion, but a plain acceptance
of what he was.

'Get up, boy,' he said. 'Wipe your face. What do you
want to take with you now?'

Gabriel stayed where he was, crouching on the floor.
'You cannot shelter me,' he said. 'The scandal—'

Foscari chuckled as if he genuinely found that funny.
'You'll learn, boy. I'm too old and fat for scandal to stick
to me. Old Foscari can do things that Leonardo Loredan
can't, especially if he wants to be Duke.' Impatiently he
added, 'Sweet saints, boy, do you think you've told me
anything I didn't already know?'

Gabriel stared, and rose shakily to his feet. 'You
knew . . .?'

Foscari jerked his head at the portrait. 'Could anybody
look at that and not know?'

He strode across the studio, took Gabriel's jacket from its hook on the back of the door, and tossed it to him. Gabriel caught it on the reflex.

'Better for you when you're out of the house,' Foscari said. 'What you need is work to do. I'll find you some commissions – no, I'll commission you myself. You can paint a portrait of Maria Dandolo, and I'll give it to my nephew, poor besotted idiot. Dammit, boy, stop gaping! Move!'

Gabriel made a desperate attempt to pull himself together. He put on the jacket, and turned almost in a panic to the work table. 'I'll need to pack—'

'You can come over with my constructs in the morning. When Leonardo is in council.'

'May I not even see him?' He was furious with himself for not being able to keep back the question.

'Not yet. When the election is over . . .' Foscari shrugged. 'We'll see. One day at a time, boy.'

Gabriel was not even surprised when Foscari took him by the shoulder and propelled him out of the studio. Going down the stairs, he could see the closed door of the study, and even hear the murmur of voices behind it. He could not stop himself from hoping that Leonardo would come out, and forbid him to leave. But the door remained closed.

Foscari chivvied him down to the entrance hall and out into the loggia. Moonlight glittered on the surface of the canal, except where the dark prow of Foscari's boat cut across it. Gabriel climbed aboard, unable to help shrinking from the dark water, remembering the lagoon. He clutched the side as the boat lurched under Foscari's weight, and then the palazzo was falling behind as the boatman rowed out into mid channel.

Gabriel kept his head turned away. All he could hear was the soft gurgle of the water as the boat slid through it, sounding like all the tears he could not allow himself to shed.

3

Dr Anhalt clasped his hands comfortably behind him, under his coat, and looked out of the window. Rain drizzled from the cold northern sky, falling slick on the steeply gabled roofs and the narrow, cobbled streets that twisted between them. The hillside fell away sharply in front of him, as far as the flat gleam of the distant river.

Flyers circled beneath the low cloud cover, and as Anhalt watched, a hawk zoomorph – no doubt under the control of a rival establishment – hovered outside the window, scanning him with lensed eyes.

Smiling, Anhalt spoke, even though he knew that the creature's controller would be unable to hear him. 'Nothing for you here, little bird. Go and spy elsewhere.'

The hawk hovered a moment longer, bright eyes boring into him, and then suddenly fell away. Anhalt watched its downward flight, and then lost it among the tangle of roof-tops.

Behind him, the door opened, and he heard the whirring mechanism of the construct before he turned and saw it. It stood a head taller than him, and had the crude shape of a man, though there had been little effort to disguise the metal casing under its overalls, or to make the painted features lifelike.

Anhalt regarded it with distaste. Fashions changed, he supposed, and following the craze for incorporating animal forms, and the sleekly abstract designs he favoured himself, it was about time for crudity to become popular again.

'Yes, what is it?' he asked.

The construct bowed jerkily. Its tinny voice issued from somewhere deep inside, while the hinged mouth made a few unco-ordinated movements. 'Geschaftsmeister Vogel will see you now, sir.'

It drew back to let Anhalt pass through the door and into the lift, closing the grille of elaborate ironwork and pressing the switch that would take them to the top of the tower. On the upper landing, another door stood open, leading to a large, circular chamber. The walls were draped in sombre tapestries, and opposite the doorway stood a suit of armour, fluted and damascened, a trap for the unwary who did not realize that it recorded everything that went on inside the room.

Stepping through the door, Anhalt almost tripped and fell as something scuttled, chittering, between his feet. He bit back a curse.

Dry laughter came from the desk at the other side of the room. Geschaftsmeister Vogel himself was seated there, fingers spidering over a control disc, while the rat zoomorph scurried back and forth and eventually came to rest beside the wall.

Anhalt suppressed a sigh: another of Vogel's new toys. 'You sent for me, Geschaftsmeister?'

Vogel nodded. He was an old man, dried up and thin as a bundle of twigs, his skin yellowish and stretched over a hairless skull. Too juiceless now for most of the pleasures of life, Anhalt assumed, except for those of wealth and power, which remained potent when all else had failed.

'Word from the south,' Vogel said, gesturing to the chair on the other side of his desk. 'Sit, Anhalt. You'll take wine?'

As Anhalt settled himself, the construct, which had followed him in, poured from a carafe on a table beneath the narrow, pointed window, and placed both glass and carafe next to Anhalt on the desk. Vogel took nothing.

He waited for Anhalt to sip the wine and nod his approval of the vintage before he said, 'My representatives in the Imperial Hostel inform me that the Duke has had a stroke. He still lives, but he cannot live long.'

Anhalt sat upright; this was more interesting than he had expected.

'He was an old man, a traditionalist, his mind closed to progress.' Vogel swept the dying Duke to one side, as if he himself were still young. 'For all our efforts, we had little success in placing our goods in his city. Now, things may change.'

'Do we know who will be the new Duke?' Anhalt murmured, taking another sip of the excellent wine.

'Not yet. Down there, they elect their rulers.' A faint sneer showed Vogel's opinion of that. 'And until the old man dies, they can't set the date of the election. Yet there are indications.'

'Which are?'

Vogel gave him a death's-head grin. 'What would you say to Count Dracone?'

'Dracone?' Anhalt could not hide his astonishment. 'Impossible! For all his efforts, he has no seat on the Council.'

The grin widened into a look of deep satisfaction. 'My dear Anhalt, you are behind the times. Have you no spies of your own down there? No matter, my secretary has prepared a report bringing you fully up to date; you can collect it on your way out. For now, take my word for it, Dracone is eligible, and he has a certain following.'

'Dracone as Duke . . .' Anhalt set down his glass, and at once the construct whirred up and refilled it. 'That would be . . . useful.'

'More than useful,' Vogel snapped. 'Dracone is ours, and he's free of that damned superstition that keeps the city out of our hands. When he is Duke, we may make what profit we will.'

'When?'

Vogel shrugged, acquiescing. 'Very well. If. Dracone is a fool. He cares for nothing but his own appetites, and does what he needs to feed them. That, of course, is what makes him useful to us. But you're right, my dear Anhalt, he may not have the subtlety to secure the Dukedom.'

'Has he a rival?' Anhalt inquired.

'Oh, indeed he has.' Vogel folded twiggy fingers and leant forward across the desk. 'And that, my dear Anhalt, is where you come in. As head of my legal department, you're going down there to speak to him.'

Anhalt smiled. This was beginning to make sense. 'Tell me about him.'

'Count Leonardo Loredan,' said Vogel. 'A young man, and poor as dirt, so I'm told; you should have no trouble bribing him. I'm told he sleeps with his genic – one of ours, if I'm not mistaken. His *male* genic, moreover.'

'Which suggests that he too has no use for superstition,' Anhalt said.

'Exactly. I don't foresee any difficulties. Naturally you may draw on the firm's account for whatever you need.'

He broke into cackling laughter, which turned into a spasm of coughing, and fought, wheezing, for breath while the metallic construct jerked its way over to him with a glass of water. As he sipped, choked, and wiped his mouth and eyes, Anhalt could still trace the flare of triumph in his face.

'Soon, Anhalt, soon,' he gasped, 'we shall have *both* the candidates for the Dukedom in our pockets.'

4

The courtyard garden still caught the occasional hour of sunlight as the last of summer faded. Gianni had already planted roses, jasmine, and a vine, but it would be many months before he would see the results of his work. He held the seed of beauty in his mind, and found it hard to wait for the time when he could show it to Alessandro.

One morning when Gianni sat at the breakfast table, wolfing Lucetta's hot rolls before going to work at the warehouse, Alessandro appeared in the old velvet bedgown, leaning against the doorframe as if he could not stand without support. He was white, with smudges of weariness around his eyes.

Alarmed, Gianni half stood up, but took his seat again as Alessandro waved him away and sat opposite him. 'Sandro, what's the matter? Are you ill?'

Alessandro shook his head. 'It's nothing. I slept badly, that's all. I think I won't go into the warehouse today.' He smiled. 'Don't look so shocked, Gianni. You can manage perfectly well without me.'

That was not why Gianni looked shocked. He was used to their routine, and breaking it made him uneasy, whatever Alessandro said.

'I'll stay with you, if you want me.'

'Don't be absurd.' Again the smile, and something in the depths of the blue eyes that Gianni could not read. 'I'll sit in the garden with a book. Sleep later, perhaps. Truly, Gianni, there's no reason to worry about me.'

Gianni finished his breakfast and took himself off. When he returned, earlier than usual, he found Alessandro lying in the garden chair, still wearing the bedgown, and with a book, unopened, on the grass beside him.

A skinny tortoiseshell cat had appeared from somewhere and was curled up in a fold of the bedgown, asleep. Alessandro was drowsily stroking it.

'You look very peaceful,' Gianni said. 'Both of you.'

Alessandro smiled, and looked a little embarrassed. 'It came in over the wall,' he explained. 'Lucetta said it would stay if we fed it – so we did.'

For the first time Gianni noticed a dish lying in the grass beside the book, with a scrap or two of meat still inside it. He grinned suddenly. 'That's very domestic of you, Sandro!'

'It's company, when you're not here.'

'But—' Gianni began to speak, and stopped. He had wanted to say, 'But you'll be with me at the warehouse all day,' and suddenly realized that perhaps Alessandro was trying to tell him something that he could not put into words in any other way.

Gianni's uneasiness returned, and sharpened into fear. He said, 'Well, at least it'll keep mice out of the kitchen. That should please Lucetta.'

Next day, Alessandro was still not well enough to go to the warehouse. Gianni could not help remembering the dark figure he had seen in the garden on the day of the sale. Alessandro's strange weakness had begun then.

Unbidden, another memory slid into his mind:

Dr Foscari, at the Judiciary, after Count Dracone left in a fury at his failure to obtain Alessandro's rights. 'You've made an enemy there, boy.'

Dracone must hate both of them, Gianni knew. Could this illness of Alessandro's be his revenge? How exquisitely appropriate, if it was. What better way to torture both of them, than to leach their happiness and security away like this, bit by bit?

But if Count Dracone had sent the shadow creature, what was it? What was Dracone, that he could command it? Gianni remembered Father Battista's long harangues on the fiends of hell, and tried to close his mind to the answers that he feared most of all.

Eleven

I

In the Palazzo Dracone, Giulietta Contarini had exchanged rose for scarlet, the colour of a cruel lily, Serafina thought, with poison at its heart. The hangings of her bed were scarlet, heavily encrusted with gold embroidery. Giulietta lay among pillows, scented with the musk-like perfume of the east. As Serafina came into the room with hot water for her mistress to wash, the daylight which crept in through the shutters made the room glow like fresh blood.

Giulietta turned her head on the pillow to watch Serafina as she poured water into the bowl on the wash-stand and dropped in scented essence from a golden flask. 'I shall wear the new gown this morning, Serafina.'

The new gown was a gift from Count Dracone. Scarlet silk, edged with gold, slashed to waist and thigh, leaving no refuge for modesty.

'Do I not look beautiful?' Giulietta asked, posturing in front of the mirror when Serafina had helped her to arrange the gown.

Serafina wanted to say, No, you look like a tavern whore, but she kept the words back. What point? In any case, the gown was the least of what disturbed her.

Since she had come to the Palazzo Dracone, there had been a change in Giulietta. Serafina had been prepared for screams or weeping when the girl realized the nature of the man she had married, but what was happening was not so simple. Giulietta seemed content enough, but she was sleepy always, her eyelids heavy, her head drooping. Her speech had grown slower, and sometimes she slurred her words.

Serafina was becoming more and more certain as the days went by that the Count was giving some kind of drug to Giulietta. She was also as sure as a third person could be that he had not shared Giulietta's bed.

Count Dracone was courteous to her in public, expressed himself affectionate in impeccably respectable fashion, and escorted her to her own bedchamber at night. No more nor less than many noble husbands did, but Serafina had found no evidence that he visited her.

She was half inclined to ask Giulietta, and embarrassed enough to keep silence when she wondered how to phrase the question. Had anyone ever told Giulietta what married people did? If not, it was time someone enlightened her, but Serafina did not want to do it.

So she was startled when Giulietta, still admiring herself in the mirror, stretched and yawned and said, 'My courses have not come. I think I must be with child.'

'It's early days, surely?'

Giulietta smiled sleepily. 'I am a married lady now. It is my duty to bear an heir to my House. Besides, my lord Count is to stand for election, when the Council chooses the new Duke.' She stood sideways to the mirror, and smoothed the blood red silk over her still-flat stomach. 'House Dracone will be the greatest of all.'

She sat before the toilet table and began to paint her face. Serafina laid out golden slippers, fetched the jewellery casket for Giulietta's choice, and thought furiously.

Giulietta was little more than a fortnight married. It was
not impossible that she was bearing, but highly unlikely,
especially as Serafina had just been speculating that she
was still virgin. Unless . . .

Serafina repressed a shiver. Unless the child was not
Dracone's. Had Giulietta been carrying on a liaison just
before her marriage, before her father's birthday festival?
But how would she have managed it, so guarded as she
was in the Palazzo Contarini? How would Serafina not
have known?

Or if the child had been conceived here in the Palazzo
Dracone, whose could it be, if not the Count's: Dr
Heinrich's, who had an apartment in the back of the
palazzo and dined with the Count and his lady almost
every night? Or Cesare, the bullet-headed pilot's? What
was Count Dracone prepared to do, to provide himself
with an heir? What was he doing to Giulietta?

Serafina could not answer any of those questions, and
she did not know why she should care. Giulietta was
nothing to her. Most likely the ignorant girl had miscal-
culated, and her courses would return in the next day or
two. But as Serafina carried away the water and left
Giulietta to finish prettifying herself, she could not
entirely believe that, or be comforted by it.

Serafina's lute remained in its case, propped against the
wall of her new bedchamber. Since she came to the Palazzo
Dracone, with her new duties as Giulietta's maidservant,
she had not managed to practise. Looking at it now, with
no time to do anything more than tidy herself and pull out
her sewing basket with Giulietta's mending, she remembered the music lessons of the Palazzo Contarini, and

wondered for the thousandth time what had happened to Hyacinth.

Since they came to the palazzo, she had not seen him. She had asked for news of him once, from Dracone's steward, a dried-up elderly man who had stared her up and down from pebble eyes before he snapped, 'Mind your own affairs, girl.'

There were no servants to ask for word of Hyacinth, for all the work of the palazzo was done by Dracone's shambling constructs; the only other humans in the place were Dr Heinrich and Cesare. Serafina had not tried to ask them, partly from fear, partly because she doubted they would tell her anything.

There were no musical instruments in any of the public rooms of the palazzo. Serafina had not heard a note of music since her arrival. She began to wonder if Hyacinth had been sent away – or, worse, killed – because if he were here, surely she would have heard that glorious voice, if only at a distance.

Horror at the thought of what might have happened was growing on her daily. She felt responsible for Hyacinth, half irritated with herself at the same time. She knew he would be as helpless here as he had been in the lagoon, struggling in an element as unfamiliar and just as likely to overwhelm him. She had saved him then; she could not ignore him now.

Tired at last of her own fears and ignorance, she let Giulietta's petticoat fall and slipped noiselessly out of her room.

The Palazzo Dracone was empty and echoing, unlike the bustle of the Palazzo Contarini, where you could not take a dozen steps without meeting a servant. The steward, Serafina guessed, would be minding his own business in his rooms on the ground floor. No one saw her as she hurried along the passages to the Count's private apartments.

She was terrified of what she was doing, looking at herself from the outside and wondering how she could be so stupid. So far Count Dracone had ignored her; she was happy about that and did not want it to change. Now with every step she took she was courting his notice.

As she passed the Count's private sitting room, she heard the murmur of voices, and pressed herself against the door, squinting through the gap between the hinges and the frame. So placed, she could see a segment of the room, but no sign of Hyacinth.

Dr Heinrich stood by the window, looking out, his burly shoulders blocking the light. He said, 'You must announce nothing until I'm sure.'

Dracone was lounging in a chair, filing his fingernails. Serafina shivered at the thought of those delicate claws. He said, 'How long, then?'

Heinrich shrugged. 'When you can look at your wife, and see.'

The Count sat upright, his features sharpening to fury, his mouth an ugly scarlet gash in the pale face. 'Too long! The old Duke could die any day, and the election will follow straight after. And that damned Loredan –' he added a casual obscenity – 'gains support every day.'

'Let me test her, then.'

Dracone's mouth twisted in revulsion. 'How you can bear to touch . . .' He made a sound of disgust, and added, 'Tested, yes, but not by you, Doctor. Your reputation . . . I'm told the men of the Empire threw you out of their laboratories because you were too depraved even for them.' He raised a hand in mock protest as Heinrich muttered a curse. 'Besides, you're here in my household; who would believe you? Find another physician – one of those damned pious sisters who test for fertility.' The disgust faded and his mouth became a thin curve of satisfaction. 'Then no one will doubt that my wife is with child. See to it now, Doctor.'

Serafina had already drawn back from the door, and as she heard Heinrich's heavy footsteps beginning to cross the floor, she whisked around a corner and into safety.

She was angry with herself for trembling. She could not understand why it should matter to the Count that he could prove Giulietta was with child, or what it had to do with the election of the new Duke. But without understanding, she knew that somehow Giulietta was caught up into evil. What was it that grew inside her? And why should Count Dracone be so eager to announce her pregnancy?

2

'I hear that you have dismissed your genic,' said Count Dandolo portentously. 'And not before time.'

Count Leonardo Loredan shifted uncomfortably in his seat. He felt he could hardly breathe in this overheated room in the Ducal Palace, or settle on the overstuffed chair. He could not forget, either, that somewhere in the private apartments above his head, the old Duke still lay dying.

'I have not dismissed Gabriel,' he said.

The Procurator of the basilica, the third man in the small, shuttered room, twitched nervously and shuffled the papers on the table in front of him. 'He no longer resides under your roof.'

'I have not reassigned his rights. He's working for Dr Foscari. It's convenient for him to live there.'

'For how long?' Dandolo asked.

Leonardo fastened him with a stare. 'For as long as it's convenient.' His patience close to snapping, he added, 'Count Dandolo, if you have anything to say about me and Gabriel, then say it.'

Count Dandolo gave him a look of cold revulsion. 'You were seen embracing it in public, out on the quayside there.'

'Seen embracing—' Leonardo needed a few seconds to understand what the Count was talking about. 'That was after the Contarini wreck, damn you. I was trying to revive him.'

'To touch a genic is mortal sin,' said Count Dandolo. 'How much more to hold it in your arms, to place your own mouth over . . .' He broke off with a disgusted sound in his throat. 'Young man, your immortal soul stands in danger of perdition.'

The Procurator held out a hand, feebly protesting, and Leonardo snapped, 'Then should I have left him to drown? Would that safeguard my immortal soul? Count Dandolo, who gave you the right to question me about my soul, or my household?'

Count Dandolo's mouth was a hard line, and his grey eyes cold under their jutting brows. 'You gave me the right yourself, when you decided to stand as Duke.'

Leonardo tried to control his rising temper. The worst of it was, he knew Count Dandolo was right. If he wished for public office – especially for this, the highest of all –

his whole life was open to question. And if Dandolo stood against him, the divided vote could let Dracone in. Leonardo knew that he needed Dandolo's support.

Carefully, he said, 'My arrangements with Gabriel must always take account of his talent. His painting is something rare and new.'

Count Dandolo snorted. He was one of those Leonardo had invited to the showing of Gabriel's first picture, but he had refused. 'Frivolity,' he said.

'But not, I think, sin,' said the Procurator, unexpectedly coming in on Leonardo's side. 'The great artists of the past glorified God in their painting.'

'And you suggest this . . . Gabriel should do so? A genic?'

'Oh, no, that would be quite improper,' said the Procurator hastily. 'Count Dandolo, may we leave this matter aside? So long as Gabriel remains at Dr Foscari's, there can be no difficulty.'

'And afterwards?' Count Dandolo said balefully. 'Are we to have a Duke who flaunts his genic in the face of all the city?'

'I think I can assure you,' Leonardo said tightly, 'that you need have no fear of that.'

Rage boiled inside him; he forced it down. 'Flaunt' indeed. When Gabriel shrank from anything that touched his privacy, even the display of his own talent. He set his teeth and imagined with great satisfaction his hands meeting around Count Dandolo's throat.

'Then let us proceed,' said the Procurator. He slid some sheets of paper across the table. 'Here is a list, Leonardo, of the Councillors whose vote I think you can count on. Here, those who would support Dracone. And here is the list of men you must convince.'

Count Dandolo seized the third list before Leonardo had the chance to look at it. He ran his eye down it, and then took up a pen, dipped it, and made a mark next to several of the names. Finished, he glanced through it again and tossed it over to Leonardo.

'Those are the men I can bring with me,' he said, paused, and added heavily, 'if I choose.'

Leonardo scanned the list. Over half the names had Dandolo's mark against them. If he chose, Dandolo could give him the Dukedom. On the other hand, if he decided to stand for the office himself, he might not win, but he could bring down Leonardo.

Why is it, Leonardo thought furiously, that I have to please this man, when he is not fit to clean the boots for House Loredan?

He was still keeping a tight rein on his temper, though he could see the Procurator looking anxious again. He said, 'What is your advice, messire?'

'You must talk to these men,' the Procurator said. 'Get their goodwill. The majority of them respect House Loredan.'

'It would help,' Count Dandolo added, 'if they could also respect you.'

'And what do you suggest I do,' Leonardo said, temper beginning to fray in spite of all his efforts, 'to earn their respect?'

'Live a godly life,' said Count Dandolo.

'Are you saying I do not?'

'Setting your genic aside . . . you are not seen at Mass as often as one might wish,' said the Count, his eyes cold and grey and condemnatory. 'You keep no chaplain. Your conversation smacks of impiety.'

Leonardo wished he could consign the man to hell,

get up, and walk out. He was not sure why he did not. No one – certainly not the head of House Loredan – needed to sit and be lessoned like this. But he had set his feet on this path, and turning aside at the first obstacle was not the way of House Loredan, either.

He sighed. 'I will think on your words, my lord Count,' he said.

Outside the palace, Leonardo stood with head thrown back, taking in great gulps of cold air. He hated this. Intrigue in quiet rooms, with men he despised. Truth that somehow became twisted. Flattery that came with difficulty to his tongue. He wanted nothing more than to throw the office of Duke back into their faces, and call Gabriel home.

But all around him the life of the city went on, quiet and purposeful. He could imagine the crushing weight of piety that Dandolo would lay on it, or the evil that Count Dracone would unleash. He knew he could do better.

Was even that worth it, when to sit in the Duke's seat he would need to say and do things unworthy of the last heir of House Loredan? When he had already broken his sworn word to Gabriel?

Instead of turning for home, he wandered aimlessly alongside the palace wall with his back to the basilica until he came out on the quayside. A merchant ship was making its way towards the mouth of the lagoon, and he stood watching it as the wind stiffened the sails and it heeled gently; he could hear, very faintly, the creaking of timbers and the shouts of the sailors, dying into silence as the ship sailed on.

Wind with the salt tang of the sea blew his hair back

and struck cold through the threadbare fabric of his suit. Leonardo faced into it as if it could scour him clean from that grubby little conference in the palace.

Further down the quayside, he caught sight of a small man in a black cassock, sitting on a bollard and gazing out at the water. He was eating a roll, and tossing scraps to the seagulls that squawked and flapped around him.

Leonardo strolled to his side and stood with hands clasped behind him. 'Father Teo.'

The little priest looked up at him, a smile crinkling his eyes but not reaching his mouth. 'Count Leonardo.'

'Your mistress – is she well?'

'My mistress?'

'Countess Contarini.'

All trace of a smile left Father Teo's eyes. 'I am no longer in the Countess's service. I left when I was expected to marry Lady Giulietta to Count Dracone.'

'Ah, yes, the famous marriage!' Leonardo said. 'The whole city seems to think that Count Dracone has done very well for himself.'

'And Lady Giulietta? What are they saying about her?'

'She has done her duty, has she not?' Leonardo bared his teeth. 'Her husband is noble, and rich. What more can a young woman do for her House?'

To his surprise, Father Teo rose and faced him, brushing away the last of the breadcrumbs. 'That does not become you, Count Leonardo. Giulietta Contarini was foolish, and her marriage should never have taken place. But do you not pity any woman wed to Count Dracone? Do you think he will use her as a husband should use his wife?'

The fierceness of the rebuke took Leonardo aback. He bowed his head. 'True, Father. I'm sorry.'

The little priest relaxed. 'I fear what may be happening behind the walls of the Palazzo Dracone. Giulietta, and those two genics – they'll be helpless in the Count's hands.'

Leonardo had not thought of the Contarinis' genics until now. They belonged to Giulietta, as her father's only heir. They must have gone with her to Count Dracone's. He remembered the last time he had heard them sing, at Count Contarini's festival: Serafina's pale loveliness, Hyacinth's almost indecent beauty and genius. Though Leonardo had not exchanged more than a few words with either of them, their fate suddenly pierced him more than Giulietta's. They would be dreadfully vulnerable to Count Dracone.

'Is there nothing anyone can do?' he asked.

Father Teo gave him a sideways look. 'They say you are to be the next Duke.'

Leonardo let out a short, humourless laugh. 'Then "they" know more than I do.' Suddenly he realized that Father Teo was not changing the subject. 'You think that as Duke . . .?'

'Who has more power over the laws of the city than the Duke? Especially a new Duke.' He spread his hands. 'New brooms sweep clean.'

'That would mean changing the whole status of genics . . .'

'Yes.' Father Teo sounded quite matter-of-fact. 'There is great suffering.'

Great suffering, Leonardo thought. Who knows that better than I do? Oh, Gabriel . . . Aloud he said, 'That comes strangely from you, Father, as a priest of Holy Church.'

That smile lit in Father Teo's eyes again. 'But I am dangerously close to heresy, everyone knows that. I even managed to shock that young woman – Serafina – and she made me look into myself.' Wholly serious again, he added, 'However the genics were created, Leonardo, they are here now and we must live with them. Would the Lord Christos turn away from pain?'

'I'm no theologian, Father.'

And no one would vote for me as Duke, he thought, if he overheard us talking now. Count Dandolo would withdraw his support. With a sudden inward grin, he added to himself, He would fall in a fit!

Something quickened inside him. He could see some purpose in being Duke, for this. Good new laws, defence for the defenceless, hope where now there was only despair. A gift that he could hold out to Gabriel, and say, This was what you suffered for.

'Church and State have always moved together,' he said, almost thinking aloud. 'Even as Duke, there would be a limit to what I could do. If Holy Church would not give her blessing . . .'

Father Teo sighed. 'I fear she would not. But is that the excuse to do nothing?'

Leonardo shrugged. 'You couldn't arrange a sign from heaven, Father?'

Count Dandolo, hearing that, would have castigated him for blasphemy. Father Teo merely said, 'Arrange, no. But I will pray for it.'

Though Leonardo had never thought of himself as a man of prayer, he felt oddly comforted. 'And keep silent, Father?' he asked. 'If Count Dandolo and his supporters knew of this . . .'

'Count Dandolo would take Saint Peter's place at the gates of Heaven,' said Father Teo. 'And the needle's eye would be very small indeed. I will say nothing.'

'And may we talk again, Father? Where can I find you?'

'I have a cell at I Frari.'

Leonardo bowed, preparing to take his leave, when another thought struck him. 'Are you looking for preferment, Father? Would you consider becoming chaplain to House Loredan? Count Dandolo is most concerned that I have no chaplain,' he added demurely.

Father Teo stared, and suddenly broke into delighted laughter. 'Count Loredan, I should be honoured. Though I fear I should not be Count Dandolo's first choice.'

Count Leonardo bit back what he wanted to say about Count Dandolo and his choice. A man who has just engaged a chaplain should guard his tongue. He smiled, and clapped Father Teo on his shoulder. 'Then come with me, Father, and let's discuss your new duties.'

His step was brisk and he felt his mind begin to clear as he led Father Teo along the quayside to where the boatmen waited for hire.

3

As days went by, Serafina's frustration grew. She was no closer to finding Hyacinth, nor learning the secrets of the Palazzo Dracone, although she had tried more than once. Always the constructs, or the old steward, were in the way, and she dared not draw attention to herself.

'My courses have still not come,' Giulietta informed her lazily one evening, as Serafina helped her into her nightgown. 'My lord Count has arranged for me to go to Corpus Domini, to be examined by the holy sisters.' She sank back among her silken pillows, and stretched luxuriously.

As Serafina was on her way back to her own bedchamber, a flash of scarlet caught her eye. Count Dracone had just crossed the passage ahead of her, unaware of her presence. He seemed to be alone.

Her breath coming faster, Serafina hurried after him, in time to see him mount a flight of stairs leading to part of the palazzo where she herself had never been. Scarcely aware of making a decision, she followed him.

Fear was rising in her throat. She did not know where the construct servants might be, but they had a habit of appearing suddenly. For now, Serafina could not hear their shambling tread; a fearful glance over her shoulder revealed the passage empty. Lifting her skirts to silence their rustling, she climbed the stair after Dracone.

At the top, another passage stretched in front of her. Serafina was just in time to see the Count open a door at the far end, enter, and close it after him.

Serafina followed. At first, when she reached the place where the Count had disappeared, she could see nothing but the panelling, until she managed to trace the shape of the door hidden in the wooden moulding.

There was no obvious handle, but as Serafina laid her finger tips lightly on the door, it swung inwards an inch or two. Startled, she moved back, ready to flee if she heard Dracone's footsteps returning.

All was silent. Cautiously, Serafina edged the door open a little further. Inside, a short passage led to an arched opening. Golden light spilled from it, briefly dazzling her. To her left was a short flight of steps leading upwards; the same golden light filtered down more faintly from somewhere above.

Rapidly, feeling that the hammering of her heart must give away her presence, Serafina entered, closed the door behind her and mounted the stair.

She emerged in a gallery, where once perhaps musicians might have played to entertain guests in the room below. Crouching, Serafina peered through one of the gaps in the gilded balustrade. In front of her eyes was a shifting of displaced light that blinded her until she grew used to it. She looked down and saw Hyacinth.

He was sitting up in the vast circular bed that filled the centre of the room. A silken sheet was clutched round him, as if he had just roused. His golden curls were dishevelled, and there was such a wild light in the violet eyes that at first Serafina thought he must be mad.

The windows of the room were covered with heavy silken drapes that shimmered in lamplight. The lamp itself, placed on a side table, was gold, a pair of satyr figures in such an obscene pose that Serafina had to avert her eyes. But the rest of the walls were mirrors, catching the gleam of gold, and the white and gold that was Hyacinth. Serafina thought she had never known a more evil place.

At first she could not see Dracone, until the sound of movement alerted her and she caught the scarlet flash of his coat in the mirror opposite. She realized he must be standing directly under her. Hyacinth was staring at him in fascinated terror, and as Dracone stepped forward he shrank away.

Dracone's silken tones said, 'Get out.'

Incredulous relief flooded over Hyacinth's face as he scrambled to obey and fled across the room, trailing the sheet, to pull back one of the mirrored panels and disappear behind it.

When the mirror had swung into place again and the room was empty, Dracone stepped forward. Serafina gazed down at his varnished black head, the flare of his scarlet coat below; if she had reached down she could have touched him.

Dracone raised his hands, palms upwards, and began to whisper. Serafina could not make out the words, though she did not think they were in any language she had heard before. She was drenched in icy terror. This was a more complex evil than the abuse of Hyacinth she had expected, and she did not know if her courage would sustain her to witness it.

Gradually, as Dracone's whispered chant went on, the golden light was changing, through vermilion and the scarlet of blood, until it settled into a thick, fuscous cinnabar. Serafina caught back a gasp of fear as she saw that the mirrors were no longer reflecting the room.

Instead they pulsed with colour, whorls of crimson and black, shot through with jagged flashes of flame, faster and faster until each one became a spinning vortex ready to suck down the room and everything in it. Sick and dizzy, Serafina tried to tear her eyes away, but she could not.

Just as she thought she must give herself away by screaming, the mirrors changed again. The vortices cleared. In their place Serafina could see long corridors of fire, edged with twisted pinnacles of rock. They stretched away into an unimaginable distance, like the spokes of a vast wheel with the room at its hub.

Down the corridors dark figures came pacing. Some were tall, attenuated beyond what could be human, others squat, with grotesquely long arms or necks twisted at the wrong angles. They were robed in shadow, their features hidden.

Serafina pressed her hands over her mouth as they drew closer. The surface of the mirrors rippled like water, allowing them through to invade the room. They clustered around Dracone until the room was packed with them.

Then another came, winged with dark flame, gliding down through curtained deeps of fire, and the lesser creatures gave back before it, bowing to it. 'Master . . .' Serafina heard Dracone's voice sighed out, a lover in the extreme of ecstasy. 'Asmodeus . . . Master.'

He fell to his knees before it, and the dark thing stooped over him and enfolded him with its wings. Serafina drew back from the balustrade and covered her face with her hands.

When she dared look up again, the light had changed back to gold. The mirrors innocuously reflected the disordered bed. The room below was empty, save for Dracone. As he turned, she saw his face, drowsy with satisfied lust, his eyelids drooping and his scarlet mouth curved in a sated smile.

If he had seen her then, she would have been helpless to flee or defend herself, but his look was all inward. He disappeared below the balcony; for a moment longer she could see his back view in the mirror opposite, and then heard the soft click of the outer door as he left.

For a long time afterwards Serafina stayed where she was, trying to stay her trembling and fighting the urge to vomit. Eventually she pulled herself to her feet and stumbled down the steps.

Every instinct was screaming at her to leave before

Dracone – or something nameless, worse – found her there, but she knew there was something she must do first. She turned back to the room, crossed it and pulled open the mirrored panel where Hyacinth had vanished.

She half expected the door to lead into one of those fiery corridors. Instead, she could see little; her own body was blocking the light from the room behind her. She heard a sudden intake of breath from someone more terrified than she was.

She said softly, 'Hyacinth?'

'Serafina?' His voice was a whisper that scarcely reached her where she stood by the door. 'Serafina, is it you?'

As he spoke, Serafina moved forward, letting in more light so that she could make out the room in front of her. It was bare, and tiny, with no window and no furnishing except for a rough bench across the far wall.

Hyacinth was crouching there, staring at her. Two tears spilled from his eyes and tracked gleaming down his face. He clutched the thin silken sheet closer as if it could be a shield.

Impatiently, more loudly than was safe, Serafina said, 'Of course it's me.'

He rose, eyes still fixed on her, and came towards her, reaching out a shaking hand. As his fingers closed on her wrist, he let out a little puff of breath. 'It is you. I've had dreams sometimes . . . I don't know what's real any more.'

Drawing her out with him, he closed the mirrored panel and sank down on the edge of the bed. He looked bewildered. 'Did Dracone bring you here?'

Serafina shook her head. Feeling stupid, she said, 'Has he hurt you?'

Hyacinth clapped a hand over his mouth, keeping

back hysterical laughter. The wonderful eyes blazed. When he had recovered a little control, he said, 'It's not what you think.'

Serafina stared. What was she to think? The silks and cushions of the bed, the mirrors . . . And everyone knew Count Dracone's tastes.

More steadily, as if he could read what was in her mind, Hyacinth went on, 'If it was only that, I think I could bear it. But he . . . Dracone . . . I think he can't . . .'

Serafina realized that what kept him stumbling over the words was as much embarrassment as fear. She saw what she had never fully understood in him before, a streak of innocence. The celibacy that his nature and his situation had imposed on him had never seemed to be a burden. Certainly, until he came here, he must have been quite inexperienced.

'What then?' she asked.

'He . . . does things . . . I can't say, Serafina, truly. Or sometimes Cesare, and Dracone watches . . .'

'That's vile.' Tentatively, not sure she wanted the answer, she said, 'Do you know what he does here when he's alone?'

Hyacinth shuddered. 'I don't want to know. Sometimes there are noises . . .' He pressed a hand to his lips again, took a gulp of air, and added, 'And there's no music, Serafina. He forbids me to sing.'

From anyone else, that last detail would have been ludicrous. From Hyacinth, it was the ultimate torment, the one thing above all others that he could not bear.

'I want to die,' he whispered. He gave her a swift, triangular smile. 'I tried to smash the mirrors. The glass would be sharp enough, don't you think? But they wouldn't break.'

'Oh, stop it, stop,' Serafina said, cold with horror. 'Hyacinth, you mustn't. I'll help you. I'll think of something.'

'There is no help.' His eyes were scornful. 'I'm a genic.'

'I'll do something. I'll tell Father Teo.'

'A priest? What would he care?'

'Father Teo would care that Dracone does this,' Serafina said determinedly. 'I'll find him, Hyacinth, as soon as I can get out. Only promise me – promise you won't harm yourself.'

Hyacinth flung himself down among the cushions and buried his face. His voice was muffled. 'No. I won't promise.'

Desperately, Serafina glanced back at the archway which led to the entrance. Already she had stayed too long, and every extra second increased the risk that Dracone would return and discover her.

'I can't stay,' she said. 'But I'll come back, I swear I will, when Dracone's out. And if I can't help, if it's the only thing I can do . . . Hyacinth, I'll find you a way, an easy way, something to drink, and stay with you until it's over. Only don't harm yourself until then.'

Still half buried among the cushions, he had begun to weep quietly. Serafina could do nothing but close the door on him and flee, trembling, to the part of the palazzo where she had the right to be.

4

The weather was too cold now for Alessandro to sit in the courtyard garden. Instead he lay on a sofa before

the fire, wrapped in the old velvet bedgown, and drowsed
the days away with Cat on his lap. Gianni never thought
to suggest now that he might be well enough to go to
the warehouse, and though he brought letters and
accounts home for him to read, Alessandro would wave
them away with a smile and: 'I'm sure you know best,
Gianni.'

Gianni did not know where he found the strength to
stay cheerful in the face of Alessandro's slow weakening.
In his room at night he turned to prayer, and yet he was
not sure what he prayed for. Everything he had been
taught told him that a genic was an abomination in the
eyes of the Lord, so what point in petitioning Him for
Alessandro's recovery?

He groped for words. 'Lord, You see the fall of a
sparrow . . .' Yet even the sparrow is God-created. In the
end Gianni could pray for nothing but the courage to
keep on.

One evening he brought supper, as he always did, to
a table by the fire, and tried to coax Alessandro to eat.

'You must,' he said anxiously, sitting by him on the
couch, ready to help him with the bowl of soup Lucetta
had prepared. 'Or you'll never get well.'

Alessandro looked up at him, his blue eyes wide, his
pale skin almost translucent. Softly he said, 'I am dying,
Gianni.'

'No!'

'Remember what I told you. I was made to be a child
. . . I was never meant to live so long.' His lids drooped,
as if his weariness was more than he could bear. 'I think
what happened – the arrest and trial, and that night in
the Ghetto – began something that should have begun

years ago.' He tried to smile. 'I should be thankful to have had so much.'

'Thankful . . .' Gianni felt rage rising inside him, a swelling anger that frightened him because he did not know how to handle it. All he knew was that he must not show it to Alessandro, and frighten him too.

'Only, it's hard . . .'Alessandro's voice quivered. 'Hard that it should come now, when I've something to live for.' He turned towards Gianni, and for the first time Gianni saw the depths of fear in his eyes. 'Gianni, I don't want to leave you.'

Gianni rested a hand on his shoulder. 'I'll do something,' he said. 'I'll find a physician . . .'

'Who would come for a genic? Besides, Gianni . . . this was meant to come. It's what I was made for. It won't hurt, or . . . or be offensive.' His mouth twisted wryly. 'A genic child dies beautifully.'

Gianni wondered if he was right. It would be kinder in the end, less terrifying, that this was no more than the result of Alessandro's genic heritage, instead of the darker thing he suspected, that a demon from hell had touched Alessandro in the garden, and was sucking away his strength into night without end.

There was no hope or reassurance that he could offer. Not for Alessandro the comfort of the confessional and the last rites that would carry him across the abyss and into the arms of God. Not for him the power of Christos to stand between him and the demon. Not for a genic. What is the God I believe in, Gianni wondered, if He will not look down on Sandro's pain, and mine, and show compassion?

And following that came the unimaginable: what if

Holy Church is wrong? What if God does care for the genics? If that was true, there must be a way to know it. And a way to show God's love to Alessandro, so that if he must die he would not go fearfully into the dark.

Between one breath and the next, he knew what he would do. He looked down at Alessandro; the little genic was already drifting away from consciousness. Gianni drew the bedgown closer around him.

'God is good,' he said, affirming his faith to himself, for Alessandro could not hear him any longer. 'God is good, and there is an answer.'

Early in the morning, while Alessandro was still sleeping, Gianni hired a boat and went, not without apprehension, to the Palazzo Dracone. One of the Count's beast-like constructs opened the door to his knock.

'I wish to speak with the Countess's genic,' he said. 'With her sewing woman.'

He did not even know the woman's name, but when she had come to the warehouse to buy silk she had seemed kind, and concerned for Alessandro. Gianni was sure that she would at least listen to his petition, even if she could not grant it.

The construct shambled off, leaving Gianni to wait in the entrance hall. He had never thought to stand here, at the heart of the evil, the place where Alessandro had forbidden him to go. Nervous, he began to inspect the peeling frescos until he realized what he was looking at, and, hot with embarrassment, studied his own boots until he heard a light footstep coming down the stair. He turned, and bowed with one hand on his breast.

'Messire Giovanni.' The genic woman stood at the

foot of the stairs, tall and composed, her silver-gold hair drawn back in a simple knot. Correctly, she dropped him a curtsey, reminding him that she was a genic, that he should not have bowed to her. Yet he did not feel that his respect was out of place. 'How may I help you?'

'Mistress . . .'

'My name is Serafina, sir.'

'Mistress Serafina, I have come to . . . to beg a favour. Sandro is dying.'

Concern leapt into her eyes, and he knew he had been right to come. 'Mistress,' he went on, 'everyone says that Count Dracone gave the holy relic of Christos to his lady, as a betrothal ring.'

'Yes.'

'Would she . . .' In his eagerness Gianni was afraid of stumbling over the words. 'Would she lend it to me, for Sandro? So that God might pity him and restore him? I swear to you, mistress, I would take such care of it . . . my life wouldn't be too much to pay . . .'

His voice trailed off as he saw Serafina frowning slightly. 'A miracle?' she asked. 'For a genic?'

'Yes, mistress,' Gianni said firmly.

He was aware of her cool gaze on him, hazel eyes appraising him with a kind of reserved sympathy. He was taking breath to renew his entreaties, when she said, 'I will ask. But, messire . . . will you do something for me in return? Not as a condition,' she added hastily, 'but for a need as great as Alessandro's?'

Gianni's nervousness returned. 'If I can, mistress.'

Serafina clasped her hands together, and he realized that she was not as calm as she had first appeared, that her surface serenity was only achieved by a conscious effort of the will.

'I may not leave this house,' she said, 'and I must send a message. Will you take it for me?'

Relief flooded over him that what she asked was so simple. 'Yes, of course.'

'I must speak with Father Teo, who was chaplain to House Contarini. He left when my lady married, and I don't know where he has gone. He has surely not left the city . . .' Her hands tightened, and Gianni caught a glimpse of a desperation as great as his own. 'Find him, messire, I beg you, and tell him . . . tell him that hideous things are done here.'

Her voice was beginning to shake. Gianni went to her and enveloped her hands in his own, reading the astonishment and hope in her eyes.

'Mistress, I will do this,' he promised. 'And anything else that can aid you.'

Serafina smiled, began to speak, and then broke off and turned swiftly to go back up the stairs.

Gianni watched her out of sight, heard a door open and close, and bowed his head over clasped hands as he waited for the result, and prayed that the new Countess would show mercy.

At last the light footsteps returned. Gianni watched her come, his heart throbbing uncomfortably, his breath uneven. 'Mistress . . .?'

Serafina had recovered her calm in the time she had been away. She opened her hand, to show the ring lying there. She smiled faintly. 'The Countess does not wear it; she says it is too heavy for her finger. And now she sleeps.'

Gianni stared at her. 'You have not asked her?'

'What point?' Serafina shrugged. 'She will sleep till noon; you can return it by then, can you not?'

'Yes, mistress . . .' Gianni felt shock crashing over him like sea water. 'But if she wakes and finds it gone . . . will she not beat you?'

'Beat me?' Serafina's voice had grown impatient. 'My lady would not see fit to exert herself so far. And if she does wake, we can spend an hour looking for it. Messire, do you want the ring or not?'

'Yes . . . oh, mistress, I thank you!'

Gianni held out his hand for the ring; before she gave it to him Serafina flicked up the lapis cover to expose the crystal below. 'I should wish to know—' she began, and broke off.

Gianni saw her face freeze into immobility. 'Mistress, what is it?'

'Look.'

She held out the ring. For the short time he had worn it, Gianni had become familiar with it, with the slender coil of dark hair set beneath the crystal. Now the crystal was a blank, reflecting the light of the hall. The hair was gone.

'Mistress!' Gianni whispered. 'Who would do this? Who would steal the hair of the Lord Christos?'

Serafina's mouth was set. 'You're asking the wrong question, messire. Try this one. Why would Count Dracone steal the hair of the Lord Christos? What could he possibly do with it?'

Twelve

I

The hall of the Great Council was a magnificent room, even now in the time of its decay. The gold leaf on the mouldings had peeled away, and the paintings which had covered walls and ceiling were little more than smudges, but nothing could spoil the noble proportions or the sheer scale of the place.

As Leonardo Loredan took his place in his carved wooden stall, he could not help imagining the room renewed, the gold leaf laid again, and the paintings – what could Gabriel not do here, given the chance! He let out a sigh. Gabriel was unlikely ever to come here, much less be allowed to paint.

'You sound anxious, Count.' That was Count Dandolo, lowering himself into the stall next to Leonardo with such rigidity that Leonardo was surprised not to hear him creak. 'Do you fear that Count Dracone may gain support?'

Leonardo contemplated saying, 'No, I'm pining for my genic lover,' just for the satisfaction of seeing Dandolo's face. But it would not be wise – most of all because it was in one sense the truth. 'I fear nothing from Dracone,' he replied shortly.

Dandolo's only response was a grunt, that could have meant belief or its opposite.

Most of the Councillors had already taken their places in the seats that lined the walls on three sides of the chamber. At the head of the great hall, on the dais, the Duke's chair was vacant, but his cap of office had been placed there in token of his authority.

In the chair beside the Ducal throne, the Procurator of the basilica was seated, wearing the black cap and deep purple robes of his office. He was fidgeting, twisting his hands nervously. Once or twice Leonardo felt his glance, and wondered why the Procurator had called this special Council, and what had happened to make him so worried.

When the last of the Councillors had drifted in from the ante-chamber, and taken their seats, the Procurator rose.

'My lords Councillors,' he said, 'I have called you here today for a special reason.' He hesitated, and Leonardo could have sworn that the man was shaking. 'A reason that may change the history of our city if not of the whole world.'

A voice a few places down from Leonardo muttered, 'What's the old fool babbling about?'

Leonardo could have echoed the question, except that a moment later the Procurator said, 'My lords, I request your attention for Count Dracone.'

The Count rose from his place – the place he occupied as proxy for House Contarini, Leonardo reminded himself – and bowed to the assembly.

'My lords Councillors, I must begin by announcing something that brings me great joy. My wife is with child.' He remained silent for one or two Councillors to call out congratulations, and for one or two bawdy comments that had Count Dandolo snorting in outrage.

'However,' Dracone went on, 'I would not waste the time of this whole Council for something that concerned House Dracone alone. Indeed, in this matter I am no more than the guardian of what is to come. The child is not mine.'

Inevitably, more ribald comments, but Count Dracone was unmoved. He was even smiling. 'You mistake, my lords,' he said. 'My wife Giulietta is yet a virgin.'

'A virgin with child!' Dandolo exclaimed.

Count Dracone inclined his head towards him, across the width of the hall. 'Indeed. Fortunate as I am to have the lovely Giulietta as my wife, I have forgone the delights of the marriage bed.'

Marriage, Leonardo thought, *is not what delights you.*

'I have placed my own desires at the service of something greater,' Dracone went on. 'I rejoice in this child, and yet the cause of rejoicing is not only mine, but yours also.' He paused again, for the Councillors to make what they could of that, and then continued, 'My wife's pregnancy has been confirmed by the holy sisters of Corpus Domini, but I ask you now to listen to my personal physician, who will explain the matter to you.'

He walked across the Council Chamber in a profound silence, and pulled open the door to the ante-chamber. Leonardo frowned as he saw the man who came in, trying to remember where he had seen him before. He was tall, broad-shouldered, with a thick bush of hair and good clothes that still looked grubby and ill-fitting.

'Dr Heinrich.' Count Dracone introduced him to the assembly. 'Doctor, will you tell these noble lords about the work we have achieved?'

As Dracone returned to his seat, Dr Heinrich strode into the hall and stood in a curious hunched posture, hands thrust into his breeches pockets, while he stared at the Councillors from beneath shaggy brows.

'I worked in the north,' he began abruptly, 'in the laboratories of the Empire, making genics. I came—'

He broke off as Count Dandolo surged to his feet from his seat beside Leonardo. 'Councillors,' he said, addressing the whole assembly, 'why do we sit here and listen to this man who has just confessed to the foulest blasphemy?'

A clamour of voices began to rise even before he had finished speaking, some echoing his question, others telling him to sit down and let them listen. Count Leonardo watched Heinrich, who stood with eyes raised, as if to ask the Heaven he did not believe in why he should be afflicted with such idiots.

The noise died as Count Dracone got to his feet again. He was smiling thinly. 'If Count Dandolo cares to listen, he will find the answer to his question.'

Count Dandolo grunted, looked as if he would repeat his protest, and then took his seat again. Dracone gestured to Heinrich to continue.

'All of you who trade in genics,' the doctor said, 'will know what my experience means. I tell you now so you can assure yourselves I know what I'm talking about. The matter before us is one in which I used my skills to get the Countess Contarini-Dracone with child.'

Leonardo heard a soft chuckle from somewhere a few places further down the hall, and a comment about the skills Heinrich might be referring to, but Dr Heinrich clearly did not hear.

'The techniques – yes, sir, what is it now? Can't it wait?'

He spoke, irritably, to a middle-aged Councillor, a

man with a narrow, hatchet face, who had risen to his
feet near the bottom of the hall. Leonardo suppressed a
sigh. Count Querini was capable of keeping them all
sitting here until night fell, while he clung fiercely to the
wrong end of the stick.

'Are you telling us that the Countess Contarini-
Dracone is pregnant with a genic?' he asked.

'Not at all.' Dr Heinrich looked as if the question
irritated him even more, and went on with a heavy kind
of patience, as if he was explaining something to a
retarded child. 'When you make a genic, you take human
tissue and analyse its genetic make-up. The qualities that
make the person what he is. You understand me?'

No reply from Count Querini.

'Then you replace the genes you want to change with
others that will give you those qualities you want in the
finished genic.'

Leonardo heard Count Dandolo mutter, 'Blasphemy!'
He tried to ignore the man, for he did not want to miss
anything that Dr Heinrich was telling them.

'You know,' the doctor went on, 'that Count Dracone
owns a ring, which held a relic of the Lord Christos – a
single hair. Now a hair, gentlemen, and especially the
root of a hair, is human tissue and can be manipulated
accordingly. In this case, I took the hair of Christos from
the ring and made a culture of the cells. I made no
changes in it. I implanted this culture in the womb of
Countess Contarini-Dracone, where it is now growing
until it comes to term. It will be a clone – clone,
gentlemen? – a perfect copy of the original owner of the
hair.'

From further down the Council chamber someone
said, rapt, 'Christos will live again!'

Uproar broke out. Heinrich did not try to make himself heard above it, but turned aside and spoke briefly to Count Dracone. Leonardo, watching the two men in tense silence, trying to ignore what Count Dandolo was yammering into his ear, saw Count Dracone nod slightly, and smile, and Heinrich turn abruptly and go out through the door that led to the antechamber.

Once he had gone, Dracone stood waiting, still with the slight smile on his face, until at last the clamour quietened. Then he spoke.

'My lords Councillors, do not imagine I am unaware of the great privilege it is for House Dracone to bring about the return of our Lord Christos. My Countess has the best of care the city can offer, and the services of the expert physician who has just spoken to you. If you as the voice of the city should choose to make some return to House Dracone, I should accept, but I do not ask for it, save to remind you that I stand here as a petitioner for the highest office you can award.' He bowed. 'Dr Heinrich and I will, of course, make ourselves available to discuss the matter with appropriate representatives, both from yourselves and from Holy Church.'

Smooth-tongued bastard, Leonardo thought.

As Count Dracone drew his speech to a close, more excited babbling broke out, quieter this time, as each man turned to discuss and exclaim with his neighbour. Not everybody, Leonardo thought, would be on Dracone's side. There would be those who simply refused to believe his claims. There would be others who believed, like Count Dandolo, yet saw the process as blasphemous. Others would believe and worship. And yet a fourth group, where Leonardo ruefully placed himself, would not know what to believe.

Still, he could not hide from himself that Count
Dracone had just taken a massive step towards the
Dukedom. If his claim was true, or if enough people
could be made to believe it, he could dominate the city
and beyond.

Out of the babble, the Procurator rose and came
forward to face Dracone at the edge of the dais. 'I have
made a report to the Patriarch,' he said. He still looked
as if the whole affair terrified him. 'You will hear from
my office in due course.'

Dracone bowed an assent, and the Procurator left.
Dracone himself stood for a moment longer, looking
round the Council Chamber with evident satisfaction.
Leonardo thought the serpent eyes rested on him in
particular, but he did not make the mistake of rising
to the challenge, if challenge it was. He would only
make a fool of himself, to speak without thought or
knowledge. Dracone seemed to pause for a moment,
then nodded slightly to him and followed the Procurator
out.

The Council was breaking up. Little knots of men
gathered and left in excited groups, talking loudly. Leonardo would have preferred to slip away, and think about
this in private, or discuss it with Father Teo, but before
he could escape Count Dandolo was hauling on his arm,
leading him over to Francesco Foscari, Querini, and
others of the anti-Dracone faction.

'We must put a stop to this!' Dandolo announced
loudly.

'What do you mean?' Francesco Foscari was looking
troubled. 'If the child is truly the Lord Christos come
again . . .'

'The child will be a genic,' Querini snapped. Leonardo

sighed; obviously Heinrich's explanation had gone into one of Querini's large ears and out of the other.

'No, the doctor told us . . .' Francesco was obviously prepared to launch into another, perhaps garbled, certainly useless explanation, but Querini interrupted. 'No sin in putting to death a genic.'

'And how would you go about it?' Leonardo asked silkily. 'Crucifixion?'

'Count Leonardo, you would do well to guard your tongue,' Dandolo said. 'Whatever the upshot of this vile experiment, Dracone will be able to manipulate it. Think of the power he will claim! To be the father—'

'Guardian,' Leonardo corrected him.

'Guardian, then. The guardian of Christos reborn! He has just asked for the Dukedom, and most of the Council will be prepared to hand it to him.'

Leonardo was still not sure, and these men were not giving him time to think. More than anything, he wanted to get away, to consult Father Teo, and to decide what his own attitude should be. He would not be pushed into anything, not by Dandolo, and certainly not by Querini, who had begun to speak again.

'What of his wife's virtue?' he asked. 'Has she no lovers? Had she none before marriage? No one who would claim the brat as his?'

For some reason, his words lit a spark of fury in Leonardo. He had never loved Giulietta Contarini, but for all her silliness the girl had never strayed. She had known her own value too well.

'I will not become Duke on the foundation of a lie,' he said.

Querini gave him a scathing glance. 'At this rate,' he said, 'you will never become Duke at all.'

2

Gianni banged on the door of the Palazzo Loredan, and stepped into the entrance hall when the elderly servant pulled the door open.

'Count Loredan is in Council,' the man said.

'My business is with his chaplain, Father Teo,' said Gianni. 'Is he at home?'

The old man gave him a perfunctory bow, and disappeared up the stairs. Gianni waited. He had left Alessandro sleeping, and he was uneasy at any delay that might mean he would wake and find himself alone.

Pacing restlessly, he missed the moment when Father Teo appeared, and started as a quiet voice spoke behind him. 'You asked for me, my son?'

Gianni turned. A small man, his dark hair silvering, stood at the foot of the stairs. He held himself erect in a plain black cassock. Gianni took a step forward and bowed, the respect arising naturally from the other's air of authority.

'Father, my name is Gianni. I have a message for you, from Serafina who was genic to the Countess Contarini.'

Father Teo was suddenly alert. He crossed the hall to Gianni and laid a hand on his arm. 'You have seen her? Is she well? And Lady Giulietta? And Hyacinth?'

The spate of questions unnerved Gianni for a moment. He said, 'I only saw Serafina, Father. She seemed well, but she was greatly troubled. She says that hideous things are done in the Palazzo Dracone, and she begs to speak with you.'

'Hideous things . . .' Father Teo sighed. 'I don't doubt it. But what to do . . .?'

His eyes grew unfocused, meditative, as if he was alone. His lips moved silently, as if he prayed. When Gianni thought he might listen again, he said anxiously, 'Father, that's not all. The ring, the holy relic that Count Dracone gave to his lady as a betrothal ring . . . Father, the hair is gone.'

'Gone? Are you sure?'

'I saw the ring myself, Father. The crystal compartment is empty. Serafina thinks that the Count has stolen the hair of Christos. Father, why should he do that? What would it profit him?'

Father Teo shook his head, and the silence stretched out again. Gianni felt it was wrong to break it, but he was desperate to be gone, back to his vigil over Alessandro.

When Father Teo spoke again, it was the last thing Gianni had expected. 'Forgive me, my son, but there is great trouble in your face. Is there anything you wish to tell me?'

Gianni's instincts told him to keep silence. For the last few weeks he had not dared to go to confession at the Innocenti, for it would have meant telling Father Battista about his love for Alessandro. And Father Battista, he knew, would have set him a harsh penance, and commanded him to dismiss the genic from his house.

Yet Father Battista's eyes glittered with the fires of hell that he saw licking around the sinful. They had never looked at him with the sympathy in Father Teo's eyes. Father Battista had never spoken to him as Father Teo did, either, as if he was a man with a man's problems and responsibilities, instead of a child to be lessoned.

He drew a long breath. 'Father, it's true I'm troubled. Do you know who I am, Father – do you know about me and Messire Alessandro?'

At the mention of Alessandro's name Father Teo's gaze grew sharper, and he searched Gianni's face earnestly. 'I have heard the story,' he said. 'You were his servant, and when he was denounced as a genic and stripped of his wealth, you took over his business and made him your bondman.' His lips thinned. 'There are those who say you denounced him. Is there guilt on your conscience, my son?'

Gianni barely stopped himself from gaping. He had never imagined for a second that such a story could be told of him. He wanted to laugh, or weep. Instead, he said, 'It was Count Dracone who denounced him. He wanted his wealth, and . . . he wanted Alessandro too.' For all his recent experience, he felt himself flushing. 'He is a vile man. What I did was to save Sandro from him. It was the only way.'

Father Teo nodded gravely; to Gianni's relief he did not question what he had just heard. 'And now?' he asked.

'Now Sandro is dying.' Briefly, bleakly, he described the thing he had seen in the garden, and how its visitation was followed by Alessandro's gradual weakening. 'He has had so little,' he ended, his words coming thick through gathering tears. 'I have given him so little. We have had such a short time. And he's afraid, Father, afraid of the dark. I'd die for him, Father, if I could, and it wouldn't be so hard for me. But there's nothing afterwards for him, Father, not for a genic.'

Grief overcame him at last and he bent his head into his hands and fought back the tears. After a moment he groped his way to the wall and sat on the bench there. He heard Father Teo's steps retreating, without surprise.

He could not blame a priest of Holy Church for not wishing to be in company with a man who could love a genic and grieve for him.

He was mastering his grief again – for he must seem cheerful for Alessandro – when he heard Father Teo coming back. Gianni looked up. The little priest stood before him; in his hands he held a Mass book and a folded silken stole. He said, 'Come.'

'To Count Dracone's, Father? I can't go there.'

'No. To your house.' As he spoke, Gianni realized that anger was scouring through him like an icy wind. 'Gianni, do you love Alessandro?'

'Yes, Father.'

'And do you dare to think that God, who is love incarnate, loves him less than you?'

Gianni was bewildered. 'Holy Church teaches us, Father—'

'Then Holy Church teaches blasphemy. Have you a boat?'

'Yes, Father, but—'

Father Teo swept out onto the loggia where the boatman Gianni had told to wait was leaning against the mooring post and whistling. Neatly the priest stepped aboard and waited for Gianni to follow more slowly.

'Father,' Gianni said, 'you're needed at Count Dracone's, and it's taken me days to find you.'

Father Teo was staring ahead at the surging water as the boatman began steering out into the canal. 'Vile things have been done in the Palazzo Dracone since the Count came there. I will do what I may to help Serafina, but I doubt the Count would allow me to cross his threshold without question. I must give the matter some

thought. But your matter – ' he swung round and looked
straight at Gianni – 'needs no more thought at all.'

As Gianni opened the front door of the house he heard
Alessandro calling his name. Hastily he went in to him
and found him struggling to sit up among the cushions
of the couch, with Cat protesting as she leapt to the
floor.

Gianni went to him and put a hand on his shoulder.
'What is it, Sandro?'

The little genic put a hand to his head, thrusting back
dishevelled hair. 'It's nothing, Gianni. Only dreams. I
thought—'

Dreams, thought Gianni, wondering if Dracone's dark
emissary could even invade Alessandro's sleep. He turned
back to face Father Teo, who was standing in the
doorway. 'Father, this is Sandro. What would you have
us do?'

He felt Alessandro stiffen as he saw the priest.

'Sandro, it's all right,' Gianni said. 'This is Father
Teo; I told you about him.'

Lucetta had appeared in the passage, alerted by the
sound of voices, and Father Teo spoke to her. 'Mistress,
I need a bowl of water and a clean linen cloth, a cup of
wine and some bread.'

When Lucetta had finished gaping, and disappeared
back to the kitchen, Father Teo said, 'Alessandro, do you
believe in God?'

Alessandro's eyes were fixed on the priest, and there
was uncertainty in his voice as he said, 'Yes, Father, in
your God.'

'But not a God for genics?' A slight shake of the head.

Father Teo went on, 'And what do you believe of Him? That He is good? That He loves us?'

Alessandro smiled faintly. 'He must love Gianni, surely. For the rest, how can I tell? I am a genic.'

'Set apart from God's love?'

'It must be so, Father. For the genics were created outside God's law. In defiance of God, so I have heard.'

Gianni listened raptly. In the answers to Father Teo's imperative questions, he saw the capable merchant reappear, the man Sandro had once been, before Dracone's darkness struck him down.

'And if I told you,' Father Teo went on, 'that nothing is created outside God's law, and nothing created is outside his love? What would that mean to you?'

'It would change everything,' Alessandro whispered. 'It would change the world.'

Lucetta came into the room, carrying a tray with the things Father Teo had asked for. Father Teo took it from her, and when she would have dropped a curtsey and left, he asked her to stay.

Then he spread the linen cloth on the small table beside the couch, set the water there, and blessed it. 'Alessandro,' he said, 'do you believe and trust in God the Father Almighty, creator of heaven and earth?'

Alessandro darted a glance, uncomprehending, at Gianni. 'Yes, Father.'

'Do you believe . . .'

As Father Teo continued, and Gianni finally grasped what was happening, he almost protested, and bit the words back, but he could not help marvelling. That a priest of Holy Church should baptize a genic! It had surely never happened before. He could scarcely believe that it was happening now.

And then he had to make his own responses, stumbling over the words out of sheer wonder, as Father Teo drew him and Lucetta into the ceremony, to be Alessandro's sponsors in the new world he entered as a true child.

With the water he had blessed, Father Teo traced the sign of the cross on Alessandro's forehead. 'Alessandro, I baptize you in the name of the Father, and of the Son, and of the Holy Spirit.'

Alessandro was white as chalk, but his eyes were brilliant.

Setting the water aside, Father Teo said, 'Have you any sin on your soul, my son? If so, confess it now and be done with it.'

His voice shaking, Alessandro said, 'I pretended to be human, Father.'

'And do you repent?'

'Of the deceit, Father, and yet . . .' Out of the shining, he looked briefly troubled. 'I did not know what else to do.'

Father Teo made the sign of the cross once more, and spoke the words of absolution. Then, under Gianni's astonished gaze, he consecrated the bread and the wine, and shared the Sacrament of Christos's body and blood among the four of them.

Not the Extreme Unction for Sandro; not yet.

When it was over, Father Teo took Alessandro's hands within his own. 'The world changed, my son?' he asked.

'Immeasurably.' The word was whispered, exalted. Gianni felt tears threaten him again as he looked at Sandro's face.

'I must go,' Father Teo said. 'I have other duties, but I will come back. Send for me at any hour,' he added to Gianni.

Gianni nodded. Alessandro said, his voice growing stronger, 'Father, you will be with me when I die?'

'I promise you, my son. And I promise you this – it will be no more than stepping into the arms of the Lord Christos.'

He took his leave. For a short time Gianni had felt that he stood within a wall built by the power of Christos to shut out all things of the dark. Now the troubles of the world began to edge their way back into his mind.

'Father,' he said, as he escorted the priest to the door, 'none of us will speak of this.'

Father Teo shook his head. 'I cannot hide it. No – I will not. I must go as soon as may be to the Patriarch, and make my own confession.'

'What will the Patriarch do, Father?' Gianni asked anxiously.

'I don't know.' Father Teo let out a sigh. 'Truly, Gianni, I don't know.'

When Father Teo had gone, Alessandro fell into a peaceful sleep on the couch in front of the fire. Gianni did not want to disturb him, so he brought a blanket to cover him, and sat in a chair close by to keep vigil. Shortly he, too, slept.

He woke with a jerk to find the fire burnt to grey ashes, and dawn light suffusing the room. Alessandro lay still. The scraping of Gianni's chair as he got to his feet roused Cat, who had made a nest for herself among the folds of Alessandro's blankets. She sprang down and scraped at the door, demanding to be let out.

Gianni blundered across the room and released her into the passage. When he turned, he saw a pale ray of

sunlight angling through the shutters and falling on
Alessandro's face. Alessandro's lashes fluttered and he
opened his eyes, to fix Gianni with a blue, bewildered
gaze, in the light of a morning he had never expected to
see.

3

Since Gianni's visit, Serafina had been more troubled
than ever. She felt she could trust the boy to take her
message to Father Teo, but she had little hope that Father
Teo would be able to help her. Count Dracone would
surely never allow him to enter the palazzo.

Besides, there was the matter of the ring. Serafina
found herself picking it up, when Giulietta was not
paying attention, and looking at the empty compartment.
She could not pretend that the disappearance of the hair
meant nothing. She knew that Dracone and Heinrich had
some plan for the ring; this must be part of it. But
however many times she flicked up the lapis cover and
stared down at the unresponsive crystal, she could not
imagine what the plan might be.

A few days later, in the evening, when Giulietta had
gone down to dine with Count Dracone, and Serafina
was tidying away her work in the sitting room, one of the
constructs announced Caterina Dandolo.

Hastily Serafina said, 'You must not disturb my lord
Count at his meal. Send Lady Caterina up here.'

The construct withdrew, and a few moments later
Caterina whisked into the room and closed the door
behind her. Serafina could not help staring at her. She
was white, her eyes brilliant, and her breath came fast.

'Serafina!' she said. 'I'm so glad – I hoped I could speak to you alone, without Giulietta. I must tell you—' She broke off, a hand pressed to her lips.

'Sit down,' said Serafina. 'What's the matter? Are you in trouble with your father?'

Caterina's eyes flashed scornfully. 'Papa! I don't care what Papa does, not any more. No, this is . . .' She took the chair Serafina indicated, and leant forward earnestly. 'Serafina, Papa came back from Council in such a rage! He says that Count Dracone has used the hair from the ring to . . . to get Giulietta with child. And the child will be Christos reborn!'

'What?' Serafina could not make sense of that.

'Oh, don't ask me how it's done. But Dr Heinrich explained it to the Council, Papa says. Once Dr Heinrich used to make genics, and the methods are the same. Giulietta will bear another Christos child! Papa says, Count Dracone told the Council she is still a virgin. He has never known her as his wife.'

Serafina sat opposite her friend, and began winding embroidery silk from the skein to an ivory holder. 'Your father told you that?'

Caterina giggled. 'He was so angry, he forgot what is fit for the ears of young ladies! Is it true, do you think?'

'I think it is. Not out of piety, though, not Dracone. I suspect he can't – not with his wife, not with anyone else,' she added, remembering what Hyacinth had told her. 'And that's not fit for the ears of young ladies either.'

Caterina had gone pink. 'Is Giulietta very unhappy?'

'No. She is . . . changed, from before her marriage. Slower, sleepier . . . I suspect the Count drugs her, though I've no proof.'

'Poor Giulietta!' Caterina twisted her hands. 'I never

really liked her, she was so silly, but I wouldn't want any harm to come to her. Serafina, does she know what her baby will be?'

'I'm sure she doesn't.' Serafina neatly finished her ball of silk, and began on another. Still astonished by Caterina's news, she considered the lesser problem. Giulietta spent much of her time now contemplating her physical sensations, and speaking complacently of an heir for House Dracone. She had never given any sign of suspecting that the child within her would be something immeasurably greater. 'Why has Dracone done this?' she asked.

'So he can be Duke! He thinks the Council will elect him because of the holy thing in his household, or because of the power the child will give him. Papa is so angry, Serafina. He is supporting Leonardo Loredan to be the next Duke.'

'He doesn't want to be Duke himself?' Serafina was astonished, knowing Count Dandolo's self-importance.

Bright spots of colour grew in Caterina's cheeks. 'He dares not.'

'Dares not? Why?'

'My mother and two of my sisters drowned in the Contarini wreck. He survived.'

Her tone was condemnation; Serafina felt puzzled. 'Did he not save your life? Could he have done more?'

'He did not! Serafina, I never saw what happened to Agate and Pia. But I saw my mother. She begged Papa to help her, and he would not. He struck her, and left her there, as the boat was going down. He saved himself.' She paused, and added, 'Serafina, I have spoken to no one of this. You will not – not even to Giulietta?'

'Of course not.'

'There's something else . . . I have told no one, because

I thought no one would believe me. Serafina, I was saved by a sea-woman!'

'What?'

'In the wreck. I cannot swim, Serafina – it is not proper for young ladies to learn.' Briefly the tight-lipped look reappeared. 'I got a piece of the broken rail, and I tried to hold on to it and get myself to the quayside, but it wasn't enough to keep me up, and my skirts were heavy. I was so tired ... And then there was someone beside me in the water. She had white skin and eyes like a fish, and her hair was green, Serafina! And her hands were webbed. She pushed me as far as a boat that was picking up some other swimmers, and then she dived and disappeared. No one else saw her, I think.'

Serafina listened wonderingly to the story. It never occurred to her to doubt that Caterina thought she was telling the truth. But in the fear and exhaustion of trying to save herself, she might have imagined it. And yet she had lived while her sisters drowned.

'How strange ...' she said. 'Have you told your father?'

'Him least of all!' Caterina said scornfully. 'He did not care what happened to me. He did not even ask!' She pressed a hand against her lips as if she would begin to weep, and then steadied herself. 'And now he dares not claim the Dukedom, in case anyone saw him, and would expose him for the hypocrite he is.' Anger driving out her tears, she added, 'Truly, if he dared, I would do it myself!'

She paused, folding her hands and breathing deeply as if she was consciously calming herself. When she spoke again, her voice was steady. 'Serafina, Count Dracone must not be Duke, and he must not have power over this child. What can we do?'

'I don't know. We're prisoners here in the palazzo, Giulietta and I. It's easy enough for Dracone to keep her here, because it's still the time of mourning for the Count and Paolo, and because of her pregnancy. And of course I must stay with her. The other day, I said I had to go and buy embroidery needles, but the Count made me give the order to his steward. There's no one I can tell about what happens here.'

'You can tell me,' said Caterina.

Serafina took a breath. She wanted nothing more than to pour out the horror she had witnessed in the mirrored room, to give up the burden of being the only one who knew the truth about Dracone. But Caterina was not the one to share that burden with her.

'Giulietta you know about, now,' Serafina said slowly. 'There's Hyacinth, too. Dracone . . . hurts him. We need to get away, all of us, but I don't know how to manage it.'

Caterina frowned. 'You and Hyacinth both belong to Giulietta now. What would happen if you told her?'

'About Hyacinth, or about her baby?'

'Either. Both.'

'I don't think she would care about Hyacinth. She never did. As for the baby . . .' Serafina let her imagination run free. Giulietta would either be enraptured by the spiritual role the Count had cast her in, or dive straight into screaming hysterics. Neither would be helpful. 'No, Caterina. Giulietta is just as much the Count's victim as Hyacinth. Even if she wanted to, she couldn't help.'

'Then we must have help from someone else. I shall ask Francesco Foscari.'

'Francesco Foscari? Why would he help us?'

Caterina gave her a sparkling smile. 'Of course, you don't know, shut up here like this! Francesco Foscari is Count Foscari now, since the Contarini wreck. And the first thing he did was to ask Papa for Maria to be his wife, even though she has no seal of fertility. Papa was angry, but he had to consent, because Maria refused to take vows at Corpus Domini, and Papa – well, Maria will be Countess Foscari, after all!'

'And you will not.' Serafina could not help but return her friend's smile.

'Even better! For I like Francesco, Serafina, very much, but I do not want to marry him, especially when I know that he never looks at a woman, except for my sister.' She clasped her hands and leant forward again. 'Well, Serafina, they must wait until a little time has passed for mourning, and until the Palazzo Foscari has been made ready. Then they will marry as soon as may be. And Serafina – so exciting! Maria is having her portrait painted by Count Loredan's genic!'

'Your father surely didn't allow that?' Serafina asked.

'Papa doesn't know!' Caterina gave a little gurgling laugh. 'Gabriel is staying with Dr Foscari, so I go there with Maria to chaperone her, and Gabriel paints. The portrait will be Dr Foscari's wedding gift to Francesco – he's Francesco's uncle, you know – and so it's all a deathly secret. And then . . .' She grew serious again. 'When Maria and Francesco are married, I shall go to live with them at the Palazzo Foscari. Serafina, I think we must wait until then – when Maria and I are free of Papa, and can claim the help of House Foscari.'

Serafina could not suppress a faintly acid smile. 'And

will Count Foscari not object if his household is enlarged
by two genics and the woman who is to bear the Christos
child?'

'Francesco is a good man.'

Serafina nodded. 'I believe it. I can wait,' she said.
'And Giulietta will be safe as long as she is carrying the
child. It's Hyacinth . . .' She shivered as she thought once
again of that room of mirrors, and Hyacinth's doomed
beauty. 'I'm not sure how long Hyacinth can bear it.
Besides,' she added as a new thought struck her, 'the old
Duke fell into a seizure at the funeral. If he should die
soon, before your sister is married, what would stand in
Dracone's way then?'

She put away the finished balls of thread in the
workbox, and began smoothing the crumpled silk that
would become an embroidered nightgown for Giulietta's
lying-in. Caterina watched her thoughtfully, winding a
tendril of hair around one finger, but she had no answer
to the question. Serafina came to a decision.

'Caterina,' she said, 'I'm going to tell you something
now that no one else knows. Be very careful before you
tell anyone else, because if this came to the ears of Count
Dracone, Hyacinth and I would be in great danger.'

She had Caterina's attention now, her friend's irre-
pressible high spirits quenched into a deep seriousness.

'I promise, Serafina.'

'I believe that Count Dracone caused the Contarini
wreck.'

Silence from Caterina, her eyes wide, her hands painfully clasped.

'Just before it happened, Dracone asked Count Contarini for Giulietta's hand in marriage, and the Count
refused. Then on the day before the birthday festival,

somebody sent Giulietta a box of sweetmeats, and she was very ill. She couldn't go to the party, and so she was never in danger when the boat sank – she wasn't there.'

'Go on.'

Serafina felt a tightness in her throat. She had to restrain herself from crushing the folds of silk that lay in her lap. What she had just said was no more than speculation. What she was going to say could kill her. 'When the boat went down, I helped Hyacinth to shore. We saw Paolo Contarini struggling towards the quayside. Then another swimmer came. Paolo thought he would help. Instead, he pulled him under and drowned him.'

'Serafina—'

'The other swimmer was Cesare, Count Dracone's pilot.'

Caterina sat looking at her, her lips parted, her face white. Another woman, Serafina couldn't help thinking, might have screamed or fainted.

'I didn't know,' she went on. 'Not until Giulietta was married to the Count.' Her hands clenched. 'If only I'd known before, I could have stopped the marriage. But I didn't know who the man was until I saw him in Dracone's service.'

'Serafina, you're sure?'

'Yes. I've had long enough to think about it. Caterina, I believe that the Count wanted Giulietta, and so he sent her the sweetmeats to make sure she would not be on that boat. Then he ordered Cesare to wreck it. Count Contarini hired extra boatmen for the day, it would have been easy enough for Cesare to be on board, and there might have been others, too. Cesare must have made sure that Count Contarini and Paolo died, so that Giulietta would have no one but her mother to protect her, and so that she would be the heiress to House Contarini and its wealth.'

Caterina reached out and pressed Serafina's hands between her own. Serafina was surprised at how comforting she found the warm clasp. 'Serafina, what can we do?'

'I don't know,' Serafina said. 'All of this rests on what Hyacinth and I saw, when Cesare murdered Paolo. The word of two genics. No court would admit that as evidence, and no one would ask questions if Hyacinth and I vanished.'

'Yet we must make it known!' Caterina released Serafina's hands, sprang to her feet and began pacing up and down the apartment, her silks rustling as she moved. 'Who would vote for Dracone to be Duke, if they knew what he has done?'

'But no one will believe us,' said Serafina.

'I know who will,' Caterina said determinedly. 'Father Teo is chaplain to House Loredan now. He will believe you, and so will Count Leonardo.'

Serafina knew a minute's panic, not knowing whether she could trust Count Leonardo to guard her secret until she and Hyacinth were safe. He was a devastatingly compelling man, but what would he be prepared to do to seize the Dukedom? Would the fate of two genics matter to him in the slightest?

Then she realized that however unreliable she might find Count Leonardo, she could trust Father Teo. She laid aside the folded silk and closed the lid of the workbox.

'Very well,' she said. 'Tell Father Teo. And let him use the story as he will.'

4

Count Leonardo Loredan attended early Mass in the basilica, and when the service was over, began to walk away quickly across the square. He pretended not to hear Count Querini, who would have buttonholed him for an hour of warming over Dracone's stale iniquities, but he could not ignore the hand that fell heavily on his shoulder. He turned to see Count Dandolo.

'How may I serve you, Count?' he asked, suppressing a sigh.

'It's more a question of how I can serve you,' Count Dandolo said.

Still with a hand on Leonardo's shoulder, he propelled him across the square to the pavement café beneath the portico of the Judiciary. A waiter hurried up; Dandolo ordered hot rolls and chocolate, but Leonardo wanted nothing. He had better ways of spending his time than sharing breakfast with Count Dandolo.

'I'm busy . . .' he began.

'I have been busy, about your affairs,' the Count interrupted, with that portentous manner that always irritated Leonardo. 'If you are still ambitious for the Dukedom.'

His gaze was heavy with unspoken criticism. Leonardo shrugged uneasily. 'Very well, then. What is it?'

'This story of the Christos child . . .' Count Dandolo began. 'Dracone will gain much support, if men believe him. So we must make sure they do not believe him. We must smear his name.'

'And how do you propose to do that?'

The waiter reappeared at that moment; Leonardo had

to wait, shifting impatiently, while Dandolo poured himself a cup of chocolate, sweetened it to his liking, and
spread a spiced roll with butter and conserve. He did not
speak again until he had swallowed the first mouthful.

'I sent a servant to find Dracone's pilot – Cesare, they
call him – take him to a tavern and get him drunk.'

In spite of himself, Leonardo began to feel interested.
Leaning forward, he asked, 'Did it work?'

Dandolo smiled complacently and took a sip of chocolate. 'Oh, yes, it worked. Cesare gave my man some very
interesting information.' He sipped again. 'Dracone's
origins are in the south. When Cesare first met him he
was involved in a scandal with a renegade priest and
several young men of noble families. There were rumours
of necromancy, and licentious behaviour I won't soil my
lips with.

'Dracone hired Cesare to steal a flyer and take him
north, to the Empire. There he fell in with the Imperial
merchants, and came here as their agent. Cesare told my
man that Dracone practises evil rites in his palazzo. He
has sold his soul for wealth and power.' Dandolo patted
his lips with a napkin. 'And this is the man who presumes
to foist a new Christos on the city.'

'But all this is no more than rumour,' Leonardo
objected. 'And God knows, there are rumours enough
about Dracone already. Most people don't believe them,
so why should they believe this? Do you think Cesare
would repeat it, sober, and give you proof?'

Count Dandolo swallowed the last mouthful of his
roll, and took another. 'Don't be a fool,' he said. 'They
don't need to believe. It's enough to sow doubt.'

Leonardo pushed back his chair and stood up. 'And

when Dracone points to us, and accuses us of lying? Of deliberately besmirching him, to win the election? What answer could we make?'

Dandolo snorted. 'Is it not enough that he commits vile blasphemies, that he has corrupted—'

'Forgive me, Count,' Leonardo said, cutting into his babbling, 'but I want no part of this.'

He walked away into the square, ignoring Dandolo's protests behind him. Head down, he plunged into the alleys that would lead him back to the Palazzo Loredan, almost running, as if he could outpace the grubby reality of his claim to the Dukedom.

Near the Merchants' Bridge, he once more felt a hand on his shoulder and spun round, startled, to find himself facing a man he had never seen before. A man in vigorous middle age, with black hair combed straight back from a high forehead, and a small tuft of black beard. He wore a merchant's respectable broadcloth.

'Count Leonardo?' he said.

Leonardo bowed stiffly. 'You have the advantage of me, messire.'

'My name is Anhalt, my lord Count. I am a lawyer.'

'Not of this city, messire?' Though the man was more fluent than Dr Heinrich, Leonardo caught the accents of the north, and guessed he was Heinrich's countryman.

'No, my lord Count. I have the honour to serve the merchants of the Imperial Hostel.' He gestured towards the building itself, a few yards further on. 'Would it please you to join me for a glass of wine?'

Leonardo's first instinct was to refuse. He had never set foot inside the Imperial Hostel, and he felt no curiosity about what went on there. It was Dracone's territory, and the men there were likely to be Dracone's friends. He was not impressed by Anhalt's genial manner, or 'My lord Count' at every breath.

'I hear that you have offered yourself for election as Duke,' Anhalt went on, when Leonardo did not reply. 'We might talk profitably for a while.'

'Profitable to whom?' Leonardo asked.

'To both of us, my lord Count.' He gestured again, invitingly. 'Shall we go?'

Still doubtful, Leonardo allowed Anhalt to cup a hand under his elbow and propel him along the street to the doors of the Imperial Hostel.

The entrance hall led into a spacious courtyard, sunny and pleasant, where a fountain played and roses climbed up the pillars that supported the arcades. Pigeons strutted and pecked among the stones. A faint thread of music came from somewhere above.

Anhalt snapped his fingers at a servant and conducted Leonardo to a bench in the sun. Presently the servant brought wine, pale and flowery, in green-stemmed glasses. Anhalt sipped, and his black eyes twinkled at Leonardo over the rim of the glass.

'Confess it, Count,' he said. 'You think I'm about to bribe you.'

'I'd be a fool if I did,' Leonardo retorted. 'What have I that you might want?'

Anhalt chuckled. 'Not what you have now, Count, but what you might have in the future.'

Leonardo swallowed the cool, fragrant wine. No point in stupidly pretending he did not understand what the fellow was driving at. 'The Dukedom?'

'Indeed.'

'Then you know more than I do, messire.'

'I fancy I have my finger on the pulse of the city,' Anhalt said complacently. 'If I were a betting man, I'd lay money on you, my lord, the head of a noble and ancient House, in preference to Dracone, who – whatever his claims may be – is no more than a stranger, after all.'

Flattery, thought Leonardo, and more persuasive for the brisk and business-like manner in which Anhalt delivered it. He would not have been surprised to learn that the lawyer had held a similar conversation with Count Dracone, and found reason enough to prophesy his success, if it would serve him.

'I might imagine, messire, that you're hedging your bets,' he said. 'What do you want from me?'

'The Imperial merchants – ' Anhalt waved a hand at the peaceful courtyard – 'prosper well here. It is in our interests that they continue to prosper.'

'Whose interests exactly?'

'The merchants themselves. Their suppliers in the Empire. My own, I confess.' Anhalt coughed. 'Perhaps yours, too, my lord Count. Though we have no vote in Council, our support would do you no harm.'

He paused, inquiringly, as if he expected a response from Leonardo, but when the count said nothing he went on, 'Count Dracone is a forward looking man. He understands that your Church cannot go on for ever ignoring the science and technology of the Empire. Or if it does, then men will not obey it for ever. We must look forward, not be tied to a time that has already gone by.'

A prepared speech, Leonardo reflected, if he had ever heard one, smooth and orotund. He murmured, 'Then if Count Dracone already understands this, why do you not support him?'

Anhalt smiled, and gestured for the hovering servant

to refill their glasses. Avoiding Leonardo's question, he went on, 'My lord Count, you're an intelligent man. You can't wish to live under the heel of superstition?'

'Superstition?'

'Your Church . . . faith . . . prayer and penances and weeping statues. My dear lord Count! Surely no intelligent man can countenance such nonsense?' The black eyes twinkled merrily. 'You yourself, Count Leonardo, defy the Church's edicts. Your genic—'

'We will not discuss my genic,' said Leonardo frostily.

Anhalt shrugged. 'As you will. But consider this, my lord Count. As Duke, you could do a great deal to lead your countrymen out of the past and forward to the future. By releasing them from superstition you would open up the city to Imperial markets, bring them the benefits of Imperial science, and your own relationship with your genic would cease to be a matter of gossip. Everyone would benefit. And – ' he drained his glass – 'you would not find us ungrateful.'

It had taken him some time to get to the bribe, Leonardo thought, but he had reached it in the end. It would have given him great satisfaction to throw his wine in the man's face and walk out, but he controlled himself.

'This science of yours . . .' he began. He felt a flame light behind his eyes. 'I have heard – no, seen, now and again, that things go wrong with genics. Minds and bodies twisted . . .? And more than that,' he went on, over-riding what Anhalt would have said, 'they say that so few children are born now, or are born only to die quickly, because your Imperial doctors made mistakes, changed what should have been left alone . . .'

Irritated, lacking the words to describe what he wanted to say, he hesitated, and Anhalt leapt swiftly into the gap.

'There is some truth in that, Count, I won't deny it. But for everything, there is a price.'

'Not being a merchant, messire, I wouldn't know. But that price my city will not pay.'

'Oh . . .' Anhalt waved a hand as if he flicked a fly away. 'That is all in the past.'

'And what is in the present, messire? Or this glorious future you commend to me? More genics, to be despised and ill-used?' Thinking of Gabriel, his voice almost quivered, and he pulled himself up. No more of that. 'Or machines like Dracone's flyer? What use are those to the boatmen and craftsmen and shopkeepers of the city? What can you offer me for them? Or is there no profit to be made from them?'

Anhalt still smiled, though the good humour had gone from the black eyes. 'Oh, if we speak of paupers and beggars . . .'

'There are those who have called me pauper,' said Leonardo. He rose to his feet and held out his glass to the servant. 'But I have never been a beggar. Not for money or for favour, and certainly not for the support of the Empire. Good day, messire.'

Stalking out of the courtyard, he felt Anhalt's eyes boring into his back, and knew he had made an enemy.

Thirteen

I

'I'm almost well, Gianni,' said Alessandro. 'I think I shall come with you to the warehouse tomorrow.'

A pale winter sun shone into the courtyard garden, bringing with it a milder air, a day borrowed from spring. Alessandro was curled up in a chair, wrapped in a voluminous black cloak, with Cat on his lap. Gianni leant on his spade, and breathed in the smell of freshly turned earth.

'If you want,' he said. 'There are a few things I'd like to ask you.'

He tried to sound casual. Ever since that day of his greatest despair, that Father Teo had turned into joy, he had not let himself look ahead. He had refused to recognize the first frail stirrings of hope, and even now, when hope had strengthened into certainty, he could not put words to the truth, even though he would have liked to shout it from the housetops. The power of Christos had turned aside the dark. Alessandro would not die.

'There's a new shipment of silk and damask in from the east,' he said, driving the spade into the earth again, bending over it to hide the grin that he could not repress.

'Good,' said Alessandro. 'All the ladies will want their Carnival dresses soon. Have we sequins and dyed feathers for the mask makers? Never mind – I'll take an inventory with Malatesta tomorrow.'

Gianni knelt to pull off the sacking from the roots of the bay tree he was planting, only to leap to his feet a moment later as Lucetta brought in Father Teo. Reaching out to take the priest's hand, he realized his fingers were sticky with loam.

'I'm sorry, Father. Would you like to go in?'

Father Teo shook his head. 'No, carry on. Sandro, don't get up. I shall do very well here.' He perched on the edge of Alessandro's footstool, and reached up to tickle Cat. 'I've come to say goodbye.'

Gianni set the little bay tree into the hole, and firmed the earth around it with his fingers. His heart was thumping uncomfortably. He said, 'Are you in trouble, Father? Because of us?'

'I don't know. I'm summoned to the Holy Father.'

'What will he do?'

Alessandro's voice was sharp with anxiety, but when he replied Father Teo sounded more amused than anything. 'I don't know that, either.'

Lucetta reappeared with a glass of wine and a plate of biscuits which she placed on the fountain rim close to Father Teo. He thanked her, sipped the wine, and went on, 'I told you that I made my confession to the Patriarch, after the day I baptized you, Sandro, and gave you the Sacrament. I thought then he would strip me of my priesthood, but he didn't. I admit, I underestimated him. He could not ignore what I had done, but he could not entirely condemn me for it. He wrote to the Holy Father, and yesterday the reply came. I must go and give an account of myself.'

With the tree planted to his liking, Gianni went to

dip water from the rain barrel and poured it around the roots. He looked at Father Teo for the first time since he made his announcement; the priest looked calm, but faintly troubled.

Alessandro said, 'We will pray for you, Father.'

'Thank you.' Father Teo hesitated, and then added, 'Of course, since the letter was written, things have changed. What I did was out of compassion, because you were dying. But you did not die. And on my soul I can find no explanation.'

'A miracle, Father?' Alessandro sounded troubled in his turn. 'I cannot believe—'

'Do you need an explanation, Father?' Gianni asked. It seemed very straightforward to him. 'God is good, and he answered our prayers.'

A spark of laughter showed in Father Teo's eyes, yet it was warmth, not mockery. 'The Princes of the Church are more . . . serpentine, in their dealings with the Good Lord. I doubt the Holy Father will find that a satisfactory answer. And yet . . .'

'Yes, Father?' Alessandro leaned forward.

'If I could use this – no, not use it, but make the Holy Father see what I believe is truth. That God had compassion on a genic, and that the genics are His children. Sandro, once you said that would change the world. You were right.'

'Oh, if it were true . . .' Alessandro was rapt, the blue eyes bright.

Father Teo took his hand. 'I believe it is. But whether I can make the Holy Father believe it . . . Besides, there may be a difference between what the Holy Father believes in private, and what the Holy Father finds it expedient to proclaim in public. These are difficult matters.'

Gianni could not see it himself, but he did not feel that he could pester Father Teo for more explanations. Enough to see Sandro expanding in the mercy of God as his new little tree would expand in the rain and sunlight.

'Father,' he said, 'will you give us the Sacrament once more before you go?'

'Of course. That's partly why I came. And partly – this is not the time I would choose to leave the city. I have other pressing matters to see to. It's not only I that need your prayers.'

Gianni sat on the grass and pulled a wisp of it to clean his hands. 'Tell us, Father.'

Father Teo let out a sigh, and Gianni realized that as well as being troubled he was also very tired. 'You have heard what Count Dracone claims about the child his wife is carrying?'

'I think the whole city has heard, Father. Is it true?'

Father Teo looked down into his wine glass, and turned the spiral stem in his fingers. 'I am not sure. It seems . . . incredible. And I would not be surprised at any lie that came from Count Dracone. But I do not think that he is lying now.' He gave a swift, impatient shake of the head. 'There are . . . currents, in the city. There could be riots when the child is born, between those who would kill the baby and those who would worship him . . .' He shrugged. 'This journey to the Holy Father could well keep me away until then.'

Gianni started counting on his fingers. 'Surely not, Father. It's not so long a journey. If you need transport we can help—'

He broke off at Father Teo's smile. The priest said, 'You forget the days of waiting in the office of the Holy Father's secretary, until the Holy Father has leisure to receive me. Besides, Gianni, it's not just that I await the birth of the child. I haven't forgotten the message you brought me from Serafina. I have tried to get into the Palazzo Dracone to speak with her, and I have failed. The Count's constructs guard her well.' His mouth tightened. 'He permits some of her friends to visit, and Caterina Dandolo has brought me news. But all the news in the world will do no good if I cannot *do* anything.'

'What do you want to do, Father?' Alessandro asked.

'To remove Giulietta Contarini-Dracone from that house, along with her two genics. She is safe until her child is born, but I would not give a pin for her life after that.'

'And is there any way for us to help you?'

Father Teo shook his head. 'I don't know, Sandro. Only to pray. And may I tell my patron, Count Loredan, that he can call on you if need be?'

'Of course, Father,' said Gianni, and added, 'They say he's to be Duke.'

'He or Dracone,' said Father Teo. 'The news of this child spreads so fast, and gives Dracone such power, I fear he will defeat Count Loredan. The longer the old Duke lives, the greater Dracone grows.'

Alessandro looked thoughtful, mechanically stroking Cat as he spoke. 'More power than he can handle, perhaps. Even he cannot know what the child will be.' Passion suddenly touched his voice. 'If he were truly Christos come again!'

'No,' said Father Teo. 'The child will not be Christos, not God Incarnate. Christos was human and divine at once, and it is a holy mystery how that could be. This child, even if he is truly brought into being from the hair as Dracone claims, will not share Christos's divinity. He will be an ordinary human child.'

Gianni felt stricken by a sudden pity for the child yet unborn. 'Father, they will never allow him to be ordinary. Not when the whole city knows where he came from.'

Father Teo looked sombre. 'No,' he said. 'He will never be ordinary. Unless someone can save him, he will be Dracone's Christos.'

2

Father Augustine stood on the quay. Wind blew back his hair, grown out of the priestly tonsure now, and sent clouds scudding across the sky where the moon rode half way from the full. He could see nothing of the city, nothing at all ahead of him except the dark blotch of one of the nearer islands, and at last a flat-bottomed boat that came whispering out of the darkness and slid silently against the wharfside. Tethys tossed up a rope and Augustine made it fast to a bollard. Below him the moonlight wavered over the boatload of bales and crates, and Rafael's silvery hair.

When some of the other genics had appeared to unload the cargo, their regular payment from the Master of the Waters, Rafael pulled himself up to sit on the quayside. The months of their stay on the island had altered him almost out of recognition. He was taller, and his slenderness now masked a tensile strength. He had shorn off the fleece of curls, leaving his hair a short, silvery helmet lying close to his head. The planes of his

face had grown harder, more masculine; the beauty that
had shocked Father Augustine had faded with maturity.
The only survival of that fearful night was a silvery scar
down his forearm.

'Any news?' Father Augustine asked.

'I kept out of sight. Tethys spoke to someone from
the Master of the Waters, and he told her . . .' He looked
up at Father Augustine with an impish sparkle in his face,
and motioned for the priest to sit beside him, even though
there was no one but the sea genics to overhear. 'There's
news of Count Dracone.'

'What news?' Augustine asked.

'He is wedded, to a noble lady, and she is to bear the
Christos Child.'

'Blasphemy!' Father Augustine whispered, crossing
himself.

'The story is that his physician – some genic doctor
from the north, they say – created the child from the hair
in the reliquary ring.'

Father Augustine was amazed. He remembered holding the ring in his hand, seeing the hair in its crystal
compartment, and found it hard to imagine that it could
ever become a child. But for someone from the Empire
in the north, where they had the skill to make genics and
no love of God to restrain them – perhaps it was not
impossible.

'What will happen to the child?' he asked.

Rafael shrugged. 'With Dracone? Guess.' He shivered
suddenly, as if he was not as nonchalant as he wanted to
sound. 'He will turn all to evil,' he said. 'But what can
we do? What can anyone do?'

Father Augustine stood up again, and stared out over

the lagoon towards the city he could not see. The night before he had dreamed again of the winged lion, but he did not know what the dream might mean.

Softly, Rafael said, 'You want to go back.'

Augustine spread his hands. 'I am a priest. How can I not want it?' Looking down at Rafael again, he added, 'You're not content here, either.'

'No. But I wouldn't go back.'

'What, then?'

Rafael glanced over his shoulder, past the warehouses and the dome of the half submerged cathedral, and across the spit of land that separated them from the open sea. He said, 'Onwards. Out there.'

Moonlight shone in his eyes. For a moment, he seemed wholly other, a creature of sea and darkness. Then he relaxed, half laughing.

'And neither of us can have what we want, Father. We shall have to make do with this island, and each other.'

'And God,' said Father Augustine. 'Always God. We must pray, and hope that He will hear us. We must pray that He will open a way.'

3

Leonardo Loredan wondered why Count Dandolo should have sent for him, on the evening before his daughter's marriage to Francesco Foscari. He had thought that the old bore would be too busy to interfere in his affairs for this one night at least.

When he arrived at the Palazzo Dandolo, the steward

showed him into the study, where Dandolo was already waiting. He sat Leonardo in an over-stuffed chair by the fire and poured him a glass of wine.

'It goes badly,' he said.

Leonardo cocked a brow at him, took a sip of the sickly-sweet concoction, grimaced, but said nothing.

'I have spoken with the Duke's physician, and he says that the old man could live for weeks yet.'

'Or could die tomorrow,' said Leonardo.

'Best pray he does,' said Dandolo heavily. 'Dracone's support grows by the hour.'

'I will pray for nothing but that God should do His will,' Leonardo said piously, secretly delighted to catch Dandolo in a brief hypocrisy. 'Besides, in many weeks, much can happen. My chaplain is on his way to the Holy Father.'

'Then let us hope the Church will scotch this nonsense once and for all,' said Count Dandolo. He tossed off his own wine. 'Dracone will have written to the Holy Father too, of course. But it looks good, Leonardo, very good, that your chaplain should go in person.'

Leonardo nodded. He had said nothing to Count Dandolo, or anyone else, of the real reason for Teo's journey to the Holy Father. The baptism of the genic Alessandro seemed not to be public property yet, and Leonardo hoped it never would be, at least, not until after the election. Keeping a chaplain who would admit a genic to the rites of Holy Church would not recommend him to Dandolo and the pious faction. Many of them could easily sway to Dracone and his manufactured Christos, hedging their bets in a divine lottery.

He had said nothing, either, of what he had heard about Count Dracone and the Contarini wreck. Even though the story had come through Caterina Dandolo, her father obviously did not know. He would have trumpeted it through the city, especially after Leonardo had refused to let him spread the grubby insinuations he had learnt from Cesare. Leonardo knew what a disaster that would be. Dracone's guilt rested on the word of two genics, and with no more proof than that he could pass off the story as merely an attempt to smear his name.

Leonardo suppressed a wry amusement. Here were himself and Dracone, both with their guilty secrets, and it looked as if neither of them would be a scrap of good in deciding the election.

'If I were in your shoes, Count Loredan, I wouldn't find it funny,' said Count Dandolo.

Leonardo thought he had hidden his feelings better than that. Not that he cared; Dandolo had no sense of humour. He rose to his feet abruptly. 'I'll take my leave, Count. It grows late, and you must have much to do before tomorrow.'

'A moment.' Dandolo did not quite push him back into the chair, but Leonardo would have needed to thrust him aside in order to leave. 'I didn't ask you to come here just to discuss your chances in the election.'

Leonardo took the seat again, barely bothering to conceal exasperation. What did the old fool want?

'There is a matter I want to discuss with you,' Count Dandolo said. 'It concerns my daughter.'

'Maria? No barrier to her marriage, I hope?'

'No.' Dandolo looked disapproving. 'Though it is an impious affair, flying in the face of God who ordained marriage for the procreation of children.' He sniffed, dismissively. 'No, it's my younger daughter I speak of. Caterina.'

Disconcerted, Leo tried to make sense of that. Caterina, the little bright-faced one. Friendly with Giulietta's genie, according to Father Teo. And none the worse for that, in Leonardo's view.

'Caterina? She is well, I hope?'

'Indeed. She has just been examined at Corpus Domini, and received her seal of fertility.'

'My felicitations.' No wonder Dandolo wanted to boast about that, his only hope now of an heir for House Dandolo.

'It is in my mind, Count Loredan . . .' Briefly Dandolo sounded uneasy. 'It is in my mind that if you and Caterina should wed, it would be a good thing for House Dandolo and House Loredan.'

To his own annoyance, Leonardo was dumbfounded, staring at Count Dandolo until he saw the gleam of appreciation in the older man's eyes, and made an effort to pull himself together. 'Forgive me, Count,' he said, 'but your opinion of me . . . I'd hardly expect you to find me suitable as a husband.'

'You are young.' Count Dandolo poured himself more wine and planted himself in front of the fire to pontificate in comfort. 'Young men are wild. And you have recently amended your life. I approve of that, indeed I do.'

Damn your approval! Leonardo would have loved to say that aloud, but he restrained himself. He needed time to consider this new proposal. He suspected Count Dandolo was less impressed by himself as a model of shining piety, and more concerned with the dearth of marriageable men after the Contarini wreck, and the chance that he might wed his daughter to the next Duke.

Cautiously, he said, 'I am not a wealthy man.'

'That can be arranged for,' said Dandolo. 'There are

ways ... And my daughter will have a handsome
settlement.'

'What does Caterina herself think?' Leonardo asked.

Count Dandolo looked shocked. 'I have not men-
tioned it to her. Besides, she knows her duty. She is
young, and will have no trouble in producing an heir for
House Loredan and for House Dandolo. The alliance of
our two Houses will be most advantageous.'

For whom? Leo asked himself. *Not that poor girl,
bargained over like a brood mare.* He made himself sip the
wine again, giving himself time to think. He admitted to
himself, there were women he would find much less
acceptable than Caterina Dandolo. In spite of her father,
she was no pious puppet; she had courage and the
character to do what she thought was right. As for love
... Leonardo frowned, wondering whether love could
grow in a marriage brokered like this one.

'You disapprove?' Dandolo asked.

'Disapprove? No.' Part of Leonardo wanted to grab
the offer with both hands. A nobly born woman, a
woman he could respect, an heir for House Loredan ...
He had enough self-restraint to say calmly, 'I should wish
to speak with Lady Caterina before taking the decision.'

Count Dandolo snorted. 'Speak with Caterina? Why,
in God's name? Not some romantic notions about being
in love? I've had enough of that with her sister.'

'No romantic notions,' Leonardo said. That was true
enough. 'But nevertheless ...'

'Oh, very well. Now?'

Leonardo had not reckoned on that. A day or two to
think about things, to let the new idea settle ...

'Then we might announce the betrothal tomorrow at
Maria's wedding dinner,' Dandolo said.

Fast work indeed. 'Very well,' said Leonardo.

Count Dandolo went out. Leonardo got up, restlessly pacing the room between sombre shelves of leather-bound sermons. While talking to Count Dandolo, he had barely let the other part of the equation surface in his mind, for fear the Count should be aware of it and demand that everything should be ripped open for his inspection.

Gabriel. Leonardo was unprepared for the pain that assaulted him as he thought of his friend. In all the world there was no one more important to him than Gabriel. Even while he had admitted the expediency of sending Gabriel away, something in him screamed that it was wrong.

Ever since Gabriel had left the Palazzo Loredan, Leonardo had missed him. He wanted nothing more than to go to him and welcome him home. Would marriage to Caterina Dandolo mean that he could never do that?

He would be master in his own house. He could do as he pleased, once they were wedded. He could fill the house with genics if he felt like it, and he guessed that Caterina would not even mind, since she had made a friend of Serafina. But that was not the same as giving a home to the one genic he wanted, when rumour had already linked his name with Gabriel's in a way that no wife could be expected to tolerate.

In a cruel snarling of an already complicated pattern, though the rumours were not true, Leonardo knew that Gabriel wanted him. They had not been given the chance to work that through, before Gabriel had to leave. Could Gabriel bear it, Leonardo wondered, to live under the same roof as the Count and Countess Loredan?

He stood with his back to the door, head bent over

clasped hands, as though he were praying. In the anguish
of his need for Gabriel, of his need to find something in
himself that he could give to Gabriel, he did not hear the
door open. His first realization that Caterina was in the
room was when she spoke behind him.

'Count Loredan?'

Leonardo spun round. Caterina was standing just
inside the door. She dropped a curtsey to him, and said,
'Good evening, sir. My father said you wished to speak
with me.'

Her tone was courteous and submissive, but her face
contradicted it in bright curiosity and perhaps a little
wariness. She was not stupid; she must know that men
did not ask for interviews with young women to talk
about the weather.

Damn her father! Leonardo thought. *He hasn't taken
the time to warn her what this is about.*

Feeling awkward, he crossed the room to her until he
could have touched her. 'Lady,' he said, 'your father has
suggested that you might become my wife.' Even as he
was speaking he cursed himself for the formality. There
should be a better way than this, though he did not know
what it might be, when he had scarcely spoken to
Caterina before, and had never been alone with her.
'Would that please you?' he finished.

Caterina's eyes had widened as he spoke; she studied
his face carefully. Leonardo thought he had never seen
anyone look at him with such grave attention, except for
Gabriel when he painted the portrait.

'Forgive me, sir,' she said at last. 'This is new to me. I
had not expected—'

Leonardo found that in undergoing her scrutiny he

had arrived at a deeper awareness of her, and he thought he could see a faint distress flicker across her face. *What stories has she heard?* he asked himself.

'I would honour you as my wife and the mother of my children,' he said.

Caterina thought about that as if there was some significance in the words that he had not intended, and then dropped the respectful little curtsey again. 'As you wish, sir.'

'But do you wish it?'

She raised her eyes to his. The candour there pleased him; he had not thought to find such openness in a woman, not when most of the city's marriageable girls were silly little hothouse orchids like Giulietta Contarini, groomed to flirt and entice but never to be honest.

'I am a woman, sir,' said Caterina, 'and it is my duty to obey. But—' She took a breath, sudden agitation breaking through. 'Sir, I will never have the right to choose. But if I did, I have seen no one . . . my heart is not engaged. I can come to you freely, sir, and hope to be a good wife to you.'

Could I say the same? Leonardo wondered. He reached out and took her hand, and at the same moment, as if he had been listening at the keyhole – *of course he was!* thought Leonardo – Count Dandolo opened the door and came in.

Caterina flashed him a look, and withdrew her hand from Leonardo's. Count Dandolo's face was creased into a satisfied smile, and Leonardo longed to wipe it away, and consign him and his support to hell.

But not yet. Not until he had Caterina safe. Until then, he must be courteous, and co-operative, and do nothing that would endanger the new prosperity and honour of his House.

As he called a boat to ferry him home, he could still feel Caterina's thin fingers warm within his own.

4

The cobbled streets were slick with rain as Dr Anhalt made his way up the hill towards the castle. Below the grey skies, its twisted pinnacles stood out as if they were etched on steel, every overlapping tile delineated with a hard edge.

In the square before the gates, stallholders were laying out their wares for the market: warm rolls sprinkled with poppy seed; gingerbread shapes encrusted with gilt patterns; second-hand zoomorphs furbished with new electroplating; illegal dartguns imperfectly concealed behind piles of cabbages.

Anhalt waved away a child who trotted over to him holding out dreamweed in a twisted paper cone, and stepped into the castle courtyard as the construct guard pulled open the gate for him.

Today, thankfully, he had no appointment with Geschaftsmeister Vogel. His business was with their guest, to feed him with the delights of the Empire and assure him of the Empire's support in his attempt upon the Dukedom.

'Dracone.' Anhalt sighed out the name as the lift construct took him up to the guest suite. He would far rather have been dealing with Leonardo Loredan. But Count Leonardo had refused his overtures, and Anhalt could not entirely acquit himself of misjudgement. Who would have expected so young a man – and one whose sins were the talk of his city – to remain so trammelled by ancient superstition and antiquated ideas of honour? He was intelligent enough to appreciate the advantages of what Anhalt had to offer. Why was he not realistic enough to accept them?

Anhalt's mouth hardened. If Count Loredan insisted on rejecting the Empire, he must take the consequences. They still had Dracone to work with, and he needed no convincing.

At the door of the guest suite Anhalt sounded the entry chime. A construct servant opened the door; it wore the golden braids, starched cap and voluminous skirts of a past age, and its painted smile was fixed in place. It dropped Anhalt a curtsey, its movement loose and uncoordinated, like a puppet with invisible strings.

Ignoring it, Anhalt strode into the room. Dracone was lounging in a chair by the window, a glass of wine in his hand. The scattered remains of breakfast lay on the table, where Dracone's pilot was still stuffing himself with hot rolls.

Reluctantly he got to his feet as Anhalt came in, wiping his mouth, while Dracone merely swivelled in his chair and gave the lawyer a faint smile.

'Good morning, Count,' Anhalt said. 'I hope you passed a pleasant night.'

'Pleasant?' A sneer succeeded the smile on Dracone's face. 'The genic you sent was a feeble creature. It was necessary for Cesare to become . . . quite rough.'

'My apologies, Count. Perhaps today you will have the opportunity to select one that will amuse you better. But meanwhile . . .'

He crossed to the table, swept aside the debris and laid on the surface the case he was carrying, fingering the lock so that the lid gaped open.

'Come and see, my lord Count.'

Dracone joined him by the table. The Count's pose of languor was gone; his eyes were avid.

Inside the case was one of Vogel's latest zoomorphs: a bat, with soft leathery wings and a face dominated by the complex lenses that served it for eyes. Beside it was the control disc, which Anhalt lifted out and set carefully on the table.

'Have you seen one of these before, Count?'

Dracone shook his head. 'What is it?'

'Something you will find very useful. Watch.'

Anhalt activated the power unit and at once the centre of the control disc cleared to show a picture, tiny but precise, of the ceiling of the room where the bat's eyes were trained. Dracone bit back an exclamation, drawing away from the table a moment later as Anhalt touched a control and the bat sprang into life.

Its wings jerked open and it lifted itself out of the case, flopping awkwardly at the edge of the table for a few seconds until Anhalt's fingertip touch on the controls launched it into the air.

Cesare cursed and ducked as it swooped across the room in crooked flight, barely missing his head. Dracone's gaze flicked from the bat to the control disc, where a view of the room swept dizzily back and forth.

'A new Empire toy?' Anhalt noted, with inward amusement, that the Count's attempt at disdain was not quite successful. 'What is the use of it?'

'What it sees, you see – here.' Anhalt indicated the control disc. To the construct he added, 'Open the window.'

Dracone fumed in impatience as the doll-like construct crossed the room. As soon as the window was open, Anhalt sent the bat out; on the disc appeared the crowding rooftops below the castle, the winding alleyways and flights of steps, as far as the river where barges plied to and fro.

'What the bat sees, you see,' Anhalt repeated. 'It can go where you cannot.' He suppressed a sigh as Dracone remained still poised between contempt and wonder, clearly failing to appreciate the possibilities. 'As, for example,' he added, 'Count Leonardo Loredan's bedchamber.'

Understanding flared in Dracone's eyes. 'You will give this to me?'

'It is a gift from Geschaftsmeister Vogel,' said Anhalt. 'I will teach you to operate it. You will find it useful, I think, in your efforts to obtain the Dukedom.'

Dracone ran a tongue over scarlet lips. 'If I could catch him with that ... filth in his bed ... They must be coupling still, for all that he pretends to have dismissed it.'

'If necessary you can record what the bat sees,' Anhalt continued. 'And replay it as you will ... in Council, perhaps?'

'In Council ... before his friends ... before the Patriarch ...' Dracone's face twisted into an expression of glee. For a moment Anhalt felt chilled to think that anyone could be the focus of such hatred.

He touched the controls again and the bat flapped its way back into the room. 'Now, let me demonstrate,' he said. 'You will quickly learn the trick of it, my lord Count. And if it succeeds in smoothing your path to the Dukedom ... I'm sure we will not find you ungrateful.'

*

Anhalt would normally have turned over the duty of escorting guests around Geschaftsmeister Vogel's huge manufactory to one of the technicians who worked there, but in the case of Dracone he thought it wiser to do the job himself.

Another creaking lift took them down below the castle. The hill underneath the town was riddled with passages and chambers where constructs, genics and zoomorphs bearing the mark of Vogel were brought into being far from the prying eyes of competitors.

On the upper levels women assembled the delicate components of zoomorphs, while in a vast foundry hammers beat out the metallic bodies of the fashionably crude constructs. Beneath that, brilliant light illuminated laboratories where genetic material was analysed and manipulated.

Yet lower, and Anhalt led Dracone and Cesare into a chamber lined with tanks, where the genics themselves were cultured.

'We make little use of the wombs of women,' Anhalt explained, as he and Dracone contemplated a foetus, curled on itself and floating in greenish nutrient fluid. 'Women can be ... erratic, as no doubt you know, Count. We find the tanks give more consistent results. And women, even if they are well paid, can be tediously curious about the fate of the genic they have borne.'

Dracone passed his tongue over his lips. The dim light filtering from the tank cast his features into harsh relief. 'You let the women live after?' he asked idly.

Anhalt did not believe he was an easy man to shock, but that question, and the casual tone of it, shocked him. Uncomfortably, he said, 'I told you, Count, we do not make use of women any longer.'

As he led the way out of the chamber he was aware of the Count and Cesare exchanging a sidelong smile.

They came at last to the lowest vault of all. Harsh lighting revealed rows of huge alembics, where the nutrient fluid for the genics was produced and matured into readiness. The air was damp, and a faint mist had gathered on the gleaming surfaces, dulling them to a soft shimmer.

Dracone looked bored as Anhalt explained the process, stifling a yawn with scarlet-tipped fingers. 'My dear doctor,' he interrupted. 'This knowledge is for slaves and constructs. What need do we have of it?'

Nettled, Anhalt replied, 'This knowledge will give you the Dukedom.'

Dracone stared at him, his lips slowly drawing back into a snarl. His glittering eyes still fixed on the lawyer, he rubbed his sleeve over the surface of the nearest alembic, leaving it mirror bright. His scarlet mouth sneered at Anhalt. 'Watch,' he said. His own gaze concentrated on the patch of shining metal, and his lips moved as though he murmured words.

At first all Anhalt could see was his own reflection and Dracone's, distorted by the curve of the metal, with Cesare a dark blur in the background. The Count's coat was a scarlet smear over the silvery surface.

Then the scarlet seemed to spread, and grow deeper, to become crimson, and the colour of old blood. Ripples passed over it, spun down into a vortex, and then cleared. Anhalt blinked. Though he knew it was impossible, he seemed to be looking down a long tunnel where even the rocks burnt. Fiery shapes swam along it. As they drew closer, Anhalt could make out grotesque faces with lolling tongues, and malformed limbs that clawed towards him.

He felt as though the alembic had become as fragile as a
bubble, with a skin that would burst to let the vile
creatures through into the world.

'No . . .' he said hoarsely.

Dracone gave him a contemptuous smile. As the first
of the creatures drew near, its hooked talons reaching into
the air, he passed his hand across the alembic and
whispered a single word under his breath. The creature's
mouth distended in a silent, malevolent howling. It spun
away, along with those that came behind it, as if they
were caught up like leaves in a hurricane. As they dwindled out of sight, the red light faded, and the reflections
of Anhalt and Dracone reappeared.

'You see, my dear doctor,' Dracone said, poisonously
polite, 'I am not dependent on all this – ' he waved a
hand – 'the *wonders* of your Empire. I have allies of my
own.'

Anhalt wanted to ask him what the things were, but
he was afraid of the answer. The rationalism he embraced
had no room for it. He pulled a handkerchief from his
coat and mopped his face, and eventually said, 'Impres-
sive, Count. But you will need more than these illusions
to give you the Dukedom.'

'Illusions!' The word cracked out. 'You did not think
them illusions a moment ago.' Dracone drew closer to
Anhalt, and laid a hand lightly on his shoulder. 'Listen,
Doctor. There are many ways to wealth and power. A
man may be born to them. He may soil his hands with
labour or merchandise, or . . .' His gaze travelled over the
ranks of alembics. '. . . or what you call science. Or he
may find allies to give him his desires.' He smiled
triumphantly.

Anhalt cleared his throat. 'And is there no price?'

'Price?' Dracone's lips opened on a bubble of raucous laughter. 'Doctor, you sound like one of these snivelling priests. I have learnt to take what I want and pay no price.'

Anhalt gazed at him and found nothing to say. Fear was foreign to him; he arranged his life so that there was no opening for it. Yet now he discovered that he feared Dracone, and what Dracone might do. He had to restrain himself from glancing over his shoulder, in case one of the huge, quietly shimmering alembics had begun to change and release horrors he had never permitted into his dreams.

'Come, my lord Count,' he said; his voice rasped for all his efforts to modulate it into normality. 'You are invited to eat at Geschaftsmeister Vogel's table, and after that your flyer will be refuelled for return to your city.'

He felt Dracone's sneer like filth spattering him as he led the way out of the vault. During the long climb in the lift back to the surface, he could not help regretting once again the unreasonable integrity of Count Leonardo Loredan.

Fourteen

I

On the morning that Maria Dandolo was married, Gabriel stood looking around the empty room. His brushes and palette were cleaned, his equipment ranked in orderly array ready for the next commission. But he had no work as yet.

With nothing else to demand his time, he had begun a self-portrait, and the result was on the canvas before him: no more, so far, than the charcoal outline of a face, marking the proportions of forehead, nose, chin, and the position of the eyes.

He was not sure he dared go further. He studied his own face in the glass, tentatively engaging with the image that gazed out at him, and did not think he had the power to translate his own darkness into paint.

He had heard what people said of him, especially the ladies who whispered behind their fans. He knew they called him beautiful. He could paint that, a likeness they might safely sigh over, but it would not be the truth. And if he did not paint truth, then what was he, and what was the use of him?

Everything was quiet. Dr Foscari had gone to church with the couple and then to join in the celebrations at his nephew's house. The portrait would be unveiled there, and the old lawyer had been quietly jubilant, rubbing his hands, at the thought of the commissions that would follow.

Gabriel knew he should be happy. He wanted to paint, and now his work would be admired, wanted. He could earn money for Leonardo.

But Leonardo would be attending his friend Francesco Foscari at the service in I Frari, and afterwards with all the company at the palazzo. He would be courted, perhaps, by the fathers of daughters, now that he was likely to be Duke. There would be an heir for House Loredan.

Gabriel felt tears pricking his eyes, and silently cursed himself. How could he be such a fool as to want those days back again, when he was struggling with the old techniques of painting, while Leonardo was reduced to washing his own shirts and neither of them had quite enough to eat. The future had seemed to hold no hope at all, and yet there had been a kind of joy.

Shaking his head he stepped back from the canvas, and laid the charcoal aside. Wiping his fingers on a scrap of rag, he went to curl up on the windowseat, and looked out of the window of Ca' Foscari to the canal below. A boat slid past, ferrying a black-robed clerk with a fat folder of papers. Two cats were fighting over a scrap of something. A pigeon fluttered onto the balcony opposite.

Gabriel brushed at tears. 'He will never be mine again,' he said.

He heard the door open behind him. Expecting the servant, he rose to his feet, struggling to hide that he had been crying. Standing in the doorway was Count Leonardo.

Something rose into Gabriel's throat and choked him.

For an instant he entertained a brief flicker of hope, that Leonardo had come to call him home. One look at Leo's face banished it. He felt suddenly cold, and started to shiver. He dropped the piece of rag onto the table and stood facing Leonardo as he might have faced his executioner.

Leonardo took a step towards him, began to hold out a hand to him, and let it fall. He said, 'Gabriel.'

'I thought you would be at church with the Foscaris.' Gabriel felt his voice was scarcely his own.

'I was.' A tight smile, a flash of the old Leonardo. 'They're well wedded, in spite of her bastard of a father.' Then the uneasiness returned. 'I came from the Palazzo Foscari, just for a while. I – I need to talk to you.'

His ice-blue eyes took in the mirror, the painting barely begun. Gabriel thought he would comment on it, but all he said, awkwardly, was, 'Your picture of Maria Foscari is very fine.'

'Thank you, my lord.' Cold formality; how else could he survive this?

'Gabriel, damn you—' Leonardo caught himself up. 'Gabriel, I came to tell you ... I would not have you hear it from anyone else first. I am betrothed to Caterina Dandolo.'

A blade driven into his heart. No pain yet, but the knowledge that the wound is mortal. Stiffly, Gabriel said, 'I wish you joy, my lord.'

'No.' Count Leonardo snapped out the single word, and came close enough to take his hands in a fierce grip. 'Not that, not from you, Gabriel.'

Gabriel turned his face away from the imperious gaze. 'Do you think I do not wish you joy?'

'Don't play with words!' When Gabriel said nothing, Leonardo released his hands, gripped his shoulders instead and shook him fiercely. 'Don't pretend!'

There swept over Gabriel an overwhelming compulsion to cling to him, to plead or to demand, to force a response that would be the fulfilment of his own need. With his last scrap of self-control he mastered it. What use, to ask from Leonardo something that was not in his nature to give?

He pulled away from Leonardo's grip, and stood breathing hard, leaning against the table with his back to him. Quietly, Leonardo said, 'I'm sorry, Gabriel. When all this is over, you can come home.'

Gabriel's head went up. 'And your lady? What will she think of that?'

'Caterina knows you. She came here when you painted Maria's picture.'

'She was very kind,' Gabriel said dully. 'It is not the same.'

He heard Leo moving towards him, and felt his hand rest on his shoulder, gently now, almost a caress. It would have been the most natural thing in the world for Gabriel to turn to him, to put his arms around his neck and kiss him. He did not move. He had already won that battle.

'Gabriel, I have to tell you . . . I do not love Caterina. Like her, respect her, yes. But love . . .' He let out a faint sigh. 'I have scarcely spoken to her alone. But you . . . we struggled together, when my father died and left nothing but debts. Gabriel, you are important to me.'

Something in Gabriel wanted to relax, to accept. Leo had saved his life in the lagoon, when so many others were in danger, including that Caterina who was now to be his wife. He knew that Leo was speaking the truth.

But it was not all the truth. And it crossed his own truth at a crooked angle.

Bitterly he said, 'One day you will love her, perhaps. You will never love me.'

Leo turned Gabriel to face him, hands on his shoulders. 'I do love you, Gabriel.'

'No.' Once again he pulled away, his breath coming short, his words stumbling out. 'No, and no. I am a genic. Your servant. Your property. Made to pleasure men like Dracone. Too filthy to share your roof. But with a talent—' He jerked a hand out towards the canvas on the easel. 'Something to make me not entirely worthless.'

He saw Leo look white and shocked as if he had struck him. Something in Gabriel felt a savage enjoyment that he could hurt as well as be hurt. He drew himself up. 'Perhaps, my lord, you would like to commission a portrait of the new Countess Loredan?'

Leo's mouth went white. The sudden gust of anger was so intense that Gabriel was terrified. He wanted to snatch the words back.

'Damn you, Gabriel,' Leonardo said softly.

He strode out and slammed the door behind him with a force that made the house rattle. Gabriel heard his footsteps rapidly receding down the stairs.

When everything was quiet again, he bowed his head into his hands and wept.

2

Very few ladies would visit the wife of Count Dracone, and fewer still since the Count's announcement in the Council. While their lords debated whether the Count

302 Cherith Baldry

might be St Joseph or the AntiChristos, they stayed at home. Neither St Joseph nor the AntiChristos was entirely respectable.

One of the few who did come was Caterina Dandolo. She came regularly to sit with Giulietta, to exchange gossip over the cordials and sweet cakes, and as occasion offered, to talk with Serafina.

Since the day that Serafina had first told her friend the truth about the Contarini wreck, they had made many plans together, and discarded all of them. Neither of them could think of a way for Giulietta and the others to escape the Palazzo Dracone.

On the day of the Foscari wedding, a day of blustery wind and flurries of snow, Giulietta had retired to her bed in the early afternoon, fussed over a headache for a while, and then fallen asleep. She had been invited to the wedding festivities, but the Count had refused, on account of her health. Privately, Serafina thought that he did not want Giulietta to speak to anyone who might ask her about the child she bore.

Serafina was alone in her sitting room, embroidering the edge of a sleeve, when Dracone's construct announced Caterina. She was surprised, expecting that Caterina would be with her sister. Sending the construct for refreshments, she asked, 'Is all well?'

'Oh, very well!' Caterina's colour was heightened, and her hair dishevelled by the wind. She wore a very pretty gown of peach coloured silk and lace, a much more frivolous garment than Count Dandolo usually permitted. 'Maria looked so beautiful! And Francesco was so happy. I wept, Serafina, like some stupid little girl . . .'

Serafina smiled. 'I didn't think you would come today.'

'No, I didn't think there would be time, but the guests were leaving, and I thought Francesco and Maria would like to be alone for a while. You know that I'm to live there now, at the Palazzo Foscari?'

'Yes. You'll be happier there.'

Caterina laughed nervously, and pushed back a straying wisp of hair. 'It won't be for long, though.'

'You'll never go back to your father?'

Caterina shook her head, but remained silent as the construct reappeared with a tray of cordial and sweetmeats which it placed on a table at her elbow. While she waited, Serafina realized that her friend's flushed face and agitated manner were not just because of the excitement of the wedding.

'Have you news?' she asked when the construct had gone.

'Is it as obvious as that? I think it must be written across my face for everyone to read.' Caterina leant forward and took Serafina's hand. 'I'm betrothed to Leonardo Loredan.'

Serafina could understand her agitation now, the almost panicky grip on her fingers. She remembered Count Loredan, the devastating charm and the good looks that had made Giulietta sigh over him, even though he was too poor to be her husband. Count Leonardo's fortunes were improving, it was clear.

'Are you happy?' she asked Caterina.

Caterina repeated the nervous laugh. 'I . . . don't know.'

She released Serafina, who took up her needle again and said, 'Did your father arrange it, or did Count Leonardo ask for you?'

'It was Papa.' Caterina's lips thinned. 'After I went to

Corpus Domini, and the holy sisters gave me my seal of fertility, he looked about for a suitable husband.'

She stopped, though Serafina thought she had not said everything. And she was not sure that a careful father would have thought Leonardo Loredan suitable. 'And then . . .' she said encouragingly.

'He gave me to Count Leonardo to help Leonardo become Duke, when the old Duke dies. He wishes to be allied with the Ducal House.' Her voice grew scathing. 'He will say that his support gave Count Leonardo the Dukedom.'

Serafina laid her work down and covered her friend's hands with her own. She said, 'You will be free of him soon.'

Caterina tried to smile, and then shook her head, making her hair fly, as if she was freeing herself now from all the bitterness against her father. 'Serafina, I'm sorry. That's not what I came to talk about at all.' She returned Serafina's clasp on her hands. 'I have thought of a way!'

Serafina felt her heart lurch. 'How?'

'It was really Maria's idea. She's so happy now, she wants everyone to be just as happy as she is! And when Francesco told her to have her sewing woman make her a gown for Carnival, that's when she thought of it. You must escape on Carnival night! The streets are so crowded, there are so many boats, and everyone is masked. You could slip away, and Count Dracone would never find you!'

Serafina felt a rising excitement, and made herself think of the plan's drawbacks. 'We would have to get out of the palazzo first.'

Caterina suppressed a giggle. 'That's my part of the

plan. You must get Giulietta to nag at Count Dracone, until he agrees to escort her.'

'Of course . . .' Serafina began to smile. 'She loves parties and festivity. Even now, she complains now and again, that she has no fun at all. She will hate to miss Carnival night!'

'You will have to make sure that you and Hyacinth go too. Then Francesco says that he will have a boat ready, and whisk all of you away to the Palazzo Foscari!'

Serafina was still trying to think, not to be carried away by Caterina's delight in the plan. 'I'm sure I can get away . . . but Hyacinth? I won't leave him.'

Caterina looked briefly at a loss. 'Would the Count invite some guests? Then Hyacinth could slip among them?'

'Perhaps . . .' Serafina could not help thinking that Hyacinth was not the easiest person to slip inconspicuously anywhere, even if he was not watched; she had to remind herself that Caterina had never seen the mirrored room, and she was not prepared to tell her what went on there. Even so, with a mask and a costume . . . 'We can try,' she said.

'Good.' Caterina's eyes were sparkling; for all her concern, it was a kind of game to her.

'What about your father?' Serafina felt she had to ask. 'Will he punish you for being involved with this? And what about Count Leonardo?'

The thought of her father, or of her future husband, sobered Caterina. She took one of the sweet cakes the construct had brought, and crumbled it between her fingers, but did not eat it. 'I don't care what Papa thinks. He knows I will never live in his house again. And as for Count Leonardo, I think he would help us if he knew.'

'Will you tell him?'

'I don't know.' Suddenly she took in a sharp breath, and looked at Serafina with that bright openness that Serafina had first liked in her. 'I must do this, Serafina, for our friendship, and for Giulietta and Hyacinth. If I failed you, I could never respect myself again. I cannot become a puppet for Count Leonardo. Afterwards . . . I shall be a good wife to him, as far as I am able.'

Serafina could not resist asking, 'Do you love him?'

Caterina shook her head, hesitated, and then said, 'I'm not sure. No, not now; I scarcely know him. I'm lucky; Papa might have chosen someone old, or ugly, or someone like Count Querini, that they say beat his first wife until she took her own life. Count Leonardo would be easy to love . . .' Suddenly she went scarlet. 'They gossip about him and his genic.'

Serafina had not heard that, but it was not difficult to guess what kind of gossip Caterina meant.

'Gabriel has left the Palazzo Loredan,' the girl went on. 'I saw him at Dr Foscari's, when he was painting Maria's picture. He is . . . very beautiful.'

Her hands were shaking as she lifted the glass and sipped the cordial Serafina had poured for her. 'I must not love Count Loredan,' she said. 'I shall be his partner, and help him as I may. If he becomes Duke, there will be duties for me too. But . . . oh, Serafina, I must not love him! For if he knew, he would find it . . . tedious. I do not think he will ever love me.' Still trying to smile, she fumbled for a handkerchief and dabbed away tears. 'I'm not a silly girl, Serafina. I know how a highborn lady should behave. I shall do my duty, and do it well.'

Serafina could believe her. All the same, it was easy to

see that Caterina's resolve not to love Count Leonardo
had come far too late.

3

When he was sure that Leonardo had left the house,
Gabriel shrugged on his jacket, trod warily down into the
empty entrance hall, and went out.

At first he walked rapidly, head down, as if he could
outpace his pain. Leonardo would have gone back to the
Palazzo Foscari, he supposed, to be with his promised
bride, to make himself pleasant to those who might
support him in the elections, now that he stood within
reach of the highest honour the city could bestow. Gabriel
knew he should rejoice for him. Instead, he wanted to
scream.

He came to himself at last on the bridge over a narrow
canal. Above his head two women were calling to each
other from opposite balconies, as they hung their washing
over the rail. Below a boat slid past, laden with baskets of
bread, the boatman yelling abuse at his assistant. Two
comfortably fat men, merchants by their dress, strolled
past in talk, eyeing the woman who leant, with lace wrap
and painted face and hair frowsy from her bed, from a
balcony over the water. Sound, smell, movement assaulted
Gabriel, who had lived so long in quiet rooms with few
people to talk to.

Not to make himself conspicuous – for why would a
genic be idling here, alone – he began to walk again,
more slowly, trying to barricade his senses against the city
that crowded up against him.

Passing a paper-maker's shop, he paused by the open door and gazed avidly at the new, clean-cut blocks of paper lying on the counter, and the damp sheets drying on lines in the room behind. He had a pencil stub in his pocket; if only he had money, he could buy paper, and try to make sense of this kaleidoscope of a city by setting it down in drawing. But he had not.

He was half turning away when a spry, elderly man appeared out of the back shop, wiping his hands on a towel. 'Yes, lad? What do you want?'

Gabriel backed off nervously. 'I'm sorry . . .'

The man had seen the genic badge, he could tell. He said, 'An order for your master? Don't look so scared, lad. I don't bite.'

'No, sir. I – I need paper, but I can't pay. I'm sorry if I've offended you.'

'No offence, lad.' The man weighed him up with sharp eyes. 'Wait.'

He disappeared into the back shop and came out a moment later with his hands full of paper, some scraps, and a couple of full sheets, carelessly folded.

'Here,' he said. 'Off-cuts, flawed sheets – take it.'

'Sir, I can't . . .'

'Here.' The man came round the counter and out of the door to push the paper into Gabriel's hands, scarcely seeming to care whether their fingers touched or not. 'I can't sell it. If you don't take it, it'll end up wrapping fish.'

Wrapping fish! Gabriel thought, marvelling. This – heavy and creamy, and smooth enough to take a line . . . He looked up, smiling. 'Thank you, sir!'

The paper-maker looked almost embarrassed. 'If you

need it that much, lad, then come back any time. There are always scraps.'

When he had taken his leave, Gabriel went on, and in a quiet corner beside the next bridge he carefully smoothed and divided his treasure. Above his head an iron lantern bracket creaked, a swooping eagle with sharp curled feathers and rapacious beak. Gabriel began to draw, and felt as if the whole of the city had been given to him.

Later he found himself wandering along the Beggars' Quay, among the bundles of rags, avid, grotesque faces and distorted hands stretched out to pluck at him – even at him! – if he could offer relief. He could not bear to draw with those eyes on him, and the clutching hands brought back dark memories of the lagoon. When he crossed the bridge and turned down the next alley his hands were shaking so that he could not hold the pencil.

At mid-day he sat in the colonnade outside the gates of San Francesco, and watched and drew as a plump brother put down a bowl of scraps for a weaving, purring mass of cats. When the brother saw him, he started back, nervous that he might have given offence, but the brother made signs for him to wait, disappeared, and came back with a crusty roll stuffed with cheese, that he pressed into Gabriel's hands with a blessing.

Gabriel savoured the meal in a patch of sunlight, his back against a pillar, and wondered wryly where a genic might fit into the holy brother's charity, and whether he ranked above or below the cats.

As the afternoon wore on he came across a bridge and into a square where shabby tenements with boarded-up windows sagged against each other and rose to block out the light. Washing hung from balconies above his head.

In the centre of the square was a fountain, long dry
and furred with green. Above the rubbish in the cracked
basin a bronze dolphin rose in the perfection of its
leaping. Gabriel took paper and began to draw it.

After a while, a door opened and a small tabby kitten
ran out into the square, scraped briefly at the flagstones
and squatted to relieve itself, and then scuttered off after
a blown scrap of paper. Amused, Gabriel watched, until a
small girl in a ragged smock came out of the same
doorway, swooped on the kitten and scooped it up.

Seeing Gabriel, she sidled across with the kitten clawing its way up to her shoulder and a filthy thumb in her
mouth. She looked down at the picture of the dolphin,
by now almost finished. 'What are you doing?'

'Drawing.'

'Draw Kitty.'

'All right,' Gabriel said, taking another piece of paper.
'And I'll draw you as well.'

The little girl gave him a luminous smile, and sat on
the flagstones to play with the kitten while Gabriel drew.
This was hard, harder than the portrait of Maria Dandolo, because the child would not keep still, and kept
coming to look, but in the end Gabriel thought he had
caught something of her energy and joy.

A door banged. A voice called, 'Gianetta! Gianetta,
where are you?'

A woman had come out into the square. She wore a
striped dress and white apron, painfully clean, and her
fair hair straggled over her forehead.

Seeing her daughter with Gabriel she hurried across.
'Oh, messire, I hope she hasn't been bothering you,
she . . .'

Her voice died away. Gabriel started up nervously,

thinking that she must have seen the genic badge, expecting her to scream accusations that he had defiled her daughter. Instead, he saw that she was looking at the picture.

'Messire, that's a wonder . . .'

Gabriel felt embarrassed. 'It's nothing.'

'It's me and Kitty,' said Gianetta, swinging on her mother's apron.

Her mother hushed her. 'Messire,' she said, 'will you sell me the picture?'

Gabriel stared down at the square of paper in his hands, and the pencil strokes that had caught the child's delight. He held it out to the woman. 'I'll give it to you.'

She reddened. 'No, messire, that wouldn't be right.'

As she fumbled in her apron pocket, Gabriel wondered that she called him 'messire', seeing the genic badge as she must, or if she realized that as a genic he could own nothing and so he could not sell it, or even give.

She came up with a handful of small coins and held them out. 'Is this enough, messire?'

Gabriel had no choice but to let her tip them into his palm, and give her the picture in exchange. Receiving it, she smiled in such joy that he caught a glimpse of the beauty that she must once have had, and now had given to her daughter.

'You see, messire,' she said, 'my man went south to work. He hasn't seen her since she was a week old. The picture will ease his heart.' She bobbed him a curtsey. 'Messire . . .'

'Yes?'

'Messire, my sister's here.' The words came out in a rush. 'Will you make a picture of her boy? Her man went with mine, and he's never seen his son.'

Gabriel smiled. 'Of course.'

The woman hurried back into the house, and soon her sister came, with the child, and after her others, from other doorways in the courtyard, some just to stare curiously, some to ask for pictures of themselves or their children, until the light began to fade and it was too dark to draw.

A heap of small coins lay on the fountain steps where Gabriel sat. He stared at them. He was not sure what to do with them. In law, he supposed, they belonged to Leonardo, but knowing what Dracone had paid for his first picture, guessing what Dr Foscari must have paid for the portrait of Maria Dandolo, he knew how absurd it would be for him to offer these scrapings of poverty. And yet in a way they were more precious than Dracone's gold.

He might go back to the paper-maker's, he thought. He could buy the paper this time – better paper, not these off-cuts. And make more drawings. Which he could sell. The problem of the money was not going to go away.

Across the square a tavern had opened, with lanterns hanging in the windows and a bench dragged out into the courtyard against the wall. The light was warm. Not many customers had arrived as yet; only the tavern keeper was outside, sweeping his frontage and watching Gabriel curiously.

After a few minutes he strolled over and looked down at Gabriel, and the first drawing of the fountain dolphin, lying beside the pile of coins.

'Could you draw that on wood?' he asked. 'And colour it, like?'

Gabriel considered. The ancient painters, he knew, had worked on wood as well as canvas. 'I think so,' he said.

'I've a fancy for a sign.' He gestured towards his tavern. 'This is the Dolphin.' He paused. 'You can stay here and work, if you like.'

'I'm a genic,' said Gabriel.

'Aye, I can see that.'

Gabriel felt suddenly bewildered. Things were moving too fast. Money, the offer of work, a place to stay . . . He knew that he should go back to Dr Foscari's, but what was there for him there, now that the portrait was finished? And it was almost dark, and he was tired, and not sure of the way.

He rubbed his forehead. 'I could pay you for a room.' He pushed the pile of coins towards the tavern keeper. 'If that's enough.'

The tavern keeper gave him a hard stare. 'Nay, I'll find you a place to sleep.' He hesitated and then stooped to pick two coins out of the heap. 'That buys you supper. Come across when you're ready.'

He went back to his sweeping. Gabriel thought for a moment and then took one of the remaining scraps of paper and wrote a note to Dr Foscari, telling the lawyer where he was and asking for permission to stay and work. Glancing round, he saw one of the children he had drawn earlier, a rather older boy than some of the others, and beckoned him over.

'Do you know Dr Foscari's?' The boy nodded. 'Will you take me a note for him?'

Another nod. Gabriel folded the note and handed it to him, adding, after a second's reflection, one of his little store of coins. The boy disappeared up the nearest alley. Gabriel collected the remaining coins and paper, and walked across the square to the Dolphin.

There was no word from Dr Foscari that night, and so Gabriel slept in a narrow space under the eaves of the Dolphin. Not even a room – barely a cupboard – but with a straw mattress and a blanket he was comfortable enough. The tavern keeper sent up bread and soup and a jug of wine harsh enough to scour the back of his throat.

Next morning he explained to the tavern keeper what he needed for the sign, and the man gave him money to go and buy materials. He directed Gabriel to a timber merchant's, where Gabriel ordered a fine wooden panel to be delivered to the Dolphin, and then went on to collect what he would need to make the paint.

He did not feel it right to go to Dr Foscari's for his equipment, not when Leonardo had paid for it. Besides, he was reluctant to go back there until the job at the Dolphin was done. Dr Foscari had still not replied to his note, and while silence was permission of a kind Gabriel wondered whether he was angry.

Returning at mid-day with his bundles he passed the paper-maker's. This time he turned in more confidently, and bought a thick block of paper, paying for it out of his own store of coins.

'All well, lad?' the man asked him.

Gabriel found himself smiling, and realized that some-how, without realizing it, he had found a shield against his own despair. 'Yes, messire, I thank you,' he said. 'All is very well.'

Fifteen

Giulietta Contarini-Dracone held the gown of golden
tissue against herself, and swirled in front of the mirror.
'Which gown do you think, Serafina? This, or the silver?
Or the blue?'

She was more animated than Serafina had seen her
since her marriage, delighting in the three gowns the
Count had ordered for Carnival. Like a child with a treat
in store, she could not wait for the night, and like a child
she could not choose which of the three gowns to wear.

'Whichever you like best.' Serafina had even less
interest than usual in Giulietta's clothes. She felt sick with
nervousness. Tonight, somehow, in the bustle and confusion of Carnival, she meant to slip away with Hyacinth
and take refuge in the Palazzo Foscari.

She had said nothing to Giulietta. She could not be
sure that the girl would leave her lord and husband,
especially when he had been so generous with the dresses.
Serafina could not risk that Giulietta would give the plan
away before the time was right. Once in the safety of the
Foscari household, she told herself, it would be easier to
convince Giulietta that she must stay there.

'The silver mask is the prettiest.' Giulietta dropped
the golden gown and pounced on the silver mask, holding
it up to her face. It covered everything except her lips and

chin, moulded around the rest of her face with a glitter
of jewels around the eyes and a soft fall of silvery feathers
to cover her hair.

'That one, then,' Serafina said. 'But be quick. Your
guests will be here soon.'

She herself was already dressed, in the seagreen gown
she had made for Giulietta to wear to Count Contarini's
birthday feast. Giulietta had given it to her, unable to
bear the thought of wearing it herself. With it went a
mask of leaves in soft woodland colours; once she put
that on, Serafina would be able to mingle with the
crowds of Carnival without anyone being able to tell
that she was a genic. Not that anyone would care, on
Carnival night.

Giulietta pulled off her silken wrap and let Serafina
lace her loosely into the silver gown, fasten the mask, find
her slippers and her fan and douse her handkerchief with
perfume.

'Go down to your guests, Countess,' she said when
Giulietta was ready. 'I'll follow you when I've tidied up
here.'

'Very well.' Giulietta gave one last twirl before the
mirror, and flirted her fan before the expressionless silver
face which gazed out at her. 'But don't be long, Serafina,
or the boats will leave without you.'

'I won't.'

Once Giulietta was safely out of the room, Serafina
bundled everything into a closet except for the golden
gown and mask. Tidying was not the first thing on her
mind. Grabbing her own mask, her arms full of billowing
golden fabric, she whisked out of the room and along the
passage towards the mirrored chamber where Hyacinth
was imprisoned.

On this night of all nights, surely the watch on him would be relaxed?

Serafina met no one on her way. The Count and his construct servants would be down in the great hall, where guests were expected for wine and sweetmeats. And Cesare? Given leave to go and drink himself senseless, Serafina hoped.

She edged open the concealed door and slid through it, half afraid of finding the room thronged with Dracone's demons. Cautiously she said, 'Hyacinth?'

'Serafina?' A sudden, convulsive movement. 'Don't – don't come in.'

'Don't be stupid. I must.'

She closed the door behind her and hurried down the short passage. On the threshold of the mirrored room she stopped, staring. In the faceted mirrors she saw herself a dozen times, and Hyacinth, crouched on the edge of the bed, the cold reflections giving back every aspect of his shame.

Someone – Dracone? – had covered half his body in swirls of scarlet, dusted with a golden glitter, as the courtesans painted their faces for Carnival and went unmasked into the streets. He had wept, and smeared the face paint, and pulled on a silken tunic, a scrap of gauze so transparent that it concealed next to nothing. Serafina thought she had never seen anything so indecent, or so exotically beautiful.

'He said he would display me in the streets.' Hyacinth struggled with hysterical laughter. 'But I think he dares not.'

'No,' said Serafina. 'Hyacinth, he only says it to torment you. He wants to be Duke – do you think he could be seen in public with you, like that?'

Hyacinth let out a sob that she realized was pure relief.

'No time for that,' she snapped. She shut the door behind her and tossed the golden gown and the mask on the bed. 'Put those on. You're leaving.'

'What?' He stretched out a hand to touch the golden tissue, but made no move to obey her.

'Put it on. Quickly. Hyacinth, the house is full of guests. Count Dracone won't know you, behind the mask. You can escape.'

He began to understand, the great violet eyes dilating with terror and hope. Fumbling, he slipped the gown on over his head, and Serafina helped to fasten it. Fear throbbed in her throat as she waited for the golden lamplight to shade into crimson, but Hyacinth was dressed, and the demons had still not appeared.

'No slippers,' Serafina said, vexed. 'Giulietta's wouldn't fit. Have you anything?'

He was recovering now, able to think for himself, and pulled out one of the mirrors to reveal a closet behind it. A moment's search discovered a pair of low, soft shoes; they would not match the gown, but under the sweeping skirts with any luck they would not be noticed.

'Tell me what to do,' he said.

'We'll go down together,' Serafina said. 'Count Dracone has invited guests to meet here and then take boats to hear the music in the square before the basilica.'

'Music . . .' Hyacinth's whisper was raw with longing.

'Later. For now, you're a fine lady, one of Giulietta's friends. Can you do that? No one will ask you who you are.'

For answer, Hyacinth took up the golden mask and fitted it on. It covered all his face; Serafina almost shivered as she met that impersonal stare. She fastened it for him, and threaded its golden ribbons through his curls. Hyacinth straightened, shook out his skirts, and examined himself in the mirror.

Serafina put on her own mask, and when she was ready took his hand. 'Come now.'

As they ventured out into the passage, Hyacinth's grip on her hand became painful. 'What if the Count sees?'

'He won't. At least, he'll see you, but he'll never guess who you are.' Serafina spoke with more confidence than she felt. 'But if anyone talks to you, be modest, and whisper. Or mysterious, and say nothing at all. Your voice will give you away.'

At the head of the stairs, the tinkle of glasses and the murmur of conversation already audible, he checked. 'Where will we go?'

'You'll see.' Serafina tugged at his hand to get him moving again. 'It's all arranged.'

The inscrutable golden mask turned towards her again, and again she shivered, as if it was not Hyacinth behind it, but something remote and incalculable, something she could not control. She wondered if he would go on questioning her, and she did not want to be any more specific. The less he knew the better, until he was away from Count Dracone, and safe.

Then Hyacinth released her hand, and led the way down the stairs. He had found confidence from somewhere; he was stately, elegant behind the shield of gown and mask. Serafina was impressed.

Knowing what he was, she wondered if he would have been happier if those who made him and trained him had presented him as a woman and not a man. The devastating beauty, the startling alto voice, would have been less remarkable. But that, Serafina thought, picking up her skirts and following, was the whole point. Hyacinth was meant to be remarkable; he would have been so much less entertaining without that delicious sense of sin that his audiences could feel just by looking at him.

He knew it, Serafina realized. He had always known it.

In the great hall below the soft shimmer of candles fell on knots of guests in the fantastic costumes of Carnival. Count Dracone's constructs, looking more grotesque than ever among the delicate silks and decorated masks, moved among the guests with wine and silver bowls of candied fruits.

Serafina paused in the doorway, sudden panic rising as she realized she did not know how Caterina would be costumed. She had described her own dress; Caterina would have to find her.

While she hesitated, a tall man, wearing a black velvet coat and a black mask with a hooked beak like a predatory bird, approached Hyacinth and murmured something to him. Hyacinth stretched out a hand for him to kiss, but turned his head away; Serafina heard the man say, 'No word for me, lady? So disdainful?'

Well, that was Hyacinth's problem. Serafina took a glass from the tray a construct offered to her, remembered that no highborn lady would thank a construct, and pretended to sip. As she moved uncertainly a little further into the hall, she saw a small, slender girl in a saffron coloured gown and a cat's mask, working her way towards her through the other guests. She breathed more easily; this could only be Caterina.

The girl caught her arm, and raised the impudent ginger cat's face to hers. 'Serafina?'

'Yes.'

Caterina giggled. 'Isn't this *wonderful*? Papa would hate it! He would never allow us out on Carnival night,' she added. 'We always had to stay at home, and read an improving book.'

She spun round, her skirts swirling. 'There's Francesco, over there in grey, with the white mask. And Maria next to him, in blue.'

Serafina glanced where Caterina pointed, and the grey-clad cavalier inclined his head slightly towards her. She dipped a curtsey in reply.

'Francesco says that when we go to the boats you and Giulietta must be close to him so that you take the same boat. Maria and I will be there too, of course. Can you part Giulietta from Count Dracone?' she asked anxiously.

'I think so. After all,' Serafina said, mimicking Giulietta's tones, 'no lady goes to Carnival with her own *husband*! That's *so* boring!'

Caterina laughed. 'Only Maria!' Then she sobered suddenly. 'Will Count Dracone think so?'

Serafina could not answer that. She could see the Count among his guests, dressed as always in scarlet, making no concession to the modes of Carnival except for a narrow black mask over his eyes. Giulietta, in her silver array, stood beside him, leaning on his arm, speaking graciously to two ladies identical in yellow with feathered masks like birds.

Caterina's hand tightened on her arm. 'I have told Count Leonardo.'

'Is he here?'

'No.' There was a catch in Caterina's voice, that might
have been laughter, or nervousness. 'How could he visit
the Palazzo Dracone? But he will be outside in a boat,
and wait for us to leave. If there is trouble, he will help.'

'He's a good man.'

'Yes . . . I thought once, it was Giulietta he wanted.'
The catch in her voice again. 'Serafina, I will not be
stupid about Count Leonardo. And especially not
tonight.'

Serafina saw that Count Francesco had begun to
manoeuvre himself and Maria closer to Giulietta. How
much longer, she wondered, before the general movement
to the boats would begin? She did not want to join the
others too soon. For one thing, she did not want Count
Dracone to recognize who she was. Serafina the genic
maid servant had disappeared for one night, replaced by
a lady in seagreen and silver who might whisk the
Countess Contarini-Dracone away without any questions
asked. Besides, Giulietta herself must not be given the
chance to wonder what was going on.

Caterina was tugging at the sleeve of her gown.
'Serafina, what about Hyacinth?'

Serafina nodded slightly to where the musician was
still flirting desperately with his cavalier in black. Caterina
stifled a squeal. 'Serafina, you *haven't*—'

'What else could I do? I had no man's costume, and I
won't leave him here. Dracone won't stop tormenting
him until he's mad, or dead.'

Caterina had subsided into scandalized giggles. A
moment's uneasiness seized Serafina. If even her sensible
friend found Hyacinth indecent . . . 'Will your sister and
Count Foscari receive him?' she asked. 'At least for a
while?'

'Of course.' Caterina smiled. 'Maria gives alms to beggar children, and takes in stray cats—'

'And genics.'

'And genics. But Serafina, don't let Hyacinth unmask until—'

Caterina broke off. Count and Countess Foscari had reached Giulietta and Count Dracone, and were engaged in a gracious conversation, with much bowing and flourishing. Some of the guests had begun to move closer to the doors of the hall.

Serafina motioned to Caterina to join the Foscaris. She herself went back to Hyacinth, and swept a provocative curtsey to the cavalier in black. 'I must claim my sister, sir.'

'Oh, no!' The man in black had an arm firmly round Hyacinth's waist. 'For tonight, she's mine.'

Hyacinth's violet eyes were gazing desperately from behind the mask. He would not dare do anything to draw attention to himself.

Serafina said, 'But we're bidden to the music with Count Dracone, sir.'

The cavalier laughed. 'Your sister shall have all the music she wants, with me.'

Serafina doubted it. Trying to project enticement through the mask – how did a girl like Giulietta do it, she wondered – she curtsied again. 'Then you must play it for both of us, sir!'

She caught the man's free arm, and tried to hurry him towards the doors of the great hall. The Foscari party, with Giulietta, were already well ahead. Serafina caught a glimpse of Caterina, glancing anxiously over her shoulder.

The cavalier laughed. 'This will be a Carnival to remember!'

You can't imagine, Serafina thought.

Then they were on the marble stairway, progressing down towards the entrance hall, the outer doors and the loggia. More guests pressed around them. One of the scarlet liveried constructs loomed up, and for a moment Serafina was terrified that it had penetrated their disguise, but it was only holding cloaks and canes that the guests had left in the hall.

She was through the door, and the cold wind of the canal was blowing against her. She took a breath of it, like rain in drought, the air of freedom.

All around the steps from the loggia boats were drawn up, moored to the scarlet and gold poles. Others waited out in the canal for space to slide in and pick up their passengers. Serafina gazed wildly around. She managed to pick out Count Dracone, handing some lady she did not recognize into a boat. The Foscaris were further away, escorting Giulietta; with a gasp of relief she tried to guide the black cavalier in their direction, but he resisted.

'My boat is here, pretty one.'

He gestured to a boat just below them, and released himself from Serafina to hand Hyacinth down into it. Behind his back, she pantomimed to Hyacinth that he should not resist; at least they were away, and they could escape later and make their way to the Palazzo Foscari.

Then the cavalier jumped down into his boat, snapped a single word to his boatman, and the boat began to draw away, before Serafina could board it. She caught back a cry. The cavalier raised his hat to her as his boat pulled out into the canal. Hyacinth, huddled in the bows in a froth of golden tissue, stretched a hand out imploringly. But what could she do?

She gazed round wildly. The Foscaris had disappeared;

there was no one else she could ask for help. Then another boat swung into the gap; the boatman was clad in black, with an executioner's hood and mask. 'At your service, lady?'

With a gasp of relief, Serafina sprang down into the boat. 'Please ... follow them,' she begged, pointing, desperately trying to fabricate excuses so he would not think she was completely mad. 'My sister ... I must go with her ... she'll be frightened.'

The boatman dug the oar expertly into the water and the craft skimmed out into the traffic of the canal. Lights glittered on the dark waves; raucous music came from a tavern on the far bank; above the rooftops a rocket shot into the sky and exploded in a shower of golden stars.

Serafina kept Hyacinth's boat in sight, but she thought that the boatman must have realized he was being pursued; at least, he put on speed. Her own boatman kept up with them, until another boat, filled with young men singing drunkenly, wallowed across their bows and made him veer sharply and lose way so as not to collide with them.

Serafina clutched the side of the boat. 'No!'

Her boatman swore, and added an apology. He fought with the oar as he manoeuvred their boat around the drunken revellers, and managed to splash one of them who was being comprehensively sick over the stern.

By the time they reached open water again, Hyacinth's boat had vanished.

Serafina raised her hands to her face, and felt only the smooth surface of the mask. She did not know what to do. Hyacinth did not know that he could find refuge in the Palazzo Foscari. There was nowhere else in the city where he could be safe, and she dared not imagine what would happen when the black-clad cavalier discovered who he was.

'I'm sorry.' The boatman was moving forward slowly now, so that she could examine the boats on either side. 'I was hoping to find someone tonight, too. Shall we look for them together?'

He pulled off the executioner's hood to reveal the pale gold hair and arrogant features of Count Leonardo Loredan.

2

Gabriel bought a cheap black cloak and a mask from a stall near the Merchants' Bridge. To walk abroad at Carnival without a mask would be to draw attention he did not want. He craved invisibility, so that he might draw undisturbed.

By now he could face the chaos of the city, wilder on this night than on any other. Different musics clashed in the air. Lights flared over stalls that sold wine, or sweetmeats, or Carnival masks and cheap jewels.

In the narrow streets passers-by shouldered against Gabriel, his genic badge hidden by the cloak. In any case, on Carnival night, who would care?

In the squares, fine ladies and gentlemen postured in extravagant costumes of silk and lace and velvet, their faces hidden behind masks of gold and black. Others were deformed: a woman with snakes for hair, writhing sinuously on wires; a man in scarlet – Dracone? – with a demon's face. A double line of children, dressed as mice and rats, jigged past to the tune of a flute. Beggars wormed their way among the crowds, their hands held out for alms.

Boats slid along the canals, their passengers seated on velvet stools, sipping wine, listening to the music of lute or violin. The dark water glittered with reflected light.

Gabriel paused, sketched unobtrusively, tried and despaired of trying to capture the packed confusion of it all, richness alongside poverty, beauty and grotesquerie mingled so that he could scarcely say which was which. His eyes were dazzled and he began to grow very tired.

Passing the dark space beneath a bridge, he heard a faint whimpering, and almost kept on, ascribing it to cats. But the tail of his eye caught a gleam of gold; he swung back. The whimpering again, and the torch that flared at the bridgehead reflected on a twist of metallic ribbon leading off into the dark. Gabriel's skin crawled.

He stooped into the narrow space between the underside of the arch and the water. A girl was crouching there, her extravagant gown of golden tissue ripped into shreds, which she was trying to clutch around herself. Her golden hair was threaded with the metallic ribbon Gabriel had seen at first, half of it dragged away and scattered. As she turned her head towards him, gasping with terror, he saw her face covered by a smooth, impersonal golden mask.

'It's all right,' he said. 'I won't hurt you.'

She shrank back against the slimy stones, beginning to sob.

Gabriel felt nervous. To help her, he would have to touch her. Would they think that he had done this? Edging a little closer, he said, 'Don't be afraid. I'll take you home. Here . . .'

He reached out to take off the mask. The girl jerked

her head away, and gasped out, 'No – don't . . .' Even in
those two words the vibrant alto struck a chord in
Gabriel; he raised the mask to reveal, not a girl, but
Hyacinth.

Touching was not a problem any more. He crawled
into the space beside Hyacinth and put his arms, with his
cloak, around him, feeling his convulsive shivering. He
had begun to weep unrestrainedly now; for some reason
he had been wearing face paint under the mask, and it
was smeared with his tears.

'What happened?' Gabriel asked.

For a long time Hyacinth could do no more than
cling to him, sobbing into his shoulder. Gabriel held him
and tried to get him warm. The raucous music of the
Carnival went on somewhere above their heads. At one
point someone poked his head under the bridge, and as
Gabriel tensed himself he laughed, offered a bawdy piece
of good advice, and passed on.

At last Hyacinth said, 'There was a man . . . he
brought me in a boat from Count Dracone's, and I didn't
dare refuse him. Then he made me come under here. But
when he found out what . . . what I am, he beat me. I
thought he would kill me. I wish he had.'

'No . . . no,' Gabriel said, hugging him in appalled
compassion. 'No need for that. I'll look after you. I'll take
you home.'

Hyacinth went rigid in his clasp. 'No! I won't go back
– not to Dracone.'

'Where, then? Tell me, and I'll help you.'

'There's nowhere.' Hyacinth began to weep again.

Gabriel said, 'You can come with me. I've a place. It's
not much, but you can rest, and tomorrow we'll decide
what to do.'

He took off his cloak and put it around Hyacinth, discarding the worst of the ruined gown. Hyacinth remained passive, too spent even to go on weeping. When Gabriel had fastened on the golden mask again and raised the hood of the cloak he did not look too conspicuous, and it was possible for Gabriel to support him, and guide his faltering steps through the crowds as far as the Dolphin.

When he had deposited Hyacinth on his bed, he went down to the tavern for hot water and towels. By the time he returned, Hyacinth was barely conscious, and made no protest when Gabriel eased away the last scraps of golden tissue, and the gauzy under-tunic, to bathe him.

There was more of the glittery paint on his body, bruising, but little blood, and the mask had saved the exquisite face from damage. Towelling him dry, Gabriel sighed. One look from Leonardo could turn every sinew in his body to water, but now, with the incomparable Hyacinth naked in his bed, he could feel not the smallest stirring of desire.

Finishing, he drew the blanket around Hyacinth and sat on the edge of the mattress, holding his hand.

'Are you feeling better?' he asked. 'Do you want anything?'

'No. You've been so good to me.'

'Tomorrow, we'll . . .' Gabriel was not sure how he would continue, or what could be done for Hyacinth when Count Dracone had all the power of the law on his side.

He was interrupted by the sound of heavy footsteps – two men, or maybe three – mounting the stairs and crossing the floor of the attic. Hyacinth started up as a fist thumped on Gabriel's door, and a voice shouted, 'Open in the name of the Duke!'

'The Lords of Night!' Hyacinth whispered.

Gabriel was bewildered. He had sometimes come across the city watch, the notorious Lords of Night, patrolling with their construct guards, but he had given no offence and they had paid him no attention. He did not know what they were doing here now.

'It's because of me,' Hyacinth said. His voice was a low murmur. 'We must have been seen, coming in . . .'

'But we're not doing anything.'

'They must think we're lovers. It's forbidden, you know it is. Gabriel—'

Looking at the lovely, frightened face, Gabriel almost dissolved into hysterical laughter, though it would have been cruel to give way to it. He reached for the discarded cloak and began to wrap it around Hyacinth. He would have to explain; better if Hyacinth was not naked for the interview. It would be embarrassing enough as it was.

The door crashed open to reveal him to the watchman with his arms around Hyacinth, drawing the cloak around him.

The watchman stood in the doorway. He was broad-shouldered, a big man beginning to run to fat, in black coat and breeches and a leather belt straining over his belly. The scattered shreds of golden silk shone in the light of his lantern.

Gabriel got up and managed to stand, ducking his head under the slanting roof beams. 'Why do you disturb us, sir?' he asked. 'We're doing no wrong.'

The watchman snorted. Gabriel saw the landlord's sharp face, peering around his bulk. 'This is a decent house.'

'But we didn't . . .' Gabriel was too shocked to explain clearly. 'He was hurt, and—'

'You're both under arrest.'

Behind him, Gabriel heard a terrified whimper from Hyacinth. Without looking at him, he said, 'Get out. Through the window.'

'I can't—'

'They'll take you back to Dracone's. Go!'

The watchman tried to interrupt, but Gabriel was blocking the narrow space and the watchman would have to seize him if he wanted to reach Hyacinth. Instead he turned and yelled for his construct guard.

Gabriel heard a scrabbling behind him and felt a rush of cold air as Hyacinth drew the curtain aside and climbed out of the window onto the leads. He wondered whether there were other guards waiting outside, but as the seconds ticked away and there was no outcry from below, he began to relax.

He was not afraid for himself. They would only return him to Leonardo's house, and what else did he want? Leo would never believe that he had done anything to be ashamed of. And perhaps when he had explained, they would be able to find Hyacinth and protect him against Count Dracone.

The construct guard had lumbered up behind his master, who stood aside to let him into the attic. Gabriel moved forward and straightened.

'Count Leonardo Loredan owns my rights,' he said. 'If you take me to him, he—'

'Count Leonardo!' The Lord of Night let out a guffaw from a cavernous mouth. 'Count Leonardo won't want to be bothered with filth like you, boy. You're under arrest.'

3

A rocket soared into the night and burst in an explosion of stars, red, blue and silver. Their reflections glittered momentarily in the waters of the canal as they slid down the sky and died. Boatmen let their craft glide to a halt as their passengers gazed upwards, crying out with admiration.

One boat alone steered expertly through the gaps. Its single passenger stood at the prow, fury in every line of him. As it nudged the steps of the loggia outside the Palazzo Dracone, he sprang up the steps, his cloak falling back to reveal the Count's scarlet coat. He flung a coin to the boatman and thrust open the doors of the palazzo.

Dracone almost ran along the passage and up the stairs, ripping off his narrow velvet mask as he went, and tossing it away. In the great hall, the old steward turned from supervising the constructs as they cleared up after the guests, and came to bow to his master. Dracone shouldered him aside with a curse, and went on without breaking stride.

As he wrenched open the door to the mirrored room, he consciously stilled himself. His fists uncurled to lightly curved claws. He took a breath, closed the door behind him softly, and walked forward into the golden light.

The room was empty. Where the genic had lain, weeping tears of humiliation, was nothing but the crumpled sheets, smeared with scarlet paint.

With a low snarl of fury, Dracone pulled open the mirrored panels leading off the central room. Nothing. The genic had escaped him, just like the stupid slut he had married.

Stilling himself, clenching his teeth on the obscenities that he wanted to pour out, Dracone returned the mirrors to their place. Raising his hands, he began the sibilant chant that would join the room to that other place and summon his dark minions to do his bidding.

His anger ebbed as the words spewed out, replaced by a roiling pleasure as he thought what he would do to the fugitives when they were recaptured. As the light in the room grew redder, darker, as the surface of the mirrors became a liquid skin separating it from the vortex, he brought the chant to an end and waited as the dark forms crowded around him.

'Find them,' he hissed out. 'My wife and the genic. Find them and bring them here to me.'

A wave of heat like the wind from a great burning rolled over him as his servants rushed past him and through the door into the palazzo. His mouth curved into a scarlet smile, Dracone followed them as far as the head of the stairs, and watched them racing down, with a muted roar like flame.

By the time he reached the open doors of the palazzo and strolled out into the loggia, they were gone.

Sixteen

I

Hyacinth stumbled along the alley, clutching the cloak around himself, his shoulders hunched and his head down as if he could hide himself and flee at the same time. He was so panic-stricken that he did not even listen for sounds of pursuit, and it was exhaustion that finally beat him to his knees.

He was crouching halfway up the steps of a bridge, looking down into dark water. The canal was narrow, the buildings on either side tall and shuttered. The only light came from the moon, peering through the space between the rooftops.

Now that he had stopped moving, the icy wind fingered him through the thin cloak and fluttered the surface of the water. Hyacinth let tears slide down his face. He had brought danger on Gabriel who had tried to help him. He had nowhere to go now but Count Dracone's, and no way to escape from the body that had become an obscenity.

Something said to him, 'One way.'

Fascinated, he stared down into the dark water below. He remembered his fear in the lagoon, the few seconds of desperate thrashing before Serafina had reached him and held him up. It would take much longer than that to die. How many minutes of helpless choking before his voice was stifled for ever?

Slowly, hand over hand, he used the iron railing to pull himself upright and mounted the steps until he stood in the centre of the bridge. There, leaning on the rail, he took a breath and sang. Improvising, letting the music pour out without words, he sang his pain. There was no one there to hear, and he owned how fitting that was.

When the last echoes had died away he grasped the rail and sought for a foothold in the ironwork, only to freeze into immobility as he heard a rustling from behind him.

Slowly he turned. Cloud had darkened the face of the moon, but there was enough light for him to see that several figures had formed a loose semi-circle around him. Others stood at either end of the bridge. They wore dark cloaks, and beneath the shadow of their hoods Hyacinth could make out grotesque carnival masks.

At first he thought they were revellers drawn by the sound of his voice. Their stance was threatening, but perhaps if he sang for them he could placate them and they would let him go unmolested.

The nearest of them started to move towards him, and he began to sing again, uncertainly at first, and then with more confidence as their forward movement stopped. For half the length of a song he held them, until, overhead, the moon escaped from the barrier of cloud and Hyacinth saw them more clearly.

His song ended in a choking gasp. What he had taken for a mask was the thing's face, twitching with revulsion that changed to an avid joy as the music died. Its eyes shone with a red light that owed nothing to the moon.

It darted forward, and Hyacinth pressed himself back against the railings of the bridge. Song poured out of him again, halting the creature before it touched him, and in its flinching he saw that music was his defence.

Somehow they would not touch him while he sang. Music was order and grace, and their chaos could not stand against it. But he was very tired, and he did not know how long he could keep on.

He must move, he knew. All around him was darkness, and silence but for his own voice. In his wild flight from the Dolphin, he had lost all track of where he was. But if he could find the carnival crowds – perhaps in the square before the basilica, where music would be playing – then surely the evil creatures that surrounded him would be driven away. And perhaps there would be someone in the crowd who would help him.

Wrapping his cloak tightly around himself, he took one step, then another. The creatures let him pass. Those who stood at the end of the bridge fell back before him, hissing as they fell in behind and alongside him. Once he was clear of the bridge some of them slipped ahead of him. They could not touch him, but they would not let him go.

He moved slowly along the canal side, every step an effort, forced under the eyes of his assailants. They passed the dark façade of a church; no help there, not for a genic.

He had not gone far when he realized they were herding him in the way they wanted him to go. When he tried to turn down a side alley, they packed the entrance. He raised his voice in song and walked towards them, but at the last instant his courage failed, and he stumbled back towards the canal.

They were close around him now, still not touching, but hemming him in. Hyacinth drew breath to sing again, and could manage nothing but a frightened whimper. One of the creatures thrust its head forward, peering at him with eyes like coals. It reached out, not a hand but a thing like a bird's claw, and stroked one talon slowly down the side of his face.

The touch burned, and Hyacinth could smell the reek of singed hair. He thrust out his hands to fend it off, and felt as though he dipped them into fire. But the thing was not solid. In a last, desperate attempt to escape, Hyacinth closed his eyes, shielded his face with one arm, and plunged straight at it.

For a second he thought that he had stumbled into a wall of flame. The air he breathed scorched down his throat. Then he was through, but he had barely felt the night chill when the ground vanished under his feet. He cried out in shock and terror as he pitched forward into the canal.

As the water closed over his head, his limbs spasmed. In some secret recess of his mind he still wanted death, but he could not control his body's frantic struggle for life. He groped for help and found nothing he could hold on to, only enmeshing one arm in the folds of his cloak. He tried to breathe, and gulped water instead.

Then his head broke surface. The canal side was no more than a handsbreadth away; he flailed convulsively with his free arm, but he could not reach it. Above him was the dark flicker of one of the forms which had hounded him, stooping over him like a bird of prey on its perch. Whether it would have held him up or thrust him under, Hyacinth never knew.

He tried to cry out, but the sound was choked off as water filled his mouth again. The surge engulfed him; the dark tide flowed over him, and there was nothing more.

2

Serafina clung to the side of the boat, scanning the other
boats around her and the crowds thronging the quayside.
There were gowns of golden tissue and golden masks in
plenty, but no one she recognized as Hyacinth.

'Sir?' she said nervously as Count Leonardo propelled
the boat forward with clean, powerful strokes. 'Sir, I lied
to you. That was not my sister.'

The Count looked down at her. He had replaced his
executioner's hood, and Serafina had to repress a shiver as
she met the cold, glittering eyes behind the mask.

'I know,' he said. Though she could not see his mouth
she had the feeling he was smiling, though there was no
warmth in his voice.

'Sir?'

'You are Countess Giulietta's genic,' he said. 'You
have no sister.'

Serafina raised her hand to assure herself that her own
mask was still in place. 'How do you know me, sir?'

'Lady Caterina described your dress to me,' Count
Leonardo said. 'And the lady in gold was Hyacinth, I take
it?'

Serafina nodded.

'Does he know that he will be safe in the Palazzo
Foscari?'

'No.' She was furious with herself now; she should
have trusted Hyacinth with the whole of the plan, but
she had not dared.

'Then we must find him,' was all Count Leonardo
said.

'I told him there would be music in the square before the basilica. If he has any choice, he will go there.' She hardly dared to think of what might happen if Hyacinth had no choice, or what the cavalier in black might do to him.

Leonardo gave a murmur of assent. He rowed on, expertly slipping through gaps between the other boats that crowded the water, round the wide sweep of the canal towards the entrance to the lagoon.

As she still examined the crowds for Hyacinth, Serafina became aware that the Count was looking too, though he had not told her the object of his search. Whoever he was trying to find, he had no more success than she.

Where the canal met the waters of the lagoon, Count Leonardo steered into a narrow space at the quayside and tied up the boat. Springing ashore, he held out a hand to help Serafina, and even in her anxiety for Hyacinth she spared a moment's wonder that he would touch a genic, without any suggestion that he was doing anything remarkable.

When they both stood on the edge of the quay, he tucked her arm through his own. 'Forgive me,' he said, his tone crisp and impersonal. 'A woman alone might be . . . annoyed. Let me appear your cavalier for tonight.'

Serafina bent her head towards him as they strolled along the quay, outwardly no more than another couple enjoying the freedom of Carnival. 'Gladly, my lord.'

There was something compelling about him, she had to admit. No wonder Caterina had been captivated, after her strict upbringing in her father's house. Serafina could not help asking herself, if she was truly human and no genic, might she too enjoy these strange dances of courtship? Or would she chafe to be handed over, as Caterina was, at the whim of her father and for the good of her House?

As they drew closer to the Ducal Palace, Serafina began to hear music coming faintly from the square. Gusts of noise from the crowd almost drowned it: laughter, cries of amazement at the tumblers in vivid, loose-fitting silks who were building themselves into a pyramid between the two columns that fronted the waterside, the shouts of wine-sellers and the makers of sweetmeats, selling their wares. Serafina put aside all useless speculation, and began to look more carefully for Hyacinth.

Suddenly Leonardo halted, gripping her hand where it lay on his arm. At the same instant Serafina heard a shrill cry from the gardens on their left. Drunken laughter followed it. In the darkness under the trees, something thrashed and was still.

'Wait,' Leonardo said, releasing her.

He darted through the gate into the gardens, and unmindful of his order Serafina followed. In his black garments he was hard to make out, and where the path divided she almost lost him.

As she hesitated someone else blundered past her, puffing fumes of wine into her face, and then was gone. Serafina cautiously followed the path where he had come from, and a moment later heard Leonardo's voice, not loud, but with a biting clarity.

'Get back! Are you animals?'

Another voice, louder and more truculent, said, 'What's it to you? Leave us alone!'

Serafina rounded a corner to see a man in striped Carnival costume and a jester's mask. Taller than Leonardo, he was threatening the Count with an upraised stick. Behind him, two or three others clustered together, and Serafina caught a glimpse of pale, naked limbs stretched out under a tree.

The jester waved his stick. 'Get out, or I'll break your head!'

Leonardo's only reply was to step forward and close with him, grasping the stick. For a moment they grappled together, and then the Count wrenched the stick away and swept it round to strike a swingeing blow across the jester's shoulders.

The jester howled and pitched forward, scrabbling on hands and knees to escape. Leonardo turned on the other three.

'We meant no harm,' one said, sounding alarmed.

'You're a fool,' said another, sounding contemptuous but keeping out of range of Leonardo's weapon. 'It's no woman – naught but a freak.' He aimed a kick at the pale creature lying among the leaves. 'We could cage her and show her for coppers.'

'I think not.' Leonardo's voice was soft, and sounded all the more dangerous for that. 'Not unless you deal with me first.'

He gripped the stick and took a step forward. The three remaining men – the jester had already disappeared – hesitated and then gave way, muttering among themselves. As they stumbled on to the path and turned to flee, Leonardo followed, but there was no fight in them. Serafina heard their receding footsteps, a grumbled curse or two, and they were gone.

Hesitantly she stepped forward and stooped over their victim. A glimmer of movement and a rustling met her, with a faint sound of protest.

'It's all right; they've gone,' Serafina said.

As she spoke, a burst of light overhead from an exploding rocket showed her a broad, inhuman face. The mouth was a gash, the eyes huge and swollen. The hand raised in a defensive gesture had webs between the fingers. Dark hair was wrapped around the naked body like a cloak.

For a moment Serafina felt a thrill of revulsion, and even – shaming herself – an echo of what the men had felt when they thought it was no sin to abuse such a creature as this. Violently she pushed the thought away. The same men would have abused her, with no more sense of guilt, if they had known her for a genic.

The light died, leaving the image printed on the darkness in front of Serafina's eyes. She whispered, 'What are you?'

More rustling as the woman sat up and smoothed back her hair with those webbed hands. 'A genic, mistress,' she replied.

'But you . . . I have never seen such as you,' Serafina said, aware of how clumsy the words sounded.

'I come from the sea.'

Serafina caught her breath. She remembered how Caterina had told her that a sea woman had saved her from the sea when the Contarini barge went down. She had not believed Caterina – not until now, when the proof was before her.

'Have they hurt you?' she asked.

The sea woman shook her head. 'Not much. You came in time.' She tried to get to her feet, unsteadily, but trying to move away as Serafina held out a hand to help her. 'You must not touch a genic, mistress. I can manage.'

'I am a genic, too,' said Serafina.

The sea genic – on her feet now and steadying herself

against the bole of the tree – stared at her from those huge eyes. Serafina reached out and touched her hand. What she might have said she never knew, because at that moment she heard a firm footstep behind her, and Count Leonardo reappeared, swinging the stick, with a gleam of satisfaction in his eyes.

Catching sight of the sea woman, he checked for an instant, and then exclaimed, 'So those old tales are true!'

'True enough.' The sea genic sank in a genuflection, an oddly graceful movement. 'I thank you, sir, mistress.'

'Can we find your friends for you?' Serafina asked.

The sea genic shook her head. 'I came alone. I wanted to see the lights, and hear the music.' Something about her voice told Serafina that she was still very young. 'I was foolish, I know.'

'Can you make your way home?' said Leonardo. 'Do you want us to come with you?'

The lipless mouth moved into a smile. 'I think you cannot, sir, unless you can swim out to the far islands. If I can reach the waterside I shall be safe enough.'

'Come then, quickly.' Leonardo led the way back along the path, motioning to Serafina and the sea genic to follow.

At the gate to the gardens he paused, but the nearby crowd were all captivated by a street entertainer, his naked skin gleaming as he swallowed fire. No one had eyes for anything else as the sea woman slipped silently across the quayside and let herself down into the water.

At first Serafina thought she was gone, until she saw her head resurface between two boats and she pulled herself up with her forearms resting on the quay. With webbed fingers she drew a bracelet of pearl and coral from her wrist, and held it out to Serafina.

'A token of thanks,' she said, as Serafina hesitated. 'My name is Phao. If you have need of me, seek me on the furthest island.'

Still half reluctant, feeling she did not deserve it, Serafina reached out and took the bracelet. 'I am Serafina,' she said, and added, 'and your friend.'

Phao laughed, and pushed herself off to fall back into the water. With a couple of swift strokes, strong and graceful now in the element she was born for, she plunged into the depths and was gone.

Serafina slid the bracelet onto her own wrist. Fingering the pearls and coral beads, she turned to accompany Leonardo into the square and go on searching for Hyacinth.

3

In his private sitting room, Count Dracone sipped judiciously from a crystal glass, and set it down on the marble-topped table where he sat. His fury was gone now, replaced by a cold determination to recover what was his.

He bent his head over the control disc of the spy-bat. The central screen showed a tiny image of dancers, wheeling with formal grace to music Dracone could not hear. He touched one hand to the controls, sending the bat up higher until he saw crowds packed along the porticos around the dancers, and he realized he was looking down on the square before the basilica.

The slut would not be dancing, not weighed down as she was by the child. A touch of the controls sent the bat hunting along the lines of watching revellers, swooping lower as Dracone looked for the mask and silver fall of feathers that would reveal Giulietta.

Some faces turned upwards, and one lady screamed as the zoomorph almost collided with the extravagant feathers of her headdress. Her cavalier raised his cane to beat it off, but Dracone had already sent it fluttering upwards to spiral around the bell-tower and then out towards the quayside where winesellers cried their wares and entertainers juggled fire or made live doves appear from nowhere to the applause of the fools who gawped at them.

Still no Giulietta. Dracone twisted the control to bring the spy-bat darting back along the wall of the Ducal Palace. Light from an upper window grazed the edge of the screen, and suddenly curious he sent the zoomorph back, making it mount higher until the bright oblong of the window swam into the centre of his vision.

A figure was seated there; as the spy-bat drew closer the Count made out the features of the old Duke. He wore a golden robe, and his cap of office. Dracone snarled a curse; was the old imbecile recovering?

Then he saw that the left side of the Duke's face had slipped out of shape, and the left eye twitched. The right side of his mouth bore a foolish smile, and a thread of spittle drooled from the corner.

'Yet he lives still,' Dracone murmured.

His fingers moved again on the controls. The spy-bat swooped down, the leathery wings flapping in the old man's face. The tiny image was clear enough for Dracone to see the flare of terror in the Duke's eyes, and his mouth distended into a soundless wail. One hand came up, feebly beating air as the spy-bat wheeled away.

Dracone let out a small sigh of satisfaction as the

Duke's body slipped to one side. A servant appeared in the window, gave the old man a single, horrified glance, and began to shout.

Smiling faintly, Dracone raised his glass and let the sweet wine trickle over his tongue. Then he manipulated the controls to bring the bat lower over the heads of the crowd, and resumed his search for Giulietta.

Seventeen

The Lord of Night escorted Gabriel, between two construct guards, through the alleyways of the city as far as the great square in front of the basilica. A cold dawn was breaking. Wind swept the square, driving scraps of bright ribbon and crumpled paper before it, stirring a discarded mask or a broken plume of feathers.

Gabriel saw no one as his escort marched him across the square to the Ducal Palace and into the central courtyard. He was afraid, but he had not given up hope of explaining what had happened. Besides, they would have to tell Leonardo, who owned his rights. Leonardo might be angry, but he would sort out the whole stupid mess.

The escort moved on rapidly up stairs and along passages, until at last the Lord of Night paused in a small, featureless ante-room. Gabriel caught his breath.

'Sir,' he said, 'I can explain everything. I'm sorry if the landlord of the Dolphin was offended, but truly we meant no harm. My friend was hurt, and I . . .'

The Lord of Night was not listening. He poured wine from a jug on a side table and took a long draught, wiping the dregs from his beard. When he had finished, he jerked his head at the constructs. 'Take him down.'

'No!' Outrage and fear poured over Gabriel. He tried

to stand his ground, but the constructs took him by the arms and dragged him out of the room. 'I've done nothing! You must listen to me. Tell Count Loredan, or Dr Foscari—'

He broke off as the Lord of Night slammed the door in his face. The constructs propelled him down a flight of steps, along a narrow passage with tiny windows looking down on a canal, and down another, steeper stair. Water lapped over the steps and Gabriel checked, unable to stifle a whimper of terror, but the constructs forced him on, down into the dark. He slipped and started to struggle in their grasp, only to find his feet on the flagstones of the lower passageway; the water scarcely reached his knees.

He waded through it, gagging on the stench that rose all around him, until the constructs halted, and one of them opened a heavy wooden door, beside an iron grille covering an arched opening in the brickwork. The other thrust Gabriel through the doorway; as he staggered, trying to stay on his feet, he heard the door thud softly closed behind him, and a key turn in the lock.

Gabriel spun round, clutching the bars, staring out at the constructs who were retreating down the passage.

'Please,' he called out, 'take word to Count Leonardo Loredan . . .'

His voice trailed away as the constructs vanished up the stair and out of his sight. He did not even know whether they could understand his plea, much less whether they would pay any attention to it.

The only light in his cell came through the iron grille, that gave onto the passageway. There was no window to the outside. The ceiling was stone, very slightly arched; the walls were partly lined with planks of wood. Rot bloomed on the surface of the planks, and where they had decayed to expose the bare stone Gabriel saw something dark scuttling in the gap between planks and wall.

The water washed around his knees. The surface was covered with scum and slime; shapeless scraps bobbed around in it. Gabriel shuddered as a few bubbles broke surface close to the wall.

The only refuge from the water was a thick slab of wood in the centre of the cell, resting on stone supports, a few inches clear of the surface. Gabriel splashed across to it and crouched there, shivering.

He was still stunned from disbelief. Everything had happened too quickly. He had imagined that he would be given a chance to explain, or at worst that he would have to answer to Leonardo. Now, as belief was forced on him, he began to be truly afraid.

For some reason Dr Foscari had chosen not to acknowledge the note he sent. Neither he nor Leo had shown any interest in sending for him. Even if they went to the Dolphin now, Gabriel could not believe that the tavern keeper would tell the truth about what had happened. He might stay here for ever, and Leo would never find him.

He had lost count of time, but he was stiff from crouching on the wooden slab, when there came a deep gurgling noise. The water swirled, washed over the slab and lapped against him. On a reflex of pure panic, Gabriel flung himself at the iron grille, splashing through the water and clinging to the bars.

'Help me! I'll drown! Let me out! Help!'

His throat was raw with screaming before he realized that the water had risen no higher, that it could never fill the cell because it would run out through the grille and into the passage and the rest of the prison. He could not drown in there.

He still clung to the bars, trembling and sweating, barely able to keep himself upright. No one had come in response to his cries. After a few minutes he waded back to the slab and pulled himself up on it again, beginning to weep softly.

After a while he realized that the dim light of day, filtering down from somewhere up above, had given way to the reddish light of torches, flecking the surface of the water with the image of the bars. He had to relieve himself, and imagined that the stench grew worse. He was climbing back onto the slab when he heard the sound of someone wading along the passage outside.

Desperately he started up, stumbling through the water to the grille. Another construct, placing on a ledge outside where he could reach it a cup of water and the end of a loaf.

'Please . . .' He choked back sobs and tried to speak coherently. 'Please, don't leave me here. It's a mistake. Don't—' As the construct turned away he stretched out a hand through the bars, trying to grasp its arm, but it moved out of his reach. It was expressionless; some last rational spark in Gabriel realized the futility of appealing to the pity of a construct. 'Help me!' he begged as it turned away. 'Tell my lord Leonardo—'

When it was gone, he took in the bread and the cup, shaking so much that some of the water spilt as he tried to drink. He carried bread and cup back to the wooden slab, shrinking away from the filthy touch of the water.

The bread was hard, and he did not feel hunger, or anything but a dull sickness. Still, he made himself choke it down, knowing that he must keep up his strength if he was to have any hope at all. As he tried moistening scraps of it in the water, he heard a noise behind him; his head whipped round and he saw a rat, scrabbling its way onto the slab, a wedge-shaped snout with bright eyes and wicked teeth, the arched body slimed from the fetid water.

With a spasm of revulsion, Gabriel threw the last of the bread away from him. It fell in the water; the rat plunged towards it, but before the creature reached it something else came up from beneath. Gabriel caught a glimpse of a gaping, pale mouth filled with spines before the water swirled and the bread vanished, and whatever had risen to claim it sank back into the dark. Shuddering, he covered his face with his hands.

Water was still slopping over the slab. Gabriel ached with exhaustion, but he dared not lie down and try to sleep. He drew up his knees and wrapped his arms around them, lowering his head as if by curling himself into the smallest possible space he could somehow convince himself that nothing outside himself was real. In a little while, a kind of blankness seeped into his mind, shutting out the worst of his misery.

He awoke with a jerk, slumped over on his side, with water lapping against his mouth. He coughed, retching, and pushed himself into a sitting position. His clothes were soaked and stinking and clung clammily to him. When he sat up water streamed from his hair and plastered it to his neck and face.

Briefly he had forgotten where he was or how he had come there. When he remembered he fell into a sudden panic that Leo had come while he slept, and somehow failed to find him, and the idea, even when he realized

how foolish it was, still made him rise and struggle across
to the grille to look out.

The passage was empty. The light was red. Time must
have passed, for someone had delivered more bread and
water to the ledge, but the cup was tipped over and only
a few crumbs were left from the loaf.

Gabriel felt light-headed with hunger now. He swallowed the last few drops of clean water, and then waded
back to the slab and collapsed on it.

As time went by, the light paled, and reddened, and
paled again, until he lost count of the passing of the days.
Sometimes the water would recede, and give him a brief
chance to rest. Sometimes he would be awake when his
food was brought to him, and be able to save it from the
rats. Whenever he saw the construct guards, he would
beg them to take a message to Count Leonardo Loredan.

His worst fear was that his messages were reaching
Leo, and Leo did not want to come.

2

Hyacinth was not in the square. Serafina and Count
Leonardo spent hours searching for him, by boat and on
foot along the crowded alleys of the city, but they did not
find him. The sky was growing pale above the domes of
the basilica when they finally admitted their failure and
took a boat to the Palazzo Foscari.

Through all their wanderings, Serafina had been aware
of Leonardo searching for someone else, but he had no
more luck than she did. He still did not tell her who he
was looking for.

When they arrived at the Palazzo Foscari, the servant

showed them into a morning room, where Caterina was seated at table with Count Francesco and Maria, and an immensely fat man Serafina had not met before. There was no sign of Giulietta.

Caterina sprang up as Serafina and Count Leonardo came into the room. 'You're safe! Where have you been? What happened?'

Serafina clasped her friend's hands. 'We lost Hyacinth.'

Caterina's eyes widened in distress. 'Tell me.'

As Serafina explained, Caterina drew her to the table and found her a seat. Count Francesco welcomed her as if she were a friend, not a genic at all, and one of his servants poured hot chocolate for her from a silver pot, and offered her a basket of hot, spiced rolls.

'We must look for him,' Count Francesco said, when Serafina had finished. 'I shall give orders at once.'

He bowed to the little gathering, and went out.

Count Leonardo had seated himself at the opposite side of the table, and sat passing his hands over his face, ignoring the steaming cup of chocolate in front of him. Serafina thought he looked exhausted, more than could be explained by their night's search.

The fat man said to him, 'Nothing, boy?'

'Nothing. Stupid to hope, I suppose.' Stiffly, speaking it seemed to Caterina more than to the others, he added, 'Gabriel, my genic, has disappeared. I cannot find him. I fear he is dead.'

Caterina gasped, and turned to look at the portrait that hung above the fireplace. Serafina's eyes followed hers. This must be the portrait Caterina had spoken of, the strange new art that Count Leonardo's genic practised.

He had painted Maria, and had not insulted her by trying to pretend that she was beautiful. But he had seen something, that Serafina could only think of as a kind of light, Maria's gentleness and warmth that were in themselves beauty. Though Serafina had barely known Gabriel, she could not help a pang of sorrow at the thought that the creator of such wonder should be dead.

Maria was also looking at the portrait, flushing faintly, though she said nothing of it. Instead she asked, 'How long ago did he vanish?'

'On your wedding day,' Leonardo answered. 'A fortnight now.'

Serafina thought there was something he was not saying. Caterina was looking troubled, too, but she sipped chocolate and said nothing.

'Francesco will find him,' said Maria.

The fat man snorted, and took a mouthful of spiced bread. When he had swallowed, he said, 'I've had my constructs out, since the day after. They've found nothing.'

'I've walked the streets, asked in taverns—' Leonardo began, and broke off, looking sidelong again at Caterina.

Her face grew suddenly brighter. Flushing a little, stumbling in her speech, she said, 'I learnt to know Gabriel – a little, when we came to your house, sir – ' she nodded at the fat man – 'and he painted Maria's portrait. If he is alive, I believe he must be painting. Have you tried asking in . . . oh, in paper-makers' shops, or wherever he would buy the ingredients for his paint?'

As she spoke, Count Leonardo fixed her with an intense gaze, almost, Serafina thought, as if he had never seen her before. Her flush deepened. 'I'm sorry. You must have thought of that already.'

'No. No, I hadn't.' Count Leonardo drained his cup of chocolate and stood up. 'Your leave, ladies, Dr Foscari.'

He went out and they all heard his rapid footsteps retreating along the passage.

The fat man, Dr Foscari, said, 'Young idiot.'

Caterina half rose, as if she would follow Leonardo out, and then took her seat again. For a minute she looked uncomfortable, and then she gave her head a little shake, as if to clear it, and said to Serafina, 'I'm sorry. You must be worried about Giulietta. She's here, and quite safe. She's sleeping upstairs.'

'What have you told her?' Serafina asked, relieved that at least part of the plan had worked as it was meant to.

'Nothing, yet.' It was Maria who answered. 'While we were watching the dancers in the square, someone frightened her – a man costumed as a demon, who tried to make her go with him.'

'A demon!' Serafina exclaimed. She could not help remembering the mirrored room in the Palazzo Dracone, and the evil creatures Dracone had conjured up.

'Some drunken fool,' Dr Foscari said dismissively, but Serafina could not be certain. What more likely than for Dracone to send out his servants to find Giulietta and bring her back?

'Francesco made him go away,' said Maria. 'After that, Giulietta was happy to come here for a late supper. She was very tired, so we invited her to stay for the rest of the night. When she wakes, Francesco's physician will say that for the sake of the baby she must rest for a few days, and not be moved, even to go home.'

Serafina nodded. The time was coming when she would have to tell Giulietta the truth about the child she was carrying, but this new plan would at least postpone the moment until she had time to think how best to do it. She asked, 'What about Count Dracone?'

Caterina gave her an impish smile. 'Francesco will invite him to visit his wife. What could be more correct?'

'Dracone isn't correct,' said Serafina.

Dr Foscari laughed. 'Dracone wants to be Duke,' he said. 'He can't afford to be anything but correct, in public at any rate. Besides, suppose he forced his wife home and she miscarried of the Christos Child! He daren't risk it.'

Serafina was not sure. 'Wouldn't it be better to hide her altogether?'

'Servants gossip,' said Caterina. 'We can't pretend she isn't here, and there's nowhere else we could take her.'

'Besides,' said Maria, 'it's true she must rest because of the child. She couldn't travel very far, not safely.'

Serafina had to agree, but she could not feel confident. Giulietta was Count Dracone's wife, just as much his possession as his constructs or his flyer. If he chose, he could demand her return, and the law would support him. No one would believe what Serafina knew of him, and even if they did, it might not make any difference. She sighed. She was beginning to realize that engineering Giulietta's escape from the Palazzo Dracone had solved only the first of a huge and complicated net of problems.

3

On the morning after Carnival, Gianni made his way to the warehouse. The night just past had brought its own problems, and he was deep in thought, not sure what his course of action should be.

The warehouse doors were open but the place looked

empty; Gianni heard the sound of voices from the counting-house.

When he went in he saw Malatesta at his desk, surrounded by clerks and warehousemen, all of whom seemed to be talking at once. The chatter died down, though it did not stop, as Gianni walked over to Malatesta.

'What's going on? Why is no one at work?'

The chief clerk gave him a thin smile. 'You haven't heard?'

'Heard what? No.'

'It's the Duke,' said Malatesta. 'The old Duke's dead.'

Eighteen

I

Count Leonardo Loredan passed through the ante-room and into the Hall of Shields where the Dukes of the city sat in audience. The old Duke now gave his last audience of all; his embalmed body lay in state on its catafalque, between the two great globes, terrestrial and celestial, that dominated the centre of the hall. Poised between earth and heaven, Leonardo thought, looking down at the sculptured face. The Duke had been a secretive man in life, and now that he was possessed of the ultimate secret, he still gave nothing away.

Leonardo felt uncomfortable in the stiff robes of scarlet silk that he wore for this duty of attendance on the corpse. Scarlet, not black to mourn a Duke, for though the man was dead, the Dukedom still survived. No one had worn this set of robes since Leonardo's grandfather, old Ercole, and Manfred had hauled them out of a closet the day before, sponged and pressed them and stitched the worst of the rents. Leonardo imagined the smell of mothballs still hung around them.

Candles burnt around the bier; the other Councillors blazed scarlet in their light, and cast flapping black shadows on the maps that lined the walls. The men moved softly, giving place to each other, speaking in hushed voices, or not at all.

As Leonardo stood with bowed head, he felt a light touch on his shoulder, and turned to see Francesco Foscari.

'I've something for you,' his friend murmured. 'Come into the ante-room.'

Leonardo followed him out, relaxing as he left the hall of flame and shadows. 'Well?'

'Have you any more news of Gabriel?'

They still spoke in quiet voices, so as not to be heard by the Councillors who passed in and out.

'A little,' Leonardo said. 'I found a shop where he bought paper – the paper-maker recognized his description. But he hasn't seen him since before Carnival.'

'Look at this,' said Count Foscari.

He led Leonardo across the room to the massive stone fireplace where he picked up a leather portfolio and put it into Leonardo's hands. 'One of my servants brought me this last night.'

Leonardo opened it, and his start of surprise almost sent the portfolio's contents sliding to the floor. It held paper – some scraps, some larger sheets – all of them covered with Gabriel's drawings. His hands shaking, Leonardo leafed through them: a bridge reflected in a quiet canal; a lamp bracket shaped like a predatory eagle; a fountain like a leaping dolphin; a balcony with intricately pierced stonework.

He looked his question at Count Francesco; he could not trust his voice to speak.

'They came from an inn called the Dolphin. My servant – bright lad – noticed the painted sign. The landlord gave him these. He said that Gabriel stayed there a few days while he painted the sign, and then left.' He reached across and drew out a sheet that showed a masked lady with an elaborate headdress in the shape of a bird of paradise. 'He was there until Carnival night at least.'

Very carefully Leonardo closed the portfolio and held it tight against his chest. He schooled his voice to say, 'Then we only missed him by a few days.' Straightening, suddenly determined, he said, 'The landlord must know more than he's telling. I'm going down there.'

He took a step towards the door. Francesco gripped his shoulder. 'Just a minute. You can't go dressed like that, and you can't abandon your duty here. Not unless you want to throw away the Dukedom. The Dolphin will keep.'

Something in Leonardo wanted to toss the Dukedom aside, if that would bring Gabriel back, but he could not start an argument here with Francesco Foscari. He was too grateful for the older man's friendship, his support in the search for Gabriel, and most of all that he had asked no questions.

He let out a weary sigh; his shoulders sagged, and Francesco tightened his grip.

'I've put a watch on the Dolphin,' he said. 'If he comes back, we'll have him.'

'Thank you.' Leonardo opened the portfolio again and sifted through the drawings as if they might hold other clues to where Gabriel had gone. 'I thought he might have run away, left the city,' he said. 'But he stayed . . . and yet he didn't come home . . .'

His voice was treacherously threatening to break, and he stopped before he gave himself away entirely.

Francesco was frowning slightly, his plain face serious, his eyes a little troubled. 'Perhaps we did wrong in sending him to my uncle's.'

'If there was wrong, it was mine.' Leonardo made

himself speak quietly, though he wanted to shout, and break something. 'Gabriel is my responsibility.' Unable to help himself, he added, 'We quarrelled, that last day.'

'Quarrelled, with—'

'With a genic, yes. Gabriel was never just a genic to me – and not what your beloved father-in-law thinks, either. No one can hurt a genic, isn't that what they tell us? But I hurt Gabriel, and now—'

His voice was beginning to rise, and one or two of the other Councillors across the room were starting to cast glances at him and Count Foscari.

'Leonardo—' Francesco began.

'I know, I know. Duty and decorum, and the elections. Don't worry, Francesco, I'm not going to make a fool of myself in public. But I can't help wondering—' He looked down again at the drawings he held, and closed the leather cover over them. 'Gabriel would never have left these behind. Not if he had any choice. So what happened at the Dolphin? If someone took him away, where is he now, and what are they doing to him?'

2

'Now the Duke is dead,' said Caterina, 'they will hold the elections soon.'

Serafina threaded her needle with gold silk, and picked up the breadth of white satin she was adorning with seed pearls for Caterina's wedding gown. 'Do you want to be Duchess?'

Caterina let out a little gurgling laugh as she paused in winding silk onto an ivory winder. 'No! But I want Count Leonardo to be Duke, and not Count Dracone.'

'Giulietta would make a wonderful Duchess, though.' Serafina could not help smiling. 'She would love the ceremony, and the beautiful dresses.'

Maria Foscari finished pinning lace to the skirts of the fine lawn gown she was stitching for the baby. She began, 'Francesco says—'

The door of her sitting room opened, interrupting her. Giulietta Contarini-Dracone stood in the doorway. Her golden hair was unbound, and her feet were bare. She still wore a nightgown, though she had pulled a wrapper hastily over it. She swayed as if the bulk of the child she carried might overset her.

'Giulietta!' Maria cast aside the gown and hurried across the room to put a steadying hand under Giulietta's arm. 'You shouldn't be out of bed. You know what our physician said.'

Serafina knew that the fiction Francesco Foscari had suggested had become uncomfortably close to the truth. Giulietta had over-exerted herself on Carnival night, and now she had to rest for her own sake and the child's.

'But it's so *boring* up there,' Giulietta complained. 'And nobody talks to me. When can I go out?'

'Not yet,' said Maria.

She helped Giulietta across the room to a seat by the fire, and rang for her maidservant. When the girl came, she sent her for a hot tisane and the sweet cakes that Giulietta loved.

'Would you like to make something for the baby?' she suggested, turning over the lace and silks in her sewing chest. 'Look, there's—'

'I can't sew,' Giulietta said. 'You're so good, Maria, you can sit stitching all day, but I want to have some *fun*, like we did when Papa was alive.'

Maria looked mildly scandalized. Caterina raised her eyes and cast a mischievous glance at Serafina.

Serafina would have liked to share her amusement, but she was feeling the weight of responsibility. She could not put off for much longer the time when she would have to tell Giulietta about her baby.

In spite of Giulietta's ill health, Serafina could see a change in her. She had lost the languor she had shown in the Palazzo Dracone, the slow speech and the heavy-eyed look that had convinced Serafina that the Count was drugging her. She was more like the Giulietta of the Palazzo Contarini, and she had begun to think back to her life before she was married, as if, on some unspoken level, she recognized that she had taken a wrong turning and lost her way.

She had spoken very little of Count Dracone. Since Carnival, he had paid one visit to his wife, and as Dr Foscari had predicted, he had behaved very correctly. Poisonously smooth was how Serafina would have described him, but he had thanked Maria very courteously for her care of Giulietta, listened with every evidence of concern to the physician's reports, and sent one of his constructs with flowers each morning to receive word of how Giulietta did.

Serafina could not help wondering how long he would wait before he began to demand the return of his wife. How long before events pressed upon them and left them no choice of when and how to tell Giulietta the truth?

Summoning courage, she took a breath. 'Giulietta . . . Giulietta, has Count Dracone said anything to you about your child?'

She was aware of Maria and Caterina giving her apprehensive looks.

Giulietta smiled complacently. 'He is pleased to have an heir for House Dracone.'

'No more?'

'What more should there be?'

'Giulietta, there's something we must tell you. Something about this child.' She paused in case Maria or Caterina wanted to take the responsibility for this, but they were both frozen like mice under the cat's foot. 'Count Dracone and Dr Heinrich made an announcement in Council. Dr Heinrich said that he had taken the hair of Christos from the reliquary ring, and ... and placed it inside you, to grow into a child. Another Christos.'

Giulietta stared at her, and to Serafina's dismay began to pout petulantly. 'Serafina, if that's supposed to be a joke, I don't think it's funny at *all*!'

'It's not a joke.'

'Oh, don't be so *stupid*!' said Giulietta. 'How could anyone possibly do that? Just from a hair?'

'Dr Heinrich used to make genics.' Maria came to Serafina's aid. 'Francesco explained it all to me. This – what he did to you – it uses the same skills.'

'It's true, Giulietta,' said Caterina.

Serafina said, 'Giulietta – forgive me – but when you were married and went to live in the Palazzo Dracone, did the Count ever ... ever come to you as your husband? *Can* this child be his?'

Giulietta let out a little tinkle of laughter. 'Don't be stupid, Serafina, of course he...' Her voice faded; she wrinkled her brow. All her laughter had vanished. 'I thought he did. I thought he came to me ... but I was always so sleepy. Perhaps they were only dreams.'

Or the drugs the Count gave her, Serafina thought. She said, 'Giulietta, I don't think Dracone could give you a child of his body. Only this one, that Heinrich made from the relic. They are using you to bear a copy of the Christos Child. When the child is born, he will belong to Dracone.'

Giulietta's eyes were fixed on her as she spoke. Serafina could see that at last she believed. She drew in air, and opened her mouth to scream.

Maria gripped her shoulders. 'No, Giulietta, no! Control yourself – think of your baby!'

Giulietta took several gasping breaths, and held her hands spread over her swollen belly as if she wanted to protect the child within. Very slowly, she crept back from the edge of hysteria.

She said, 'I don't want this! I don't *want* it!' Eyes wide, she looked from one face to another. 'What will they make me do?'

Serafina did not know who 'they' were. She was not sure that Giulietta knew, either. 'They'. The ones who would take this baby and make it into what 'they' wanted it to be.

Answering the thought behind Giulietta's question, she said, 'Count Dracone will use the child for his own power. Already he is saying that he must be Duke because he will be the guardian of Christos reborn.'

Childlike, Giulietta said, 'Is he a very wicked man?'

Maria exchanged a swift glance with Caterina. Serafina could almost read her thought: *Her own husband!*

'Yes,' Serafina said. No point now in hiding anything. 'He wrecked the boat and drowned your father and Paolo. He did it to marry you so you could bear this child.'

She could see the struggle as Giulietta took in what she had heard, and pitied her. What had there ever been in her life to help her face this now?

'How do you know?' Giulietta asked.

'I was there. I saw.'

Maria reached out and took Giulietta's hand in both her own. 'But you're safe here now.'

Giulietta stared at Serafina, lips parted, astonished but not, any longer, disbelieving. She said, 'He is my husband. He will make me go back to him.'

'Not if you don't want to,' said Maria. 'Francesco will help you.'

'I don't want to,' said Giulietta. She looked down at the curve of her belly where the child nested. Desolate, she whispered, 'I don't want to.'

Serafina said urgently, 'Then what do you want, Giulietta? What do *you* want your child to be?'

Enormous tears gathered in Giulietta's eyes, and spilt down her cheeks. She said, 'I want an heir for House Contarini.'

3

Gabriel was drowsing uneasily, huddled on the slab inside his cell, when the constructs came. Water lapped around him, lifting his hair like seaweed on the tide. The jangle of keys roused him as the first of them unlocked the door and swung it back.

He started up, his heart racing. The guard motioned to him to come out, and at first he stared in stupefaction, hardly able to believe that something might change at last.

'Is my lord Leonardo here?' he asked.

The construct's only reply was a jerk of the head in the direction of the passage. Terrified that it would leave and lock him in again, Gabriel let himself down from the slab, but he was so weakened by the days of his imprisonment that his knees buckled under him and he almost fell forward into the fetid water.

The construct grasped him by the arm and thrust him out of the cell, along the passage and up the flight of stairs that led to the bridge. Gabriel stumbled along between the two of them, blinking as true daylight pierced his eyes, shivering and gulping at the clearer air that flowed through the narrow windows. A final struggle up the last flight of steps, and he stood once more in the ante-room where he had last faced the Lord of Night.

The same man was seated at the table, writing, and did not look up as Gabriel was brought in. No one else was there.

The construct let Gabriel go, and he fell to his knees, close to fainting, while water streamed from his clothes and hair and puddled on the marble floor. He fought to remain conscious, to hold back the babble of pleas for help or mercy that wanted to break from him, until he should discover what the man meant to do with him.

At last the Lord of Night put down his pen and stood up so that he could look at Gabriel over the table that separated them.

'Please, lord . . .' Gabriel said. 'Send word to Count Leonardo Loredan. He owns my rights, he will—'

The Lord of Night interrupted him, though he spoke to the constructs, not to Gabriel. 'Very well. Take him.'

'Where?' Gabriel cried as the constructs hauled him to

his feet again and propelled him towards the opposite door. He fought to hold back, grabbing at the doorpost, to make the Lord of Night listen to him. 'What are you doing with me? Why? I told you, I've done nothing!'

The Lord of Night had already picked up his pen again, and Gabriel did not have the strength to go on struggling. The constructs half carried him out, down the stairway and through the courtyard into the square in front of the basilica.

It was very early in the morning; cold, pale sky arched above the city. The square was deserted. Gabriel had stopped trying to resist, half from exhaustion, half from a wild hope that they were, after all, returning him to Leonardo. But instead of escorting him down the street that led to Dr Foscari's, or taking a boat to the Palazzo Loredan, they marched him across to the bell-tower.

In the doorway, Gabriel checked. 'What's happening? Where are you taking me?'

No reply. The constructs had never spoken. Gabriel did not know if they could speak. Instead, they thrust him through the entrance hall into the tower, and up the interminable stair.

He had to crawl up the last few steps on hands and knees, and collapsed on the floor of the room below the bellchamber, chest heaving as he tried to get his breath. He heard the constructs' feet heavy on the floor, and a metallic clanging, but he did not look up until they laid hands on him again.

Across the room, beside the window, was an iron cage, its door standing open. The roof of the cage curved up to a point, from which a length of chain dangled and coiled untidily on the floor. The constructs half lifted Gabriel

and dragged him over to it; he caught at one of the bars
as they tried to push him inside.

'No!' He began to sob, giving way to panic at the last.
'Don't – please . . . Let me go!'

He tried to cling to the bars, to the constructs, in a
final frantic effort to escape. Silent, implacable, they broke
his grip and bundled him inside; the door clanged shut.

The chain shifted like a rusty snake. It ran through a
pulley and out along a bar that projected from the
window above the square. As one of the constructs turned
a handle the cage lifted and moved jerkily outwards,
swaying until it reached the end of the bar.

Gabriel clutched at the bars, staring down at the
paving far below, and screamed as the cage suddenly
dropped, seeing himself broken on the stones. Seconds
later the cage jolted to a stop at the end of the length of
chain, leaving Gabriel suspended a few yards above the
square.

Twisting around, he peered upwards, but the window
was empty now; moments later he saw the constructs
leaving by the door. They crossed the square again and
vanished into the Ducal Palace.

The only sounds were the creak of the chain, the cry
of gulls above the lagoon, and Gabriel's own quiet
sobbing. The cage was too small to lie down or even sit;
he tried vainly to curl himself into a more comfortable
position.

Soon the single, cracked bell began to toll, and a few
people appeared in the square, hurrying into the basilica
for the early service. Gabriel was torn between shame that
they would see him like this, and the desperate need to
beg their help. He stretched a hand through the bars,

crying out if anyone came close to him; most ignored him, though one or two replied with laughter or a snarled obscenity. After a while the bell stopped, the last worshippers scurried inside the basilica, and the square was empty again.

Yet Gabriel could not help but feel a small stirring of hope. Sooner or later, someone he knew would pass through the square. Perhaps even Leonardo himself. Surely Leonardo — even if he no longer wanted Gabriel at all — would never leave him here, if he knew.

As the day wore on, and the square began to fill, Gabriel peered down, trying to read each face. Councillors, robed and dignified; vendors of spiced rolls and sweetmeats; an entertainer with a little dog; ladies and boatmen and street urchins. Never the face he wanted.

Once he caught sight of Dr Foscari's bulky figure, stumping across the corner of the square between the basilica and the Judiciary, but though he screamed with all his strength the old lawyer did not hear him.

Hours passed; exhaustion overcame Gabriel and he dozed uneasily, only to jerk awake, stiff and shivering, terrified that Leonardo had passed by while he slept. The square had almost emptied again. Clouds were massing overhead; an icy wind swept in from the lagoon; sleet whipped stinging across his face. Then, though he thought he had barely blinked his eyes, it was night. He grew more frightened still as he realized that he had lost consciousness for several hours.

He began to weep softly. *I shall die here*, he thought. *Leo will not come. No one will help me.*

The creaking of the chain and the clanging of the bell slid together in his mind so that they seemed to become one continuous noise. Light merged into darkness and back into daylight. He lost count of the days. Cramp seized his limbs so that even trying to move was agony. His lips cracked with thirst. His head drooped against the bars of the cage, and he had barely strength left to raise his heavy eyelids and scan the crowds for the face that never came.

Nineteen

I

Count Leonardo Loredan knelt on the cold marble tiling of the basilica floor, and listened to the droning of the Patriarch somewhere at a distance. When the service was over, he and the other Councillors would withdraw to the hall of the Great Council and cast their votes to decide who would be the next Duke. Leonardo genuinely did not know whether he or Count Dracone had more support. And as the days had slipped by with no further word of Gabriel, he was finding it harder to care.

The silver hanging lamps woke gleams of gold from the mosaics that decorated the walls and the inside of the domes. The Lord Christos and the saints looked down in dark, jewel colours. Leonardo gazed back, but if they had any message for him, he did not know what it was.

He wore his Councillor's robes for the voting ceremony that was to follow. The other Councillors knelt all around him, with those of their ladies who had chosen to attend. Leonardo had seen Caterina there, with the Foscaris. He wondered whether, if he lost the election, she and her father would wish to withdraw from the betrothal.

At last the Patriarch came to the end of his long blessing. Leonardo was able to rise from his cramped position, stretch discreetly, and wait for the Procurator to chivvy him into his place in the procession.

He and the other Councillors formed up in the narthex, ready for the short walk to the Ducal Palace. The Procurator, in his official purple gown, led the way, with Leonardo and Count Dracone, as the Ducal candidates, following just behind him.

Dracone bowed and smirked with that scarlet mouth as he came to stand by Leonardo, and murmured, 'Is it permitted to wish you good fortune, my lord Count?'

Leonardo shrugged. 'As you please.' He could hardly believe that Dracone's wishes were sincere, or summon up more than the barest civility.

'This is hard for you, when so much rests on your success. The restoration of your House . . .' The black eyes glinted amusement as Leonardo gritted his teeth, scarcely able to restrain himself from cursing the fellow under the basilica roof. As if he had no other motive for seeking the title of Duke, except for the mercenary one.

'Don't worry.' Dracone's voice was softer still. 'If I should prevail, I will find you a . . . suitable office.'

'I thank you,' Leonardo said shortly. 'I shall return the favour.'

An office that Dracone deserved . . . he could have entertained himself with choosing one, if he had been in the mood. As it was, he shifted restlessly, chafing for the formal proceedings to begin, so that he did not have to listen any longer to Dracone's poisonous courtesy.

At length the Procurator was satisfied with the ordering of the procession, and led the way down the steps from the narthex out into the square, swinging out towards the bell-tower and back to the door of the Ducal Palace.

Crowds thronged the square, and broke into cheering as the Councillors made their dignified way through their midst, flanked by the lion-headed constructs of the Duke's personal retinue bearing ceremonial falchions. Leonardo heard his own name shouted, but he also heard Dracone's. Count Dandolo had told him that Dracone's pilot Cesare had spent several nights and a large amount of money buying wine in every tavern along the canalside from the basilica to Corpus Domini, and though the people could not vote, their enthusiasm might influence the Councillors who could. Leonardo was quite ready to believe that some of the men in the procession still did not know into which urn they would drop their ivory voting slip.

He kept his eyes fixed on the Procurator just ahead of him, the purple folds of his robe billowing out in the breeze that blew off the lagoon. He was making the turn that would lead the procession back towards the Palace, when Leonardo heard his own name cried again.

Not the cheerful shouts of his supporters, but a hoarse, cracked scream, from somewhere above his head. 'Leo – Leo, help me!'

Puzzled, still pacing slowly after the Procurator, he turned his head in the direction of the voice. The wretched creature in the cage suspended from the belltower had hardly registered on his consciousness, taken up as he was with his own affairs. Now he looked closer.

An emaciated creature, limbs drawn up at crazy angles in the confined space. One arm stretched out to him, the fingers crooked into a claw. 'Leo – don't leave me! Leo!'

'Gabriel!'

He halted. The Councillor behind him cannoned into him and muttered something. Leonardo stared up at the cage, reached upwards, but could not touch the straining fingers. He snapped at the nearest construct, 'Get him down.'

The construct hesitated, confused by the break in the expected ceremony.

'Now.'

The force behind the single word seemed to resolve the construct's dilemma. It bowed clumsily, and pushed its way through the suddenly thickening crowd to the door of the bell-tower.

The Procurator glanced back, saw that the rest of the procession was held up, and retraced his last few steps until he stood beside Leonardo. 'Count Loredan, what—'

'That is my genic.' Leonardo's voice was icy; he felt himself shaken by a blast of fury so cold and powerful that it frightened even himself. He did not know what he was going to do.

'Your *genic*?' the Procurator repeated. 'My dear Leonardo, are you out of your mind? The election—'

He broke off, recoiling, as Leonardo swung round on him. 'Damn the election.'

There was a creaking from far above, as the cage began to sway and jerk in its uneven descent, until it jarred on the paving of the square. Leonardo knelt beside it, gathered Gabriel's hand into his, and beckoned to another of the constructs.

'Open it. Get him out.'

There was no hesitation this time. With more than human strength the construct took hold of the bars of the cage door and bent them until the lock snapped. The door swung open; Leonardo caught Gabriel as he fell forward, cushioning him against the paving stones.

Gabriel was sobbing in feeble spasms, fingers scrabbling at the folds of Leonardo's robe. Waves of convulsive
shivering shook him. His clothes were stiff with filth, his
hair matted, and a sour stench came off him. He was
pale, his eyes sunken with red and crusted lids.

Leonardo held him close, hardly aware of the silence
that spread through the watching crowd like ripples in a
pool, or the protests of the Councillors. He only looked
up when he heard Count Dandolo exclaim, 'Are you
quite mad?'

The Count was standing over him, face congested
with anger, as if he was about to throw a fit. Behind him
the procession had broken up, and Councillors were
standing here and there in little knots and casting doubtful glances at him. The Procurator looked completely
helpless. Dracone stood close by, not bothering to hide
his contempt, and a growing exultation.

Leonardo felt a great weight lift off him. It was over.
The lies and hedging and compromise, unworthy of
House Loredan. He would not be Duke, but he would
regain the honour of his House. He hugged Gabriel.

'Don't cry,' he whispered. 'You're safe now. I won't
leave you.'

Before he could begin to think of what he must do
next, he saw Francesco Foscari pushing his way towards
him, with Maria and Caterina behind. Briefly he felt
sorry. Francesco had done his best; this must seem like a
betrayal. But Francesco did not have first claim on his
loyalty.

His friend stooped beside him. 'I've sent for my
servants. They'll take him home, and later you can—'

Closer to consciousness than Leonardo had thought,
Gabriel clutched at him in a panic at the suggestion. 'It's

all right,' Leonardo reassured him. To Francesco he said,
'I can't leave him.'

'You can't stay here,' said Francesco.

'Do as he tells you.' That was Count Dandolo again,
grasping frantically at any hope of regaining control.
'Leave that ... filth where it belongs. You must sit in
Council, and speak for the Dukedom – if you haven't
already thrown it away. If every member of this Council
isn't disgusted at the thought of what kind of Duke you
would make.'

Leonardo's roiling anger and compassion found a
focus, and as he looked up at Count Dandolo he felt a
smile of unholy delight spreading across his face.

'Very well,' he said. 'At least they know what kind of
Duke I would make. Let's see if that is the kind of Duke
they want.'

'What do you mean?' asked Dandolo.

'Let's proceed to the great hall. But if I go, Gabriel
goes with me.' Ignoring Dandolo's apoplectic protests, he
bent his head over Gabriel and said, 'Can you walk, just
a little way?'

Gabriel's limbs were still drawn up in the cramped
position from the cage, and though he tried to rise he
had to sink back into Leonardo's arms. Leonardo began
to lift him, and then he realized that Caterina was there
beside him, pulling off her velvet cloak and thrusting it
into his hands.

'Here, take this. He looks so cold.'

Leonardo stared at her, lips parting on an instinctive
protest, to keep her out of danger at least as his life came
crashing down around her. She gestured to silence him.

'If I do this,' she said, 'they cannot say those things of
you.'

Her words took his breath away. He could not calculate how much she knew, or thought she knew, but he could understand the compassion that drove her.

'Oh, thank you, lady,' he breathed out.

'Caterina!' Dandolo was certainly going to throw a fit. 'I forbid this!'

His daughter turned a cold look on him. 'Don't be foolish, Papa.'

With her to help him, Leonardo worked the cloak around Gabriel, folds of blue velvet that hid the filthy rags and shielded him from the chill breeze. Murmuring encouragement, he helped Gabriel to stand, and supported him across the square and through the archway that led into the Palace, beneath the grave regard of the winged lion.

Silent now, from outrage or apprehension, the other Councillors followed.

In the ante-room to the hall of the Great Council, Leonardo settled Gabriel on one of the couches that lined the walls, and sat beside him, still letting Gabriel hold on to him. He was aware of the other Councillors passing him in a rustle of stiff silk, to take their places in the room beyond.

The Procurator hovered briefly in front of him, and Dr Foscari, who as Secretary of the Voices had charge of the conduct of the election, stood looking down for a moment and then snorted and continued into the hall.

Caterina brought a footstool and sat close by, arms clasping her knees, eyes wide now in a rapt seriousness. The doors of the hall were closed.

Leonardo bent his head so he could speak softly to

Gabriel. 'Why did you run away? Did I make you so unhappy?'

The dark eyes were fixed on him wonderingly. 'I sent a note to Dr Foscari. He knew where to find me, but he never sent for me.'

Briefly Leonardo felt a stab of anger, ready to believe that the devious old lawyer had engineered all this, for the sake of getting rid of Gabriel. Then he realized how absurd that was. 'The note never reached him. We've been looking for you.'

Gabriel breathed out a bubble of laughter that might have been a sob. His eyes closed, flickered open, and then closed again. Leonardo realized that he was too exhausted for questioning now. He drew Caterina's cloak around him, and listened to the murmur of voices that came from the hall beyond the door.

In a little while Maria Foscari came with a steaming cup that held a tisane; Leonardo coaxed Gabriel to sip the warm liquid, and felt him gradually begin to relax, while the two sisters murmured together and cast apprehensive glances towards the hall.

To Leonardo it did not seem long before the door opened again, and he heard movement beyond it. Was it over already, then, he asked himself, unable to deny a tug of regret at the thought of what he had cast away. But if it was to do again, he could not have changed his mind.

Then Francesco Foscari appeared, his uncle treading close on his heels.

'Leonardo,' Count Foscari said, 'you must come and address the Council, and make your plea for the Dukedom.'

Leonardo had almost forgotten the speech, although he had discussed what he should say with the Foscaris,

Count Dandolo, and others of his supporters, he had rehearsed it and carried a slip of paper with notes on it.

'Gabriel,' he said, 'I must go into the hall. I won't be long, I promise.'

Gabriel half roused, clutching at him again and gasping in a panic. Leonardo could feel terror quivering through him, and knew it was too early to expect him to be rational.

'I'm sorry,' he said to Count Foscari. 'I can't leave him.'

Dr Foscari muttered, 'Young idiot.'

'Leonardo, you must,' Francesco said desperately. 'It's that or let the city go to Dracone. If you don't care for yourself . . . what laws will he make for genics, do you think?'

Leonardo knew he was right. His determination flaring up again, he rose, drawing Gabriel with him. He found time for a quick smile at Caterina, as he heard her indrawn gasp of understanding.

'Gabriel, forgive me. You can rest again in a few minutes. This won't take long.'

Francesco said, 'Leonardo, you can't take a genic into the hall of the Great Council.'

Leonardo bared his teeth. 'Both of us or neither, Francesco. You choose.'

Francesco made a wild, helpless gesture, while his uncle broke into sudden, wheezing laughter. 'Let him have his head, boy. All's crazy today.'

Supporting Gabriel, Leonardo made his way into the hall. The Councillors were seated in their stalls, and the golden voting urns stood one on each corner of the dais, the gold leaf peeling off the handles and the winged lions in relief on the sides.

The murmured conversations died as Leonardo mounted the dais; he could have cut the silence into slabs. The Procurator rose from his seat, started to speak, and broke off, looking just as helpless as Count Foscari. Dracone, back in his seat after making his own speech, fixed bright, avid eyes on him.

Leonardo let his gaze travel around the hall. 'If you elect me Duke,' he said, 'I will be required to swear that I will uphold peace, justice and freedom in the city. And yet I do not know how I can swear this oath, for truly I see no peace, or justice, or freedom here, where the innocent are tortured and piety is the cloak for slander. Elect me or not, as you will, for a Loredan does not swear falsely, or with empty words. And if I can only redeem my oath by making a city where the words of it will be true, then by God I will do it, or die trying. I swear that to you now, by the honour of House Loredan. Gentlemen, cast your vote.'

His gaze scoured the chamber once again before he led Gabriel away. The Councillors looked stunned. Scarcely caring, Leonardo settled Gabriel again on one of the couches in the ante-room. He heard Dr Foscari's rumbling voice beginning the instructions for the voting procedure, and then the door to the hall was shut, and he heard no more.

By the time the doors opened again, Gabriel was sleeping, his head in Leonardo's lap. Leonardo looked up to see Dr Foscari beckoning to him. He could read nothing of the result in the old lawyer's face.

Caterina touched his arm. 'Go,' she whispered. 'It's only for a moment. I'll take care of Gabriel.'

She raised Gabriel's head and found a cushion for him as Leonardo rose. Gabriel stirred, and sank back into unconsciousness.

'Call me if he wakes,' said Leonardo, and strode into the hall.

The Procurator and all the Councillors were seated in silence, but a low murmuring broke out as Leonardo appeared and walked to his own seat, not looking at any of them. He could not believe they would elect him after what he had done, and he almost hoped they had not. Then he would be free to take Gabriel home.

Dr Foscari moved ponderously to the centre of the dais, the floorboards creaking under him. He glanced at the piece of paper in his hand, and cleared his throat.

'Gentlemen, under my authority as Secretary of the Voices, I announce that you have chosen Count Leonardo Loredan to be your new Duke.'

Leonardo stopped himself from gaping. Dr Foscari was continuing, something about numbers of votes cast, but it was all a clanging in Leonardo's ears. He sat in frozen disbelief, until he realized that Dr Foscari was beckoning him, and the rest of the Councillors – all but Dracone, he realized – were rising to acclaim him Duke.

In a daze he crossed the floor of the hall and mounted the dais to stand beside the lawyer.

'A landslide, boy.' Dr Foscari spoke into his ear, chuckling under cover of the Councillors' applause. 'Most of Dracone's supporters swung over to you in the end. It's courage, boy, courage. We may forget it, but we know it when we see it.'

*

Still stunned, Leonardo was finally able to withdraw into the ante-room, to meet Caterina, excitement flashing into her eyes as she read the result in his face, and to rouse Gabriel gently from his sleep.

He picked Francesco Foscari out of the crowd that surrounded him, and said, 'Francesco, can you have a boat ready at the water gate? I want to go home.'

'All in good time, my lord Duke,' said Dr Foscari. 'First we have to show you to the people.'

'I'd forgotten.' Though that was less than true; he had just failed to think of it. His mind was not working as it should, and Gabriel's need was still more important than the duties of his new office.

Raising Gabriel to his feet he guided him out of the ante-room and down to the colonnade above the inner courtyard of the palace.

With Dr Foscari he paused at the top of the staircase, the massive statues on either side, and the Councillors ranged behind him. Gabriel, still bewildered, leant on his arm and turned his face away from the gaze of those who stood below.

The whole of the inner courtyard was filled with the citizens who had come to hear the result of the elections, and for the final ceremony which would secure the new Duke in his place. Leonardo knew that there would be, shortly, a magnificent service in the basilica, but here, now, was where it mattered.

The crowds below were quiet. Looking down, Leonardo could not see any faces that he knew; they were starting to blur together, and to keep his self-control he looked instead at those close to him, at Gabriel, and Caterina standing bright-eyed a pace or two behind him.

Dr Foscari reached out and laid a hand on Leonardo's shoulder. 'This is your Duke,' he said, 'if you will have him.'

A legal fiction, perhaps, that the people of the city had a voice in choosing their own Duke, but Leonardo knew that if they rose against him now he would find it almost impossible to impose his authority. He waited.

A low murmuring rose from the crowd, that swelled into a roar, a tide of acclamation rising to engulf Leonardo and leaving him, ridiculously, blinking back tears. His mouth wanted to move into an inane grin, but he managed instead what he hoped was a dignified smile, and raised a hand in acknowledgement as his people cheered him.

Beside him, Count Dracone pushed past, clattered down the stairs and thrust his way, a scarlet blur, through the press of the crowd, to vanish under the archway that led out into the square.

2

Gabriel rose slowly to the surface of consciousness, knowing that he had slept long, without any nightmares. He lay somewhere soft, and warmly covered. His limbs felt weak and relaxed; he was naked, and clean. Instead of the stink of his own body and the fetid water of his cell, he could smell the faint scent of sweet herbs. His head felt light and strange without the mass of matted curls.

He opened his eyes, and did not know where he was. Not his room at Dr Foscari's; not the Palazzo Loredan. A high ceiling, painted walls, a window with a blind softening bright sunlight.

As he tried to sit up, his head swam alarmingly. Sinking back, he heard movement somewhere in the room, and a moment later a face came into view, looking down at him. He struggled to remember, and caught hold of a name: Caterina Dandolo.

Gabriel knew that he should say something courteous, something fitting for a highborn lady. Instead, what came out was, 'Where is Leo?'

Caterina smiled. 'In Council.'

Gabriel turned his head restlessly. He could not remember what had happened since they took him out of the cage, but he knew he had been with Leonardo. No longer. He wondered what that meant.

'Leonardo will be back later,' Caterina said. 'This is the Palazzo Foscari. You're quite safe here.'

He tried again, just as unsuccessfully, to sit up. 'I want to go home.'

Caterina laughed gently. 'That's what Leonardo said. Francesco told him he couldn't take you back to that barn of a place – he meant the Palazzo Loredan! – and you could both stay here until Leonardo moves into the Palace.'

'The Palace?'

'Leonardo is Duke now. Don't you remember?'

Bewildered, he shook his head. Caterina withdrew, leaving him to think. Partly he felt joy, so great that it almost overwhelmed him, and with it a desperate desire to weep. The old Duke had been remote, almost like a carved statue carried in procession; would that be Leo now?

In a few moments, Caterina was back, with a small cup in her hand that she placed on the bedside table.

'Francesco's physician said you were to have this when you woke.'

'His physician . . .?' Confusions were piling up around Gabriel. 'Lady, no physician will treat a genic.'

'Leonardo said –' Caterina looked half-scandalized, but her eyes sparkled – ' "Do as you're told and you can be the Duke's physician. Refuse, and I'll see you selling boluses outside the fish market." The man saw reason.'

Gabriel collapsed into weak laughter, so he was off his guard as Caterina slipped an arm behind his shoulders and began to raise him.

'Lady, this isn't fitting . . .' He clutched the sheet to him, embarrassed by his nakedness. 'You know I am a genic.'

Caterina slid a pillow behind him and let him lie back against it. 'Yes, I know. And I don't care. I'm Serafina's friend, Gabriel, and yours too, if you will let me.'

He could find no reply to this, but he made no further protest as she sat on the bed beside him and held the cup for him to drink the physician's vile tasting concoction.

When it was finished, she asked him, 'Do you want to lie down and sleep?'

He shook his head. Searching her face, he could see nothing there but interest and good-will. Slowly he said, 'You are to be Leonardo's wife. His Duchess.'

'Yes.' She flushed under his gaze. 'Gabriel, I know that he must wed for the honour of his House. I will not—' She broke off, biting her lips, her fingers twisting together.

Gabriel guessed what she had wanted to say. Something that no gently reared girl could say to the man she thought was her husband's lover. A wonder that she had come so far.

It was just as difficult for Gabriel, but in response to

her pain he could not remain silent. He said, 'Leo does not love me.'

The words lay between them like a gift. Tentatively, Caterina offered him one of her own. 'Yes, he does.'

Gabriel shook his head, furious as all the old desires and despairs came swelling over him, so he could not trust his voice. 'Not – not as they say of him. There is no reason why he may not . . . may not love his wife.'

He turned his head away. A moment later, he felt her caress, a fingertip touch on the stubble of his hair. She said, 'Gabriel, do you have any idea what happened yesterday?'

He could not look at her. 'I don't know what you mean.'

'When Leonardo found you in the cage? You don't, do you? Oh, Gabriel . . .'

She began to speak. She told him how Leonardo had heard his cries while the Councillors were walking in procession to the palace for the election. She told him how Leonardo had halted the procession to free him, and insisted on taking him into the palace because he would not leave him, not even to claim the office of Duke.

'And then he took you into the Hall of the Great Council, and told them all that he would not swear to uphold freedom, peace and justice unless he could make a city where his oath would be a true one.'

Long before she had finished, Gabriel had turned to stare at her, to read in her face the truth of what she told him. He could feel his tears spill over, and he could scarcely care.

'And that is how I know he loves you,' Caterina said gravely.

Impulsively, she reached out to hug him, and they were laughing and weeping together.

A little later Caterina found a handkerchief for herself, and one for Gabriel, and as he wiped his face she said, 'A good thing Leonardo didn't come back. He would think we're both quite mad.'

'Lady . . .' Gabriel felt embarrassed, and confusedly happy. 'Lady, there's something I want to ask you.'

'Of course, Gabriel, anything. And my name is Caterina.'

'I would like . . . may I have my painting things sent over from Dr Foscari's? I would like to paint you, Caterina. I would like to paint you as a gift for Leo.'

On the following day Gabriel felt well enough to get out of bed and sit in a borrowed bedgown in a chair by the window where he could look out on a quiet view of rooftops and pigeons. A servant brought him a silver pot of chocolate, and a basket of sweet rolls. He ate and drank a little, but began to feel sated after a few mouthfuls.

Drowsing peacefully, mind drifting, he heard the door open and close. A voice said, 'Gabriel.'

He was out of the chair in an instant, and swayed with unexpected weakness. His vision blurred; before he knew it strong hands were supporting him, and the first thing he saw, as he blinked to clear his sight, was the intense blue gaze fixed on him. Leonardo's eyes blazed with such joy that Gabriel was bereft of all words.

After a few moments, Leonardo said, with deep satisfaction, 'You're safe. You're getting well.' Gently he lowered Gabriel back into the chair. 'Do you want to tell me what happened?'

Uncertainly at first, but with growing confidence, Gabriel began to tell the story, while Leonardo sat on the arm of his chair and filched one of the rolls from the basket. He did not interrupt until Gabriel came to his discovery of Hyacinth under the bridge.

'Hyacinth!' he exclaimed. 'You've seen Hyacinth?'

'Yes, I took him back with me to the Dolphin. He was hurt. That's why I was arrested. They thought we were . . . I'm sorry, Leo.'

'I don't know what you have to be sorry for. But go on – did they arrest Hyacinth as well?'

'No, he escaped. I don't know what happened to him after that.'

'Nor does anyone else.' Absently he took another roll and bit into it. 'He hasn't been seen since Carnival night.'

Anxiously Gabriel looked up at him. 'He must be dead.'

'Perhaps. Or perhaps he was arrested later. I can make sure of that, at least, if I have to search every cell of the prison myself. And I can have his name cried in the streets. I'll find him, Gabriel, if he lives.'

'You won't send him back to Dracone?'

'He doesn't belong to Dracone. He belongs to Giulietta Contarini, and she is here, under Francesco's roof, along with all the other street sweepings.' His laughter leached the words of any contempt they might have carried. 'We won't stay long, Gabriel. Soon we'll go home.'

'Home?'

'To the Ducal Palace, now. Once it's fit to live in.

The old Duke was alone there for years, and the place is like a damned mausoleum.'

As if he had seen the pang that struck at Gabriel's heart, he added, 'But I thought you might use the studio again, not to live in, but to work. Would you like that, Gabriel?'

'You know I would.'

The sudden contentment, the sense of a future scrolling out in front of him with work that he could do and a place where he could belong was not disturbed even when Leonardo said, 'I'm to be wed to Caterina tomorrow. Gabriel, I wish you could be there. But they will never allow a genic into the basilica.'

'Better not, perhaps,' said Gabriel. 'Oh, Leo, I wish you joy.'

And if he could still have wished that the joy was one that he could share, he would not despise what Leo had given him, or leave any space for bitterness to grow in his heart.

3

Caterina waited in the salon, pretending to embroider, while Leonardo spoke to Gabriel upstairs. At last she heard the quick footstep in the passage, and half expected him to go by, until the door opened to admit him.

Half embarrassed, she got up and dropped him a curtsey. Leonardo stood there, looking awkward in his turn, and fumbled out of his coat pocket something wrapped in a scrap of silk.

'I wanted to give you this,' he said, 'to wear tomorrow, if you will.'

He held it out to her, and Caterina saw that it was a heraldic rose, finely worked in silver, with a silver chain to hold it. 'I will have many jewels to give you, once we are wed,' he said. 'But they will be for the Duchess. I wanted you to have this, for . . . for Caterina.'

Wonderingly she realized that he, whose confidence had always seemed impregnable, was not confident now.

He went on, 'My father diced away all the jewels of House Loredan, except for this. It was my mother's. Will you wear it?'

Formal speeches about honour and duty flickered across her brain. She said, 'Yes, Leonardo.'

He fastened the chain around her neck; she shivered at the touch of his hands on her skin, lifting her hair. When the pendant was in place, he took her hands in his own and looked deeply into her eyes.

'Caterina, it's still not too late,' he said. 'Do you truly wish for this?'

A few days ago, before the election, she might not have known how to answer. She had not been sure that she truly wished to be the wife of a man whose heart was given elsewhere. But since then she had learnt what Gabriel had told her, and more than that. She had seen Leonardo in the square, in the palace, defying everyone and ready to throw away the dukedom, her dear Leonardo, desperate and dishevelled, and needing her – not her wealth and the status of her House, or her seal of fertility that would bring him a son – needing her, Caterina, for what was in her to give.

'Yes, love, I truly wish it,' she said.

He bent his head and kissed her.

Twenty

I

Caterina felt the cool touch of Leonardo's hands as he slid the ring onto her finger, and listened to the Patriarch pronouncing them man and wife. She was Caterina Loredan now, the Duchess, Leonardo's lady. Almost as if the old demure Caterina Dandolo had split her chrysalis and emerged, this new, glittering creature, into the sun.

As she let her fingers rest in Leonardo's hand, as the Patriarch spoke the final blessing, she let her other hand trace the embroidery on the skirts of her wedding gown. Serafina had stitched it for her, a wedding gift, and the only shadow on Caterina's happiness now was that her friend could not be there to see her married. She wondered if Leonardo wanted Gabriel, as she wanted Serafina.

Above her head the organ burst into triumphal music. Leonardo turned her, and as they began the slow, dignified walk down the aisle towards the central doors of the basilica Caterina could see the assembled guests. All the Councillors, in their ceremonial robes – notably her father, whose face was so suffused with pride that Caterina quite expected him to have a fit. Her sister Maria, weeping a little with happiness, alongside Giulietta Contarini, who was heavily pregnant now, yet still deliciously pretty in a new gown. Dr Foscari, who gave her a wink as she went by, almost shattering her formal gravity.

She and Leonardo were to lead the way to the reception and wedding dinner at the palace, but they were barely half way to the doors when Caterina caught sight of a movement among the congregation, a figure that slithered through the crowd until it emerged into full view beside Giulietta Contarini.

Count Dracone. Caterina restrained a gasp, and knew by the sudden tightening of Leonardo's fingers on hers that he had seen too. Dracone bowed, murmured something, and took his wife's hand. Giulietta let out a little shriek, and Maria, turning to hush her, caught sight of the Count and put an arm protectively around her.

Movement rippled out from them as heads turned, followed by a low-voiced babble of comment. Francesco Foscari pushed his way out of the ranks of the Councillors and joined his wife. Leonardo drew to a halt, with Caterina at his side, as they reached the little group. The formal pattern of the ceremony broke up.

Count Dracone bowed, to the Foscaris, and then to Leonardo. He wore the Councillor's robes over his scarlet coat, and piously carried a prayer book in one hand. 'I am delighted,' he said, 'to see my wife recovered from her indisposition. However, I fear that the formal dinner will be too much for her. My dear Giulietta, let us go home.'

'No!' Giulietta tried to pull away, and the Count fastened his fingers around her wrist. 'Maria, I don't want to go!'

'My dear, you make yourself conspicuous,' Count Dracone said silkily.

Giulietta screamed. Caterina tugged urgently at the sleeve of Leonardo's coat. 'Leonardo, don't let him!' she begged.

Leonardo stepped forward. 'Count Dracone, this is unseemly.'

'Unseemly?' Dracone's mouth twisted in an ugly smile. 'And it is not unseemly for the Duke of the city to connive in keeping my wife from me? She belongs to me and she will go with me.'

'No!' Giulietta cried.

Leonardo beckoned to the nearest of the construct guards, who were drawn up in formal order near the doors of the basilica to escort the Duke and Duchess and their guests to the palace for the formal wedding dinner.

'Arrest him,' he said.

The construct stepped forward with a hand outstretched to lay on Dracone. Count Dracone swivelled. The prayer book in his hand spat fire. Someone in the congregation let out a shriek. The construct jerked, and began to fold over itself. As it went down on its knees Dracone stepped forward and deliberately placed another shot into the leonine head from the concealed pistol. The construct crashed in ruin onto the tiles, its ceremonial falchion clattering beside it.

Leonardo gripped Caterina's shoulders and swung her round so that he protected her. He snapped out, 'Stop him!'

But for a few seconds everyone was too shocked to move. Count Dracone backed away towards the doors, his fingers still tightly around Giulietta's wrist. Giulietta had begun to sob hysterically, and though she struggled to free herself her efforts were feeble, as if she did not believe that she could do anything to save herself.

'Be quiet, my dear,' Dracone said. He pressed the prayer book hard against her belly. 'Or I'll put this through you and the brat with you. Move!'

They had almost reached the doors when Caterina saw a flicker of movement underneath the archway that led out to the narthex. A man in a black cassock stepped into the basilica. Caterina had to press her hands to her mouth to keep back a cry. She knew him: Father Teo.

With barely a pause, the little priest came up behind Dracone, hooked a foot around Dracone's ankle, and grabbed for the hand that held the book. Dracone cursed, tried to spin round, and lost his balance. The book flew out of his grip and skidded across the floor tiles as he fell, dragging Giulietta down with him.

Giulietta screamed. Caterina darted forward to hold her and protect her. As she raised Giulietta in her arms, her friend's eyes rolled back in her head and she went limp, in a faint. Caterina supported her head in her lap, while Maria slid quickly through the crowd and knelt beside her, fumbling for her vinaigrette.

Dracone was thrashing like a scarlet fish, pinned down by Father Teo and Count Francesco. Leonardo stooped to pick up the prayer book, which had come to rest at his feet, and moved forward until he could look down at his enemy.

'Count Dracone, I arrest you in the name of the city.'

Dracone's face was a mask of hatred. As Father Teo and Count Foscari hauled him upright, he spat. Unmoved, Leonardo gestured towards the constructs who still stood waiting to take their part in the formal procession. 'Take him to the prison.'

'On what charge?' Dracone asked. 'What have I done, except reclaim my wife, that you stole from me?'

Leonardo glanced down to where Giulietta was still prostrate in Caterina's arms. 'Your wife seems . . . reluctant to go with you.'

'But she is my wife. Women who are bearing have strange fancies.'

For a moment Caterina thought she could see uncertainty in Leonardo's eyes. He gestured towards the fallen construct. 'Destruction of property,' he said. 'Violence in this holy place.'

Dracone laughed. Even though he was still securely prisoned by the men on either side of him, he was recovering himself. 'I will pay for the construct,' he said. 'And a fine for the violence. Though how many of this holy company – ' his voice was sneering – 'would not do the same to reclaim what belongs to them?'

'Dracone, I will—' Leonardo began.

'You have nothing to charge me with,' said Count Dracone. 'Unless you choose to fabricate a charge. Is that how you choose to begin your rule, *Duke* Leonardo?'

As Leonardo hesitated, a new voice spoke from the narthex. 'Charge him with attempted murder.'

Caterina looked up from where she still sat on the floor, the skirts of her wedding gown spread out around her and Giulietta slumped in her lap. Two others had entered through the archway: a tall young man in a tattered black cassock, and a silver-haired boy in the linen shirt and breeches of a fisherman.

Francesco Foscari exclaimed, 'Father Augustine!'

Caterina could not stop herself from gaping. The young priest from I Frari, the one who had disappeared so long ago, after setting out for the Palazzo Dracone to beg the Count to gift the ring to the Church. The man everyone thought was dead. Bewildered, she could not begin to guess how he came to be here, now, or what his accusation might mean.

Father Augustine bowed awkwardly to Count Foscari

and the rest of the noble company. 'Count Dracone tried to kill me,' he said. 'Once in his palazzo, and once afterwards, out there at the quayside. I will swear to this in court, my lords, or however you will.'

'And other crimes,' the silver-haired fisher boy added. 'Sins I will not speak of in this holy place.'

Caught up in wonder as she was, Caterina had still watched Count Dracone's face. There was a flicker of cold knowledge that screamed his guilt to anyone who could read it, but almost at once he had recovered himself.

'Lies,' he said. 'Or the vapourings of the mad. Must we listen to them?'

He sounded so sure of himself. Caterina could see the Councillors looking uncertain, as though they found it hard to believe such accusations against a man who was, after all, one of them. She felt something swelling up inside her, and knew it was the time to speak.

'Yes, my lords,' she said, taking in Leonardo with her gaze, and Francesco, and her father, and all the rest of them. 'You must listen, to that and more. I know that Count Dracone is a murderer many times over. It was he who sank Count Contarini's barge.'

In the hush that followed she sought for the blue intensity of Leonardo's gaze, but before he could speak the silence was broken by Dracone's sneering laugh.

'And how did I do that? I was not even there.'

'The orders were yours,' Caterina flashed back. 'And you—'

'More vapourings,' Dracone interrupted. 'My lord Duke, will you not lesson your wife when to speak and when to be silent?'

'Indeed.' Leonardo's eyes were gleaming appreciatively. 'Speak, Caterina.'

'I will speak,' she said. 'For my mother, and sisters, and all those who have no voices, now. Your wives and sisters, fathers and sons, my lords Councillors. Drowned in a plot laid by Count Dracone, to destroy House Contarini and clear his way to Giulietta.'

A faint murmuring spread through the ranks of Councillors, and there was a ripple of movement among those who stood closest to Dracone, as if they might have fallen upon him, if the holy place had not restrained them.

'And your proof?' Dracone asked. 'Evidence for this . . . fantastic assertion?'

'Your pilot drowned Paolo Contarini,' Caterina said. 'Serafina saw him.'

Raucous laughter spilt from Dracone's mouth. 'Serafina? The genic Serafina, my wife's waiting woman? Will anyone take her word above mine – even if a genic could testify in court, as assuredly she may not.'

'As assuredly she may,' said Father Teo.

He left his place beside Count Dracone, and approached the Patriarch, who was standing in shocked silence beside Leonardo. Father Teo bowed to him and kissed his ring. From inside his travelling cloak he took a heavy parchment, that crackled as he laid it in the Patriarch's hands. Caterina was close enough to see that it was sealed with the device of the Holy Father himself.

'My lord Patriarch,' said Father Teo, 'I have laid my case before the Holy Father as you commanded. You will find his answer written there. But with your leave I will speak the gist of it before the Councillors here, since it has a bearing on this matter.'

The Patriarch inclined his head, as if he could not find words to give permission.

'Then, my lords,' said Father Teo crisply, 'the Holy Father has declared a miracle, that the genic Alessandro recovered from the brink of death when I baptized him and gave him the Holy Sacrament.'

More murmured comment, louder now and more urgent. Most of the Councillors had heard nothing of this until now. Caterina could not help seeking for her father's face in the crowd, and saw his eyes starting out of his head. No doubt, she thought, he was struggling not to cry 'Blasphemy!'; to submit gracefully to the will of the Holy Father would be more than he was capable of.

'Further,' Father Teo went on, raising his voice to be heard above the babble, 'the Holy Father rules that such a miracle shows that the genics must be regarded as God's children. For God would surely not save what He does not love. So from now on no one may own the rights of a genic. They are to be free citizens, with the same rights that we all enjoy – including, my lord Count,' he said to Dracone, 'the right to give evidence at a trial.'

Dracone spat a blasphemy. Ignoring it, Leonardo gestured to the construct guards. 'Take him to the prison.'

Two of the constructs moved up, one on each side of Count Dracone, and pinioned him by the arms. The rest formed into position around him, their ceremonial falchions a cage of steel.

'And what of the child?' Dracone asked. His voice was raised, growing desperate. 'What of the Christos Child that is to be born again into my House?'

'The Holy Father has pronounced on that also,' said Father Teo. 'As I thought, he has decreed that the child is not the Christos. He may bear Christos's human body, but God alone could infuse that body with the divine, and how He might do so is a holy mystery.' His voice hardening, he added, 'The child will not save you, my lord Count.'

The constructs, under orders from Leonardo, had not waited to hear Father Teo's pronouncement. Already they were dragging Dracone back, under the archway, and though he struggled furiously he could not break their inexorable grip on him. As he vanished into the narthex he burst out into a stream of oaths and obscenities; Caterina heard the sound gradually die away until it ceased.

Leonardo stooped beside her. 'My dear—'

At that moment, Giulietta Contarini stirred. All this while Maria had been waving the vinaigrette under her nose, without result; now Giulietta gasped and let out a feeble cry, and struggled wildly to raise herself.

Caterina held her securely. 'Lie still, Giulietta. You're safe now. The Count has gone. He won't hurt you again.'

Giulietta sighed, and for a minute let herself relax into Caterina's arms. Her golden hair was tangled over her shoulders, tendrils clinging to her face. She was a little flushed, and her eyes looked very bright.

Suddenly she let out a whimper, and clutched with both hands at her belly. 'The baby – oh, Caterina, my baby!'

'Giulietta, not here!' Maria sounded exasperated, quite unlike herself, while Caterina struggled with a mad urge to giggle. 'Not in the basilica! Francesco—'

'I'll call for the boat,' Francesco said, and disappeared into the narthex.

Maria took Giulietta's hands. 'Don't be afraid. You shall come home with us. Francesco's old nurse is there, and she will know what to do. Everything will be all right.'

Giulietta was staring down at the mound of her belly, looking terrified. Maria coaxed her to sit up, and then to stand, and two or three other ladies crowded round to help her out to where the boat would be waiting.

Caterina was left with Leonardo. He reached a hand to her, to help her to her feet, and they stood together for a moment as the other Councillors, deprived of the procession, milled uncertainly around them.

'My lady Duchess,' Leonardo said, bowing to her, 'will it please you come to your wedding dinner?'

2

In the Palazzo Foscari, Serafina sat beside Gabriel on a satin-covered couch, while Father Teo explained to them how their world had changed. She felt uneasy. It was the evening of Caterina's wedding day, and Caterina, along with Maria and the other women of the household, were upstairs with Giulietta, who was in labour. Serafina would rather have been with them.

'And so I suggest,' Father Teo finished, 'that I go with you, now, to the chapel, and baptize you.'

Serafina glanced at Gabriel, but he was silent. His eyes were fixed not on Father Teo, but on Duke Leonardo, who was prowling restlessly from window to fireplace and back again.

'I'm not sure,' she said. 'To be baptized is to promise to belong to God. I don't know if I'm ready for that.'

Father Teo inclined his head. 'You are wise, Serafina.

But think of this. Baptism will not only seal you to God, it will seal you to the city. You will have all the rights of a human being; you will *be* human. You will be able to give evidence at Count Dracone's trial.' As though he could still read uncertainty in her face, he added, 'My daughter, at your baptism God will reach down to you and say, "My child". It is for you to decide to take His hand and say, "My Father".'

Still hesitating, still finding it hard to cross the gulf, she said, 'Very well, Father. As you will.'

Father Teo smiled. 'I hoped you would say that. And Gabriel?'

Gabriel tore his eyes away from Leonardo; they looked dark and tragic. He said, 'I cannot, Father. It . . . it does not matter. I know nothing that would be useful at the trial.'

Leonardo stopped his prowling and swung round to look at him. He said, 'Gabriel? What troubles you?'

Gabriel swallowed; his distress was becoming clearer with every passing moment. He spoke to Father Teo. 'Father, I was made for . . . for pleasure. You would say for sin. I do not think that God would receive me.'

Leonardo let out a single oath; Father Teo raised a hand to silence him. His mouth had hardened into a thin line, but Serafina understood that it was not Gabriel he was angry with.

He said, 'Gabriel, my son, God does not care what men have made you.' The anger dissolving, he smiled a little and bent over Gabriel to take both his hands up into his own, and examine the thin fingers with the paint stains ingrained around the fingernails. 'God does not care what men have made you,' he repeated, 'for He made you a painter.'

Serafina saw Gabriel's hands convulsively return the priest's clasp. His eyes widened in sudden wonder. He whispered, 'Truly?'

'Truly.'

'Then – yes, as you and my lord will.'

'I hoped for this,' said Father Teo, releasing Gabriel. 'And so I sent a message to Alessandro, the genic I first baptized. I thought that he might wish to be here, and that his presence might perhaps make it easier for you. When he comes, we shall go to the chapel.'

'Then while we're waiting,' said Leonardo, 'tell me how you came upon that priest . . . Father Augustine, is it? The one everyone thought was dead.'

'That was strange,' said Father Teo. 'On my journey back from the Holy Father, I waited for the ferry so that I could cross from the mainland, and no ferry came. In the end, I hired a fisherman to bring me over, and he told me of another priest who had been seen on one of the outer islands. No one knew who he was or where he had come from, the man told me, and some of the fisher folk thought he was a ghost. I have no patience with superstition, and so I made him take me there to find out the truth.'

'And the truth was Father Augustine?'

'The truth indeed, for he brings the truth about Dracone. And a very strange tale of sea people, who rescued him and the boy with him from Dracone, and hid them all the while on the island.'

'Hid them?' Leonardo asked impatiently. 'Why should they hide?'

'For fear of Dracone. And in Father Augustine's case, out of guilt that he failed to obtain the ring. As though Dracone would ever have given it! The man who needs reprimanding is Father Augustine's superior at I Frari, who sent him on such a hopeless errand – but that, thank God, is not my affair. And so, Leonardo, in the morning you can—'

The door opened to admit a servant, who said softly, 'Messire Alessandro,' and went out again.

Three people came into the room. The first was the little genic merchant, the second the huge youth Messire Giovanni. The third was a figure in a dark cloak who raised exquisite hands to put back the hood.

'Hyacinth!' Serafina cried joyfully.

She sprang up and hugged him, not noticing, until she drew back, that his golden curls had been sheared off into a ragged halo around his face, and his exotic beauty was marred by a scar that stretched from ear to chin on one side.

'You're hurt – what happened?' she asked.

Hyacinth shivered. 'There were creatures . . . evil things, following me. They were dark, but they burnt.' He raised a hand to touch the scar. 'One of them did this. I tried to escape, but I fell into the canal. I would have drowned, but Gianni and Alessandro saved me.'

Alessandro and Giovanni were beaming with pride, like a mother showing off a talented child. In spite of the scar, Hyacinth looked even more impossibly beautiful in the sober black of a merchant.

'It was fortunate we were there,' Alessandro said. 'And you have Gianni to thank for the rescue, not me. As to these dark creatures . . .' Turning to Leonardo, he said, 'There was something, on the canal side, but whatever they were, they fled when we came.'

'Dracone's demons,' said Serafina. A wave of thankful-

ness swept over her as she realized that now she could tell
the truth of what she knew.

'Demons?' Leonardo sounded disbelieving.

'Would it surprise any of us,' Father Teo asked, 'to
learn that Dracone trafficked with the powers of hell?'

'I have seen them, sir,' Serafina said. 'And when I am
baptized – ' a little nod to Father Teo – 'when I am fully
human, I will tell you everything.'

Leonardo shrugged, as if he still needed to be convinced. 'Where have you been since then?' he asked
Hyacinth. 'I've had men combing the whole city for you.'

'I stayed with Gianni and Alessandro.' Hyacinth was
flushed, over-excited, the violet eyes too big and bright. 'I
was ill at first – my hands were burnt, and for a few days
I could not sing.' His eyes grew momentarily dark; for
him, Serafina knew, there could be no greater pain, to
fear that he would not touch lute or keyboard again, or
know the mastery of song. 'But soon I healed. And then
your message came,' he said to Father Teo, 'and I knew
Dracone was in prison, and I could come home . . .'
Imperiously he added, 'You wish me to accept baptism?
And then I may play and sing again? Now?'

For a moment even Father Teo looked mildly scandalized, but laughter won the battle with orthodoxy.

'Yes, my son,' he said. 'Now. And may God take joy
in your music.'

As they withdrew to the chapel, Gabriel held back,
and spoke softly to Leonardo. Serafina, just behind them,
felt that perhaps she should not listen, but she could not
help hearing.

'Leo, you don't own my rights any more.'

Leonardo faced him. 'No, Gabriel, I don't own you.'

He drew the shorn head against his shoulder in a gesture of such tenderness that tears pricked behind Serafina's eyes. 'But you will always belong to me.'

3

When the baptism was over, and he had heard all the story of Dracone's evil from Serafina, Father Teo took his leave of Duke Leonardo, and walked meditatively in the moonlight, through the city from which he had been so long absent. At length he found himself on the quayside in front of the Ducal Palace.

Lights burnt there, but he turned away and faced the darkness of the lagoon, the black waves faintly silvered and shifting in the breeze that blew in his face.

He raised his arms and cried, 'Tethys!'

There was no response. The sea woman he had spoken with on the far island where he had found Father Augustine was most likely still out there, with her brothers and sisters of the sea.

Still he called again, 'Tethys? Anyone? Can you hear me?'

He thought, though he was not sure, that he saw a disturbance out on the surface, that might have been a bobbing head, or a webbed hand raised.

He cried out, 'You are free! You belong to no one but God!'

After a while, when there was no reply, he lowered his arms, turned away, and went back to the Palazzo Foscari.

4

On the same night, Gianni went to the Ghetto to find a one-eyed genic who once, long ago, had given him bread and a blanket, and brought him home.

Twenty-one

I

As Gianni stepped into the counting-house, he was aware once again of the buzz and ferment of gossip, as it had been on the day the old Duke died.

He looked for Malatesta, and saw the old clerk hurrying out of the warehouse, a worried look on his face.

'Messire Giovanni, thank God!' he exclaimed.

'What is it, Malatesta?' Gianni cocked his head towards the gossiping scriveners. 'What's the matter with them?'

'Them? Haven't you heard? Dracone is arrested.'

'Yes, of course.' The upsurge of relief that Gianni had felt when the news first reached him swept over him again. The threat over, the lurking anxiety that he always felt for Alessandro lifted at last. Hyacinth, too . . . The news was still too new for him to have worked out everything that it would mean.

'They say he wrecked the Contarini barge,' said Malatesta.

'Yes, it's true.' Gianni crossed himself. 'So many lives . . .'

'But that's not all, Gianni,' Malatesta went on, forgetting respect in his anxiety. 'Come and look at this.'

He took Gianni by the arm and towed him into the warehouse, past the counters where customers were served, and into the storage bays beyond.

In the darkest corner, among bales of cotton from the
Indies, a candle had been wedged. Only a stub remained;
wax was spilt over the thin fabric. The cotton itself was
soaked in oil; the air reeked of it.

'I always said this warehouse was damn' draughty,'
said Malatesta. 'But it's the draughts saved us. The candle
blew out. If the flame had reached the cotton the whole
warehouse would have gone up.'

Gianni stared. 'But who . . . Please God, not one of
our own men.'

'I think not.' Malatesta's look was grim. 'More likely
a rival, if we were rich enough to have rivals. But my
guess would be Dracone. He lost the Dukedom. Yesterday
he tried to take his Countess from the basilica. Suppose
he meant to quit the city altogether, and leave a gift or
two behind him? You and Messire Alessandro were never
his friends.'

'But then—' For a moment Gianni was paralysed,
body and mind, gazing down at the burnt out stub. Then
he forced himself into action. 'Malatesta, we might not
be the only ones favoured with . . . a gift. Go and tell the
clerks, send them with messages, to all the warehouses –
oh, dear God, and paper-makers, sellers of oil and candles
. . . Anyone, Malatesta.'

The old clerk was already hurrying out of the warehouse, and Gianni followed. 'I shall go myself and inform
the Duke,' he said.

On the wharfside, Malatesta stopped and looked up.
Gianni followed his gaze to where, further down the canal
in the direction of the basilica, a single column of smoke
rose up, smudging the sky.

'I think my lord Duke already knows,' said Malatesta.

2

A newly married man, in the opinion of Duke Leonardo
Loredan, deserved time to acquaint himself with his wife.
When he awoke in the pale light of early morning, roused
by Caterina's movement, he was dismayed to see her
rising from his bed.

'Come here,' he said drowsily.

Caterina bent over him and kissed him, her fragrant
hair falling all round his face, but she evaded his hands.
Casting a mischievous glance at him as she pulled on a
silken wrapper, she said, 'I must find out about Giulietta's
baby.'

She went out. Cursing under his breath, Leonardo
gazed at the closed door, and then called for hot water to
bathe and shave.

The servant informed him that the Countess Contarini was still in labour. Yawning, Leonardo allowed the
man to attend him, scandalized him by pulling on the
shabby black suit that was his only alternative to the
magnificence of his wedding clothes, and called for a boat
to take him to the Ducal Palace.

In the entrance hall, he found Manfred waiting for
him, looking much more respectable than he did himself,
in the livery of the ducal steward. Leonardo slapped
him on the shoulder. 'Manfred – when can I move in
here?'

'As soon as Your Serenity wishes,' Manfred replied
with dignity.

Leonardo grinned at him. No one but Manfred would
think of addressing him by that ancient title of the Dukes;
he felt not at all serene.

'Tonight, then.' Under his own roof he might stand a chance of getting his wife to himself. 'Meanwhile, send word to Dr Foscari to attend me. We must draw up the charges for Count Dracone's trial. And find me some breakfast.'

Manfred bowed, and said, 'Your Serenity, there is a man waiting to speak with you.' He nodded towards the ante-room. 'In there.'

'Who is it? Can't he wait?'

For some reason Manfred was looking grave. He said, 'I think you had better see for yourself, Your Serenity.'

He bowed again and withdrew, leaving Leonardo to push open the door of the ante-room and go in.

Sitting beside the fireplace, where once Francesco Foscari had given him Gabriel's portfolio of sketches, Leonardo saw Dr Heinrich. He was seated on a gilt chair too small for his huge frame, kneading his hands together rhythmically as he stared at the floor. His shirt was grubby and he had not shaved.

'Well, Doctor?' said Leonardo.

Dr Heinrich lumbered to his feet, sending the chair spinning. 'My lord Duke!' he exclaimed.

Leonardo gave him a guarded look. He was not at all sure that he wanted to speak to this man, to listen to what would no doubt be a plea for Count Dracone.

He said, 'What do you want?'

Heinrich hesitated. Observing him, Leonardo realized that the man was afraid. He said, 'My lord Duke, I knew nothing of Count Dracone's crimes. I did as he asked me, that's all.'

'All?' Leonardo's voice was bleak.

'I made a culture of cells from the hair in Dracone's

ring. I implanted that culture in the womb of Countess
Contarini-Dracone—'

'Without her knowledge or consent.'

Heinrich shrugged. 'She is a woman. Bearing is her
duty.'

Leonardo set his teeth. As Duke, he could not horse-
whip the fellow, and he knew of nothing – yet – that
would justify his arrest. He said, 'If you wish to dissociate
yourself from Count Dracone, you have done so. Now
get out.'

Heinrich made a wild gesture. 'No – my lord Duke,
you must listen to me.'

'Then say something that I want to hear.'

'Count Dracone has planned to burn the city.'

Silence fell, in which Leonardo could hear Heinrich's
breathing, like a man who has been running. 'Go on,' he
said.

'He planned it with Cesare – that he would take the
Countess from the basilica at the end of your wedding
ceremony, and fly out leaving the city to burn. He has
destroyed the ferry and killed the ferryman to cut off
escape to the mainland.'

The ferry. Leonardo frowned, trying to remember
what he had heard recently about the ferry. Then he
recalled Father Teo, when he returned, explaining that
he had needed to hire a fishing boat because the ferry
had not come. A detail, that he had disregarded at the
time.

'But now Count Dracone is in prison,' he said,
reminding himself to add this murder to the crimes
Dracone must answer for.

'But his plan goes on!' Heinrich said desperately.
'We'll burn – all of us will burn!'

'Cesare . . .?'

'I think he's mad! Or he has another plan I know nothing about.'

Leonardo stared at him. Heinrich was sweating, and his fear was evident in his eyes.

'So you betray him,' Leonardo said icily. 'For the good of the city, for the sake of your civic duty?' Sarcasm lashed in his words. 'But you are not of this city. Why should you care if we burn? Unless you are to burn along with us? Did the Count not include you in his plan to escape?'

'He would have left me here.' Heinrich tossed his head from side to side, like a baited bull. 'And he will burn the Palazzo Dracone first of all, to spread the blaze on either side. My laboratory – my work! Gone, all of it. And the fire will take us.'

He slumped into the chair again, and buried his face in his hands. Leonardo watched him, his body immobile while his mind worked rapidly. If he had to evacuate his people to the mainland, the ferry was the key. The canal boats were not built to sail at sea, there were few fishing boats, and fewer still of the ceremonial barges kept up by some of the Houses. But now the ferry was gone. He could save some of the population, but those who were left would panic. And how to choose?

Leonardo crossed the room to Heinrich and hauled him to his feet. 'Tell me, what has he done?'

Heinrich was shaking; a reek of stale sweat and fear came off him. 'Candles, burning down into oil . . .'

'Where, man?'

'The Palazzo Contarini, and your Palazzo Loredan, my lord, and some of the warehouses . . . I don't know!'

Leonardo watched him with distaste as he started to

sob. Still keeping a grip on him, he called for Manfred. When the old steward appeared, he said, 'Take this . . . down to the water gate. Tell the guards he is to have a boat.' He shook Heinrich, and spoke fiercely. 'If I see you again, I swear I'll kill you with my own hands.'

Dr Heinrich tried to clutch at him. 'My lord, I don't know how to sail!'

'Then I suggest you learn — quickly.' He evaded Heinrich's grasp and thrust the man towards his steward. 'Take him, Manfred. And when he has gone, come straight back to me.'

He paced the ante-room, thinking frantically, as he waited for Manfred to return. Candles burning down . . . They must have been lit during the night just past. How many could there be, how many places did Dracone's pilot have access to? Surely not enough to burn the whole city. Heinrich had panicked; Leonardo knew that he must not.

When Manfred came he was not alone; the huge youth, Messire Giovanni, Messire Alessandro's partner, followed him into the ante-room.

'Your Serenity,' said Manfred, 'there's smoke rising . . . and this young man brings news.'

'It's the Palazzo Dracone, my lord,' said Giovanni, ducking his head respectfully. 'And this morning my clerk found a burnt out candle in our warehouse.'

'Burnt out?' Leonardo said hopefully.

'Put out by the wind, my lord. I sent the clerks and warehousemen to warn as many others as they could.'

Leonardo clapped him on the shoulder. 'Good man! Manfred — see that we do the same. Send messengers. Ask Father Teo to inform the Patriarch, and get his people to warn the churches. Everyone must search for these things, and get ready to fight the fire. Send boatmen to the ferry crossing, in case we need to evacuate.' He felt energy begin to course through him. 'We'll contain this yet.'

'And the Palazzo Dracone?' Manfred asked.

'Damn the Palazzo Dracone.' Leonardo remembered speaking with Hyacinth the previous night, as the beautiful genic told his story. 'Let it burn.'

3

In her bedchamber at the Palazzo Foscari, Giulietta Contarini struggled to give birth. Serafina had been in attendance on her ever since she had returned, in the early stages of labour, from the basilica.

Serafina had to admit that she was surprised. She would have expected Giulietta to fall into a faint, or the vapours, when faced with the inexorable process of childbearing. Instead she had borne the pain. With shrieking and loud demands of her attendants, and language so profane Serafina wondered where she had learnt it, but she had borne it.

Benedetta, Francesco Foscari's old nurse, had taken charge, and knew exactly what to do. Maria and Caterina, when they returned from the formal wedding dinner, came in to help, through the rest of the day and the long night.

Serafina left her mistress only to speak with Father Teo, and to receive baptism at his hands in the Foscari chapel. Though she knew the momentous step she was taking, she found the ceremony a distraction, and was glad to return to the bedchamber, folding away the experience until she should have leisure to consider it.

She was aware of footsteps on the stairs, comings and goings along the passage and in and out of the ante-room, hushed voices and the occasional banging of a door. She shut it all out, concentrated on Benedetta's brisk orders and encouragement, and Giulietta's demands as she strove to bring the child to birth.

She was bathing Giulietta's forehead with lavender water, as Giulietta relaxed on her pillows between two pains, when she felt a hand on her shoulder, and turned to see Caterina.

Her friend murmured, 'Let me do that for a while. Go and rest in the ante-room. There's food, and cordials.' As Serafina hesitated, her eyes danced, and she added with the old mischievous smile, 'I am Duchess now; you must do as I bid you.'

Serafina returned the smile, and gave her place at the bedside to Caterina. When she went out into the ante-room, she saw Maria, who was directing a servant to lay food on a table beside the window.

'Come, Serafina,' she said. 'There's hot soup. You must take care of yourself.'

Serafina allowed herself to be drawn over to the chair. More footsteps passed the outer door, and Maria cast a worried glance in that direction.

'There is fire in the city,' she said. 'One of Francesco's boatmen brought word. He said the Palazzo Dracone is burning, and there's more smoke towards the Merchants' Bridge.'

Serafina paused, gripping the back of the chair. 'Fire?' she repeated. 'Is this Dracone's doing, do you think?'

'Francesco thinks so,' said Maria. 'And that's not all. People came to stand outside, thinking that the baby would save them. Francesco told them to go home, that the child was not the Christos, but they wouldn't listen.'

'But the Holy Father has decreed it,' said Serafina.

Maria spread her hands. 'Decrees . . . a decree is a cold thing, Serafina, when you fear for your life and your home. They were so afraid, and the fire is spreading . . . When they wouldn't leave, Francesco said that we should let them in. They'll be safe here – as safe as anywhere. But . . .' She bit her lip. 'Serafina, they brought gifts! Just what they had with them. Gifts for the child. A gold sequin, or an embroidered kerchief, or a ring. We did not wish to take them, but how could we refuse?'

Serafina sat down and dipped her spoon into the bowl of soup. Its warmth and aroma drifted around her, and she realized how tired she was. 'They want to worship the child?' she asked.

'They do worship him,' Maria said. 'And he isn't even born yet.'

She went quietly into the bedchamber. Serafina spooned soup, ate a roll and some cheese, and thought about what she had just heard. She thought she understood why the child was not the Christos. She did not understand how she or anyone else could explain that to frightened people who needed something to believe in.

If the city was saved, they would believe in a miracle.

There would be no hope for Giulietta's baby ever to live a normal life.

Her meal finished, Serafina went to the window and pushed it open. She had lost count of time, there in the birthing room; the light showed her it was mid morning. There was an acrid smell of smoke in the air.

She could see nothing of the burning, but from

somewhere below a babble of voices rose up, as if more of the citizens were gathering for the protection of the Christos Child.

As she closed the window again, she heard the door open behind her, and turned to see Francesco Foscari. Dropping a curtsey, she asked, 'May I help you, sir?'

'Have you seen Maria?' he asked.

'She is in the birthing chamber, sir.' Serafina went to the door of Guilietta's room and opened it in time to hear a spate of lurid curses from Giulietta, ending in a gasp of pain.

Beckoning Maria, she drew back as Francesco said abruptly, 'The fire grows worse. There's a crowd outside again. We can't house them all.'

Maria went to her husband and took his hand. 'We must do what we can. Is Father Augustine still here? You could ask him to speak to them, and pray with them.'

Francesco nodded. His plain, good-natured face was creased into a frown. 'It may take more than prayers,' he muttered. 'Soon all we will be able to do is burn alongside them.' He turned to go.

'Sir—' said Serafina.

'Yes, what is it?'

'Sir, there may be a way.' She fingered her bracelet, the cool beads of pearl and coral that Phao had given her on the night of Carnival. 'Father Augustine told us that the sea genics live in the lagoon, to rule the tides and control the level of the water. If they would send the sea to save us—'

She heard Maria draw in her breath sharply, while Francesco shook his head, still frowning.

'But how to call them?' he said. 'If they would even agree to help us. They have no cause to love the city.'

'Someone must plead with them,' said Serafina. The resolve was in her mind before she was aware of it; she drew herself up. 'I will go.'

Francesco stared at her, for a moment unable to stop himself from gaping. 'Nonsense,' he said, when he had recovered himself. 'That is no task for a woman, and no woman under my roof will take such a risk.'

'I am under your roof, sir,' Serafina said, bobbing a tiny curtsey. 'But not under your command. Not any longer. I am human, sir, since last night.'

Francesco still stared, looking affronted, as if even he, the most easy-going of men, had boundaries beyond which he would not permit anyone to go.

'Sir, I must go,' Serafina went on, before he could forbid her to speak, or stalk out of her presence. 'The sea genics owe a debt to me, and to Duke Leonardo . . .' Eagerly holding out the token as a proof of what she said, she told him about the encounter on Carnival night, and how Leonardo had beaten off the men who were attacking Phao in the gardens. 'Someone must do this, for the sake of the city,' she said. 'I will go, sir, with your leave or without it, but you can make it easier for me. Lend me a boat, and a boatman to sail it.'

For a few seconds she did not know whether Francesco would give in, or break into a towering rage. Maria reached out tentatively to lay a hand on his arm, but he did not look at her. At last he broke into shocked laughter.

'I'll do better than that.' He strode across the room and tugged the bell rope. When the servant appeared, he said, 'Tell Michele to make my skiff ready. And send Father Augustine to me here.'

When the man had gone, Francesco turned back to

Serafina. 'You shall have your boat. And Father Augustine knows where the sea genics may be found. He shall go with you.' As Serafina bowed her head in thanks, he added, 'And may God go with you too, for I fear we have no other hope.'

Twenty-two

Once Gianni had taken his leave, swept along with Father Teo to tell the Patriarch what he had seen, and Manfred had ordered messengers to warn all parts of the city, Leonardo found himself without anything to do. Unable to stay still, or wait for his servants to do his bidding, he left his apartment and ran down the stairs to the water gate.

The boatman who had brought him from the Palazzo Foscari was still waiting for him. Leonardo stepped into the boat and ordered the man to take him back there. He had to make sure that Caterina and Gabriel would be safe, and he remembered that among his possessions at the palazzo were the keys to the Palazzo Loredan. He would send some of Francesco's men to look there, and see if they could put out the fire before it took hold.

As the boat pulled away from the palace water gate a fluttering movement high above him caught Leonardo's eye. A bat, flying in daylight, he thought, before he realized it had emerged from the window of one of the cells under the roof, where Count Dracone was confined.

Watching it more closely as it flapped away, he caught the glint of metal, and noticed the jerky movement, a copy, but not a perfect one, of natural flight. He let out a soft curse as he understood that he was observing a mechanical creature.

Another of Dracone's bribes from Anhalt and the damned Imperial merchants; Leonardo wondered how long Dracone had possessed it, and what it was used for. It could take a message, that was plain enough, and no doubt there were messages that Dracone would not wish to pass through his gaolers. Messages to Cesare, Leonardo guessed, to tell him where and how to set the fires.

As his boat passed along the quayside and into the mouth of the main waterway, Leonardo tried to keep the bat in sight, but soon it disappeared into the growing pall of smoke over the rooftops. A billowing black column that must be the Palazzo Dracone. Two or three other smudges on the skyline, showing where other buildings were burning. But not the inferno Heinrich had feared. Or not yet.

The waters of the canal were still and dark. Oily rainbows broke and re-formed as the boat slid onwards, and there was a tang of oil in the air, making Leonardo feel faintly sick. Everything was quiet. There was not the usual traffic on the canal, but no sign of panic as yet. It was as if the whole city was waiting.

Then, as if at a signal, Count Dracone's flyer appeared, swooping down the length of the canal. It came in low over the water; fire spat out of it, and in its wake the whole of the canal sprang into flame. The flyer screamed over Leonardo's head. Below, a river of fire rushed down upon the boat, ripples dancing.

The boat rocked wildly. The boatman yelled something, and sent the craft skimming towards the mouth of a side canal. The flames were there before them. For a moment Leonardo felt fire all around him, searing and scarlet, and then the boat rammed hard into a stone quay.

He grabbed the boatman, thrust him up onto the quay-side, and pulled himself up after.

Coughing, gulping in cool air, he crouched on the canal side. He was soot-blackened; his face and hands stung, but he was unharmed. The boatman was cursing steadily as his boat burned. Flame leapt and quivered over all the surface of the canal. In the distance, someone was screaming.

After a few moments, Leonardo struggled to his feet. Wordlessly, he jerked his head at the boatman to follow him to the Palazzo Foscari. As he led the way up the narrow street he saw the flyer again, circling over the rooftops, raining fire over the city.

At the Palazzo Foscari, Francesco had ordered his servants to fill what vessels they could with water, but fire spread-ing up the canals on two sides had driven them indoors. The palazzo itself was still undamaged.

A crowd had gathered in the square outside, and Leonardo had to thrust his way through. Their eyes were fixed on the palazzo, and some of them were praying. None of them realized that he was their Duke.

As he waited in the entrance hall for the servant to announce him, he heard a door open somewhere up above. A few notes from a harpsichord drifted into the air, followed by Hyacinth's glorious alto, singing scales. Leonardo felt as though he stood in a shaft of sunlight; the touch of transcendence was followed by an impulse to laugh, which he quickly stifled. Even as the city burnt around him, Hyacinth would sing.

A moment later, Francesco Foscari came hurrying down the stairs.

'We got your message,' he said, breathing hard in anger, so unlike the patient and practical man Leonardo knew. 'All's well here – for now.'

'Caterina?'

'With Giulietta, still. Lord, Leonardo, why do babies take so long in coming?'

Laughter came from the stairs above, and Caterina ran lightly down to join them. 'I heard your voice, my lord.'

Leonardo caught her hands. 'You're well? You're not afraid?'

She shook her head. 'I have too much to do.'

'We may have to evacuate the city,' Leonardo went on. 'I've ordered boats to the ferry crossing. If you—'

'No,' said Caterina. 'Giulietta can't go anywhere, and we must stay with her.'

'I might send some of the servants,' Francesco said. 'Maybe Hyacinth . . . But what would they do, out on the water, or on the mainland without shelter? Here is as safe as anywhere. Besides, there may be help you don't know about, Leonardo.'

Leonardo listened as Francesco told him how Serafina and Father Augustine had gone to beg help from the sea genics. 'I tried to forbid her,' Count Foscari finished, 'but she wouldn't listen. Should I have tried harder, Leonardo? I could have—'

Caterina smiled, laying a hand on his arm. 'You could have locked her in, and even then she might have climbed out of a window. Francesco, I don't think anyone could stop Serafina once she has made up her mind.'

'She's a brave woman,' Leonardo agreed.

'I only pray she gets there safely,' said Francesco. 'And that the sea genics listen to her.'

'We have given them little cause,' said Leonardo

grimly. He touched Caterina's hand to his lips. 'I must go, but I should speak to Gabriel first. Where is he?'

Francesco and Caterina exchanged a glance.

'He went to the Palazzo Loredan,' said Francesco.

Leonardo felt as if every drop of blood had drained out of his heart. He said, 'When?'

Francesco gripped his arm. 'When your message came. He's surely there by now, Leonardo. He wasn't caught in – that.'

'You let him go?' In some part of him Leonardo knew that his friend was not to blame, any more than he was to blame for Serafina's leaving, but fear was making him unjust.

'I'm sorry, Leonardo,' Francesco said, 'but he insisted. He said something about a painting that he had to rescue. I gave him your keys, and sent him with a boatman I can trust.'

His own portrait, Leonardo thought. Of course. Gabriel would risk anything to preserve it, even his life.

He said, 'I have to find him.' He took Caterina by the shoulders and kissed her urgently. 'I have to.'

'Yes, I know,' Caterina said. 'Go safely, love.'

Leonardo ran down the stairs and pushed open the entrance doors at the back of the palazzo.

In the short time Leonardo had been inside, the crowds had grown thicker, packing the square and the street behind the Palazzo Foscari, and flames were licking around the boats huddled together beneath the bridge over the side canal. Leonardo halted in the doorway, and called, 'What's this? Why are you here?'

When no one replied to him he pushed through the crowds as far as the bridge and grabbed the shoulder of the nearest boatman. 'You – tell me what's happening.'

The boatman turned with a curse on his lips and went white when he realized he was face to face with his Duke. He whipped off his hat and stood turning it nervously between his hands. 'They say – begging your pardon, my lord – they say the Christos is to be reborn here. We reckoned we'd be safe if we came where He is.'

'That's not true,' said Leonardo. He raised his voice so that all the crowds could hear him. 'The Holy Father has decreed that the child is not the Christos! Go home, and save what you can. Go home, I tell you!'

The crowds stared, and muttered, and one or two people slunk away, but most stayed where they were, refusing to meet his eyes.

Leonardo bit back an oath. He knew he would never convince them with rational argument, and he was wasting time. He climbed the steps of the bridge, took a last look back over the heads of the crowd, and began to run.

Smoke billowed through the air, across the water. Leonardo blinked as it stung his eyes, and tried to peer through it. More smoke than flame as yet, he thought, praying in frantic silence as he hurried onwards. The Palazzo Dracone when he approached it was like a torch, with flame slashing into the sky; the buildings on either side had begun to burn. The blazing canal was like a pair of redhot pincers, closing around a peninsula of fire.

As Leonardo stumbled across the bridge to skirt the back of the buildings, the main door of the Palazzo Dracone burst open, and a tongue of flame licked out of it. One of Dracone's shambling constructs, wreathed in flame, arms raised to shield its face, blundered down the steps and fell headlong into the canal. The water hissed; steam rose from the roiling surface, but the construct did not reappear.

A dull roar came from somewhere above as part of the palazzo's roof fell in. Leonardo scarcely gave it a glance, only to stop and look back as instead of fading away it swelled louder and louder, became a blast that shook the sky. Glittering shards of mirror fountained into the air.

After them came more fire, but these flames were dark, licking upwards with nothing to feed them, whirling into the sky like a tornado. Within the spinning spiral Leonardo could make out eyes and claws, the flapping of ragged wings, grotesque creatures jerking as they danced on air.

For a moment his limbs turned to water and he slumped against the wall at his back. His hand moved in the sign of the cross. His courage, his pride in his new office, the honour he upheld for House Loredan, all were leached away as he stared up into the vortex of hell.

But the swirling maelstrom of demons had no interest in him. As they surged out of the burning building and into the sky they seemed to gather, darken, and then poured away over the rooftops, in the direction of the Palazzo Foscari where the new Christos was to come into the world.

3

Father Augustine heaved the tiller over and the little skiff tacked into the wind. Serafina ducked as the sail swung over and pulled hard on the rope. The flapping sail stretched taut, the wind filling it, and the skiff skimmed over the waves.

'You sail well, sir,' Serafina said, glancing back at the young priest where he sat in the stern.

He smiled at her. He had changed his ragged cassock for a new one, but his hair was still long, not returned to the priestly tonsure yet, the straw coloured strands whipping back and forth in the wind. 'The sea genics taught me,' he said.

Something about him teased at Serafina; she had seen him before, and now she remembered where. 'Father,' she said, 'it was you that day, was it not, on the quayside when the Contarini barge went down? You helped me and Hyacinth from the sea.'

Father Augustine bowed his head. 'Yes, mistress.'

'And the sea people were with you, too – Caterina said a sea woman saved her.'

'Yes, mistress, some of them. Some were too far out, on the distant islands. And others . . . others did not care that humans were drowning.'

His face grew shadowed and he said no more. Serafina let him be, biting back the question she wanted to ask. Would they care now that the city burned?

Huddling into the cloak that Maria Foscari had given her, Serafina gazed back the way they had come. The city was a smudge on the horizon. She could hardly believe it looked so small.

A stiff wind blew towards it as the heat of the fires rose into the sky. Father Augustine had to tack again, sending Serafina scrambling for the ropes. If they capsized now, there would be no help for them, or for any of those they had left behind.

The lagoon was sullen, steel-grey, the sky clouded. The boat scudded on, away from the inner islands that huddled around the city. There seemed nothing ahead but grey water and grey sky.

Then as the boat tacked again Serafina saw that they

were drawing close to a larger island, where a jumble of abandoned buildings stretched down into the sea.

'This is the place?' she asked.

Before Father Augustine could reply, she saw movement ahead of her; a shape – human or sea creature, she could not be sure – had slipped from one of the tumbledown walls and dived into the waves.

'They know we're here,' said Father Augustine.

Something in his voice made Serafina uneasy. 'Surely they won't harm us?' she asked. She had expected nothing but friendship from Phao.

'Harm us, no,' said Father Augustine. 'They are not evil. But some of them are bitter over their service to the city, and want nothing to do with us.'

'But I am a genic too,' said Serafina.

She said nothing more as their skiff approached the island, drawing closer to a domed building half submerged by water. She had time to realize that long ago it must have been a church, before the boat surged forward underneath an archway.

At once the wind dropped. The boat slid softly forward, losing momentum. Serafina gazed around at grey walls, lit by a grey light filtering down from windows high above, light caught by the surface of the sea, to send glancing reflections on walls and roof, so the whole building shimmered.

Above Serafina's head, on the inside of the dome, vast faces, gravely formal, stared down at her, and as a shiver ran through her she recognized the figures she had seen the night before in an icon on the altar of the chapel in the Palazzo Foscari.

The boat began to move again as Father Augustine paddled towards the far end of the church. As they drew closer, a head bobbed up from the water, then another, figures slid from balconies on ropes of twined sea wrack, until an escort of sea genics swam beside the boat towards a throne where one of them sat crowned with pearl and coral, and the waves lapping around him.

'That is the sea-Duke,' Father Augustine murmured in Serafina's ear. 'Call him "my lord". He is no friend to the city, but he may be persuaded.'

He brought the boat to a halt before the throne, and shipped the paddle. The other sea genics gathered round it. Serafina knew there was no way back, no escape from here if the sea people did not wish it.

The sea-Duke leaned forward. 'Augustine, why do you return? And why do you bring this woman with you?'

Serafina got to her feet, holding on to the mast to steady herself as the boat rocked beneath her feet. In the grey light, shifting with the ripple of reflections on the water, she hoped the sea people could not see her fear. 'The city is burning, my lord,' she said, trying to make her voice sound strong and confident. 'We have come to beg your help. Send in the sea to save us!'

For a moment there was utter silence, except for the sea sucking at the base of the pillars. Then the sea-Duke spoke. 'Why should we help you? What is it to us if the city burns?'

'Everyone will die!' Father Augustine sounded outraged.

The sea-Duke shrugged. 'We do not care for the deaths of humans.'

There was some murmuring at that, and Serafina realized that not all of his people agreed with the sea-Duke. She glanced around at them, willing sympathy to appear in those alien faces.

'There are genics in the city too,' she said. 'I was born a genic, but now I am human too. No genics are enslaved in the city any more.'

The sea-Duke paused at that, regarding her intently with dark, secret eyes, but she could see no belief in his face.

'Draw my genic blood, if that will convince you,' she said. She held out her arm towards the sea-Duke, her wrist bearing Phao's bracelet of pearl and coral. 'And see this token. See, and tell me whether there can be friendship between the city and the sea.'

Still there was no reply from the sea-Duke, but towards the back of the crowd, someone called out, 'My lord Duke!'

There was a disturbance as she began to swim forwards, through the ranks of her people, who parted for her, until she reached the clear space around the boat and reached for the side with one webbed hand.

Serafina had expected to see Phao, but this woman was unknown to her.

'Tethys!' Father Augustine exclaimed, relief in his voice.

The sea woman smiled her lipless smile at him, and then addressed her Duke. 'My lord, I told you of this, of the man I heard yesterday, calling to us from the quayside. He told us we are free.'

'And you believe this?' The sea-Duke did not speak contemptuously. The question was thoughtful, rather, as if he wanted Tethys's opinion and would respect it. For the first time Serafina began to believe that Father Augustine was right, and the Duke was someone who could be persuaded.

'It's true, my lord,' she said urgently. 'No one may

own a genic now. We have a new Duke who will make this into law and enforce it.'

'We should try this, at least,' said Tethys.

While they had been speaking, more of the sea genics had been swimming in, crowding curiously around the boat. Now, before the sea-Duke could reply, a voice cried, 'Serafina! Serafina!' and suddenly Phao was swimming towards her, clinging to the prow and reaching up to her. Serafina reached down and their hands met.

'What is this?' the sea-Duke asked, an edge of displeasure in his voice. 'Phao, you are too young for this council.'

Phao's curtain of wet hair flicked back as she turned to face him. 'My lord, I must speak.' She sounded nervous, but determined. 'You know what happened to me when I went to the city on Carnival night. It was Serafina who saved me then – Serafina and a human man.'

The Duke sat up straighter, and the water around him rippled. His eyes were fixed on Serafina. 'That was you?'

Again Serafina held out her arm to him. 'That is how I wear this token. And the man with me was Count Leonardo Loredan, he who is now Duke.'

A hush fell again. Amid the soft lapping of the sea, the shifting light, Serafina waited for the word that would save or destroy her city.

Twenty-three

Leonardo Loredan forced himself to stand erect, to turn his back on the dark cloud funnelling down the sky towards the Palazzo Foscari, and to stumble on across the square and towards the bridge over the next canal.

Beside the steps a man was standing, a lanky, raw-boned youth in a boatman's jacket. He was cursing in a low monotone as he looked down at the burnt-out wreck of his craft, nudging against the arch of the bridge.

Leonardo grabbed his arm. 'Leave that – go to the Patriarchal Palace and tell the Patriarch that the forces of hell are loose over the Palazzo Foscari. Go now!'

The boatman gaped at him. Leonardo wrenched off the ring the Patriarch had placed on his finger when he was made Duke, and closed the man's hand tightly around it. 'Give him that.'

The man stared at the ring, and then at Leonardo; understanding suddenly lit his face. 'My lord Duke—'

'Take the message,' Leonardo interrupted. 'Afterwards, return that ring to me at the Ducal Palace, and you shall have the finest boat in the city.'

Clumsily the man saluted, and went scrambling off up the canal to where another boat lay moored, abandoned by its owner. Leonardo did not wait to see him cast off, but sprang up the steps of the bridge, and hurried on.

The shops on the Merchants' Bridge, when Leonardo reached it, were untouched, though black smoke rolled out from the Imperial Hostel on the left hand side. A few men – Leonardo recognized the lawyer Anhalt among them – were loading armfuls of papers into a handcart.

Ignoring them, he plunged into the maze of alleys alongside the canal. A woman pushed past him, carrying a huge bundle; someone was screaming from a window high above. As Leonardo passed San Giovanni, the bell was ringing, and crowds streaming in through the open doors.

He hurried on, and could not restrain a cry of relief as he emerged from the alleyways to see the Palazzo Loredan still untouched by fire.

As he drew closer, he could see that the side door had been broken open. By Cesare, he wondered, setting fire? Leonardo pushed his way inside, and shouted, 'Gabriel!' Silence. 'Gabriel!'

Knowing where he must be, if he was here at all, Leonardo ran up the stairs and burst through the door of the studio.

Gabriel was standing by the window, looking down on a city wreathed in flame. He turned as Leonardo thrust back the door.

Leonardo strode across to him, and gripped him by the shoulders. 'You're safe!'

'Yes – Count Foscari's boatman searched, and found a candle among the wine barrels, burning down into a dish of oil.' Gabriel shivered. 'If he had not . . .'

'Where is he?'

'By then the canal was burning, so he went back to the Palazzo Foscari on foot. I said I'd wait. I knew you would come here.'

'And the painting?'

Gabriel nodded towards the wall. Leonardo's portrait was leaning against it, swathed in the blanket from Gabriel's bed, and fastened with cord.

Leonardo hugged him. 'Stupid.'

'I wanted it.'

'Bring it, then. We've work to do.'

Leonardo and Gabriel threaded their way through the alleys towards the basilica. Smoke drifted on the air, but as yet the worst of the fire had not reached this part of the city. As they crossed squares and bridges, and Leonardo could catch a glimpse of the open sky, he could see the vortex spreading like a bruise. It hung above the city like a storm cloud, seething within, tattered at the edges, where winged spirits of hell flapped against the sky like scraps of rag.

When they reached the square they saw a sheet of water covering it, fluttered by wind blowing in from the sea. There was no flame here, but the water reeked of oil and fire. It was barely ankle deep, but as they began splashing through it towards the basilica and the palace beyond, it grew deeper, with waves lapping inwards.

'A flood?' Gabriel said nervously, clutching the painting. 'Are we to drown as well as burn?'

'The sea genics . . .' Something in Leonardo's mind expanded like a burst of light.

Against fire, water. Serafina had reached the sea genics, and they had listened to her. They had opened the sluice gates across the mouth of the lagoon. The incoming tide would save the city.

Laughing exultantly, he took Gabriel by the shoulder

and propelled him across the square. The water was knee-deep by the time they reached the bell-tower. As Leonardo gathered himself for a final dash to the entrance of the palace, he saw movement on the roof, a flash of scarlet, and a rope snaking down the wall at the end nearest the sea.

Gabriel grabbed his arm. 'Dracone!'

The pilot Cesare let himself over the edge of the roof and climbed down to the square. Dracone followed, and the two men began to wade towards the flyer, which was moored at the quayside.

Leonardo shouted, but the wind whipped the sound away, and it was drowned by the steady roaring that was growing from the sea. Neither of the escaping men heard him.

'Damn!' said Leonardo. 'We should have expected this.'

In the crisis over the burning city, he had scarcely thought about Dracone in his cell below the palace roof, or thought to ask himself what his pilot was doing after he sprayed the city with fire. No one else had thought about them either, and now they were slipping away from justice.

As he began to cross the square to the palace to give the alarm, in a rapidly vanishing hope of recapturing his enemies, Gabriel cried, 'Leo, the sea!'

Beyond the flyer, out in the lagoon, the water was swelling. A green wave rolled inwards, slowly, but with gathering speed and power. Leonardo spun round, and pushed Gabriel through the door of the bell-tower. 'Too late!'

He flung himself up the stairs. Gabriel thrust the painting into his arms and hurried on ahead, up to the bell chamber. A moment later Leonardo heard the bell begin to sound a rapid note, the age old warning against the encroaching sea.

He himself set the painting safely at the turn of the stairs and stepped out onto the terrace above the entrance hall. Dracone and his pilot had disappeared; they must have boarded the flyer.

The engine powered up and the flyer began to move over the surface of the water. But before it could lift off, the surge came. The powerful swell caught the craft, swept it inshore, and casually, like a hand swatting a fly, drove it against the palace wall. One wing buckled; a float was sheared off; the craft wallowed, trapped between two columns by the force of water, and began to sink.

Leonardo saw the hatch open, and Cesare emerge and throw himself into the water. The surge took him, and half swimming, half swept along by it, he was carried past the base of the bell-tower and towards the entrance to the basilica.

Water foamed through the arches and into the narthex. The pilot struck out for the safety of the basilica, but he never reached it. As Leonardo watched, two – three – heads surfaced beside him, and he recognized the floating hair and white faces of the sea genics. One of them raised an arm as if to salute him.

Cesare had seen them. He tried to turn, and as they closed with him he began grappling with the nearest. There was a swirl of water, a moment of mad struggling, and then all four heads disappeared beneath the surface.

Only Leonardo was left to see as Count Dracone, slower than his pilot, pulled himself out of the flyer cockpit.

One leg dragged uselessly, as if it was broken. He

clambered out on top of the sinking flyer. Faintly, Leonardo could hear his shrieking. 'Come to me – help me! Master! Asmodeus!'

He stretched out an arm towards the writhing vortex, spreading now to cover half the sky. Leonardo thought he saw a face coalesce from it, and two red flares that might have been eyes, looking down on the Count with a vast, amused satisfaction. There was no help, no hand or wind from hell to bear Dracone to safety, nothing but that pitiless gaze.

Dracone shrieked again. Clawing at one of the columns, he managed to hold himself upright and clung to the carved acanthus leaves as the support gave way under his feet.

But before the flyer went down, flame blossomed from its fuel tanks. Dracone was sheathed in it. Beating at it wildly, he lost his hold on the column, tottered briefly on the foundering roof of the flyer, and was swallowed up in the sea as it sank.

As Leonardo was drawing a breath of relief that it was over, he caught a flash of scarlet, and saw Dracone fight his way back to the surface, closer now, as the incoming tide swept him nearer to the doors of the basilica.

He was trying to swim, but between panic and his injuries he could do no more than thrash convulsively, like a drowning scarlet spider. Leonardo gripped the rail of the balcony. He wanted Dracone dead, but not this manner of his dying. He wondered if he would ever sleep sound again.

Three heads resurfaced further out into the square, but this time the sea genics moved no closer, only pacing Dracone as he fought furiously for life, cursing the demons who were leaving him to drown, screaming with rage against the sea that eddied around him, drawing him back again from the refuge of the basilica.

Leonardo would have turned away, but he had to bear witness. He felt himself beginning to tremble. An eternity seemed to pass before the frenzied struggles grew feebler. Pawing impotently at the smothering water, arms weighted by pulpy velvet, Dracone sank, became no more than a scarlet blur under the tide, and then was gone.

2

Caterina slipped quietly out of the bedchamber where Giulietta Contarini-Dracone still laboured to give birth. Her head spun from weariness and her anxiety for Leonardo and Serafina and Gabriel. She had to find out whether there was any word.

On the table by the window someone had left fruit and sweet cakes and a silver pot steaming with the aroma of a hot tisane. Silently blessing Francesco's servants, Caterina went to pour herself a cup.

The room was dark; had evening come so soon? Caterina glanced out of the window and almost dropped the pot. The hot liquid inside splashed over the table.

A foul stench flooded into the room. Staring at her from outside, misshapen hands pressed against the glass, was a creature Caterina had never thought to see outside nightmare. Its bulging eyes shone red. Veins throbbed scarlet on the surface of its skin. Ragged wings webbed its fingers and hung to conceal its body.

As Caterina stared back, too shocked even to scream, a third eye opened up in the creature's forehead and winked at her. Its mouth gaped open. A forked scarlet tongue protruded from between needle-sharp teeth, and licked the glass.

Moving as if the air was thick, slowing and deadening her limbs, Caterina set the pot down and backed away. As she did so, she saw that the creature was not alone. More were behind it, jostling for space near the window, peering and pointing. Their mouths distended in uncontrolled laughter that was all the more horrific for being silent.

Caterina had almost reached the door when she heard it open behind her. She did scream then, a faint, gasping cry as she fought to hold on to her senses. Then she felt a hand grip her shoulder and heard Francesco's voice say, 'Caterina, what is it?'

Wordlessly she pointed at the window, and felt Francesco's hand tighten and then release her.

'Dear God . . .' he whispered, and made the sign of the cross.

As if the holy sign had angered them, Caterina saw the demons swirl faster, flinging themselves against the window. The whole sky was dark with them, as if they were engulfing the whole of the palazzo.

'If they get in . . .' she said, in a rasping voice she did not recognize as her own.

'Giulietta?' Francesco asked hoarsely.

'Her windows are shuttered.' Caterina grasped for self-control. 'She mustn't see . . . oh, she must not . . . Her baby—'

'That's why they're here,' said Francesco. 'They want her baby. They want the Christos.'

He had not finished speaking when Caterina heard a scream, coming from some distant part of the palazzo. Someone else had seen what was outside.

Francesco pulled open the door and stepped onto the landing outside. The screaming continued. At the same moment, rapid footsteps sounded on the stairs, and Hyacinth appeared.

'They are the same.' His violet eyes were huge, the red weal of his scar standing out against the pallor of his face. 'They are the ones I told you of, the ones I saw on Carnival night.'

'Hyacinth—' Caterina went to him, her hands held out, only to halt as something like excitement flared in his eyes.

'Music!' he exclaimed. 'Music will hold them back.'

Turning, he hurried back upstairs. A moment later, Caterina heard the harpsichord, and Hyacinth's glorious alto raised in song.

It seemed absurd, but when she stepped back into the antechamber and risked another glance at the window, she saw that the demons were drawing back. They still packed the sky in a seething canopy, but close to the palazzo was a clear space of air. The unnatural darkness had lifted slightly.

She dared approach the window again. Everything in the city was still. Distantly she could hear the cracked note of the basilica bell, sounding fast and urgent.

As Caterina stood there, the stench of the demons gave way to the salt tang of the sea. The air felt warmer, and heavy. From far away, she heard a soft roaring sound. Below her window she could see the canal; the floating, blackened debris began to move, in uncertain eddies at first, and then swept along faster as the tide came in. The colour of the water changed to a deep jade. The canal brimmed full, and water began gurgling up between the paving stones. A salt wind began to blow.

From the bedchamber there came a raw shriek from
Giulietta; silence; then another cry, a thin wailing that
gradually strengthened. Caterina turned, lips parted,
breath coming short, as she heard the cry of the newborn
child, and the world began anew.

3

Wind whipped in Serafina's hair, soaking it with spray.
With one hand she gripped the side of the skiff, and held
her cloak around her with the other, as the tiny craft rode
the surge, skimming swiftly back towards the city.

On every side, the sea genics plunged through the
waves, exulting in the power of the sea. Ahead, the walls
and towers of the city seemed to rise like magic from the
lagoon, the domes of the basilica floating above the
tossing sea like silver bubbles.

As they drew closer, Serafina could see water foaming
around the columns of the Ducal Palace, eddying past
the bell-tower as it rushed on into the city. Above, the
sky roiled with the smoke of the burning.

'See — over there!' Crouched in the stern, Father
Augustine lost his grip on the tiller and grabbed for it
again as the boat yawed wildly. 'In the sky . . . dear God,
what is it?'

Serafina gazed in the direction he was pointing. At
first she thought she saw only thicker smoke over to the
left; then, gradually, she began to discern movement
within the darkness, and flashes of dull crimson and
scarlet. The sky was writhing.

'Dracone's demons!' she cried.

Had he loosed them, she wondered, to set the seal on

his destruction? Or had they broken free, to feast on terror as the city burned?

Father Augustine's lips were moving in prayer as he guided the boat between the two columns at the edge of the square. The cracked bell was beating out a rapid note. More sea genics swam to meet them, crying out in welcome and triumph.

Then Serafina heard someone shouting her name. She looked up to see Leonardo Loredan leaning over the balcony of the bell-tower terrace.

'Serafina! Here!'

Serafina loosened the ropes as Father Augustine had taught her to let down the sail, and the young priest steered towards the bell-tower, managing to bring the boat alongside the tower wall, out of the main force of the incoming sea.

Standing erect, steadying herself with a hand against the wall, Serafina looked up at Leonardo. 'My lord Duke, have you seen . . .?'

He did not need to ask her what she meant. 'They are laying siege to the Palazzo Foscari,' he said tensely. 'They want the Christos.'

'Caterina . . . Giulietta . . .' Serafina fought a gush of pure panic. 'My lord, we must go there!'

Leonardo gave her a curt nod, and drew back from the balcony rail. She heard him shouting, 'Gabriel! Gabriel!' The beating of the bell broke off, and a moment later Leonardo reappeared with Gabriel at his side.

'Do you want to stay here?' he asked the genic. 'There's danger . . .'

Gabriel shook his head. His eyes were dark with fear, but he did not hesitate. 'I want to come with you.'

'Get in the boat, then.'

Awkwardly, Gabriel climbed over the rail, and Father Augustine helped him into the skiff, where he huddled in silence, his eyes fixed with growing wonder on the sea genics who breasted the surge with almost lazy power, thronging the sea between the tower and the basilica.

Leonardo followed more nimbly, and took Serafina's place, tightening the ropes until wind tugged the sail again. 'Go,' he snapped at Father Augustine.

Father Augustine used the paddle to fend the skiff off from the tower wall, and managed to bring it head to wind. The sails flapped madly and then filled as the skiff tacked across the square and back towards the lagoon, hugging the line of the quay until Father Augustine could turn it into the main waterway, out of the worst of the surge.

Most of the sea genics stayed behind, but a few still followed; Phao was close to the boat, and Serafina spotted Tethys further out, pacing them along the line of the canal as they drew closer to the Palazzo Foscari.

Cold grey daylight gave way to dusk as they sailed beneath the outer edges of the canopy, deepening to darkness shot through with dull flame. A hot stench swept over the boat as one of the winged demons swooped low over it. Serafina looked up into burning red eyes and a mouth gaping in grotesque laughter. The dark fire that wreathed it could have reduced them to ashes tossing on the water, but it climbed upwards again on beating bat wings, not even trying to attack.

We are not important, Serafina thought. *There will be time enough for us, when they have the Christos.*

Father Augustine had half risen from his seat by the tiller, tracing the sign of the cross in the air, only to sink back again as he saw that the creature paid him not the slightest attention. Instead he began to intone a chant, the words unfamiliar to Serafina, though she found the sound comforting as the priest's voice strengthened and the boat bore them on into the dark.

Leonardo's mouth was a hard line, his eyes intent on the waterway ahead, not sparing a glance for the twisting horror in the sky. Gabriel, crouched close to him, was gazing upwards. His face was white; he looked quite ill with fear, and yet there was a spark in his eyes that was more than a reflection of the fire overhead. Serafina wondered where he would find a canvas big enough to paint what he saw.

Phao still swam close to the boat, but Serafina had lost sight of the other sea genics; they were gone, or hidden by the encroaching darkness. Peering forward, she could just distinguish the façade of the Palazzo Foscari, beginning to appear from the clinging webs of twilight. In front of it, another boat was drawn up, a small man standing erect at the prow, while the larger figure of his boatman bulked behind him.

Wonder threatened to overwhelm Serafina as she recognized Father Teo and Gianni.

The priest held up his pectoral cross, flinging words of abjuration at the swirling vortex, but as Father Augustine brought the skiff alongside, Serafina could hear his voice cracking with fatigue, his erect stance beginning to waver. The demons could not reach him; they kept their distance, sweeping past with an angry chittering, but they still prowled the air above the Palazzo Foscari.

Father Teo broke off with an exclamation as Serafina reached out to draw the two boats together.

'Father!' she said urgently. 'Tell us what to do.'

'I do not know.' He let out a sigh of weariness,

sinking down to a seat in the boat. 'They cannot over-
come the power of Christos. They cannot enter. But I do
not know how to banish them from the world.'

Serafina looked up at the forbidding façade of the
palazzo. Demons whirled around it like leaves in a storm,
but they made no attempt to break their way inside.
What held them, she asked herself. Giulietta's baby, born
at last? Yet the Holy Father had decreed that he was not
the Christos. What held back the demons from crushing
the palazzo, from destroying the child along with everyone within, or taking him if they pleased, to make him a
shadow Christos, a demon like themselves?

As she gazed, the vortex parted. Even the demons
seemed afraid, peeling back and scattering to leave a clear
space above the rooftops. A shape formed out of the
darkness and came stalking down the sky, the one she
had seen in Dracone's mirrored room, the one the Count
had called Asmodeus. He spread his arms, and a cloak of
dark flame shrouded the palazzo, shedding flakes of fire
to fall hissing into the canal. Yet still he could not enter.
Serafina saw frustration blaze in his eyes.

Father Teo, in a low, exhausted voice, began to speak
a prayer. Serafina heard Father Augustine join with him,
and Gianni, and, after a moment's pause, Leonardo.
Words of power: and yet the little group of them,
huddled together under the mocking gaze of Asmodeus,
seemed powerless to oppose the vast might of hell.

Then, above the words of the prayer, above the dull
roar and crackle of the demonic assault, Serafina heard a
voice. Like a pure thread of water it sprang into the sky,
and the fire could not quench it.

'Hyacinth!' she whispered.

Now she knew what to do. Rising to her feet, she

steadied herself against the mast, and sang, defying the dark. Without her thinking about it, the melody that rose to her lips was her part in the duet, that Hyacinth had written and rehearsed with her so long ago in the Palazzo Contarini.

Hyacinth heard her. His own voice joined hers, stronger and more joyful, and they flung the music back and forth, weaving a net of protection around the Palazzo Foscari.

Angry whirlpools formed in the canopy as the demons lashed the air in fury. Asmodeus spread his wings and let out a shriek of defiance, but it sounded curiously faint, as if it rose and spent itself far in the distance.

Closer to Serafina was a spurt of shocked laughter from Leonardo. 'They give way! Sing, Serafina!'

The duet came to an end, and at once Hyacinth began another song, one that Serafina knew, so she could add her voice to his. There were others singing too, inside the palazzo, and from all around her Serafina became aware of a queer, wordless melody, shiveringly high, and realized that the sea genics were clustering around the boats, joining the harmony.

Father Teo held out his cross; he and Father Augustine began to chant, a deeper, more solemn strain, a ground to Hyacinth's soaring song. Leonardo joined them, and Gianni in an unexpectedly strong bass, and at last, hesitantly and without words, Gabriel.

The demons seemed to struggle in a surge of air, tossed helplessly to and fro in a frantic beating of shredded wings. The vortex lifted from the palazzo roof. As if a monstrous flower could shrink its petals back into the bud, it was sucked upwards, gathering in on itself until it became a pulsing knot in the sky, and winked out.

Asmodeus swept free of it, stooping over the two boats like a vast bird of prey. Serafina felt his searing breath, and smelt the stink of him. For a hideous eternal second she met the smouldering eyes, and her heart almost failed her, but still she sang.

The demon lord let out another shriek, a distant wailing, dwindling to nothing as lightning crackled across his wings and he dissolved into the cool shine of day. His eyes flashed hatred for a moment longer, and he was gone.

Cool air touched Serafina's face. All was silent, except for the lapping of water against the steps to the palazzo loggia, and Hyacinth's voice, alone once again, threading the clean sky.

Blinking like someone just awoken from sleep, Serafina looked around her, dazed, as if she saw her companions for the first time. Around the boats the sea genics trod water, reaching hands to each other. Serafina saw a dark head among them, crowned with pearl and coral, and realized, amazed, that the sea-Duke was with them.

The sound of heavy bolts being drawn roused her. At the top of the steps, the doors of the palazzo were swinging back, and in the opening stood Francesco Foscari, his hands outstretched in welcome.

Twenty-four

The waters were receding. Leonardo Loredan stepped out into the square from the Ducal Palace. His eyes stung after a night without sleep, as reports had come in from all the quarters of the city, as the flood fought with Dracone's fire. As the sun rose, he knew that they had won.

The Palazzo Dracone was burnt out; the fire had spread to the buildings on either side, but there it had stopped.

In the merchants' quarter there had been little damage, thanks to the prompt action taken by Messire Giovanni. There were, however, a number of merchants waiting at the Palace to complain about goods ruined by the high water.

Fire had swept through the ground floor of the Palazzo Contarini, but the flood had put it out before it did irrevocable damage. The theatre had burnt to the ground, and there was fire damage at I Frari and Corpus Domini. A row of tenement buildings had collapsed when sea water had scoured through them.

From what Leonardo could hear, gossip was rife about the thunderstorm and lightning that had accompanied the flood.

There was surprisingly little loss of life.

A skin of water still covered the square. Seaweed lay washed up on the flagstones, along with the occasional stranded fish. There was a strong smell of the sea.

Leonardo rubbed his strained eyes as the brightness of sunlight on water dazzled him, and began to walk slowly towards the quayside. Without his ducal robes, dressed in the comfortable and shabby black of the days of his poverty, he drew no attention from the few people already up and about.

He stood on the quayside and breathed in the cold, salted air. Out in the lagoon, two sea genics played in the waves, leaping joyfully in the sunlight. He raised an arm in greeting, but did not know if they saw him.

As he turned back towards the Palace he saw the body of Count Dracone, a small heap of scarlet wreckage, thrown up at the base of the column where the city's first protector slew the dragon in immemorial stone.

Leonardo walked towards it and stood looking down. The scarlet coat was blackened and half burnt away, and flesh sloughed off the limbs beneath. Arms and legs were contorted as though the surge had tossed him until the bones snapped. Vomit trailed from the scarlet mouth. The eyes stared, but all feeling, of rage or fear, had long since died from them.

Though Leonardo did not think of himself as a pious man, his hand moved in the sign of the cross.

He half turned to go and find someone to take up the body. For a moment he hesitated. Then he stooped, and drew from the dead finger the reliquary ring.

2

Giulietta Contarini-Dracone lay back against a mound of
lacy pillows, her golden hair loose, her nightgown a froth
of silk and ribbons. She cradled her newborn child, as he
sucked eagerly at her breast.

Though he knew it was the custom to visit a lady new
delivered, Leonardo Loredan could not help feeling
uncomfortable in the soft, stifling bedchamber, among
the women: the genic Serafina at the bedside with her
stitching, while Maria Foscari and his own Caterina sat
with heads together by the window.

Giulietta had gracefully accepted his offering of flowers. 'So kind, my lord Duke,' she murmured.

'My pleasure, Countess,' said Leonardo. 'My chaplain,
Father Teo, would be glad of a talk with you, when you
feel able.'

Giulietta opened her eyes wide. 'Of course, I'd be
delighted to see dear Father Teo again. But what can he
possibly want to talk to me about?'

'About the child.' As Giulietta still looked beautifully
bewildered – was the girl really *that* stupid? – Leonardo
added, 'To discuss what must be done for him, and how
he should be brought up. If he is truly a copy of Christos's
body, grown from His hair—'

Giulietta went pink, and let out a little tinkling laugh.
'*Surely*, my lord Duke, you don't believe *that* story?'

Leonardo stiffened. In all the speculation about the
baby, no one, to his knowledge, had thought to ask
Giulietta what she believed. He asked her now. 'Is it not
true?'

More silvery laughter. 'Of course it is not! How could

it possibly be? A baby, grown from a single hair? My dear lord Duke!'

'The child is Dracone's, then?' Leonardo was not sure he liked the sound of that. Count Dracone was dead, the Palazzo Dracone burnt, and House Dracone no more than a memory. He had no intention of restoring it under his rule, but if this child was the heir, and Giulietta chose to insist on his rights . . .

Giulietta had gone pinker than ever. She shot a glance at Serafina, who kept her head bent over her embroidery, though Leonardo thought he saw a faint tightening of her lips.

'No,' said Giulietta. She gave Leonardo an imploring look. 'Forgive me, my lord. This is hard for me . . . shameful, indeed.'

'What do you mean?'

'The child is the son of Lucio Venier.' Giulietta reached for a lacy handkerchief and dabbed delicately at her eyes. 'He drowned when poor Papa's barge went down.'

Leonardo stared at her. He was aware that the soft murmuring talk from the two sisters behind him had stopped; he did not turn to look at Caterina. 'Explain,' he said.

'Lucio and I were . . . very much in love.' Giulietta lowered her eyes modestly and cast a look at Leonardo through her lashes. 'Papa hoped for a better marriage for me, for Lucio was not the heir to House Venier, and so we . . . we became betrothed in secret. We . . .' She cleared her throat in embarrassment. 'We did not wait for our marriage vows, and . . . and just at the time that Lucio died, I realized that I was with child.'

She dabbed with the handkerchief again.

'Go on,' said Leonardo. He felt anger building in him, but tried to keep it out of his voice and his demeanour.

'I knew I had done wrong,' Giulietta said. 'And I knew that if anyone found out I would be sent to Corpus Domini, and have to repent, and pray, and be *good*! So when Count Dracone asked for my hand...' She shrugged and her silks rustled. 'It seemed for the best. I never *dreamt* that he would tell such a fantastic story about the child!'

She lay back against her pillows, pulled the baby's shawl closer about him, and fixed blue eyes on Leonardo. 'Forgive me, my lord. I did it all so that my child should have a father.'

'No doubt, madam.' Leonardo almost spat the words out. 'And now that once more he has none...?'

Delicately Giulietta stroked the dark fuzz of hair on the baby's head. 'He shall be brought up as the heir to House Contarini.'

Feeling so furious that if he stayed he would have said something unseemly for a lady's bedchamber, Leonardo bowed and withdrew. At the door he snapped, 'Serafina!' and jerked his head towards the passage outside. The genic woman rose and followed him; as he left the room he heard Giulietta's silvery laughter break out once again.

When the door was closed, Leonardo turned on Serafina, to meet a composed look from clear hazel eyes. 'Well?' he said.

'Well, my lord?'

'Don't play games with me. Was it you who thought up that ... that farrago?'

'Farrago?'

Leonardo's fingers twitched; if she echoed him again he would have a hard time keeping them from her throat. 'That story about Lucio Venier.'

'I believe he was much enamoured of the Countess,' said Serafina calmly. 'I saw them together at Count Contarini's *soirée*, soon after I entered his service. You may remember the occasion, my lord?'

Leonardo did. At the time when he himself had nourished a hopeless ambition of wedding Giulietta Contarini, and she had infuriated him by flirting first with Lucio Venier, and then with Count Dracone.

He took a deep breath. 'Giulietta Contarini,' he said, 'would never have rushed into a secret betrothal and love-making before her marriage. Not for virtue's sake, but because she estimated her own worth too highly. And however she might have flirted, she would never have lost her head over a younger son with no hope of inheriting his House.'

'No?' said Serafina innocently.

'No. So I ask you again, madam, was the story yours? I don't believe Giulietta is clever enough to have thought of it all by herself.'

Serafina gave a little shrug, as she might have gracefully turned aside a compliment.

'Clever,' Leonardo repeated. 'Lucio Venier and his elder brother Marcello both died in the Contarini wreck, and Count Venier is now Marcello's son, a boy of ten. There's no likelihood that this child of Giulietta's will be called upon to inherit House Venier. But with her father and brother dead, Giulietta can pass to him the lordship of House Contarini. And that is why I call the story clever, and convenient, and why I don't believe a word of it!'

Briefly Serafina looked anxious. 'Do you think no one will believe it? Why should Giulietta tell a story to her own shame, unless it is true?'

'For an heir to House Contarini.' A thought struck him, and he asked, 'Does Caterina know anything about this?'

Serafina hesitated. 'What you know,' she said at last. 'No more.'

'Then there is more? You admit Giulietta is lying?'

Amusement leapt into Serafina's eyes; outraged, Leonardo realized that she was laughing at him. 'My lord Duke, I admit nothing,' she said. 'But consider this. Either Giulietta lies, or Dr Heinrich lied when he said he used Giulietta as a vessel to bear the Christos Child. Which lie, do you think, is more likely to be believed?'

Leonardo opened his mouth to reply, and paused. He had himself been uncertain of whether to believe Dr Heinrich when the man had made his speech in Council. Nothing more likely than that Dracone should order him to lie, for the sake of power. Or perhaps Heinrich had lied to Dracone too, and pretended to have done what in truth was beyond his skill. Different possibilities crowded into Leonardo's mind, but one thing stood out: a young girl's indiscretion was much easier to believe than the twisted tale that came from Heinrich's lips.

As he hesitated, Serafina stepped close to him and gripped his arm. 'Listen. If Heinrich spoke true – if Dracone still lived – what would they have done with this child? What will happen to him now, if people believe he is the Christos?'

She was not amused now. Her eyes were lit with a passionate questioning.

Slowly Leonardo said, 'The Holy Father has decreed that he cannot be the Christos. He cannot be infused with the divine. At most, a copy of Christos's humanity.'

Serafina released him, and spread her hands. 'How many people would understand that? You saw yourself how they came here for protection when the city was in danger. Will they lay all their sin and grief on him, as they did on Christos Himself? How can a human child bear it, how could he live, when Christos Himself was crucified?'

Listening to her, the last of Leonardo's anger died, leaving not just admiration for her cleverness, but more than that . . . for her understanding and compassion.

She must have seen his face change, for she smiled. 'I admit nothing,' she said. 'But Giulietta's story will pass for truth, and it will save the child. To be truly human. To be whatever he can be.'

She dropped Leonardo a deep curtsey, and went back into the room to Giulietta and the young Count Contarini.

3

Hardly knowing whether he was furious, amused, or grateful to Serafina for removing an enormous problem from the early days of his Dukedom, Leonardo went to look for Count Foscari.

A servant directed him to the study, where he found Francesco at his writing table. Francesco bade him good day, and gestured towards the letter he was engaged on.

'I am writing to the Holy Father,' he said, 'to report the safe delivery of the child.'

'And which version of his parentage are you including?' Leonardo asked.

Francesco looked gravely earnest. 'I must, of course, report the story Giulietta tells. I would not presume to dictate the Holy Father's decision.'

'I could make a guess.' Leonardo was sure that the Holy Father, too, would be grateful to be rid of the problem. 'But that's not what I want to talk to you about, Francesco.'

'No?' Francesco rose from his seat again. 'Shall I call for wine?'

'No need. This won't take long. I have a job for you.'

Francesco reseated himself, laid down his pen, and clasped his hands. 'What job? I'm at your service, of course.'

'The Imperial Hostel.' Leonardo did not reply directly. He walked across the room to the window and looked down on the square below. A pedlar was stationed there, bright ribbons and laces fluttering from his tray, and a young servant girl, eagerly bargaining. 'I confess,' he went on, 'my first thought was to revoke the lease and drive every last one of the Imperial merchants out of the city. They might even be glad to go. There'll be no market for genics here now.'

'But . . .?' Francesco prompted him.

'You remember I told you about that slippery lawyer Anhalt? He wanted my support, if and when I became Duke. And now, here I am – and as Duke, I'm just minded to give him what he asked for.'

He could not help grinning at Francesco's bewildered expression. 'The Imperial merchants have used us,' he explained. 'They sold us luxuries – wonders! – for profit. I'm of a mind to use them in return.'

'And how can I help?' Francesco clearly did not understand what his friend was driving at.

'The Church has set itself against the science of the Empire,' Leonardo said. 'With some justice, when all they had to offer was genics, and machines like Dracone's flyer. Their science brought no good, and much pain. But need it always be so?'

He came and leant over Francesco, his hands flat on the writing table. 'Think of it, Francesco! They can do so much, and I don't want to stay in ignorance any longer. I want to know what the Empire has to offer us, so that we can choose what is good and useful.

'And so, my friend,' he said with a smile, 'I am offering you an appointment. You are to go north, you and your lady, to be my ambassadors to the Empire. And when I truly know what is going on there, then maybe we, and all the city, and the Imperial merchants – even Anhalt, damn him! – might profit from their skills. Perhaps we can even learn them here.' He laughed at Francesco's amazement. 'You shall go, and bring a new world home to us!'

4

When he had taken leave of Francesco Foscari, Leonardo collected Gabriel and ordered his boatman to row to the Ducal Palace.

'Why do you want me there?' Gabriel asked.

Leonardo smiled affectionately at him. 'I've something to show you.'

Gabriel still looked too thin, he thought, and the dark eyes were enormous in the wasted face. His hair was beginning to grow back in fine dark tendrils, lifted by the wind from the sea as the boat skimmed along the canal. He was wearing a fine linen shirt and a heavy cloak that must have been provided by Francesco Foscari; the shirt had a smear of paint down the front.

At the palace, Leonardo led the way into the Hall of the Great Council. He stood Gabriel in the middle of it, took him by the shoulders and turned him round so that he could see all four walls with their ancient frescos peeled away and barely visible.

'There,' he said. 'A gift. It's yours.'

Gabriel turned his head to look at him. 'Leo . . . to paint?'

'Yes.' He laughed. 'I will have this chamber as fine as it ever was. Finer.'

He was afraid Gabriel was about to faint, he had gone so white. 'What shall I paint?' he asked.

Leonardo drew him over to the carved seats by the wall, where he had already placed, in anticipation of this moment, the portfolio that Count Francesco had recovered from the Dolphin.

Gabriel hugged it to him. 'I thought it was lost.'

'No – look . . .' Gently Leonardo prised the portfolio away from Gabriel's grip and began to leaf through the sketches. Faces, buildings, reflections in water . . . 'It's there, Gabriel, all there. Paint me the city.'

Twenty-five

Serafina knelt on the uneven floor of the basilica, the marble tiles striking cold through the skirts of her gown, and tried to compose her mind to prayer. A good God would forgive her, she suspected, if she was not proficient at it yet.

She could not help wondering if God would forgive her the lie she had created for Giulietta Contarini. To lie was a sin, was it not, and to be forgiven you would need to repent. Serafina could not repent when her lie had saved the child – another Paolo, like his dead uncle and grandfather – to live and grow and be free.

Serafina let out a faint sigh. Being a good daughter of the Church was more complicated than it had first appeared. 'Lord God,' she said silently, 'show us Your will for this child. I leave him in Your hands.'

In her own thoughts, she had lost the thread of the prayers the Patriarch was intoning, somewhere in the higher reaches of the basilica. Cautiously she raised her eyes and looked around.

Gabriel, beside her, was rapt, his gaze fixed on heaven – or, more likely, on the gold mosaics within the domes, the ancient, sacred images shimmering in the light of silver lamps. Far from a mind set on holiness, Serafina suspected, he was trying to work out if the same effects could be reproduced today.

Yet was not reverence for beauty at least a step on the path to holiness? Perhaps God would see it so.

Beyond Gabriel, Serafina could see the genic Alessandro – Messire Alessandro again, now – and his business partner, Messire Giovanni. Both in their merchants' sober black, both intent on their worship. With them was Hyacinth, enveloped in his dark cloak with the hood thrown back to reveal his golden curls and the scarred perfection of his face.

As Serafina observed him, the Patriarch's prayer came to an end. In the silence that followed, a single voice was lifted up, somewhere high in the galleries above the choir, a pure, soaring treble that filled the whole basilica.

Hyacinth started as he heard it, and Serafina saw Gianni put a hand on his arm, hushing him. Another voice, a warm alto, answered the first, and then suddenly the whole air burst into music, a complex polyphony interweaving and tossing the melody back and forth from all sides.

Instruments joined the singers: the clarion call of brass like a shaft of sunlight, a silver wave of strings, lighter and faster, and drawing all together the deep sonorities of the organ.

Serafina felt as though she floated in a bubble of music and light. Hyacinth's violet eyes were wide, his lips parted, and tears were flowing down his face. His hands were clasped at his breast; with his beautiful, marred face he looked like a fallen angel brought beyond all hope or expectation to the open gates of Heaven.

*

The single cracked bell was tolling repeatedly. As she left
the basilica, Serafina saw that crowds of people had
gathered in the square, waiting for the Ducal procession
to appear. The rest of the congregation began to melt
among them; Serafina saw Father Teo, and drew Gabriel
over to him. He faced her, smiling.

'Well, Serafina?'

She returned his smile, feeling as though she greeted
an old friend. 'I thought you would be in there, with the
great ones, Father. You're the Ducal chaplain, aren't you?'

'Yes, but this is the Patriarch's day. I won't—'

He broke off as Hyacinth rushed up to him and
clutched at his hands. His hair was dishevelled and his
cloak fluttered in the sea breeze. Tears still streaked his
face and clung to his lashes.

'Father, the music!' he said. For once the exquisite
voice was stripped of its modulations; he sounded very
young and eager. 'Father I must – I may sing there now,
may I not?'

Amusement sparked in Father Teo's eyes, but his face
was grave as he said, 'Of course, my son. The man you
want to speak to is the Master of the Chapel.'

'Where?'

Father Teo glanced around, and – his hands still
captured – nodded towards a tall, balding priest who
stood a little way off with some of his choristers. 'There.'

'Thank you!' Hyacinth pressed his hands and darted
off.

Father Teo called after him, 'His name is Father
Claudio!'

He stifled laughter and exchanged a glance with
Serafina as Hyacinth bore down on the elderly priest,

who looked taken aback to be the target of so much urgent beauty.

'I happen to know,' Father Teo said, 'that Father Claudio is thinking of retiring. Would Hyacinth make a good Master of the Chapel, do you think?'

'Would he have to become a priest?' Serafina asked, startled.

'It's usual.'

'But Hyacinth is—' Serafina stopped. It sounded absurd. Count Dandolo would probably think it blasphemous. Hyacinth had never shown whether he believed in God or not, or given any sign that God was important to him. But now that he was baptized into Holy Church, surely that could change? The celibacy of the priesthood would be no burden to Hyacinth. And it would give him the security he had never had before, and a meaning in his music that would heal his heart.

'He has a great deal to give,' said Father Teo.

Hyacinth and the Master of the Chapel had their heads together by now; from being flustered, Father Claudio had an expression of intense interest. Serafina caught a scrap of their conversation.

'. . . music for the great Church festivals,' Father Claudio was saying.

'Yes, yes, I can do that.' Hyacinth was excited. Then, suddenly, out of what had always been an impenetrable pride, a touch of humility. 'Father, you must teach me what the words should be.'

Serafina and Father Teo looked at each other, and had nothing to say.

A silver trumpet sounded, drowning the repeated calling of the bell. The crowd stirred, and fell silent. From

the basilica the Ducal procession appeared, headed by
construct heralds with banners of scarlet and cloth of
gold. Behind them came the trumpeter, followed by the
Patriarch in his ceremonial chair.

The old man bowed from side to side, acknowledging
the acclamations of the crowd with a grave, somewhat
bewildered courtesy.

Behind his chair came a construct bearing a cushion
on which rested the Ducal cap, and behind that another
construct with a drawn sword.

Following them was another ceremonial chair with
construct bearers, this time carrying the new Duke.
Leonardo Loredan wore cloth of gold. His pale hair was
drawn back from a face paler still, remote and dignified.
He too acknowledged the cheers of the crowd with a
lifted hand.

As the procession continued towards the quayside, the
Procurator, the Councillors and their ladies following the
Duke, Serafina could not stifle a pang of regret for the
impoverished young nobleman who had gone now, sub-
sumed somehow into the office of Duke. She remembered
his exhaustion on the night of Carnival, when he had
sought in vain for Hyacinth and for Gabriel, and even his
recent fury as he confronted Giulietta's lie about her
child. He had been real then, a man, not a political
puppet, and she wondered whether the man could survive
the ceremony of the office.

She dared not look at Gabriel.

'Serafina! Serafina!' It was Caterina's voice, and Serafina turned to see her friend hurrying towards her, skirts
picked up, ribbons fluttering, with none of the dignity
proper to a great lady.

'Serafina, Leo is asking for you – and you, Gabriel,

and Father Teo. Everyone – he wants everyone who brought us to this today. You're to come with us on the barge. Hurry!'

Like a butterfly she flitted away, alighted briefly beside Hyacinth and Father Claudio, and went on to Messire Alessandro and Gianni. They bowed to her, smiled at each other, and walked slowly towards the quayside. They were so perfectly attuned to each other that Serafina scarcely realized how strange they looked together.

Following them was Father Augustine, neatly tonsured again, with the silver-haired boy, Rafael, at his side. Like Leonardo, the priest had changed, casting off the dishevelled, desperate man who had sailed out to the islands with Serafina to bring help from the sea genics. Yet the memory of their journey together was warm in his eyes as he bowed to her.

'What will you do now, Father Augustine?' asked Father Teo. 'Will you return to I Frari?'

The younger priest ducked his head, embarrassed. 'No, Father. I have begged the Patriarch, and he has consented – I wish to go back there, to the island, and build a new church. I wish to bring God to the people of the sea.'

'Do they want that?' Serafina asked, surprised into being less than tactful. She could picture in her mind this earnest young priest toiling to set one stone on another, while the sea people danced in the waves. And yet what he wanted was not entirely foolish; he should have the chance to speak the word, and they to hear.

Father Augustine smiled. 'Perhaps not, or not yet, mistress. But I must go and tell them of the mercy of God, and that they are all His children. What they decide will be in His hands.'

'And will you go with him, Rafael?' Father Teo asked his companion.

The boy drew himself up. 'No, Father. I'm to sail in one of Messire Alessandro's ships – to sail East, Father, for silk and spices, to the lands where the sun rises.' His eyes shone. 'They say there are wonders to be seen.'

Caterina hurried past again, chivvying them towards the barge. Father Augustine and Rafael bowed and moved on.

'And you, Serafina?' Father Teo asked, as they turned towards the quayside last of all. 'What will life hold for you, now?'

'I shall stay with Giulietta,' she said. 'To help her care for little Paolo. To see he grows straight, and safe.' Seeing Father Teo's encouraging nod, she went on, 'We mean to have the Palazzo Contarini repaired and open it up again.'

'And I suggest you persuade Giulietta to recall the old Countess from Corpus Domini,' Father Teo said. 'Two young women living together need a chaperone.'

'But I—' Serafina began, and stopped.

'Exactly. There will be young men hovering around Giulietta, just as they used to. And now they will be hovering around you, as well. You're very lovely, Serafina. There's no reason that you should not wed.'

The compliment was all kindness, nothing to make Serafina feel embarrassed, and yet she felt as if something of her ease with him had slipped away, as if she had remembered that he was a man, for all his cassock, and she a woman.

'I had never thought of this, Father,' she said, frowning slightly. 'Genics are not made for marriage. I do not know why I was made, and I think my heart will never be quiet until I find the answer.'

Father Teo broke into delighted laughter. As they drew to a halt at the end of the procession slowly embarking on the Ducal barge, he took her hand in both his own.

'Dear Serafina, what else is it, to be human? I do not believe that we will find the answer until God speaks it to us at the last, and meanwhile we may find joy in the seeking. I pray that you will find great joy, Serafina.'

She felt his grip on her hand, and the pathway stretching out before her, to an unimaginable end.

The Ducal barge was moored along the quayside. On the lower deck the oarsmen were ready, while the Councillors and their ladies were already assembling on the upper deck below a silken canopy. Near the bows, beside the figurehead of Justice with her balance and sword, stood Leonardo Loredan.

Caterina was beside him, sparkling with happiness and excitement, and seized Serafina's hands as she drew close. 'You're here now, all of you, and I have everything I've ever wanted.'

Serafina kissed her, and she turned to greet Gabriel. As she curtseyed to Duke Leonardo, Serafina realized that her fears had been unjustified. Though he kept the grave demeanour appropriate for the occasion, his eyes were dancing. His formal, correct words of welcome were warm with friendship. Perhaps, Serafina thought, he had forgiven her for the lie about the child.

She boarded the crowded barge and found herself a seat; Father Teo had moved away to attend the Patriarch, but Gabriel remained with her. His eyes were wide and dark; he looked afraid, remembering, perhaps, the day of the Contarini wreck, or perhaps simply overwhelmed to find himself in this company. She found his hand and held it reassuringly, and caught his look of startled gratitude.

The Councillors' ladies had brought baskets crammed with flowers. The humid scent made Serafina's head spin. She looked around for familiar faces and saw Maria and Francesco Foscari, Giulietta with little Paolo swathed in lace and silk, Father Claudio chivvying his choir into position – with Hyacinth, now, in the midst of them – Dr Foscari surveying everything with a fat and satisfied grin.

The trumpet sounded again, and the barge began to move away from the quayside. The waves surged under it as it made for the outer reaches of the lagoon, and the entrance to the open sea. In its wake a fleet of smaller boats followed. Wind fluttered the silken canopy, and the clouds parted to reveal the dazzling sun.

At the gateway to the sea, where the ancient lighthouse stood, the boatmen backed their oars and brought the barge to a halt. The Councillors' ladies tossed their flowers overboard, to strew the sea with perfume.

Gazing across the waves, Serafina saw a lifted hand, then more than one, and heads bobbing above the water. The genics of the sea were present, too, to take part in this dedication.

Then silence fell as the Patriarch rose and spoke a prayer. The company murmured responses. Father Teo brought a bowl of water for the Patriarch to bless, and sprinkled Duke Leonardo, his attendants, and all the company with drops of holy water shaken from a spray of rosemary. It was strange to Serafina; the meaning of the symbolism had never been explained to her, and yet she felt it calling to something deep within her.

When the ceremony was over, the choir rose to sing. The words of the psalm, a prayer for cleansing, soared above the water. Hyacinth's pure alto rose higher still, like a lark ascending, dominating the voices around him and yet blending with them. Serafina could see an astonished happiness in his face, and imagined that it touched his voice as well, and led him to greater heights than ever before.

When the psalm had ended, Duke Leonardo rose. He held something small within his hand.

'My friends,' he said, 'in former times the Dukes of this city wedded the sea in token of their domination over it. I dare not speak those words. For the sea saved us, and we all saw its power. It is not for us to rule.'

His voice rose clearly, and Serafina wondered if the sea people could hear it. They were gathered around the barge, among the floating flowers; she thought Leonardo's words must carry so far.

'So I will wed our city to the sea,' he continued, 'but not as a lord to rule over her. As an equal partner, so land and sea may work together, bring life and happiness to all those who live here, and give honour to God.'

As he spoke, Serafina could not help asking herself who had prepared his speech, and whether Caterina had any hand in it.

Now Duke Leonardo held up the object he carried, and Serafina saw that it was the reliquary ring.

'This ring belonged to my ancestors,' he said, 'and it was most precious because it carried the hair of the Lord Christos. It carries it no longer, and all of you know how

evil men tried to use it to gain dominion over the city.
They failed, and each of you here played a part in their
failure.

'Yet the ring is still precious. Not because it held the
relic; God is not contained in gold and crystal. It is
precious because it brought us here, to this moment, and
to the future that lies ahead of us. And so I give it now; I
wed us to the sea; I dedicate land and sea and all of us to
God.'

He drew back his hand, and threw the ring. It arched
upwards; sunlight glinted on the gold. Then it fell, and
the sea received it with a tiny spurt of foam. A long sigh
went up from all the company.

All around the barge the sea genics raised their arms
as if in acknowledgement. For the first time Serafina saw
that the Sea-duke was among them. She caught a look,
passing between him and Leonardo, as though they
recognized each other as equals.

Not far away from her, she heard Father Augustine
say to Rafael, 'Last night I dreamed again of the winged
lion. He stood with his forepaws in the square and his
hindpaws on the sea, and his wings covered the city.'

The Patriarch spoke a final blessing. The sea churned
around the boat as the oarsmen turned it. The sun was
rising to its zenith, glittering on the surface of the sea,
and a few drops of rain spattered down. As the barge
faced inland once again, Serafina saw the city.

It lay as she had seen it before, from the Contarini
barge, and again from Francesco Foscari's skiff, looking
inconceivably small and flat on the horizon. Yet the sky
shone blue above it, and over it stretched an arch of
quivering light: a rainbow.

Someone cried out. Serafina heard Maria Foscari say,

'God's promise, given again.' There was the sound of laughter, and a gurgling cry from little Paolo Contarini. Beside Serafina, Gabriel whispered, 'To paint such light . . .'

The boatmen picked up a rhythm and the oars dug into the water, sending the barge surging back towards the inner lagoon and the quayside. On either side the sea people escorted it, leaping through the waves in the joy of their strength.

Serafina gazed at the band of pure colour arching over the city, and wondered what this new world of humanity would be, and how much she still had to learn.

OTHER BOOKS
AVAILABLE FROM PAN MACMILLAN

JULIET MARILLIER
WOLFSKIN   0 330 49354 X   £6.99

ANDY SECOMBE
LIMBO   0 330 41161 6   £5.99

JEFFREY FORD
THE PHYSIOGNOMY   0 330 41319 8   £6.99

STEVE CASH
THE MEQ   0 330 49315 9   £6.99

All Pan Macmillan titles can be ordered from our website,
www.panmacmillan.com, or from your local bookshop
and are also available by post from:

Bookpost, PO Box 29, Douglas, Isle of Man IM99 1BQ
Credit cards accepted. For details:
Telephone: 01624 677237
Fax: 01624 670923
E-mail: bookshop@enterprise.net
www.bookpost.co.uk

Free postage and packing in the United Kingdom

Prices shown above were correct at the time of going to press.
Pan Macmillan reserve the right to show new retail prices on covers
which may differ from those previously advertised in the text
or elsewhere.